LUST TAKES THE WHITE HOUSE

LUST TAKES THE WHITE HOUSE

By

Benson Lee Grayson

CHAPTER 1

The President leaned toward me, a big, toothy smile on his face. He looked just the way he did in his photos on the covers of the news magazines during the campaign. His press aide had once described it to me as the endearing sort of smile you might see on the face of a small child on Christmas Eve as he expectantly told his parents what presents he hoped Santa Claus would bring him. I disagreed. To me it was the type of smile you would see on the face of a used car salesman. Not one that was completely corrupt. Rather, one who had managed to convince himself that the junk heap he was about to sell to you at a ridiculously high price was really the finest new car offered at the lowest price ever available.

"Mr. Shultz," he said. "I would be very pleased if you would accept the job of Director of the Central Intelligence Agency."

I stared at him, amazed. I had never indicated to him that I wanted any government post, let alone that of Director of CIA. Initially, I had helped him win the presidency out of whim. Later, I realized that having someone in the White House who owed me a favor would be helpful in persuading the Federal Communications

Commission to stop attacking my company's advertising.

"I'm sorry, Buck," I said. "I'm sure you can get someone else to do it. I'd rather go back to running my company."

The incongruity of the President of the United States addressing me as "Mr. Shultz" while I called him "Buck" struck me. Of course, it accurately reflected our respective power positions. Without my help, he never would have become President. And I possessed enough detrimental information on him to be confident of being able to force him from office at any time I decided to do so. I wondered if he was shrewd enough to realize that fact.

I stood up. He got up from the sofa on which he was sitting and walked over to me, placing his arm around my shoulder. He was well over six feet in height, towering over me. Like many other big men, he had gone to fat. He was fortunate that his large frame helped to conceal his weight. Together with his thick head of curly grey hair, his height and grin had helped him win a majority of the women's vote.

I didn't know which I envied him more, his height or his hair. Those two features, added to his grin and his ability to tell anyone with whom he was speaking exactly what they wanted to hear had propelled him into the White House. That, plus my money, help and advice. Not that I would have changed places with him. While he was not stupid, he certainly was not bright. I wondered if I had not made a mistake, foisting him on the American people. The fact that he could be elected President bolstered my doubts over the soundness of the American political system.

As I looked up at Buck, I could not help thinking that if he wished, he could have crushed me with one hand. Not for the first time in dealing with him, I felt like the trainer of a huge bear.

"I'd better get back to my hotel," I said. "I have to pick up Pergamon and dress for dinner."

Pergamum and I were due to join the President and his wife and a few of his close friends who had helped him win the presidency. It was a dinner Pergamon had persuaded me to attend. I would have preferred to have spent the evening in our hotel room, watching a western on TV. I would have preferred even more to have gone back to our home at Watsonville. I had no interest either in putting up with what passed as conversation between Buck and his friends or in attending that evening's inaugural balls. I reminded myself that it was my own fault. I could easily have avoided letting Pergamom meet Buck's wife. I would certainly have done so if I had thought that she and Tammy would become fast friends.

Buck stepped back, extending his hand. The big grin was back on his face. It reflected one of his strongest assets, his unwillingness to accept defeat.

"Please think it over, Mr. Shultz," he said.

"I will," I said, shaking his hand. It was a polite lie. I had no intention of re-considering my refusal. Tomorrow, or the next day at the latest, Pergamom and I would be back in Watsonville and I would have resumed running my company.

He escorted me to the door. As I left, the Secret Service men standing in the corridors stared at me, watching my every move until the elevator arrived. I congratulated myself at not heeding Pergamon's arguments that we take a suite in the same hotel as the President's. I certainly would not want to put up with the intense security requirements the Secret Service was imposing on the hotel and on anyone who entered or left it.

When the elevator reached the lobby floor and the elevator door opened, I was struck by the luxury of the hotel lobby. I could understand the appeal this had for Pergamum. The hotel in which we were staying, a moderately-priced one about two miles away from that housing the President, was shabby compared to this one.

However, I felt loyal to the friendly little hotel in which I always stayed during my trips to Washington. The staff there knew me and always welcomed me on my arrival, making me feel like a valued friend. And I enjoyed the delicious blueberry muffins served as part of the hotel's complimentary breakfast buffet.

Passing through another cordon of Secret Servicemen in the lobby, I left the hotel. I looked at my watch. I had just enough time to walk the two miles to my hotel. Declining an offer by the hotel doorman to call a taxi, I strode out along 16th street in the direction of my hotel. As usual when I walked, I felt relaxed, enjoying the opportunity to be alone with my thoughts. Most of my best thinking was done during my walks, something Pergamum found inexplicable.

As I walked, I recalled my first meeting with Buck. It was a week before the New Hampshire presidential primary and I was in the state to meet with one of my distributors. I had been persistently disappointed in his sales of my company's products and thought it best to deliver my warning to him personally. If he didn't significantly increase sales, I informed him; I would find or establish another distributor. This was not the first warning. I had already passed this message to him via my sales manager. Unfortunately, the latter lacked my ability to be brutally frank. This time, I felt certain; the distributor could not mistake the meaning of my warning.

The hotel at which I was staying in New Hampshire was typical of those I always chose on my trips. It was small, friendly, and modestly priced. As I entered the lobby after having dinner nearby, I passed the hotel bar. It was about 7:00 p.m., a bit too early to go up to my room to watch television. I decided to enter the bar and have a beer. The bar was virtually empty. Just one man was sitting there, talking to the bar tender.

As I entered the bar, the man swung his stool around and addressed me.

"Don't you agree?" he asked.

"Agree to what?" I answered. I thought he looked familiar.

"That what this country needs is a new education program, free college tuition for all students and payments to high school students to attend class."

I considered and discarded the thought that the man was drunk or pulling my leg. He was apparently sober and quite sincere. I stared at him, wondering how anyone could be so foolish.

Then I recognized him. It was Robert "Buck" Porter, a one-term governor of Oklahoma and one of the candidates in the state's Republican presidential primary. He had been reduced to driving a cab in Oklahoma City when he decided to enter the New Hampshire primary.

I recalled the press reports that he had based his decision on his need to get out of the state to avoid being forced by an aggrieved husband to testify in a lurid divorce case. Most of what I had heard about Porter suggested that the reports were correct.

In an unusual demonstration of political good judgment, New Hampshire's Republican voters had largely dismissed Buck's poorly financed and ineptly managed campaign. The latest polls showed him dead last among the seven candidates. He was even behind the TV comedian, who had entered the contest as a joke. It was no wonder that his limited funding had dried up. Unpaid, virtually all of his campaign workers had quit. As thing stood, he had less chance of winning the primary than a snowball in hell.

Behind his back, the bar tender was moving an extended finger in a circle next to his head, indicating that Buck was crazy.

"Buck," I said, "You can't win a Republican primary in New Hampshire talking about spending taxpayer money on free college tuition. The Republicans in this state think the government is already spending too much."

"What do you think I should do?" he asked, in a pleading voice. It was hard to be contemptuous of him, because of the pathetic look on his face.

I motioned for him to leave the far and follow me to a booth at the far end of the room, where the bar tender couldn't hear me.

"Buck," I said. "If you want to win this primary, there is only one thing that would work."

"What's that?" he pleased, "Mr. ....?"

"Shultz," I introduced myself. "Melvin Shultz. From Watsonville, Illinois."

"Look, Buck," I continued. "All Americans hate taxes and New Hampshire Republicans hate taxes more than anyone else. What you have to do is promise that the first thing you will do after becoming President will be to immediately end the federal income tax."

"How do I do that," he asked.

"I don't know," I replied. "Frankly, I don't think it can be done. But if you say it often enough and loud enough between now and the primary, you have a chance of winning."

"But won't people see through it? " He asked.

I thought of stating to him the maxim that had made me rich, if you fool some of the people all the time and all of the people some of the time, that's usually enough. Thinking it over, I decided he wasn't smart enough or devious enough to accept the truth of that statement.

"No, Buck," I assured him. "There are many ways for the government to replace the federal income tax. The only problem is to find the best one. It's always possible to cut out waste and corruption."

He thought it over for a moment and nodded in agreement. I was glad he didn't realize that one person's waste and corruption was another person's priority for government spending.

"Why that's wonderful," he said. "I'll use your suggestion as the basis for my campaign speeches tomorrow."

"It won't do you any good if you say that to a few people on the street," I said. "Do you have any money left for television ads?"

"I don't think so," he admitted. "My campaign manager quit two days ago. We don't have any up-to-date account of our finances."

I quickly analyzed the situation in my mind. Then I came to a decision.

"Look, Buck," I said. "If you agree to say exactly what I write for you, I'll bankroll the rest of your campaign in New Hampshire, including a massive TV blitz."

Buck grinned, the massive smile spreading across his face.

"You bet I will, Mr. Shultz," he said. "And you'll be glad you did. I'll be the best President this country ever had. We'll make a difference."

I looked at him carefully. He really believed what he was saying. I decided it would be wiser for me not to reveal what I expected as the quid pro quo for my help in the unlikely event he actually did become President. It would be an interesting experiment to see if I could actually accomplish my goal. However, what was more important was the opportunity to gain more favorable treatment of my company's advertising than it regularly received from the Interstate Commerce Commission. With Buck in the White House, the FCC would be instructed to steer clear of me. I would be free to go as far as I liked in my advertising on radio and TV. With even more blatant commercials for my Lust Cosmetics, I would have virtually every female in the country using them.

"All right, Buck, "I said, speaking as though to a small child. "You go upstairs to your room and wait for me. "I'll make a few phone calls and arrange for the money. Then I'll write your speech. It shouldn't take me more than two hours, at most."

I looked at my watch. It was almost 8 p.m.

"I'll be at your room before 10. Remember, don't tell anyone about this. If the other candidates in the primary get wind of what we're planning, they'll buy up the television time and we won't be able to get your message across."

Buck assured me he would follow my instructions to the letter. He gave me the number of the room and I realized we were on the same floor. He stood, smiled again and headed off to the elevator to go up to his room.

As he left, I thought for a minute of what I had gotten myself into. The amount of money I had committed myself to spend on his campaign was not small, although I could comfortably afford it. Moreover, I had no intention of raising it all, myself. The major disadvantage to helping Buck was really the fact that he was at best a mediocrity. As President, he would be a joke. Still the likelihood of that occurring, even with my help, was not great.

Walking to the phone booth to start making my calls, I realized I could just as easily have made the phone calls from my hotel room. However, using pay phones was a life-long habit it was hard to break. In my younger days, when money was short, I had always relied on pay phones to make long distance calls. I would inform the operator to notify me as soon as my pre-paid three minutes was up. That way, by hanging up immediately after receiving the operator's warning, I had been successful in terminating calls before they became too expensive.

Feeling foolish at my unnecessary frugality, I started to leave the phone booth, and then sat down in it again. If I made the phone calls from my room, there would be a clear record. Given the fact that I was starting out to manipulate the New Hampshire primary, I would be far better off not leaving a clear record of my calls.

Checking my pocket, I found I did not have the necessary small coins. I gave the bar tender a five dollar bill and asked him to change it into quarters. He looked at me curiously as he gave me the coins, but said nothing.

Returning to the phone booth, I made the first call to Max Behrman, head of the agency that handled advertising for Lust Cosmetics. Max and I went back a long time together. I had gone to see him shortly after taking over Lust Cosmetics. My newspaper, which financed itself largely by doing commercial printing, had become the largest creditor of the cosmetics firm. Learning it was about to file for bankruptcy, I had acquired most of the remaining shares in Lust Cosmetics, paying off other creditors with pennies on the dollar. In part, I hoped that by taking over the company, I might be able to recover some of the money the firm owed me. In part, I did it to save the jobs of the four hundred employees who would have been laid off if the company had closed its doors.

When I first contacted Max, his company was a small one. I turned to it after the larger advertising agencies I contacted turned down the ad campaign I proposed, dismissing it as tasteless, crude and vulgar.

Max initially reacted the same way. The campaign I was proposing, he pointed out, was based on the slogan "add lust to your life."

"You can't say that in print," he said, "let alone on radio or television. Why don't you let me draw up something better?"

"Mr. Behrman," I said, "sticking to tasteful advertising helped put Lust Cosmetics into bankruptcy. Do you recall their old advertising pitch? It was 'use Lust Cosmetics, the brand your mother used to use.' That didn't do the trick. Nothing like that will do the trick."

Max nodded in agreement. "I'm sure we can think up something better than that and still be tasteful," he said.

I stood up to leave. "I'm sorry you can't help me," I said. "If I can't get an ad agency to work with me to pull the company around, some four hundred people will lose their jobs. And most of them will not be able to get another one."

Max shrugged. "All right, Mr. Shultz," he said. "I'll do it your way. But I don't like it."

Despite his initial reluctance, Max had done a good job. He had been correct in warning that many newspapers and radio and television stations in Illinois would refuse to carry our ads. However, enough did and we were able to fill the gaps with billboard ads. The adverse publicity the campaign inspired gave my company millions of dollars in free advertising. Within a few years, Lust became a billion dollar corporation.

As Lust's sole owner, I became a millionaire many times over. Max had not done badly either. With my company as his largest client, his advertising agency had grown until it was one of the largest in the Middle West.

I rang Max's home number. When his wife answered, she put him right on the phone.

"Max," I said, "I apologize for calling you at home. I need your help on a crash project."

"What's the problem?" he asked. "Your current campaign seems to be going well."

The campaign was based on the slogan "use lust in bed." I smiled as I thought about it. It seemed that the more tasteless my advertising was, the better were the results.

"It's something else," I explained. "Do you know who Buck Porter is?"

"I can't say that I do," he answered.

"He was a one-term governor of Oklahoma a few years ago. He entered the New Hampshire Republican primary and is currently dead last, moving rapidly in reverse. With your help, we're going to have him win the New Hampshire primary and then the presidency."

There was silence on the phone. Then Max asked, "Are you serious?"

"I couldn't be more so. But we have to work fast. There is less than a week before the primary. The first thing I want you to do is to buy up every available minute of advertising time available on every radio and television station in New Hampshire. If any of the nearby Massachusetts stations would be useful, buy up their time too. Then buy a full page of advertising every day in every daily newspaper in New Hampshire through to Election Day. Can you do it?"

"I can," he said, "but it will be very expensive."

"Don't worry about the cost," I said. ""I'll send you funds to use as working capital. In a few days I will give you the names and addresses of the people to actually bill for the work. When you receive the funds you can repay me for my advance."

"Another thing," I went on. "The theme of the campaign is as soon as he is President; the first thing Buck Porter will do is end the federal income tax."

"Are you sure, Mel?" he asked. "Do you really want to do this? You will have every reputable politician, economist and newspaper in the country, every talking head, calling Buck crazy."

"You're right," I said. "But how many of them vote in the Republican primary in New Hampshire? The primary voters up here will love it. Do you remember the last time we disagreed over a campaign?"

I was referring to our discussion some three years before. I had laid out the new Lust Cosmetics campaign, based on the slogan Lust makes the world go round. Accompanying the slogan in our ads was the figure of a voluptuous naked Greek goddess.

Max had argued that the naked goddess would arouse too much adverse publicity. I had pointed out that the picture of the naked goddess was a replica of an ancient Greek statue, housed in one of the world's leading museums. Anyone criticizing the picture would open himself to the charge that he was ignorant of art and culture. Max had reluctantly gone along with me. He had been perfectly correct in predicting that the criticism of the campaign would be unprecedented. However, it accomplished everything I had hoped for and more. It resulted in Lust Cosmetics becoming a member of the Fortune 500 companies and made me a billionaire.

"Now Max," I went on. "For the newspaper ads I want a picture of Porter, looking presidential. He is wearing a white shirt, striped tie and suit, seated at a large desk. Behind him is a large window through which you can see the Capitol. Until you can get a more recent photo of him, retouch one of the official ones he used when he was Governor of Oklahoma."

Max interrupted. "But you can't see the Capitol from the White House."

"You know that and I know that," I answered. "But the voters in New Hampshire don't. In any event, it doesn't make any difference. We're not selling reality. What counts is the image. On either side of the window," I went on, "I want large American flags. Above Porter's head, in large letters, I want a slogan in quotes saying 'THE FIRST THING I WILL DO AS PRESIDENT IS END THE FEDERAL INCOME TAX.' Under the picture, I want in smaller capital letters 'STOP CONGRESS FROM GIVING YOUR DOLLARS TO THEIR MINK-COATED MISTRESSES.'"

"Mel," said Max with something close to disgust in his voice, "Not only is that a non sequitur, it's the lowest, most vulgar advertizing I have ever heard of."

"You're right, Max, I said. "I won't try to deny that. But it just might work. I can't think of anything else which would. Remember when I reminded you of the old quote attributed to P.T. Barnum, 'Nobody ever went broke underestimating the intelligence of the American people.' You thought I was joking. It took a long time for you to realize that Barnum was right, whether we like it or not. The only modification I would make now is to add, you also don't go broke underestimating the good taste of the American people."

"You're the boss, Mel," he said. He was obviously not happy about my planned campaign, but he would go along.

"OK," I went on after a moment. "For the subsequent days I want the full-page newspaper ads to be basically the same, but with a different slogan each day. Use things like 'STOP HAVING TO FEAR AN IRS AUDIT,' ' THROW THE IRS INTO THE GARBAGE,' ' STOP CONGRESS GIVING YOUR MONEY TO FOREIGNERS.' "

"I've got all that," Max said. He sounded a bit wore confident about his role.

"Also, get a crew to New Hampshire to have Porter do the radio and television ads. In the interim, have announcers make the pitch. You know, various voices saying 'Had enough?' 'The first thing Porter will do as President will be to end the federal income tax.' And try to have the actors sound like New Hampshire residents. Can you do all that?"

"I can," he said. "And if you pull this off, they should fire every advertising professor in the country and have you teach their courses."

"Thanks", Max," I said, and hung up. I no longer had any doubts Max would carry out my instructions in his usual skillful manner.

My next phone call was to my lawyer, Sol Sugarman. The timing of my call was fortunate. Sol had just been named partner in his firm, Quincy, Nixon and Faulkner. It was one of the most prestigious law firms in the country. I had been primarily responsible for Sol making partner. I had not told him of that fact, but he was smart enough to realize it and had thanked me most profusely.

I had started using Quincy, Nixon and Faulkner about three years earlier, when I decided to expand Lust Cosmetics' operations overseas and had purchased cosmetics plants in Hong Kong, Poland, Ireland and Mexico. The Chicago law firm, Murphy and Chamberlain that had been handling my company's legal affairs, did not have sufficient international expertise to handle my foreign operations.

My first step was to see Chamberlain, the managing partner and ask him for his suggestions. I had told him I was very happy with his firms' work and that it would of course continue to handle Lust's legal affairs in the U.S. The only change I had in mind was to hire a law firm to handle my company's foreign operations. What I wanted, I explained, was the best law firm he could recommend for the purpose.

Chamberlain had looked puzzled. "What do you mean by best firm?" he asked. "There are many different criteria you can use to evaluate the different law firms."

"Let me put it this way," I explained. "What I want is a firm that believes if it's worth winning, its worth it's fighting dirty for."

As soon as I said that, I realized I should never have been

so blunt. In effect, I had burned my bridges with Murphy and Chamberlain. Chamberlain was a devout Episcopalian who had served as warden of his church several times. He also had no sense of humor. He stared at me as though I was a piece of excrement he had found on his shoe.

I regretted my choice of words for a minute, and then concluded it was just as well. Pat Kelly, the jovial red-faced Irishman who had handled my legal affairs at the firm until his death a few months before, had been an easy man to work with. After winning an important case for me, allowing me to use the slogan 'Lust rules the world,' he had laughingly told me that representing Lust Cosmetics had given him more fun than any other legal work he had ever performed. Chamberlain, since had taken over as managing partner, had been distinctly less helpful in handling my firm's work.

"I should think," He said coldly, "That the firm you want is Quincy, Nixon and Faulkner. They are an old line New York law firm that specializes in international work. I believe they also have a reputation for doing the sort of work you require. However, I doubt they would consider adding Lust Cosmetics as a client. Virtually of the firms they represent are much larger, members of the Fortune 500."

"That's all right," I told him. "If you can set up a meeting for me with their managing partner, I think I can convince him to take me on as a client."

"I'll see what I can do," he said. A few weeks later he called me. He told me in a cold tone that he had arranged for me to meet with Prescott Cooper, the managing partner of Quincy, Nixon and Faulkner at their Manhattan office the following week. I thanked him and hung up. Thinking about it, I concluded that Chamberlain had used whatever influence he could muster to arrange the appointment, in the hope that I would transfer all of

Lust Cosmetics' legal work away from his firm.

On the day set for my meeting with Cooper, I took an early morning flight to New York, checked into my hotel just off Times Square, and walked the several miles up to the officers of Quincy, Nixon and Faulkner. The firm was located in a large, modern building on Park Avenue. Reportedly, the building charged the highest rents for office space of any in Manhattan. The firm occupied six entire floors of the building.

When the elevator doors opened and I walked to the receptionist's desk of the firm, I was struck by the impressive decor. It could be best described as in elegant good taste. Rich oriental carpets covered the parquet floors. The walls were paneled with fine, dark wood. Full length oil paintings in antique gold frames hung from the molding, many of them of the firm's senior partners. Among the latter were at least two former senators and a former Attorney General.

The receptionist matched the décor. Seated behind a large mahogany desk she was beautifully dressed and one of the most attractive women I had ever seen. When she addressed me, I was not surprised that she had a cultured English accent.

I gave her my name. She spoke on the intercom and then told me that the managing partner would see me. As she led me into Prescott Cooper's office, I enjoyed both looking at her figure and catching her pleasant perfume.

Cooper's office was even more impressive than the receptionist area. On one paneled wall was a full-length oil portrait of one of the firm's deceased partners, Trowbridge Faulkner, wearing the robes of an Associate Justice of the United States Supreme Court. On the opposite wall, behind Cooper's desk, hung his law degree. I was not surprised to see it was from Harvard Law School.

Cooper was a tall, handsome man, with distinguished gray hair.

His suit was tailor-made. On his finger was a Princeton class ring. I thought that if God deigned to take human form, he would have looked very much like Prescott Cooper.

Cooper stood up and motioned me to sit in the arm chair next to his desk. I was conscious that he made no move to shake my hand. He sat down as I did. The look on his face was one of amused contempt. I was wearing walking shoes, relatively expensive, very comfortable, and quite scruffy. My wrist watch was a twenty dollar one I had bought at our local drug store.

As he took in my appearance, I recalled the many lectures Pergamon had given me to improve my appearance. She told me repeatedly that people were put off by my careless dress, I had always shrugged off her criticism with the comment that anyone who was as rich as I was could jolly well dress as he damned please. Now, I was not quite so sure.

After a few minutes of silence, it was clear that Cooper was not about to speak first.

"Mr. Cooper," I said. "My law firm in Chicago has recommended Quincy, Nixon and Faulkner as the best firm to handle Lust Cosmetics' foreign operations."

Cooper nodded in agreement. He obviously shared my high opinion of his firm.

"Mr. Shultz," he began, in a deep cultured voice that was what I would have expected God to sound like. "We are naturally quite pleased when any firm wishes to use us as counsel. As is our practice, we have conducted an initial review of Lust Cosmetics. I am afraid; our conclusion is that we would not be a good fit. Virtually all of our clients are Fortune 500 companies. I do not think that your firm's sales are at a level where we can efficiently handle your work. We would, of course, be pleased to recommend some smaller law firms which might be more suitable."

"Mr. Cooper," I replied, "What are the average annual billings you receive from your clients, just a ball park figure?"

"Cooper gave me a figure. It was an impressive one.

"Mr. Cooper," I said, "My company's earnings and also its need for high quality legal representation are substantially above what might be expected from its annual sales. I am quite prepared to guarantee you billings from my firm equal to your annual average."

Cooper looked at me with obvious distaste, as though gentlemen did not haggle over money.

"Mr. Shultz," he said coldly, "perhaps I should be more frank. Your firm has, how shall I put it, a somewhat unsavory reputation. We are afraid that if we accepted you as a client, it could have a detrimental effect on our relations with our other clients."

I smiled back at him, my confidence returning. I was beginning to enjoy this.

"I certainly appreciate your frankness," I said.

He looked at his watch and at the door, expectantly. He clearly wished me to leave. Instead, I leaned back in my chair and relaxed. I had not expected to have difficulty in securing the services of Quincy, Nixon and Faulkner, but I had prepared for this eventuality. I do not like to be crossed. I dislike even more to be treated with contempt.

"Perhaps you can refresh my memory," I began. "I seem to recall that several years ago your firm was involved in a bit of nasty business. One of your partners defended a young man accused of multiple counts of child molestation. The victims were quite young, some really tots, with both boys and girls involved. Your partner was able to get the more serious charges reduced, including several for aggravated rape.

Cooper glared at me, his face flushed. I went on. "Your partner then was successful in having the remaining charges dismissed by the judge on a technicality. A few weeks after he was released, your client kidnapped, raped, tortured and murdered two young girls. The story made all of the tabloids, but the earlier association between the man arrested, tried and convicted for the crime with your firm was never mentioned. Interestingly, the judge who dismissed the earlier charges had been a congressman before his appointment to the bench and had received several large contributions from your firm. Even after he became a judge, he was the guest of several of your partners at sports events, including the Kentucky Derby."

Cooper was by now unable to conceal his anger.

"Just what exactly are you driving at, Mr. Shultz?" he asked in a cold voice.

"Only this," I said, attempting to sound meek. "I would consider it a personal favor if you would reconsider and accept Lust Cosmetics as a client. All I want is a law firm that will protect my little, unsavory company as successfully as you protected the rapist and murderer who, as I recall, was the son of the CEO of one of your major clients."

He stared at me. "Perhaps I have been hasty," he said. "We certainly would not wish to turn down a firm that felt strongly about our representing their interests. I believe we do have a young associate who would be able to add your firm to his client list."

Cooper clicked his intercom. "Please ask Mr. Sugarman to come to my office immediately," he said. He began a polite discussion of the weather in New York, which continued for a few minutes. There was a knock on the door and a tall, lean young man entered Cooper's office. He was wearing an expensive suit, but the effect was undermined by his round shoulders.

Cooper introduced us and told Sugarman he was to take over as my company's counsel and that I could explain in Sugarman's office what I wanted him to do. I thanked Cooper and followed

Sugarman to the elevator.

The elevator took us down four floors and the elevator doors opened, revealing a corridor far less well decorated that that which led to Cooper's office. I gathered this was the floor that housed the more junior associates of the law firm.

Sugarman then led me down the corridor to the far end and ushered me into a small, windowless office. Sugarman, I realized, was the firm's token accommodation to outside pressure for an equal opportunity policy. The accommodation only went just so far.

"Mr. Sugarman," I began "how long have you been with the firm?"

"Three weeks," he answered.

"Do you have any other clients?"

"No, sir."

"What law school did you attend?" I pressed further.

"NYU." came the reply. I was editor of the law review and first in my class."

I smiled at the young lawyer. "Sol, "I said, "It must be hard on you, trying to squeeze in among all those Harvard and Yale Law School graduates."

He swallowed hard, but said nothing.

"Sol," I continued. "I don't care what law school you attended. All I am interested in is results. What I want is a lawyer who won't be telling me how I can't do things, but how I can."

"I can't help you break the saw," he said softly.

"I don't expect or want you to do that, what I want you to do is to stretch it, to go as far as you can without actually breaking it. Find the loopholes. If you have to go back to Sixteenth Century English Common Law for a precedent, so be it. Do we understand each other?"

He smiled. "I think we do," he said.

"I found Sol to be a very effective and innovative lawyer who had no problem handling most of my firm's legal work, although I kept a small part of it with another firm as a contingency. Sol was particularly helpful in negotiating for me advertising agreements in Western Europe, which saw Lust Cosmetics garner arising proportion of the market. Part of this involved our heavy advertising in the hard-core pornography channels.

After Sol had handled Lust Cosmetics for two years, Cooper had called me to suggest one of the partners of the firm could replace Sol as my lawyer. I had thanked him politely, but assured him that I was very pleased with Sol's work. I had added that I thought it would be appropriate for our work to be handled by a full partner and that I expected Sol to be made a partner at the earliest possible moment. Cooper had simply said goodbye and hung up. However, Sol's elevation to be a full partner was announced not long after. I was glad I did not have to force the issue to achieve that.

I was on the phone for several minutes with Sol before I was able to interrupt his expressions of gratitude for my help in having him made partner. "You deserve it, Sol," I said. We chatted for a couple of minutes before I broached the subject of my call.

"I need your help in an urgent matter," I said. "I've decided to help Buck Porter win the New Hampshire Republican presidential primary. It's going to take a lot of money. I know there are various limits on the amount of cash that can be furnished by a single donor to a candidate. I don't wish to break any laws. We to find loopholes and set up whatever committees and bank accounts to funnel money into the campaign. And see what the distinctions are between hard and soft money and how we may be able to use them"

"OK, sir," Sol, said. "It's not my area of expertise, but I'll get started on it right away. I gather that time is vital."It sure is, Sol," I said. "Hire whatever assistance you think you may require. The theme of the campaign will be Porter's pledge to immediately end the federal income tax as soon as he becomes President. So label any organizations we establish accordingly. You know something like the Coalition for Economic Justice and Prosperity or the Anti-Income Tax Crusade."

When I said goodbye to Sol and hung up, I thought of calling some of my suppliers and distributors, to tell them how much money they would be levied upon to help fiancé the Buck Porter campaign. But I was almost out of change for the pay phone and it was getting late. I decided to postpone the other phone calls until tomorrow and to instead go to my room and draft the speech Buck would make tomorrow.

CHAPTER 2

When the elevator stopped and the door opened on my floor, I was so deep in thought planning the speech that I almost bumped into a young woman standing in the corridor. I was startled to hear someone say good evening and looked up. I found myself addressing a good looking woman, about thirty. She was wearing the uniform of a chambermaid.

"Good evening," I automatically responded.

As I looked at her I realized she was surprisingly attractive. Her light green uniform was tight, emphasizing her figure. Below the hem of her short skirt, she was wearing black stockings and black, high-heeled shoes. Over one breast was a name tag identifying her as Tanya. Raising my eyes to her face, I noticed lovely blond hair, slightly askew. I remembered Pergamon once remarking to me that some woman's hair looked as though she had just tumbled out of bed. I wondered idly if that applied literally to Tanya.

I passed her, heading to my room. She leaned back provocatively, stretching her uniform even tighter over her attractive breasts. "Is there anything you need?" She asked with a warm smile.

"No thanks" I answered, smiling in return. She certainly was pleasant to look at. I wondered if she had been assigned by one of the other candidates to spy on Buck, or perhaps to entrap him. But that was unlikely. Buck was so far behind in the polls that no candidate would waste resources on him. I decided that she was either a professional hooker or a semi-pro, supplementing her earnings as a chambermaid.

It struck me she spoke with an East European accent. "Are you from Russia?" I asked.

"Yes," she responded proudly, "from Moscow."

"It's a great city," I said to her in Russian, using the few words I recalled studying the language a few years before, when Pergamon and I had gone to Russia as tourists.

She gave me an even warmer smile. I returned her smile and entered my room. It was one of the hotel's minimum price ones I always reserved. The meager furnishings were quite adequate and I couldn't see wasting the money on anything better.

At home, I did most of my typing on an old manual typewriter, using the two finger, hunt and peck system I had learned as a youngster, working on my father's newspaper as a reporter.

Pergamon, who was always attracted to the latest technology, had bought me a lap-top computer for Christmas one year. I had used it only a few times, preferring my familiar manual typewriter. However, I had not wanted to hurt her feelings when she had suggested that I take the lap-top with me on this trip. I was glad now, since I could use it to write Buck's speech.

Since there was no desk in the room, I placed the lap-top on one of the twin beds and tried to use it. I found this unsatisfactory. Then I moved a lamp from the night stand and put the lap-top there. This was far better. It took me a few minutes to learn the word processing capability of the lap-top. Once I mastered this, it took me no more than an hour and a half to complete the draft of Buck's speech.

I had no way of printing the speech until I could find a printer. The simplest expedient would be to have Buck read it on the laptop screen. Picking up the machine, I left my room and walked down the corridor to Buck's room.

I knocked at his door and waited. There was no response. I knocked again, louder. This time I thought I heard a noise inside. I waited but Buck still did not open the door. I was becoming rather annoyed. I thought I had sufficiently impressed on him the importance of remaining in the room until I drafted his speech.

As I knocked for the third time, the door opened. Buck's head emerged, his face looking flushed and embarrassed. He opened the door further and I could see he was wearing a bathrobe. Without waiting for an invitation, I entered the room. The first thing that struck me was that it was far more luxurious than mine. The furniture and draperies were better and there was a large, king-sized bed. The bed was unmade. On the floor beside it I saw a pair of women's black, high heeled shoes.

"If you're entertaining someone right now," I said, "You had better get her out of here. We have something important to discuss. Where is she?" I asked, "In the bathroom?"

Buck nodded and smiled sheepishly. He walked to the bathroom door and opened it. As I expected, Tanya was inside. She walked out, still buttoning her uniform. Keeping her eyes fixed on the floor, she put on her shoes and started to leave the room.

I thought that if I was going to back Buck's campaign, I had better prevent any scandal arising from his roll in the hay with Tanya. The easiest way to win her silence was probably to offer her cash. However, I was still uncertain whether she was a hooker. If she wasn't, offering her cash might only infuriate her and cause the very scandal I was trying to avoid

"Tanya," I said with a smile. "I wish I had been free earlier. You're certainly an exceptional young woman."

She looked at me with curiosity.

I took my wallet out of my pocket and opened it. As I don't like to use credit cards, I usually carry a reasonable amount of cash with me when I travel. Removing five hundred dollar bills from my wallet, I handed them to her.

"I come to this hotel often" I said. "Please take this from me as a present and with the hope that we can get to know each other better when I am next here."

She smiled at me. "Please make it soon," she said.

As she left the room, I stared at her, enjoying the beautiful picture of her figure in the close-fitting chambermaid's costume. If I ever decided to play around, which I have never done since I married Pergamon, Tanya would be on the top of my list.

When the door closed behind her, I turned to Buck.

"You fool," I said, letting my anger show. Don't you realize that you may have thrown away any chance you have left to win the primary? If she talks to the press, you are finished."

"I'm sorry, Mr. Shultz," he said. "I never thought of that. Do you think she will talk to the reporters?"

"I hope not. If we are lucky, the money I gave her will keep her happy and silent."

I turned on my lap-top and gave it to Buck. This is the speech you will deliver on television as soon as we have the time arranged on the stations. Read it to see if you have any questions. Then memorize it."

Buck read it intently. He looked up. "It's a great speech," he said. "But Tammy thinks it would be a mistake to end the federal income tax. She says the government needs the money, particularly if we want to fund our education program. And she thinks most people would be against ending the income tax."

I looked at Buck appalled. "How did Tammy find out about this?" I asked. Didn't I tell you not to talk to anyone?"

"But she called me," he said. "She wanted to find out how the campaign is going. And she's smart. Don't you think we ought to listen to her?" He seemed frightened by my obvious anger.

This was the first indication I had received of the very strong influence Tammy exercised over her husband. After I met her, I could understand why. She was very intelligent, far more so than Buck. She was also very able and very forceful. She was relatively pragmatic. However, her views were influenced by her attachment to liberal policies, at least as compared to most Republicans. I wondered if she had gained her political views while a student at Harvard Law School and whether she had become a Republican, only after going out with Buck.

"Buck," I said, "Let's get one thing straight. Unless you follow my instructions without any deviation I'm not spending a cent on your campaign."

"Mr. Shultz," he said contritely. "I'm sorry. I'll follow your instructions to the letter."

He looked surprised that he had aroused my fury and to be quite sincere in his assurances. I regarded them as worthless. I didn't think I could trust Buck not to spill whatever was on mind to anyone he might meet or to keep his pants on if he was anywhere near an available woman. In short, I couldn't let him out of my sight.

"Buck," I said, "let's go to my room. I have an extra bed. You can spend the night there."

"But why, Mr. Shultz?" He seemed honestly puzzled.

"Because I want you to memorize that speech. And I want to

be there to answer any questions you may have about it. This way, I'll be sleeping in the next bed, able to answer anything right away."

I stood, reached up to place my arm around his shoulder, and steered him to the door. I deliberately left the lap-top behind. When we entered my room, I motioned him to take the spare bed. As he sat down on it, I quickly removed the phone jack out of the room phone. I hoped he would not realize what was wrong if he tried to make a phone call.

I looked at him with mock anger. "Buck," I said, "I've left the lap-top in your room. Give me your key and I'll go and get it."

Ignoring his offer to retrieve it himself, I practically grabbed the room key from his hand and went back to his room. I did not want to use his room phone, but decided it was less risky than leaving him alone for as long as it would take to go down to the pay phone in the lobby.

It took me several phone calls to Chicago to reach James Barlow. Barlow was what could be called a political hired gun. He had successfully managed state races in Illinois for both Democratic and Republican candidates and had the reputation of being effective.

When he came to the phone, I apologized for calling him so late. I introduced myself, explaining that I had never met him personally, but knew him by his reputation.

"Mr. Barlow," I said, "I have decided to back Buck Porter in the New Hampshire primary. I would like to hire your services. Are you at liberty at this time?"

"I'm not working now, Mr. Shultz," he said, "But I'm afraid I can't accept your offer. Buck Porter has no chance of winning the primary, or even of coming close. I don't want to waste your money and I can't afford to be associated with too many losing campaigns. If I do, it ruins my reputation and I won't get new clients."

"I certainly understand that," I said. "However, there are several unusual factors that may affect your decision. I'm personally backing the campaign, so there will be no lack of money. Secondly, there is no need for you to have any official position with the campaign. You can be an adviser, a consultant. Hell, you can be here for the skiing. If you decide to join the campaign officially, the timing and title will be completely up to you."

"Additionally," I went on, "while I would appreciate your political advice, I have already decided what the basis of the campaign will be. What I really want you for is hand-holding. I can't trust Buck Porter out of my sight. Your primary job will be to see that he doesn't talk to anyone I haven't OK'd. I'm trying to do that myself right now and it isn't easy. I don't expect you to do that yourself either. Bring along a couple of assistants you can rely upon, as many as you need. But I'd like you here as soon as possible."

"What is the theme of your campaign?" he asked.

When I told him, he began laughing "I don't think it will work," he said, "but it should be damn interesting. OK, "I'll do it if you can pay my fee."

He quoted me the figure he would charge. "No problem," I told him. "Get here as soon as you can."

"I'll be there tomorrow morning, as early as a flight can get me up there."

I gave him the name of my hotel and hung up. Picking up my-lap top, I returned to my room. I found Buck stretched out on the bed. He had turned on the television and was watching a movie on the hotel's porn channel. I looked at it for a minute and found it much less explicit than the porn channels in Europe, which were carrying the Lust Cosmetic's advertising.

I turned the TV off. "OK, Buck," I said. "Time to get to work."

I turned on the lap-tap and handed it to Buck. "Memorize the speech," I ordered. "And wake me up if you have any questions."

I got into my bed and turned my head away from the light, expecting that my mind would be too active from the evening's events for me to sleep. I was mistaken. Then next thing I knew, it was morning, with daylight streaming in the window. Buck lay sleeping in the other bed. The lap-top was on the floor. I wondered if he had actually worked on the speech I had written for him.

I got up, shaved and got dressed. Buck was still sleeping peacefully. I reconnected the telephone and shook him until he awakened.

"Buck," I said, "I'm going to order breakfast from room service. What would you like?"

He told me. It was more food than I could imagine anyone eating for breakfast, but I said nothing. I called in the order. I regretted not being able to go down for the hotel's complimentary breakfast buffet, but I was afraid Buck might get into trouble in public.

Buck suggested that he get dressed. I didn't want to let him out of my sight to go back to his room. I asked him to wait until I called the hotel reception desk. After instructing the desk to send Barlow to my room as soon as he arrived, I accompanied Buck back to his room. He looked surprised, but said nothing.

As we entered the room, the telephone rang. I grabbed it before he could and asked who was calling.

"Mark Goldsborough," came the reply.

I turned to Buck. "Who is Mark Goldsborough?" I asked, placing my hand over the phone's speaker.

"Oh my God!" he said. "I forgot all about him. Mark is a political science professor at Harvard. He is helping out in the campaign. I am scheduled to go with him to meet voters today."

I removed my hand from the speaker. "Mr. Goldsborough," I said, "Mr. Porter says he can't make any of the events scheduled for the day. Something important has come up. He wants you to go out and speak for him."

I then hung up before Goldsborough could reply. I didn't like turning him loose to speak on his own, but I doubted if he could find enough potential voters for the events he had arranged to matter.

"Shouldn't I go with him?" Buck asked plaintively. "He says it is necessary for me to get my message out to the voters."

"That's right," I said, as though I were speaking to a child. But how many people are you meeting at a time, two or three? I have arranged for you to record that speech and to have it broadcast all across the state. You will reach thousands of voters at a time. It's a matter of spending your time where it will do the most good. Now take your shower and get dressed!" I continued. "We'll then go back to my room to wait for Barlow, the man who will help arrange your campaign from now on."

I waited in his room until Buck got dressed, then went back with him to my room. We sat there, watching television as he became increasingly anxious.

"Shouldn't we be doing something? He said. To keep him occupied, I asked him what hobbies he had.

"Golf," he answered, explaining he had taken it up while governor. "Of course," Tammy made me give it up after I left office. She said it was too expensive."

I didn't ask why. I knew he couldn't have made much, driving a taxi.

I was running out of things to say to Buck when there was a knock on the door and the waiter from room service brought in the two breakfasts I had ordered. Buck finished his, then looked longingly at mine. I had eaten only a muffin with my hot tea, leaving untouched a large piece of toast and an order of bacon and eggs.

"If you're not going to eat that, Mr. Shultz," he said, "would you mind if I did?"

"Help yourself," I told him. He methodically ate all of the food I had left, slathering the toast with both butter and jam. It was clear to me why he looked so pudgy.

Shortly after 10 a.m., as we were watching TV, the room phone rang. I was pleased to hear Max inform me that he had obtained the radio and television time I had asked him to get, as well as the space for the newspaper ads. He also had secured actors to record the commercials I had asked him to prepare.

"I should have enough radio ads completed by this afternoon to fly them to you to broadcast tomorrow," he informed me. "It will take longer to prepare the newspaper ads, but I think I can also get them in shape to start the press campaign tomorrow, as well. I talked to an advertising firm in Concord to have Porter use their facilities to personally make the radio and television commercials. I have tentatively arranged the time. But you probably should speak to them to make sure the arrangements fit into Porter's schedule."

Thanking Max, I hung up and told Buck about the appointment. I then directed him to keep practicing his speech. As he appeared to do so, I called the Concord firm and confirmed Buck's appointment. About noon, as I was wondering whether to have lunch sent up, the phone rang again. It was the hotel desk, informing me that Barlow had arrived. I gave instructions for Barlow to be sent up.

A few minutes later, there was a knock at the door. I opened it and saw four men standing there. Barlow entered and introduced himself. He was younger than I expected, in his mid-thirties. I introduced Barlow to Buck. Barlow, in turn, introduced us to his three companions, all men he had worked with before on previous campaigns. It was a relief to have help in minding Buck.

"You made good time," I told Barlow.

"That's because we took an early flight into Boston," he explained, "then chartered a private jet to fly us here."

"I'm glad you did," I said. Then I excused us and led Barlow out into the corridor, closing my room door behind me.

The corridor was empty and I felt I could safely speak to Barlow, without our being overheard.

"Do your men understand their job?" I asked. "Porter must be prevented from speaking to anyone, in person or on the phone, unless they clear it with me. That includes his wife, Tammy. And they must insure he is not left alone with any female. That includes waitresses, chambermaids, anyone. He has the sex drive of a rabbit."

"As bad as that?" Barlow asked smiling.

"You don't know the half of it," I said. "Thank God you're here. I couldn't let him out of my sight for a minute. Now," I continued, "I want your men to be in his room if he is there. We'll have an extra bed moved in. Also, I think it would be wise to have another man out in the corridor watching the room. I don't put it past him to wait until your man inside is asleep and then try to slip out. If necessary, bring in more people to help you."

"I get you," Barlow said.

We reentered the room. I reiterated to Buck that he was to follow without the slightest deviation instructions from Barlow and his assistants. Buck was further to permit them to handle all phone calls and visitors and that it was up to them to decide which of them it would be safe for him to meet,

"I want to make this crystal clear," I said to Buck. "If you screw up in any way, I pull out immediately. Do you understand?"

He nodded in agreement. I hoped my determination had gotten through to him.

Turning to Barlow, I told him to have his men accompany Buck to his room and have him get ready for the recording session. I then turned on the lap-top and brought up the speech I had written for Buck.

"I know this isn't part of what I asked you to do, Mr. Barlow" I said, "but I would be grateful if you could look at this speech I drafted for Buck. The theme has to remain the same. I know it is pretty raw stuff. If there is anything you can do to make it more effective, I would appreciate your suggestions. Naturally, if you care to help out, bill me extra for your work."

He read the speech and smiled. "It is strong stuff!" he said. "Frankly, I doubt it will work. Still, with a poor candidate in last place and so little time left, you don't have much leeway to try anything else."

He made a few changes in the draft, slightly improving it. "If you can," I said, "Have one of your men take the lap-top to a printer and have copies of the speech printed up for Buck to use. Also, go with Buck to the recording studio where he will make the ads. I have some other arrangements to take care of."

Leaving Buck in the hands of Barlow and his assistants, I went down to the hotel lobby and out to the street in search of a bank. After obtaining change at the bank for my phone calls, I returned to the phone booth in the hotel lobby. My first call was to Sol Sugarman. He informed me that he was still researching the campaign finance regulations, but felt confident he could create a series of funding mechanisms that would permit me to channel whatever sums I wished into the campaign.

I then called some half dozen of the largest distributors and suppliers associated with Lust Cosmetics. None of them found the prospect of contributing to Buck's campaign appealing. Each of them, however, enjoyed the highly profitable work my company provided. Faced with my not-so-veiled warning that they would lose the work if they refused, all but one agreed to go along. To heighten their enthusiasm, I noted that having a President in the White House who could be counted upon to do us a favor would benefit all of our companies. In this, I was following my usual tactic of relying both on the carrot and the stick. The combination, I have found, is far more effective than relying on either one, alone.

The only holdout was my West Coast distributor, Warden Brothers. When I warned him of the consequences of a refusal to cooperate, Warden's President, Burt Warden, just laughed.

"Come now, Melvin," he said, You know you can't afford to replace me."

Unfortunately, he was right. Warden Brothers had a distribution system no other firm in the area could match. If I shifted to another distributor, Lust Cosmetics' sales would suffer.

"Furthermore," he added, "I think the discounts you are giving me are too low. When our current contract is up next month, I expect a forty percent increase in my discount."

I was ready to explode. I don't know which angered me more, Warden's refusal to contribute to Buck's campaign or his use of my first name. I have always hated to be called Melvin, the name bestowed on me by an otherwise wonderful father. Unfortunately, my father came from Gretna, Louisiana, the same home town as the old New York Giant's star outfielder, Mel Ott. A die-hard baseball fan, my father had named me after his home-town idol.

Possibly, my father later regretted his decision. He had never called me Melvin or Mel. Instead he and all my relatives and friends had always called me "Scoop." The knick name stemmed from my father's owning and editing the "Watsonville Weekly Courier," the only newspaper in Watsonville.

"Warden," I said, "I have to agree with you. Warden Brothers is irreplaceable."

I was silent for a moment, letting him savor his victory. I laughed to myself, visualizing the smile spreading across his face.

"However," I went on after a suitable interval, "I have a little puzzle for you. I believe you own about two percent of Warden Brothers' voting stock. Guess who is the largest stockholder, with eight percent of the voting shares? Let me give you a little hint. He's a short, bald, nasty God damn son of a bitch who is going to use his shares to wage a proxy fight and remove you as president if you don't send a very large contribution to Buck Porter's presidential campaign."

For a moment there was silence. Then Warden spoke in a hoarse voice. "All right, you bastard," he said. "I'll do what you want."

I couldn't resist driving the knife in a little deeper.

"Oh, Warden," I said. "You'd better double the contribution I said you'd give."

When I hung up, I thought for a moment, then called my stock broker. I told him to buy another hundred thousand shares of Warden Brothers stock, adding that it was no longer necessary to conceal the fact that I was the buyer. It might keep Warden from giving me any further difficulty if he was aware his control of the company depended upon my good will. Moreover, at the recent price of the stock, the purchase was a good investment.

My next call was to the office of Lust Cosmetics, to my executive vice president, Walter Byrd. He was bright and reasonably efficient. However, what I valued most was his loyalty. Some years before, when his son had been diagnosed as having as fatal brain tumor, I had located the doctor reputed to be the finest brain surgeon in the country and arranged for him to operate on the boy. Byrd and his wife had been pathetically grateful. Their son had survived the operation and was still alive and in good health. I was reasonably confident that Byrd's loyalty would continue, at least as long as his son survived.

I asked Byrd to update me on developments at the company since I had left for New Hampshire. His report left me thinking that all was going well and that I could safely extend my stay in New Hampshire until the primary was over.

After finishing my call to Byrd, my final call was to my home. I was uncertain about how to tell Pergamon that I would delay my return until after the New Hampshire primary. To my surprise, our housekeeper Milly answered the phone, rather than my wife. When I asked Milly if I could speak to Pergamon she reminded me that as she did every Wednesday afternoon, she had gone to the meeting of the Episcopal Churchwomen.

"Thanks," I said, asking her to inform Pergamon that I was delaying my return home until the following Wednesday.

"I hope nothing is wrong," she said.

Milly's concern touched me. I had originally been reluctant to hire Milly, telling Pergamon that nobody could cook as well as she did. I had added that it would be foolish to spend the extra money to no purpose.

I should have anticipated Pergamon's reaction. She exploded, berating me for being cheap. As usual, she went on to complain that we were still living in my parents' old home instead of moving to one of the new mansions being built on the north side of Watsonville. From there, she had gone on to criticize my car, a seventeen year old Buick that I had purchased used.

The old Buick was an eccentricity, but one based on the fact that it was the peppiest car I had ever driven and I saw no reason to give it up, just because it was old. Although the exterior was rusted, I had found an expert mechanic who took pride in maintaining it and I never regretted the amount of money I paid him to keep the motor in superb running order.

"What must the neighbors think," Pergamon had demanded, "seeing that old wreck parked in front of our house? It's the shabbiest car in the neighborhood as well as the shabbiest car in your company's parking lot."

That of course was true, but of no consequence.

"Who cares what the neighbors think?" I had answered. "They don't seem to care what I think. If the Hunters' dog shits on our lawn again, I may shoot the mutt. Besides, when my workers see my old car, they think twice about asking for more pay than I want to give them. It makes a lot of sense to have the boss drive the oldest car in town."

However, I don't like to argue, particularly with Pergamon. I had finally agreed to hiring Milly on condition that Pergamon stop complaining about my car. Pergamom had kept our bargain for a few weeks before starting up about the car again. Still, I did not regret my surrender. Milly had proved to be a cheerful, pleasant person to have around the house. As a bonus, she had turned out to be almost as good a cook as Pergamom.

I reassured Milly that my extended stay in New Hampshire was not the result of any trouble and asked her to make pork chops and an apple pie for dinner on Wednesday night. I suspected her pie crust was so good because she made it with lard, something Pergamom had stopped using years ago when it was reported to be bad for your health. I was not prepared to ask Milly if that were in fact the case, and hoped Pergamom never looked into the subject either.

As I left the phone booth, I looked at my watch. It was past

2:20 p.m. If everything was going according to plan, Buck would be making his ad recordings at the studio under the watchful eyes of Barlow and his assistants. I felt exhausted by my efforts to revive Buck's campaign, on edge, and in need of exercise.

I decided a walk would relax me. The weather was excellent for walking, and I enjoyed looking at the shops. Stopping off at the Historical Society, I inquired if they had any materials on Franklin Pierce, a governor of the state and America's fourteenth president. Pierce, along with other less well known presidents like Hayes, Arthur and Benjamin Harrison, had always been of interest to me. I was told the archivist was out and hoped I would have some free time while I was in Concord to stop by the Historical Society again.

As I walked along the streets, I saw posters of the various presidential candidates in many store windows. There were none of Buck's, reflecting the lack of resources and poor organization that had marked his campaign. I made a mental note to arrange for posters advertising Buck's virtues to be printed and posted.

By 4:30, I felted mentally relaxed and ready to return to the hotel. As the elevator opened on my floor, I saw one of Barlow's men in the corridor, watchfully controlling access to Buck's room.

"Is Mr. Porter inside?" I asked.

"He sure is."

I knocked at the door and was admitted by another of Barlow's assistants. Buck was seated in an easy chair, drinking a coke.

"How did it go, Buck?" I asked.

"Very well."

I turned to Barlow's assistant.

"Is Mr. Barlow in my room?" I asked.

"Yes," he answered.

I turned and entered my room. I found Barlow writing down his expenditures.

"Let me know the total and I'll write you a check," I told him. "How did the recording session go?"

"Porter was excellent. A real pro. If I didn't know better, I'd think he was sincere. But I have to admit you were right about his being a lady's man. I found him propositioning the receptionist. We really do have to keep him under tight control."

"Mr. Shultz," he continued. I think we ought to find some way of getting him out to meet the public. Not so much for what he can accomplish but to prevent him from going stir-crazy. I don't think he will sit for too much longer in a hotel room."

"What would you suggest?" I asked. "I don't trust him to talk in public. There's too great a risk he will blow the campaign."

"How about photo ops?" Barlow suggested. "You know, situations in which he can be photographed meeting the public but not saying anything."

"That's a great idea," I said. "We can have him distributing gifts of playing cards to hospitalized patients in veterans' hospitals, giving a donation to the Mothers Against Drunken Driving, that sort of thing. Can you take care of it?"

"Yes," he said, "I can arrange it. I think it will probably work."

"One more thing," I added. "Hire people to provide a crowd of supporters. Get them in various sizes and shapes, whatever looks good. Have the crowds gradually grow in size as the week progresses, so that we create the impression his campaign is gaining momentum"

Barlow smiled at me. "You know," he said, "It's fun getting involved in a presidential campaign, even one as screwed up as this one." He sat down and began making the phone calls to set up the operation.

I was not looking forward to spending more time with Buck. However, it was foolish to let myself become fed up with him while

I was devoting so much effort to getting him elected President. Deciding that if things got too bad, I could talk to Barlow, I invited Buck, Barlow and his assistants to dine with me at Concord's best restaurant.

I thought the price of the meals far too high for what we were served. Still, the decor was pleasant and I was able to place Buck at the far end of the table. There he talked to two of Barlow's assistants, while I was able to enjoy a interesting conversation with Barlow about political campaigns he had been involved in.

I said goodnight to Buck early, after instructing Barlow to continue to keep a close watch on him. I relaxed in bed, watching an old western movie on TV until I fell asleep.

A loud knocking on the door awakened me. When I opened the door, I found one of Barlow's assistants.

"Jim wanted you to know right away," he said. "We were watching TV and saw one of Buck's ads."

I quickly put on my bathrobe and went to Buck's room. Buck and the others were drinking cokes and he was eating potato chips. A science fiction movie was on the television. I wondered if Barlow had persuaded Buck not to put on the porn cable channel.

When Barlow saw me, he grinned. "That ad was really good," said. I waited until the next commercial break to see if the station would repeat the ad. There were numerous ads, but not Buck's. I was getting tired.

"I'll take a look at the set in my room. Thanks for alerting me," I said.

Back in my room, I considered turning on the television, but decided I was too sleepy. The ad could wait until tomorrow morning.

Early the next morning, I awakened and turned on the TV, switching from channel to channel. I was disappointed until I reached one of Concord's stations. The local 7 a.m. traffic report carried one of Buck's ads. I was surprised that Max had been able to obtain such a desirable time slot. I learned later that he had used many of his chips to persuade other ad agencies to relinquish desirable time slots to him.

After watching two more of Buck's ads, I dressed hurriedly and went to Buck's room. I was surprised to find him already up, in conversation with Barlow about the photo ops Barlow had arranged for the day. We had a quick breakfast at the hotel buffet, with Buck surrounded by Barlow and his assistants. They were discussing the scheduling of the events. It felt good to be freed from that task. I felt reasonably confident that in Barlow I had somebody I could rely on.

The days leading up to the primary sped by. Each day, Barlow and his assistants steered Buck to photo ops and other events at which he could be protected from inconvenient questions as well as from making impolitic statements. The task quickly became too much for Barlow and his assistants and I readily agreed to Barlow's request to bring in more helpers.

As the campaign went on, the number of television and radio ads urging voters to choose Buck increased until it was almost impossible to watch or listen to any program for more than fifteen minutes without being subjected to one of his commercials. To further bombard the voters with our message, I approved Barlow's proposal to print and distribute campaign posters, including paying shop owners to place them in prominent positions in their windows,

During Buck's public campaign appearances, I left handling him to Barlow, mingling with the audience to catch their reactions. These could not be taken at face value, as many of the bystanders had been hired by Barlow to create the impression for the media covering the event that Buck was attracting a growing number of voters. However, from time to time I picked up reactions which I thought might possibly be genuine.

Most of these were favorable and I mentioned them to Barlow. When I asked him what he thought Buck's chances were, he paused for a moment to reflect.

"Mel," he said, "the limited polling we have available indicates that he has moved from last to fourth position in the race. By today, I would guess he is now in third spot."

"Do you think he can win?" I asked.

"Honestly, no. Sure, that ad campaign is stimulating a lot of built-in resentment against the income tax, and some of those people will vote for him. He also is showing himself to be a natural campaigner. A lot of people viewing his public appearances, particularly women, see him as an attractive candidate."

"However," he continued, "he is still only a one-issue candidate. His stand on the income tax has roused vigorous opposition from all of the other candidates, as well as ridicule in the media. I think many voters sympathetic to his views will decide to vote for one of the other candidates when they get into the polling booth. I can't see him finishing any better than third."

"Then we need another issue," I said. "Something to give voters a reason to overcome their doubts about the anti-tax campaign."

I went over in my mind everything I knew about Buck, hoping to find an answer to our problem. Then, I suddenly recalled the first time I had seen him. He had been trying to explain to the bar tender the virtues of his education program.

"That's it," I told Barlow. "Our second campaign theme is interest free tuition loans for all college students."

"Isn't that going to play into the hands of those who are arguing that the abolition of the income tax will cause the budget deficit to soar?"Barlow asked soberly.

Refining my plan as I spoke, I said, "To answer that we say that students qualify for loans after their first year in college only if they have passing grades. Repayment begins as soon as a student gets a job after graduation. Repayment comes from the student's social security withholding, with his loan repaid before the withholding is applied to his social security account. That way we can say that all we need is seed money for the first four years, with repayments after that covering new loans."

"Does that work out mathematically?" Barlow asked.

"I doubt it," I said, "but that's unimportant. The plan will appeal to all those parents who are worried about financing their children's college education. We release the plan the day before the primary, so there is a minimum of time for critics to focus on it. It's fortunate that Buck will be convincing when he springs it. He really believes something like that would work."

"Well," said Barlow, "I have to admit it's no worse that the income tax policy. If that worked, this one might just, too. However, if you do it, I suggest that Buck make the announcement on TV on Sunday night. That would give more people a chance to learn of it and still not give the critics much time to attack it."

"Let's do it!" I decided quickly. See if you can write a draft for Buck along the lines of what I said. I'm going to try and arrange for the TV time.'

When I telephoned Max, I was delighted to find him optimistic over the prospects of acquiring the additional time we needed for Buck's speech on Sunday. Max was confident he could get five minutes on Sunday evening on the leading New Hampshire stations for Buck to announce his education program, although not necessarily the same time on all stations. A fifteen minute slot would be more difficult, he would see what he could do.

Returning to Barlow, I found he had already completed a draft of Buck's speech. I made a few alterations, then we jointly drafted a fifteen minute version.

On Sunday evening, we gathered in Buck's room to watch his filmed announcement. Max had obtained a fifteen minute time slot on only one New Hampshire station, but had managed to secure coverage on all of them. The speeches had been recorded several hours earlier. Buck was the only one in the room who did not appear nervous. He alternatively was taking large handfuls of potato chips from a large carton and gulping coke from a can.

I wondered how he could consume so much food. Only a few hours before he had eaten a large steak and several helpings of French fries.

We got our first look at Buck's education speech on the evening news. It was only a thirty second clip, too brief to evaluate its effectiveness. When the news was over, we found the five-minute version of his speech broadcast as an ad on another channel. I thought it impressive. Buck came across as friendly, intelligent and totally sincere. Barlow was right. Buck was a natural politician or actor; the two seemed interchangeable in our society.

I looked at Barlow. He was grinning and nodding his head in approval. One of his assistants flashed me a victory sign.

"Buck," I said, "You were great!" I meant every word.

Throughout the evening, we watched repeats of his speech, mostly the five-minute version. I thought that the longer version was no more effective than the five-minute one.

I motioned Barlow to follow me out of the room.

"You're right," I said, "He is a great politician. Let's take a chance. Have him make longer and more frequent appearances tomorrow. It's a risk, but hopefully he won't put his foot in his mouth."

"I think it's a chance we have to take," he said, "if we hope to have any chance of winning the primary." He began writing on a yellow pad, scheduling additional public appearances for Buck.

I said goodnight and went back to my room. My watch showed it was past 9 p.m. "Just forty-eight more hours," I thought, "and it will be over, one way or another."

The next two days went quickly. Buck spoke at innumerable meetings, attended photo ops, introduced himself to pedestrians on the sidewalk. He chatted to patrons at cafes and coffee shops, munched numerous hot dogs purchased from street venders to the amusement of the bystanders. Barlow and his expanded group of assistants prevented most gaffs. When he veered off script to speak about his initial education plan rather than the one we had carefully drafted for him, Barlow was close and was able to quickly stop Buck and lead him away.

On Tuesday, Buck had a full schedule of meetings, lasting until the polls closed. Barlow had told me that many politicians believed that such last-minute campaigning was a waste of time, but agreed when I told him we had to try it anyhow.

I ordered the hotel to send up drinks and sandwiches to Buck's room, and we gathered there to watch the election returns on TV. Unlike the other candidate camps. I had not bothered to hire a hall for the campaign staff and Buck's supporters to await the election results. I had, however, ascertained that the hotel ballroom would be available if we needed it. I knew rationally that I was being superstitious, but felt it would jinx our chances if I acted as though Buck had a chance of winning.

The earliest returns showed Buck in the lead. However, he quickly fell behind Ross Tobin, viewed by most of the media as the probable winner of the primary. The senior Senator from North Dakota and a retired Marine Corp General and decorated war hero before that, Tobin might have been my preferred candidate too, if I had not decided to back Buck. Tobin came across as intelligent and able. Comparing his campaign platform with the wish list of the major contributors to his campaign, I found an interesting similarity. This was disillusioning but, given the way political was conducted, not surprising.

I decided that like Buck, Tobin was a puppet. The major difference was who had the ability to pull the strings.

As the returns came in, Buck became increasingly depressed by Tobin's lead. He clearly expected to win, and by a big margin. His optimism, it was clear, far exceeded his intelligence.

More returns came in and Buck regained the lead. Then it shifted again in favor of Tobin.

The race was obviously going to be a close one between Buck and Tobin, with the other five candidates some distance in the rear. I looked at my watch. It was going to be a long night.

The closeness of the race showed that the advertising blitz we had orchestrated for Buck had been effective. It would be ironic, I thought, to have moved so far, only to have him finish behind Tobin, in second place. I had no illusions that a second place finish would enable Buck to battle on to eventually win the nomination. New Hampshire would mark the end of my involvement in the race if Buck lost.

About 9 p.m., with Buck holding a razor-thin margin in the vote count, the phone in the room began to ring constantly. The callers were primarily from the media, wishing to interview him and to station TV cameras at his campaign headquarters to cover the activity there during the night. I assumed that the media's delay in contacting us earlier was due to their reluctance to admit their earlier predictions on the outcome had been wrong. None of them had revised their earlier estimates, which showed him dead last.

I instructed Barlow to tell all callers that Buck would not be available for an interview until later in the evening. I did, however, say that they might set up cameras in the ball room of the hotel. I then called the night manager of the hotel and arranged to rent the ball room and to install there large TV monitors to permit watching the election returns come in. I also ordered sandwiches and soft drinks to be sent there, hoping to convey the impression of confidence in Buck's headquarters. I was amused to see the pleasure of the night manager in this unexpected business.

When we left the hotel room to go down to the ball room, Buck was still in the lead over Tobin. His margin was still so small, a handful of votes could quickly shift the vote back in Tobin's favor.

As we took the elevator down to the ground floor room, I was praying that Buck would still be ahead when we reached the ball room. To my relief, entering the hall, I looked at a TV monitor and found that Buck's lead had not faltered.

It had passed through my mind that we might bring into the hall some of the people we had hired to appear as Buck's supporters at photo ops during the campaign. I was now happy I had not done so. The ballroom was crowded by TV cameramen and reporters, accompanied by what seemed to be actual real members of the public. I knew that none of them would have been there if Buck was not leading in the votes counted.

By 11 p.m., virtually all of the votes had been counted. Buck still held on to his narrow lead, and the TV networks had declared him the winner. Tobin still refused to concede defeat, but Buck's other rivals had all done so. I ordered champagne brought to the room and drafted a short announcement for Buck to deliver, expressing thanks to all those who had supported him.

I had Barlow deflect all questions from the reporters and

instructed his assistants to escort Buck back to his room. I cautioned Barlow to impress upon his staff that it was even more important than ever for Buck to be carefully watched to prevent his speaking with anyone without my prior approval. After arranging for the hotel to provide food and drinks to the ball room until the last of the media left, I said good night to Barlow and went back to my room to turn in.

I made some instant cocoa, using the electric water heater I always take with me when I travel. The hot cocoa never fails to help me fall asleep quickly. It did so this time. I was very pleased with my success in manipulating the New Hampshire primary to achieve Buck's victory.

Before dawn, I awakened with my mind dwelling on two unpleasant incidents from the night before. The first concerned the unexpected arrival in the hotel ball room of Mark Goldsborough, the Harvard political science professor who had been acting as Buck's impromptu campaign manager until I had taken charge of the campaign. I had deliberately kept him from contacting Buck, fearing that he might be successful in persuading Buck to depart from the script I had written for the campaign.

Goldsborough's appearance had resembled that of a lunatic. He had been disheveled, needed a shave and had smelled of liquor. Seeing Buck, he had rushed toward him, gesticulating wildly, shouting obscenities. He shouted that Buck "Had raped the Constitution." Fortunately, I had succeeded in having two of Barlow's assistants grab Goldsborough's arms and escort him politely but firmly out of the hotel. None of the media appeared to have noticed the event. I wondered if I should attempt to neutralize Goldsborough's possible danger to the campaign by buying him off with some sort of research grant, but decided against it.

The second problem had been phone call from Buck's wife

in Oklahoma City. I had prevented Buck from talking to her for a week, afraid of her interference in the campaign. However, when one of Barlow's assistants informed me she was once again on the phone trying to reach Buck, I decided that I had stalled her as long as possible and that the time might be as good as any to permit Buck to talk to her.

To help control the conversation, I arranged for the call to be switched to Buck's room and had Barlow escort him there. Then I stationed myself close to Buck as he picked up the phone. His end of the call, which lasted a good five minutes, consisted of little more than periodic repetitions of "Yes, dear."

When he hung up, Buck turned to me with a glum expression his face.

"That was Tammy," he said.

I nodded gravely, as though I had been unaware of the identity of the caller.

"She's very angry," he continued. "About the campaign. She says the plan to eliminate the federal income tax is stupid and that we should have pitched it on the need to revitalize the inner city schools. She also said she has gotten David Ames to take over as my campaign manager."

"Who is David Ames?" I asked.

"He's a senior partner in her law firm. He also handled financial matters in my Cabinet when I was governor."

"Buck," I said, "Your wife is a very intelligent person. But she is in Oklahoma City. It's difficult for her to be as up to date as we are on the situation in the states where we plan to campaign. I think it would best if I continue to decide on the spot what themes we ought to stress."

Buck looked sulky. I could see there was no point in trying to persuade him to reject any advice he might receive from Tammy.

"Why don't you let me talk to her?" I told Buck. "Once I explain what is going on, I'm sure she will agree to keep things as they are. Besides," I went on, "It wouldn't be fair to Jim. He has really acted as the campaign manager since he arrived. Do you think it would be proper to kick him out now, after he's won for us in New Hampshire?"

"No," he said. "I didn't think of that. Do you really think Tammy doesn't understand the situation here? She's very smart."

"Just let me talk to her," I replied confidently. I obtained Tammy's phone number from Buck, then suggested that he discuss with Barlow our campaign strategy for the next few days. Excusing myself, I went back to my room and called Tammy.

"Mrs. Porter," I began, "I'm Melvin Shultz. As you know, I have been helping Buck campaign in New Hampshire."

"Yes," she said.

Her voice was cold and her manner crisp. Clearly unfriendly.

"I've heard about you. I think Buck's performance in New Hampshire after he met you was vulgar, stupid and disgraceful."

"But he won," I said, trying to sound friendly.

"He would have won without your help."

"Mrs. Porter," I said, choosing my words carefully. "When I met your husband he was in last place in all the polls. His campaign had no funds. I provided him with all of the financing and organization that enabled him to win. Unless I continue to do so, his campaign will collapse. And, unless I retain full control, I will immediately stop my support, all of it."

"Nothing could make me happier," she snapped back. "Please do so!"

I decided that any attempt to be cordial to her was futile.

"Mrs. Porter," I said. "I appreciate your frankness. Let me be equally frank with you. Not only will I withdraw from the campaign. I will go downstairs to the campaign headquarters and speak to the radio and TV media there. I will announce my complete severance of ties with Buck's campaign, stating that I made a horrible mistake in supporting him. I will emphasize that he would be a fiasco as President and that I am throwing my full support to Senator Tobin."

"You wouldn't dare," she said.

"Oh yes, I would. And then I would say that my breaking off support for his campaign was due to his duplicity and opportunism in proposing programs that he did not believe in. I would cite his previous public statements on education as proof of that fact. I would add that in addition, Buck was morally unqualified to be in the White House."

"Exactly what do you mean by that?"

"I would describe finding Buck in his room in bed fucking a whore. And, Mrs. Porter, I would then have her confirm my comments."

"You bastard!" she almost shouted.

"Mrs. Porter," I said, "Lots of people have called me that. But they're wrong. My parents were married in church four years before I was born. The only difference between you and me is that you wear a skirt and I wear pants. Now I suggest you shut up about what Buck should and shouldn't do in the campaign and let me run it. And tell Mr. Ames that his services as campaign manager will not be needed. That also goes for your involvement. Do we understand each other?"

"You win," she said. I could sense that I had won only a skirmish. More confrontations between us were clearly going to come.

CHAPTER 3

The morning after the primary, I had breakfast with Buck and Barlow. Before speaking to Buck, I had made sure to speak privately with Barlow, offering him the title of Campaign Manager. In part, I did this to make it more difficult for Tammy to move someone of her choice into the post. It was a necessary precaution. I could not be sure of how long I could keep Buck from acceding to her demands. In part, I thought it only fair to Barlow to reward him for the hard work he had done in the campaign.

There was also a third reason. During my acrimonious phone conversation with Tammy, Barlow had entered the room and overheard part of it. I had caught a glimpse of his face. He had seemed shocked and unhappy about the harsh tactics I had used with her. I had a lot of respect for Barlow and no reason to distrust his loyalty. Still, if I could make him grateful to me by offering him the post of Buck's campaign manager, it made sense to do so.

I was pleased by Barlow's eager acceptance. Apparently, there was a clear distinction in his mind between taking on the job, when Buck was in last place, and after he had won the New Hampshire primary.

During breakfast with Buck, we drew up plans for the forthcoming primaries. Buck had virtually no organization in any state. At my direction, he drew up a list of contacts he had and we worked out what positions and salaries and titles we could offer them. Buck seemed pleased by the arrangements after I told him that Tammy had agreed to Barlow's serving as campaign manager under my overall direction. Naturally, I did not mention the means by which I had obtained her acquiescence.

We decided that Barlow would fly with Buck to Delaware, the site of the next presidential primary, to establish an organization there. From there, the two of them would fly to Arizona, where the primary would be held three days after Delaware's. Because of the strong anti-tax sentiment in both states, Barlow thought we had some chance of winning if we could build adequate campaign organizations in time.

I assured him we could spend as freely in those states as we had done in New Hampshire and that I believed a massive advertising campaign would be effective. Barlow was not as optimistic as I was.

"Remember, Mel, "he said. "Nobody thought Buck could win in New Hampshire. Nobody even thought of attacking him. Now that he is the front-runner, Buck will be the target for all sorts of media scrutiny and political attacks."

"Cairns," I said, thinking aloud.

Barlow and Buck both looked at me.

"Of course," I said, "How could I have been so slow? Cairns is the answer."

I was referring to Senator Cairns, senior Senator from Delaware, Chairman of the Senate Foreign Relations Committee, and one of Buck's rivals in the New Hampshire primary. Cairns had conducted a thoughtful, statesman-like campaign, stressing his skill and experience in foreign affairs. The low priority voters give to experience in foreign affairs when choosing their candidates and Cairn's lack of financial resources to support his campaign had resulted in his finishing in sixth place in the primary, ahead only of the television comedian.

"Jim," I said. "I want you to contact Cairns. Tell him that the results of the New Hampshire primary show he has no chance of winning the nomination. If he drops out now, endorses Buck, and places his Delaware organization behind Buck, Buck will appoint him Secretary of State."

"I doubt Cairns would accept such a deal," Barlow said thoughtfully. "Maybe if he doesn't win the Delaware, but not now."

"After Delaware, his help would be worthless," I said. "Tell him that. The offer stands only if he accepts it today. And promise him anything else you have to, except the vice presidency. Tell him that Buck will give him free rein in handling foreign affairs. He can name all of his deputies. Tell him he will go down in history as America's greatest Secretary of State. If he still refuses, tell him we'll cover any debts his campaign has from the New Hampshire primary."

I glanced at Buck. He was following the conversation closely. I wondered how he felt, having his Cabinet appointments used as trading material to obtain the nomination.

"I'll take care of it," Barlow said, as I stood up.

"Gentlemen," I said, "May God be with us in our endeavor."

As I said this, it sounded pretentious to my ears. I hoped that God had a good sense of humor when he regarded presidential politics. If not, I might be in serious trouble.

After saying goodbye to Barlow and Buck, I collected my suitcase, checked out of the hotel, and took a taxi to the airport. Although I was taking an early flight, I had to change twice and did not arrive in Chicago until late in the day. It was already dark when the airport shuttle dropped me at the satellite parking where I had left the Buick.

I hoped I would have no difficulty in starting the car. It had been parked there since I drove from Watsonville to the airport some two weeks before on my way to New Hampshire. I was glad when, as always, it treated me with the same regard I always treated it, turning over almost immediately.

As I headed to Watsonville, I turned on the car radio. I was overjoyed when I heard on the news that Senator Cairns had unexpectedly withdrawn from the race for the Republican presidential nomination, throwing his support to Buck. Jim had done his work well. With Cairns' support, Buck had an excellent chance of winning the Delaware primary.

There was little traffic and I pulled up in front of my house in Watsonville a little after 7 p.m. I got out of my car and looked around me. I loved the street. The houses on it had been built before World War I. They were solidly built and well cared for. My home was the smallest on the block. This reflected both the fact that I was an only child, so that my parents did not need a larger home, and the relatively low income my father earned from his newspaper.

A thick canopy of old trees shaded the street. Pergamon's car, a new BMW, was parked on the driveway.

I reached the front door and took out my key to unlock it. Before I could do so, the door swung open and I saw Pergamon illuminated by the light from the living room behind her.

We had been married for almost forty years. Pergamon was sixty-four, my own age. Her once-blond hair was gray, but she had added only a few pounds since I had first met her. I thought she was just as pretty as the first time I had seen her.

"Dear," I said, putting my arm around her and attempting to kiss her on the lips. She moved her head, so that I kissed only her cheek. I felt the desire I always did when holding her.

"Pergamon," I said, "Let's go to bed."

"Don't be silly," she said. "Dinner's ready."

Her refusal did not surprise me. While she was still passionate at times, it had become increasingly less frequent. I blamed this on her involvement in volunteer work and church activities. In fairness, however, I had to admit that it really dated back to the time the doctors had told her it would unwise for her to become pregnant again. It had been a relatively minor disappointment to me at the time, although I wanted to have children. But, coming on the heels of a miscarriage, it had left her depressed for almost a year.

"It was sweet of you to welcome me at the door," I said, trying to maintain a cheerful manner. With luck, I might still be able to persuade her to go to bed after dinner.

Pergamon, was having none of it.

"How could I miss you?" she said. "That Buick makes enough noise to awaken the dead."

I saw no purpose in getting into an argument with Pergamon.

"Dinner smells great," I said. "Let's eat."

We ate in the dining room, as Pergamon preferred. My choice would have been to eat in the kitchen. It was the largest room in the house and had a wonderful old fireplace along one wall. In my mind, the kitchen was associated with warmth and companionship, ever since as a child I used to chat with my mother as she cooked.

Milly had prepared the pork chops I had asked her to make when I called from New Hampshire. I found them delicious, as always. Milly welcomed me warmly, and hovered over me to make sure I was enjoying my meal. We ate silently for a time and then

Pergamon looked up.

"Did you find the New Hampshire primary interesting?" she asked.

"Yes, I did."

"Melvin, did you have anything to do with Porter winning it?" she asked.

As always, I found being addressed as Melvin irritating. It was particularly annoying when Pergamon called me that. Shortly after I started taking her out, I had asked her to follow my family's example and call me Scoop. She had readily agreed. Unfortunately, she had reverted to calling me Melvin shortly after her miscarriage.

"A little," I admitted. I thought it unwise to tell Pergamon the extent of my involvement.

"I thought so," she said. "His campaigning was the most dishonest I have ever seen. Can you imagine, calling for the abolition of the federal income tax? As though that could be possible. If you had to meddle in politics, why didn't you back Tobin?. He seems like an honest sort."

"I thought so, too, until I compared his campaign positions with the list of his biggest contributors."

Pergamon got up from the table.

"I'll be running," she said. "It's the vestry meeting at St. Marks."

"What's that got to do with you?" I asked. "You're not a member of the vestry."

"No," she replied. "But they are discussing the church budget. They asked me to explain the budget for women's affairs."

She left and a few minutes later I heard her BMW pull out of the driveway. I was feeling a bit depressed, when Milly brought in the apple pie she had baked.

"Have some," Mr. Shultz," she said.

I cut a large slice. As I had expected, it was delicious.

"Nobody can make apple pie like you can, Milly," I told her.

"You say that every time," she said. It was true.

"That's because it's good every time."

She smiled with pleasure at my compliment.

After finishing the pie, I helped myself to a second piece, ate it, and went upstairs to the bedroom. Undressing, I got into bed. My usual practice was to relax in bed watching a movie on TV. I tried the channels, but there was nothing good on. Fortunately, I had several old westerns I had taped, using my VCR. I selected one, an old black and white western, and watched it till the end. I particularly enjoyed the older movies, finding the language in many of the newer ones annoying.

I very much wanted to call Barlow at his hotel in Dover, Delaware, to find out how the state looked for Buck. I desisted until the movie was over, thinking that Barlow and Buck might be having a late dinner. When I called, he immediately picked up the phone. I began by congratulating him on persuading cairns to endorse Buck.

"He at first refused to pull out of the race," Barlow said. "What finally convinced him was our promise that as Secretary of State, he could name all of his senior assistants. I didn't have to offer to cover his campaign expenses."I

"Great!" I said. "How are things going in Delaware? Has Cairns turned his campaign organization over to you?"

"He has. He flew back here this morning and personally introduced me to his people here. I think we are in good shape to win the state."

"What about Arizona?" I asked.

"I really haven't had time to do much on that," he said. "Do you have any other Cabinet posts you can offer to get that state?"

"I'm afraid not," I said. "Unfortunately, there are more states we have to win than there are Cabinet jobs available. Seriously," I went on, "There are a large number of retirees living in Arizona. Let's have Buck promise that as President, he will push through legislation making every retiree above sixty exempt from federal taxes on car purchases. Oh, and have someone out there find out what the Republican voters in Arizona are particularly angry about. Then draft a speech for Buck promising to delivery whatever they want. Can you do that?"

Barlow laughed. "Before New Hampshire, I would have said you were crazy. But, hell, if it worked there, that sort of advertising might work here. I'll get the research done right away."

When I finished thanking Barlow and hung up, I looked at my watch. It was almost 10 p.m., too late to all anyone else. I went down to the kitchen, made my nightly cup of instant cocoa, and went back to bed. Pergamon was still not home. Apparently, the vestry meeting was a long one. I decided it would be foolish to wait up for her and turned off the light.

The next morning, I awakened at 5:45 as usual. I turned off the alarm so as not wake Pergamon and shaved in the bathroom with the door closed, so that the light would not bother her. I looked carefully at Pergamon, but she was still asleep. Sometimes when she woke up early, she felt like making love, but this was apparently not one of those days.

I had my usual breakfast of juice and coffee in the kitchen. Milly had offered numerous times to get up early to make it for me, but I saw no reason to bother her. I then walked out. It was still dark and I admired the stars as I got into the Buick.

There was no traffic on the road at that early hour, and I arrived at the Lust Cosmetics plant some fifteen minutes later. The plant had been expanded several times since I took over the company, but not recently. One reason was the lack of adequate space for further expansion. A more important one, however, was the fact that it was cheaper to acquire or enlarge other plants rather than to have the work done at the Watsonville facility, parts of which were over seventy years old.

Indeed, I had been advised by my accountants to close the plant and transfer all of its operations elsewhere to increase the company's profits. I had rejected their suggestion. I did not wish to be a party to firing the thousand or so workers at the plant, many of whom would have been unable to obtain other jobs. Lust Cosmetics already provided me with a healthy profit, a good part of which I put in the employee profit sharing plan. As the sole owner, I was not responsible to any stockholders or board of directors and was free to follow my own inclinations in this area.

I parked the Buick, as usual, in the first space by the door. It was mine by virtue of my being the first to arrive at the plant. I had rejected suggestions that I set aside reserved parking spaces for the senior officials. Every space was available on a first come, first serve basis. I believed this policy encouraged the workers to arrive early and was good for employee morale. It also resulted in blue collar employees parking next to senior executives, giving them a chance to see and greet each other.

The fact that my car was always in the best parking space let my employees know that I was the first one at the plant each morning. I knew I was regarded as a character by the workers. Not only did I drive the oldest car in the lot, but my policy was to pay the lowest wages in the industry and the lowest, for comparable work, of any large company in the Watsonville area. I also did my best to insure that no plants of Lust Cosmetics were unionized, although this was not always successful in some of the foreign facilities acquired by the company. When Pergamon had gotten wind of my policy and questioned me about it, I had told her it was based on my unwillingness to have any unions dictate to me what I was going to do with my workers.

Despite low wages, jobs at the company were highly prized. I had established a profit sharing plan under which all employees received a share of the profits, an incentive which had raised worker productivity to the highest level of any company in the industry. Many of the workers who had been employed by Lust Cosmetics since I had taken control of the firm received each year almost as much in profit sharing than they did in their basic wages. And the company credit union that I had established made it possible for the workers to buy homes and cars at subsidized interest rates.

As I entered the plant, the security guard at the reception desk handed me that day's copies of "The Wall Street Journal" and the "Chicago Tribune." I had these delivered them to the plant so that I could read them first thing in my office. The "New York Times" was not available for home delivery, so that I had to depend on a mail subscription. This frequently resulted in my getting that paper several days late. I believed firmly that knowledge is power. My regular reading of these papers had enabled me to make many wise decisions over the years.

Going upstairs to my office, I made a cup of coffee using the electric coffee maker I had installed in my office. I had installed similar coffee makers in the offices of all company executives and throughout the plant for the other employees to use. The coffee packet's, supplied by a local service, did not make nearly as good coffee as Milly did, but that was hardly to be expected.

I then sat down at my desk and carefully scrutinized the papers. It was a habit I had inherited from my father. Each day he had read the daily newspapers in the belief that they helped him publish better stories in our weekly. I went through the papers carefully, checking the domestic, foreign and business news for information that might affect Lust Cosmetics. I also read the style and sports news, since events there could be helpful in preparing more timely advertising. I found I was spending far more time on political news than before, looking at events from the point of view of how they might affect Buck's campaign.

Shortly before 8 a.m., I heard the rest of the work force begin to arrive. My office window looked down on the prized parking spaces in front of the building, so that I was aware of which executives arrived early. Typically, Walter Byrd's was the next car to arrive after mine. As my deputy, Walter loyally followed my example of arriving early. A few minutes after 8 a.m., he arrived at my office, carrying a folder of papers for me to sign. He briefed me on developments at the company since I had been gone. Everything had gone well; production and sales were up and he had been successful in settling a potential problem with an environmental advocacy group over alleged contamination in our plant on the west coast.

After Walter left, I telephoned several of my senior executives. I thought it desirable to keep in personal contact with them, to more accurately evaluate their loyalty and performance.

Feeling confident that things at the company were going well, I turned my attention back to Buck's campaign. My first call was to Max Behrman. I thanked him for the great job he had done handling the advertising for Buck in New Hampshire.

"Without your work, Max," I told him, "We never could have pulled it off." I meant it sincerely. I then instructed him to obtain all the advertising time he could in Delaware and Arizona, so that we could repeat the massive effort we had in New Hampshire.

"We'll stress the same themes we did in New Hampshire," I told him. "We hit hard on eliminating the federal income tax and providing tax free loans for tuition for college students. For Arizona, also prepare ads promising to exempt every retiree over sixty from federal taxes on the purchase of a new car. If you can think of something that will appeal to gun owners in Arizona, do that, too."

After completing the call to Max, I telephoned Sol Sugarman. I was very pleased when he informed me that he had set up the funding apparatus we needed to finance Buck's campaign.

"With the various mechanism we've established, he explained, "You can contribute as much as you want without going afoul of the election finance laws. Of course, we had to use every loop hole in the regulations and some of the cash may have to be funneled via various intermediaries. But it's all strictly legal!"

"Sol," I said laughing, "You're amazing."

My final call was to Alan Barnes. Barnes and I went back a long way. I had first met him when he was a waiter in a Chicago fast foods restaurant. I had gone there for a quick and cheap meal. I was feeling depressed. I had just had an unsuccessful meeting at a Chicago bank, failing to persuade the loan officer to lend me money to purchase new equipment I needed to make Lust Cosmetics' production more efficient. The meal had cost about six dollars and I had left what I thought was a generous dollar tip.

Walking from the restaurant, I heard someone shouting, "Hey Mister."

Turning, I saw it was the waiter. He was holding a bill in his hand. I wondered if he was going to give me an argument for leaving too small a tip. It wouldn't have done him any good. I certainly was not about to increase it.

Instead, he told me that I had left a ten dollar bill, which he assumed had been a mistake. He handed it back to me and started to leave. Gratefully taking the ten, I looked in my wallet and found I had two singles. I called him back and gave them to him, thanking him for his honesty. I liked his demeanor and apologized that I did not have more cash I could spare for a generous tip.

"That's OK Mister," he said, with a rueful smile, "We all have problems."

As I regarded him more closely, I realized he looked a bit scruffy, in need of a haircut and a shave. He also seemed to be too old to be a waiter in a fast food restaurant; all of the other waiters had been teenagers.

Are you the manager?" I asked him.

"No sir," he said.

He looked embarrassed. "I just got out of the army. I'm looking for another job, but this pays the bills until I can find one."

When I pressed him, he told me his names was Barnes, that he had served sixteen years in the military police and had been a Captain in criminal Investigation.

"You look young to be retired," I said.

His face reddened. "I didn't retire," he said. "I was court-martialed for allegedly fabricating evidence against a suspect. It was a trumped up charge and I was quickly acquitted. But even with an acquittal, I realized my superiors would always remember I had been charged. I had no future left in the army, so I retired. It's ironic, I was probably the most scrupulous investigator the army had "

I felt a sense of pity for the man. I didn't know much about court-martials, but I didn't think defendants were ever acquitted. Any man who had gone to the effort Barnes did to return a large bill he thought had been given to him by mistake, particularly when he needed the money as much as Barnes obviously did, was unlikely to be dishonest.

I suggested that he might do better using his army experience as a private investigator. Barnes bitterly answered that when prospective employers learned of his court-martial, they refused to hire him.

"Look Barnes," I had told him, touched by his situation, "I own a small cosmetics company. I can't pay you a lot, but you can do some security work for me. It can help you get into the field."

Barnes had gladly accepted my offer and had performed well. His firm had grown to modest size, aided by the increased work I had given him as Lust Cosmetics had prospered. He could have expanded further, but Barnes had not wanted to handle the additional supervisory responsibilities this would have entailed. He had been particularly helpful in conducting background security checks on individuals I was considering hiring for senior positions and in weeding out applicants for lower jobs whom I suspected might be undercover union organizers sent to unionize my plants.

When I got Alan on the phone, I arranged for him to come out to the plant for lunch. He was prompt, as usual. I took him down to the plant cafeteria, where I normally ate. Several of the company executives had urged me to establish an executive dining room, but I had refused. I thought it good for the workers to see the senior officials of the company sharing their eating place and their fare.

Alan and I obtained our food from the cafeteria line and seated ourselves at a table. After looking around to make certain that nobody was close enough to overhear our conversation, I turned to him.

"Do you have time to undertake a major investigation for me?"

"Yes, sir," he replied. I laughed to myself. Although he had been out of the military for some dozen years, he still used the military 'sir' when addressing me.

"Good, Alan," I said. "I want you to go to Oklahoma City. You will be there for some time, so you had better set up a temporary office there. I want a complete background investigation of the fellow who won the New Hampshire primary, Robert Porter. I want to know everything about him, from the day he was born. About his parents, his uncles and aunts before that. If he got fresh with a girl, I want to know that, even if it occurred when he was in grade school. Ditto if he knocked over a neighbor's ash can on Halloween when he was five."

Alan took out a small pad and began making notes.

"You certainly want a thorough job."

"More than thorough. I don't want a book on Porter. I want a twenty-volume encyclopedia. On his wife, political associates, on his roommates in college. And I want the same sort of investigation on his wife. If you find anything detrimental, dig further. Spend whatever is necessary to get notarized statements substantiating detrimental information. If there are any unfavorable photographs, buy them, too.

"That will take time," he said.

"I know it will. After you get it, I want you to stay in Oklahoma City until the presidential election, assuming Porter wins the nomination. Keep your ears open for anything that may affect his chances."

I noticed a puzzled look on Alan's face.

"Is there some problem?" I asked him.

"Just this. Why do you want notarized statements if I uncover any detrimental information? I thought you were backing him?"

I realized it would be foolish to tell Alan the truth.

"If I get notarized statements, it allows me to check further and show they are lying if their allegations are untrue."

I was glad he seemed satisfied with my answer.

After lunch, I walked with Alan back to his car. As I said goodbye, I handed him a check to cover his initial expenses and his regular fee and told him to bill me further payments as convenient.

Then I had an afterthought. I had no reason to distrust Barlow. Still, as campaign manager for Buck, he was in a sensitive position. I really didn't know enough about him to completely relay on his loyalty.

"Alan," I said. "Have one of your assistants do a similar background investigation on James Barlow, Porter's campaign manager."

Once again, Alan made notes in his pad.

"Goodbye, sir," he said, "I'll arrange to leave for Oklahoma City tomorrow."

As he drove away, I was glad, as I had been many times before, that I had encouraged him to go back into investigative work.

Over the next week, I spent as much time on the Delaware and Arizona primaries as I did on running the affairs of my company. I was on the phone several times daily with Barlow, clearing statements for Buck to make, approving large expenditures of funds, allocating personnel and resources between the primaries in the two states. I had Barlow add as many new personnel as needed and the campaign staff swelled almost daily.

Thanks to the backing of the Cairns' organization, Buck came in first in the Delaware primary by a large margin. The Arizona primary was a lot closer, but he managed to eke out a slim lead.

Buck's successive victories in New Hampshire, Delaware and Arizona caused a profound change in the media's treatment of him. His victory in New Hampshire had been regarded as a fluke, due in large measure to the state's conservative Republican voters. Three consecutive primary victories and his impressive lead over Tobin in the matter of pledged delegates made the media reappraise his campaign and his chances of winning the Republican presidential nomination.

Buck's smiling face began to appear on the covers of the nation's leading news magazines. He was invited to appear on the Sunday morning TV talk shows. We arranged for him to accept some of the invitations, in those cases in which the conditions could be carefully controlled to minimize the risk of his committing serious blunders.

The newspaper columnists and talking heads began treating Buck as a serious contender. Their comments, almost always critical, attributed his primary victories to his appeal to the "selfish, baser instincts" of the voters.

As we approached the South Carolina primary, Tobin and the other candidates remaining in the race concentrated their attacks against Buck. His popularity in the polls began to drop, as Tobin concentrated his fire on Buck's military record, or rather, his lack of one. Buck had not just avoided military service. Tobin's investigators uncovered the fact that Buck had dodged the draft by claiming conscientious objector status. Frankly, if I had been aware of this fact when I first encountered Buck in New Hampshire, I never would have involved myself in the least way in his campaign.

This was hardly the sort of background voters would want in someone who was seeking to be elected commander-in-chief. Tobin was naturally stressing this in his ads. The generally conservative, pro-military voters in the southern states saw this as a convincing reason to favor Tobin, who lost no opportunity to underscore his record as a decorated Marine Corps General.

In my phone conversations with Barlow, I had detected a rising note of concern. When I flew to meet him in Columbia, I was shocked when he showed me the latest polls. Not only was Tobin far ahead in South Carolina, but he was also leading in the other southern states.

Meeting with Barlow and the other senior campaign aides in our hotel, I was surprised at how many unfamiliar faces I saw.

Barlow had put together a large team. Their resumes had appeared impressive when I approved his choices. I hoped they would live up to their resumes.

"Gentlemen," I said. I realized that several of those gathered around the table were women, and amended this to "ladies and gentlemen. The polls show we are facing a serious problem. Does anyone have any suggestions?"

I looked around me. One young man raised his hand tentatively.

"We could have Buck visit some military bases, be photographed riding a tank. That sort of thing."

"Thank you," I said. I hoped the rest of the team recruited by Barlow was more efficient. No one else spoke.

"All right," I went on. "As I learned from my old football coach, defense doesn't win football games."

A few of the individuals seated around the table chuckled appreciatively. I wondered what their reaction would have been if I had said what was really on my mind. What I felt like saying was when you are in peril, aim for the jugular vein.

"Jim." I said, addressing Barlow. "What unfavorable information do we have on Tobin and Atwood?"

Atwood was Chester Atwood, the Governor of California. He had won the Iowa caucuses before coming in third behind Buck and Tobin in the next three primaries. His delegate count was behind Buck and Tobin. He now was tied with Buck for second place in the South Carolina polls and the other southern states and was rapidly gaining on Buck.

There was a loud silence in the room. I looked directly at Barlow.

"None," he said.

I stopped myself from criticizing him. He should have had the information as a contingency measure, but there was no point in stating this obvious fact. He was a good man. More important, it would be awkward to replace him at this juncture. It was really my fault for not paying closer attention to the campaign.

"All right," I said. "Here's what we do. I want a massive ad blitz in all the southern states. Buck stresses that as President, he will immediately end all government affirmative action programs."

"That will kill us with the black and liberal voters," piped up one of Barlow's aides.

"It can't be helped," I snapped back.

"And it's probably unconstitutional," another piped out. "Certainly, it will get embroiled in the courts."

I shuddered inwardly. The new crop of campaign aides Barlow had brought on board were certainly less practical than the first arrivals had been.

Ignoring the interruption, I went on.

"Secondly, I want another massive ad campaign in which Buck comes out in favor of protective tariffs for domestic textile industries. Third, he proposes tax credits for tobacco farmers shifting from tobacco production to other crops. That one ought to gain us some support from the liberals. We stress this will help the economies of all the southern states. Both the pro and anti-tobacco lobbies should like that one. Finally, pass the word to all of our media contacts that during the Vietnam War, CIA and the FBI recruited patriotic young people to penetrate anti-war groups believed to be under foreign control. Frequently these undercover agents had to pretend to be conscientious objectors to gain access."

"Was Buck one of those people?" asked one of the individuals around the table.

"Not as far as I know," I said. "But spread that story anyway. It's all we have to counter those attacks by Tobin."

Another of the campaign aides spoke up.

"I don't think I can buy that argument that tax credits to tobacco farmers will aid the local economies."

You don't have to believe it," I said. "Your thoughts are your own. But if you can't act as though you do, your resignation is accepted.

I looked around the table. The man stood up and left the room.

"Anyone else?" I asked.

No one said anything.

"All right," I said. "We're agreed. You all have your instructions. Let's get started!"

I delayed my return to Watsonville for a few days to insure that my orders were being carried out. I need not have worried. Barlow showed the same skill he had exhibited in the earlier primaries and Buck came through with another sterling performance, delivering the speeches and ads I had crafted for him.

Reasonably confident that we had reversed Buck's slide in the South, I flew back home before the South Carolina primary. I arrived at my house to find Pergamon livid. The media had learned more about my involvement in Buck's campaign, although nowhere near the full extent. As soon as I entered and greeted Pergamon, she rushed to show me articles in the news magazines and newspapers that some of her friends had clipped out and brought to her.

All were critical. One was headlined "Cosmetics tycoon manipulates presidential primaries." It described me as a "self-made millionaire who amassed his wealth by using pornographic advertising to sell tawdry merchandise to gullible teenagers." Another described Buck as the "failed one-term Governor of Oklahoma," whose presence on the campaign trails is welcomed by the husbands and fathers of Oklahoma as keeping him from attempting to seduce their wives and daughters."

"See what your meddling around in politics has done,"

Pergamon told me in an icy voice. "All of our friends are laughing at us. I could see people whispering and pointing at me at church last Sunday."

I realized that no displays of affection or explanation would appease her. What she wanted was a humble apology and my promise to withdraw at once from all involvement in the campaign. This, I was not about to do. Instead, I fell back on an appeal to her sense of fairness.

"It's one of the things you have to expect in politics," I said. "Honorable people can't stay out of politics for that reason. Would you prefer to have our Presidents chosen only by the professional politicians, who are inured to this sort of abuse?"

"I'll tell you what," I went on. "Let me introduce you to Buck and his wife. They are pleasant, likeable people. They will be campaigning in Illinois this month, and I'll have us get together. You can form your own opinion of them, instead of depending on this filth."

She scrutinized me. I tried hard to return her gaze, while refraining from laughing at what she would say if she knew all of the details concerning my dealings with the Porters. Fortunately, my diversion succeeded. While not completely convinced, she seemed ready to give me a chance to prove her wrong. Not for the first time, I congratulated myself on choosing a wife who, despite her other flaws, always tried to be fair.

The next day at the office, I called Alan and got the first report of his investigations in Oklahoma City. I learned Buck's parents had been killed in a car accident when he was a child and he had been raised at an orphanage. The rumors that Buck was a womanizer and had deliberately sought a draft deferment by claiming to be a conscientious objector were correct.

Alan then added with a chuckle, "How do you think he got the nick name Buck?"

"A childhood nickname?" I suggested. "Or perhaps he liked hunting deer."

"Nothing like that," Alan said. "Actually, he got the name when he was in college, working part time at a fast food restaurant in Oklahoma City to pay his tuition. He was a ladies' man even then. The owner of the place bet one of the patrons that Buck could lay three of the waitresses within an hour. The girls were willing, and Buck performed the feat with several minutes to spare. When the owner collected his winnings, he referred to Buck as 'that young buck' and the name stuck. "

"Who told you that?" I asked. "And were you able to get a notarized statement confirming the story?"

"I learned that from a friend of Buck's who was one of the other waiters. He personally witnesses the incident. And, yes, he did give me a statement which we had notarized. I didn't talk to the girls Buck laid. Two of them are no longer around. The third is married and a mother. I didn't feel right to ask her about it after all those years."

"Good work, Alan," I told him. "Keep on. And have you learned anything about Mrs. Porter?"

"Nothing adverse. She's regarded as very bright, hard-nosed and liberal. Her law firm is the biggest and most prestigious in Oklahoma City. She came to Oklahoma City after she graduated from Harvard Law School to work for a poor peoples' advocacy group. She met Buck here, married him, and acted as de facto campaign manager when he was elected Governor."

"What about their marriage?" I inquired.

"From what I hear," Alan said, "It's been pretty rocky. There are lots of stories about his fooling around with a large number of women. I am trying to confirm them. No indication that she has ever played around. They have no children. Word is that she's totally concentrated on her career."

"She made partner two years after she joined the firm" Alan went on. "It was unprecedented for any associate to make partner in the firm in such a short time. However, I've been unable to uncover any hint of impropriety about it. Everyone I talked to says she's a damned good lawyer. Of course, she was born and lived in Massachusetts until she came to Oklahoma City, so her activities there should be investigated as well. Do you want me to have it done?"

"No, thanks," I said. "I'll take care of that end. Just keep on with what you're doing."

When I hung up, I called Lou Masters. He was a private investigator I sometimes had work for me. I did not have the same liking for him that I had for Alan. On the other hand, his ethical sensitivity was less, a very important consideration given the sort of work I was going to be obliged to ask him to do for me. I told him to immediately begin thorough investigations of Tammy Porter's life while she lived in Massachusetts and of Buck's two most important rivals for the Republican nomination, Ross Tobin and Chester Atwood.

I did not return to Columbia to watch the South Carolina primary results come in on election night. For one thing, I had work to attend to at Lust Cosmetics. Equally important, Buck and Barlow and the rest of the campaign staff were scheduled to fly early the next morning to New York to campaign there for that state's all-important bloc of delegates.

All things considered, we did reasonably well in South Carolina. Buck, Tobin and Atwood each ended up with about the same number of delegates. Buck's lead in delegates from New Hampshire, Delaware and Arizona enabled him to hold on to first place in that most important category, but the momentum he had exhibited was now gone. Stories in the media began commenting that Tobin and Atwood would probably move ahead of Buck as a result of the next primary.

I was reasonably confident that Buck could regain his momentum by winning in New York. I approved another massive advertising campaign for that state. It was proving expensive, but the mechanisms Sol had established for gathering funds from Lust suppliers and distributors was proving equal to the task, thanks to the muscle I was able to apply from behind the scenes.

Our chances in New York were aided by the fact that one of Lust Cosmetics largest suppliers was headquartered in the state. I contacted the president and persuaded him to place his excellent contacts with the upstate New York Republican organization at Buck's behalf.

CHAPTER 4

Disaster struck the first day Buck began campaigning in New York. He and the other candidates were scheduled to speak at an outdoor rally in New York City's financial district. Buck won the coin toss and was the first speaker. As he moved forward on the platform to take the microphone, a man in the crowd drew out a revolver and fired, trying to kill him.

I heard the news at my office, when Pergamon phoned to tell me. I was surprised when my secretary told me my wife was on the phone. Not only did she rarely call me at the office, but it was a Tuesday afternoon, which she regularly devoted to going to her Episcopal Churchwomens' meeting.

"Melvin," she said, her usually calm voice excited. "There's been an assassination attempt against Governor Porter. I don't know if he was hit. The church secretary was listening to the radio and told me."

I hurriedly thanked her and hung up. Turning on the television set in my office, I switched from channel to channel. There were repeated news bulletins on all of them reporting the assassination attempt, but firm facts were still lacking. Several people had been wounded, but the gravity of the injuries was not stated. I could find no word about Buck.

I was tempted to go home and watch the cable news there. It seemed likely that one of the cable news channels would be carrying a fuller coverage of the incident. However, I decided against it. Barlow would most likely try first to reach me at my office with word of what happened. I tried the television again. Additional details were coming available. All of the presidential candidates had escaped unhurt. The attempted assassin had been apprehended and was in police custody.

I breathed a sigh of relief. Then my secretary informed me that Barlow was on the phone.

"Did you hear what happened?" he asked.

"I understand there was an assassination attempt, but that Buck is unharmed."

"Yes," he said. "I'm afraid it's bad news. The attempted assassin was Mark Goldsborough. Buck told me he had been working on his campaign in New Hampshire. Before he tried to shoot Buck, he was screaming that Buck had betrayed their friendship by trying to buy the election. It was the screaming that alerted the people around him. They realized he was a nut and grabbed his gun hand as he tried to shoot. That's why Buck wasn't hit. However, two other people on the platform were, one seriously."

"That's sure a mess," I said.

"You don't know the half of it," he went on. "When Goldsborough started firing, Buck hid behind the speakers' podium. I don't know what protection he thought it would provide. It was made of wood."

"Buck's was a natural enough reaction," I interrupted.

"Sure it was," he said. "I probably would have done the same if they were shooting at me. The trouble is, Tobin didn't. He jumped right off the platform and helped the police throw Goldsborough to the ground. He was a God-damn hero!"

"Was any of this on television?" I asked.

"There was no live TV coverage of the event. However, the networks had camera crews there. The footage will almost certainly be on every TV news show tonight."

"OK," I thought for a moment. "The important thing is not to panic. Whatever you do, don't let Buck or the others get depressed. Tell them that I am handling it and I'll be there tomorrow to work out the details."

When I arrived home that evening, I found Pergamon watching the news on television. The footage of the assassination attempt was worse than I expected. Tobin came off as a hero, taking charge of the situation. All that was missing was footage of Buck cowering behind the podium. I supposed I should be grateful for small favors.

Pergamon turned on me. "You sure picked a great candidate," she said. "I told you it was stupid to get into politics."

I decided it was wiser not to answer her. We ate in silence. Early the next morning, I got up, packed and left for the airport. My departure was marred by an argument with Pergamon. She had offered to call me a cab. When I thanked her and said I would drive my Buick to the airport, she had begun her familiar litany about the shabbiness of the car. As I headed to the airport, I thought bitterly that our truce over the Buick had been of a remarkably short duration.

The flight to New York was uneventful and I found Barlow waiting for me at the airport. As he drove to the Manhattan hotel in which we had established our campaign headquarters, he brought me up to date.

"It's as bad as it can be," he said. "Most of the media have hailed Tobin as the candidate who has shown the fitness to be President."

"Do you think we have lost New York?"

He shrugged. "I think we have lost the campaign. My best advice to you is to have Buck throw in the towel and withdraw from the race."

In retrospect, I probably should have accepted Barlow's advice and folded Buck's campaign. It was clear that he was not the best candidate. Indeed, there was considerable evidence that he was not even qualified for the job at all. However, I had already expended considerable time and effort in trying to win the nomination·for Buck. We had come so close to winning. I was not about to back away.

It was no longer a question of the financial advantages that would accrue to my firm if Buck won the presidency. It had become a personal challenge to me. I had been successful in turning Lust Cosmetics into a powerful and profitable firm. I wanted to see if my intelligence was up to manipulating the election process to elect Buck Porter President of the United States.

"Jim," I said. "We're not going to quit. My experience has taught me that if you're too stupid to know you're beaten and continue to slug it out, sometimes you win."

Barlow shrugged again. It was clear that he was not convinced. We entered the hotel room in which the senior staff of the campaign had gathered. Their downcast expressions mirrored Barlow's. Only Buck looked cheerful. I knew that he was an inveterate optimist. I had not been not surprised when Barlow told me that after the failed assassination attempt, Buck had gamely gotten to his feet and had delivered his scheduled speech.

The first thing I said after entering the room was to Buck. "I'm glad you were able to duck. It would have been hard to replace you."

He smiled. "They loved the speech," he said. "There was a lot of cheering."

I thought it better not to tell him that the cheering almost certainly came from the people we had hired to attend the event and to act like enthusiastic supporters.

"All right," I said. "If the press wants to attack Buck because someone tried to kill him, we go over their heads directly to the voters. We'll double our advertising campaign. Don't forget to tell the media that the reason Buck hit the floor instead of going after the attempted assassin was that our security people pushed him down."

Sitting next to me, Barlow wrote something furtively on a pad and passed it to me. I glanced at what he had written. It said, "There were no security people near Buck."

I leaned over and wrote underneath his comments "So What?" The only way we were going to fool the voters, I thought, was to convince our own campaign staff first.

"OK," I continued. "Here's our game plan. First, we spread word to all the pro-Israel groups that as President, Buck will have the United States recognize Jerusalem as the capital of Israel."

"That will mean a break with past American policy," someone interrupted.

"So what?"

"Cairns won't like it," Barlow said. "We promised him a free hand in running foreign policy."

"Right," I said. "But the free hand starts after Buck names him Secretary of State. If Cairns objects, tell him that he won't get to be Secretary of State if Buck isn't elected, and Buck won't be elected unless we make a decent showing in New York. Next," I continued,

"Buck comes out in favor of affirmative action programs and set-asides in any city or state in which the level of unemployment for minorities is sufficiently higher than the local level to constitute a serious social problem. Make the percentage high enough to cover the big cities in states where the primaries have not yet been held, particularly New York, Illinois and California."

"Doesn't that open Porter up to charges of double dealing?" asked one of the campaign aides. "He came out against affirmative action programs during the southern primaries."

"Not at all," I said, trying to keep from smiling. We explain that he is in favor of them only where the unemployment rate for minorities is sufficiently large to require them."

"Finally," I said, "We need the women's vote. Buck comes out in favor of freedom of choice."

"That will cost us heavily among our core supporters," Barlow said. "It's a complete break from past Republican policy."

"I know it is," I said, "But we have to do it. I realize it's a gamble, but it's our only chance. We have to attract the liberal pro-choice voters in New York City. I'm counting on the contacts we have upstate to keep the conservatives there on our side, no matter how reluctantly."

I stood up. "All right," I said, "Let's get started. You know what to do."

The people around the table stood up, reluctantly, I thought. Only Buck looked happy. I felt someone grab my arm. I looked. It was Barlow.

"Can I speak with you?" he said.

"Sure, Jim."

I waited till we were alone in the room.

"What's on your mind?

Barlow turned to me. "I'm sorry," he said. "I can't buy your campaign. I'm resigning as of now."

"Jim," I said, "What's wrong? If you quit now, it will sink Buck's campaign. Isn't there anything I do?"

"No," he said slowly, shaking his head. "I'm a hundred percent opposed to abortion. It's a matter of conscience."

I looked at him. He was dead serious. His performance in the campaign had been superb and I had come to regard him as a friend.

"All right, Jim," I said. "If you feel you must leave the campaign over this, I won't try and dissuade you. I can appreciate and respect your convictions. In part, I share them myself. But I must ask you not to resign. We can say you're taking a leave of absence because of health. You just never return to the job."

"I'm sorry," he said quietly. "I can't do that. It's a matter of principle."

I realized what I had to do, and I regretted it sincerely. I respected Barlow and liked him. Still, there was no alternative. I was being forced against my will to use some information Alan Barnes' firm had gotten for me when I had asked him to do a background check on Barlow.

It was something Barnes would probably not have passed on to me. He was too honorable for that. But when he had left for Oklahoma City, he had one of his associates in Chicago handle the background investigation of Barlow. The associate had uncovered reliable evidence that Barlow's teenage daughter had an abortion.

"Jim," I said, "It pains me to have to bring this up. I don't know if you are aware of this, but your daughter Elizabeth had an abortion last year. Your wife accompanied her to the clinic."

The expression on his face was one of hatred.

"Is there nothing too low for you to do? Do you think you can blackmail me?"

"I'm sorry, Jim." I said. "You leave me no choice. I can't let you resign from the campaign. If you do, or if you let on in any way that your support for Buck is anything less than a hundred percent, I will publicize the information about your daughter. Not because I want to, but because I will have to counter the effect of your action, give people something else to think about you when you say something."

"Just take that leave of absence because of ill health," I went on. "As long as you appear to remain a Buck supporter, I swear to you my lips will be sealed about your daughter."

He nodded his agreement and left. I realized I had created in him a bitter enemy. All I could do was never turn my back to him and to tell myself I had no other choice.

With Barlow gone, I realized I would have to take a much more active role in running Buck's campaign. However, I preferred to conceal my involvement as much as possible. I thought of brining in someone completely new, but it would take time to locate and check out a potential replacement. Reviewing in my mind Barlow's various aides, I selected Eric Baxter as the best available fill-in for Barlow. He was the most competent of the senior associates Barlow had brought on board. He had done an excellent job of escorting Buck to campaign events and had been skillful in preventing Buck from making untoward statements. From time to time he had expressed sound views on campaign strategy.

Baxter was oily and not someone I could ever like, as I had Barlow. On the other hand, I thought I could rely on him to do whatever had to be done. This was the deciding factor. I didn't want to have to use the same tactics I had employed against Barlow to control anyone else. I contemplated replacing those campaign staffers who shared Barlow's dislike of my campaign strategy and tactics, but disregarded the idea. Any significant number of departures from the campaign of aides on the heels of Barlow's leaving would make it clear that his going did not result from the health issues I had identified as the cause.

Baxter, when I offered him the title of director of operations and the de facto post of campaign manager, accepted eagerly. Together, we worked on the detailed program for added campaign appearances by Buck.

In the days that followed, Buck called at every Jewish, Afro-American, Hispanic and women's organization to which we could wangle an invitation. We spent money lavishly, to the extent that our campaign funds were virtually exhausted. I had scaled back use of my own funds, utilizing the contributions I had levied on Lust Company suppliers and distributors. Now this supply trickled off, despite my efforts to push them further and I was forced to myself make up the gap between contributions and expenditures.

As we gathered in our campaign headquarters on election night to watch the returns come in, I felt less than confident. The media had come out strongly against Buck, accusing him of attempting to buy the election by massive spending, an accurate assessment of our campaign tactics. Equally valid was their pointing out that Buck was pandering to the selfishness of special interest groups. Apart from the support I had been able to garner for Buck in the upper New York State Republican apparatus, thanks to my contacts there, the state party organization had worked for Buck's rivals. In terms of negative sentiment among the public, polls showed almost two-thirds of the prospective voters were strongly opposed to Buck.

Fortunately, opposition to Buck was divided almost equally between his two major rivals, Tobin and Atwood. Bad weather in parts of the state in which Buck had the lowest support held down the vote there. The early returns showed all three clustered together, each with about a third of the votes. Gradually, Buck's strength in the northern part of the state and in heavily black and Hispanic areas helped him gain a tenuous lead which clung to throughout the night. It was clear that the money we had dispensed liberally to sway prominent individuals and their voting constituencies had done its work.

As the last votes were counted, I turned to Buck and congratulated him on winning.

"Thanks, Mr. Shultz," he said, with a big grin. "I was always sure we would." I stared at him in amazement, realizing that he was totally sincere.

The next morning, carefully shepherded by Eric, Buck and the rest of the campaign team headed off to the south, to begin campaigning in Florida, Texas and the other southern states. Barlow, before his departure from the campaign, had been able to build a fragmentary organization in those states. I instructed Baxter, now handling the day-to-day functions of campaign manager under my close supervision, to spend whatever was necessary to complete the organization.

When I arrived home, I was pleased to find Pergamon in a relatively cordial mood. She had been asked to head our church's annual fair and had thoroughly immersed herself in preparations for it.

The next wave of primaries approached, obliging me to make numerous phone calls each day to Baxter and Buck. I also made several quick trips to meet with them and to see for myself the actual state of events on the ground. Our massive advertising campaign was under way, but things did not look good. The polls showed Buck far behind Tobin and Atwood in all the states. Buck's support for affirmative action, which had helped him regain support in New York, was hurting him badly among white conservative voters in the South. Equally harmful was his behavior during the assassination attempt, which reinforced his image as a draft dodger and coward.

I tried offering a Cabinet post to the governors of various southern states in exchange for their support, but all refused. Finally, in desperation, I targeted the lower level Republican leaders, hoping to break the almost complete lack of support Buck was facing from the Republican organizations in the southern states.

My offer of appointment as Secretary of Defense was successful in winning the endorsement for Buck of Davis, the junior Senator from Florida. Miller, the Texas Attorney General , came out in favor of Buck in return for the promise of his being the first appointment Buck would make to the Supreme Court, if a vacancy arose.

On the day of the primaries, I flew down to join Buck and the campaign staff in watching the election returns come in. Overall, we did not do as poorly as we might have. Buck came in third behind Tobin and Atwood in the Georgia primary.

Buck's call for subsidies for the tobacco farmers and tobacco industry were well received the tobacco growing states. In Florida and Texas, the two most important states, he came in second. In Florida, Davis's support helped, as did Miller's in Texas, although not as great as the offices I had offered them should have provided. We were fortunate in that Tobin and Atwood were slugging it out, with each winning several primaries, so that neither of them was able to grab a good lead in delegates. Buck continued in first place in the number of delegates, but his margin over Tobin and Atwood was further reduced.

We now turned to the cluster of primaries in the Middle West. I felt more confidant here, as I had good personal contacts with Republican Party circles in Illinois and has been successful in obtaining Governor McAndrews' support in return for the promise he would be named Secretary of Commerce. Ohio was more of a problem and I was relying on an important supplier I had in the states to use his political influence on behalf of Buck.

It was much easier for me to direct Buck's campaign, now that the scene of operations was closer to Watsonville. I traveled to meet with him and Baxter almost daily. In the Mid-West, Buck really hit his stride as a campaigner. The crowds that gathered at his appearances now included many actual supporters, in addition to the individuals we paid to attend. Even though Tammy had rebuffed all Buck's requests that she join him in campaigning, I was optimistic concerning the outcome of the Mid-Western primaries.

Meanwhile, I was receiving regular reports from Alan concerning the results of his investigations in Oklahoma City. He had obtained numerous reports, backed up by solid proof, of Buck's amorous activities, both before and after his marriage. However, he had not been able to uncover anything derogatory about Tammy or any indications that Buck had engaged in illegal or unsavory business practices, either before he became Governor or subsequently. Buck's behavior in claiming conscientious objector status to avoid the draft, while unpopular, could not be proved to have been fraudulent.

A phone call from Alan one evening shattered m complacency.

"Mel," he said, "We're in trouble. Buck's about to be dragged into a nasty divorce suit!"

I had never heard Alan so excited.

"What's it all about?"

"Peggy Terrell, Buck's old secretary when he was Governor, is suing her husband for divorce. She's charging, among other things, adultery. George, that's her husband, is counter-suing, alleging adultery with Buck. He claims to have pictures proving it."

"Have you seen them?" I asked.

"No," he said, "But George Terrell sounded as though he had them. I think it's all going to go public in a day or two. What do you want me to do?"

"I'll be out there by tomorrow afternoon," I said. "Meet me at the airport."

Alan met me at the airport and filled me in on the situation as we drove into Oklahoma City.

"Peggy Terrell," he said, "Was very close to Porter when he was Governor. Apparently, she functioned as a sort of office manager. When his term was over, he got her a job with the State Employment Service. However, she got into an argument with her boss. Out of office, Porter was unable to protect her and she was fired. Her appeals were rejected and she has been unable to get another job."

"Her husband, George," he went on, "operated one of the largest auto dealerships in the state until it went bankrupt. After it failed, he began hitting the bottle and gambling. Ran up heavy losses and signed IOU's he was unable to honor. He tried to get Peggy to sign a contract selling their home so he could pay his gambling debts. She refused and sued him for divorce on the grounds of adultery. He doesn't deny the truth of her charges."

"The problem is," continued Alan, "George Terrell counter-sued. He alleges she committed adultery with Porter while he was Governor."

"Have you talked to them?" I asked.

"Yes," he said. "Each is very bitter about the other. She is still living in their home. Although I don't know for how long. Her savings are all gone. He is living in a cheap hotel in the downtown area."

"Did you try to see if they might be willing to delay their divorce suit until after the election?"

"No," he said. "I don't think it would work. I can take you to George Terrell's hotel room so you can talk to him yourself. He hardly ever leaves it, so we'll probably find him there."

We drove into a rundown section of the city and Alan parked in front of a small, dilapidated hotel. When I entered the lobby, it struck me as the kind of hotel that rented its rooms by the hour. Wallpaper hung from the walls. Several of the lights were out and the single elevator had a sign on it stating it was out of operation. The clerk at the desk gave us a disinterested glance and returned to reading a magazine as Alan and I climbed up two flights of stairs.

The corridor on the third floor was even shabbier than the lobby. Alan led me to a door and knocked. In a minute the door swung open and I found myself facing a man of about forty. The smell of liquor hit me as we entered. I was not surprised to see an almost empty bottle of bourbon on the cheap dresser, which was the only piece of furniture in the room apart from the bed. Terrell very much needed a haircut and a shave. His pants looked as though he had slept in them. I extended my hand to Terrell.

"Mr. Terrell," I said. "I'm Melvin Shultz, president of Lust Cosmetics. This is my associate, Alan Barnes."

Terrell looked surprised. He didn't appear aware of my extended hand. I don't think anyone had addressed him politely in many months and he seemed unsure of how to respond. He looked at the empty glass near the bottle of bourbon, obviously wanting to take another drink.

"What do you want?" he asked. His voice was hoarse and his words slurred. I didn't know how drunk he was, but his mind was certainly not functioning properly.

"I'm interested in expanding the market for my company's cosmetics in this area," I said. "I think you might be the right man for the job. Since I had to come here on business, I thought I'd take the opportunity to discuss it with you."

As I finished speaking, I caught a glimpse of Alan's face. He was frowning. Alan clearly thought I was deliberately lying to Terrell. It was possible I was. I preferred to be truthful, but I might have to lie. I didn't know what would work with him, but above all I had to keep Terrell from taking any action that would threaten Buck's campaign. At any point there was no reason to involve Alan in my effort. He was my friend. I didn't want to see our friendship end the way mine had with Barlow.

"Alan," I said. "Why don't you go and get Mr. Terrell a cup of coffee. Make it black."

Alan left on the errand and I turned back to Terrell.

"Please sit down," I said. He obediently sat down on the bed. There was no chair in the room, so I leaned against the dresser.

"Let me describe the job," I began "I need someone who is experienced in sales to do market research and then draw up a marketing plan based on his findings. It also will involve contacting the various retail chains to persuade them to handle my products."

Terrell struggled hard to comprehend what I was saying.

"I was the owner of an auto dealership," he finally said. "I have no experience in cosmetics."

I was surprised at his honesty in admitting his lack of experience, given his desperate need for a job.

"That's all right, Mr. Terrell," I reassured him. "I know that. I had you thoroughly checked out before coming here. I had to make sure you are the kind of person I want. I am confidant you have the necessary qualifications for the post."

I rapidly calculated in my mind what salary to offer him. A high five-figure one seemed most appropriate. It was less than he had earned as owner of the auto dealership, but enough to live decently and to pay off his debts.

When I mentioned the figure, Terrell shock his head as though he couldn't believe his good fortune. "Of course," I added, "you will receive a bonus based on the new business you obtain."

I could see from the look on his face that he was eager to accept the offer. Now, I had the harder job, which was the purpose of my visit.

"There's just one thing, Mr. Terrell," I said smoothly, hoping that I sounded convincing. "I know that you and your wife are suing each other for divorce on grounds of adultery."

His face fell, but I went on.

"Of course, your personal life is no concern of mine, nor is it if you get divorced. However, I can't afford to have one of my officials involved in a scandal. It would reflect poorly on my company's image. Because of Governor Porter's presidential race, anything involving him would immediately be picked up by every newspaper in the country. He simply must not be mentioned!"

"But he laid my wife!" Terrell said, almost crying. "What else can I do?"

I sincerely pitied Terrell, but there was no alternative. I had to press on.

"Things like that happen," I said. "They can't be helped. It would be foolish to throw your life away by insisting on mentioning him. All you have to do is delay your divorce until after the election. Then get a quiet one. I can obtain a good lawyer for you, one that will find some grounds other than adultery. He will then save you a lot of money by getting a good financial settlement."

"But she's suing me for divorce," he said in a low voice. "She's charging me with adultery." He began to sob.

"I may be able to persuade her to use other grounds," I said. "Anyhow, how did this adultery business come up? Did you do it?"

"Yes, but it was only once. I was out of town at a convention.

You know how those things can get out of hand."

I nodded sympathetically.

"But why are you charging her with adultery?" I asked."Was that made up?"

"No," he said. "She told me. With the Governor. And more than once."

He got up and headed toward the bottle of bourbon. I stepped in front of him, blocking his way. I didn't want him to get any drunker.

"How do you know she wasn't just making it up to get even with you? Women sometimes do that."

He stared at me. "I found the photographs. Her and the Governor! I have proof!"

"Come on now," I said. "People don't take pictures of things like that."

"She did!" he said emphatically. He stepped in front of me and opened a dresser drawer. From underneath a pile of dirty clothing he extracted a manila envelope and handed it to me.

I opened the envelope. Inside were three black and white photos. The lighting on them was not good, but there was no mistaking what they showed. All three of them were of Buck and a buxom blond on a bed, stark naked. The photos appeared to have been posed. In one of them, Buck and the woman stared at the camera, grinning. Buck was fondling one of her breasts. She had her hand on his penis. Another showed Buck's naked rear, as he mounted her. One of her arms was stretched behind her head, in a provocative pose.

I wondered how they could have been so stupid, posing for photos like that. Terrell had been correct about one thing. He certainly did have hard proof of his wife's infidelity.

"You're right," I said to him. "These photos leave little doubt she committed adultery."

There was a knock at the door. It was Alan, bringing the coffee. I thanked Alan, took the cup and handed it to Terrell.

"Drink it up," I said.

Terrell grimaced, but drained the cup.

"Alan," I said, "Do you have anything to write with?"

He opened the attaché case he carried and took out a yellow legal pad and a pen. I turned to Terrell.

"I'd like you to write down exactly what your wife told you about her affair with Porter. Begin with the day it happened and the circumstances under which you found out."

Why do you want that?" he asked, his suspicions aroused.

"So I can use it when I see her. I hope I can persuade her to drop the adultery charge against you."

Then a thought struck me.

"Do you think you two can be reconciled? Would you drop your divorce suit and take her back, if she agrees to do the same?"

"Yes," he said, starting to cry again. "I really love her."

Terrell wrote for about fifteen minutes and then handed the pad back to me. I read it carefully. It was just what I wanted, a detailed statement of how he had found the photographs in his wife's dresser, demanded to know the full story, and listened as she detailed her affair with Buck. As Terrell recounted it, she had been brazen in her statements, probably out of shame at being found out and resentful at him for his own behavior. I turned to Alan.

"Is there a notary near here. I want Mr. Terrell to sign this and have it notarized."

"I think I saw a notary nearby," Alan said. "But I don't know if it's still open."

"Let's go," I said. I was thinking of pocketing the envelope with the photographs, but Terrell quickly returned it to the drawer from which he had taken the envelope. The determination with which he did so left me with no illusion that he would voluntarily relinquish the photos, even if it meant losing the job I had offered him. He took from the closest a rumpled suit jacket and put it on. The three of us left the room, Terrell carefully locking the door behind him.

We walked down the stairs to the lobby, past the desk clerk, and into the street. Alan led us to a building that had once housed a liquor store. In the window was a sign offering to prepare tax returns and promising immediate tax refunds. We entered and found a bored looking woman seated at a desk, eating a sandwich.

"Can you notarize something?" I asked her.

"Sorry, Mister," she said, still chewing her sandwich. "We only notarize things connected to the tax returns we prepare."

I removed a twenty dollar bill from my wallet and put it on the desk.

"That's for you, in addition to your regular fee, if you notarize something for me."

She put down the sandwich, opened her desk drawer and removed a notary stamp.

"Sure, Mister," she said. "Glad to oblige."

I removed from my pocket the account Terrell had written describing his wife's adultery and watched as he wrote his signature at the bottom of the sheet. The woman then stamped it with her seal and signed it. She returned it to me, and I carefully folded it and put it back in my pocket. I experienced a feeling of great satisfaction. While I hoped never to have to use Terrell's statement, it went a long way to guarantee that Buck would always be responsive to my guidance.

As we left the shop, I let Terrell leave first and caught Alan as he was about to follow.

"I'm going to take Terrell to my hotel," I said, "and get him a room there. I'd like you to go back to his room and get that envelope of pictures he hid in the middle drawer of his dresser under some clothing. Did you see him do it?"

"Yes, I did," Alan said softly, "But I can't take them without his permission. That would be stealing."

I looked at Alan and realized I had a erred in asking him.

"You're right," I said. "I don't know what I was thinking of. Anyhow, with that statement he signed, I have no need of the photos."

We walked out and joined Terrell. Crossing the street back to Terrell's hotel, I stopped at Alan's car.

"You know," I said to Alan, as though I had just had s fresh thought, "This is foolish. Mr. Terrell shouldn't have to stay at a dump any longer. Why don't you take him to my hotel and book a nice room for him? If the barbershop is still open, get him a haircut and a shave. And if the hotel cleaning service is open, have his suit cleaned and pressed."

I handed Alan some cash.

"This should cover it. Anything more, have them charge it to my room."

I then turned to Terrell. "Mr. Terrell," I said. "I know you'll be happier in my hotel than in this place. I want you to make yourself comfortable there. I'm going to your house and tell your wife about your new job. I think I can talk her out of suing you for divorce now. Possibly I can persuade her to agree to reconciliation between the two of you."

I didn't give Terrell a chance to object. "And Mr. Terrell." I added, "You can't go around without any money in your pocket."

I had no idea how much cash he still had. Giving him a few dollars would hopefully keep him from thinking about returning to his hotel room. I stuck some bills into his jacket pocket.

"Use some of this to buy a shaving kit. We'll pick up the things you left in your room tomorrow."

I then walked around the car and stood by the driver's side until Alan opened his window. I gave him the name of the hotel at which I had made a reservation. In a low voice I told Alan, "Stay with Terrell until I get there."

I stepped back, giving Alan no opportunity to respond. After what seemed like an eternity, he started the car and drove off. I waited until they turned the corner, then entered the hotel and climbed the stairs to Terrell's floor. Reaching his room, I tried the door. As I feared, it was locked.

The door lock looked simple to pick. Unfortunately, lock picking was not a skill I possessed. Standing there, staring at the door, I wondered if I should try opening it with a credit card, as I had seen done in TV movies. Hearing something behind me. I turned and saw a chambermaid.

"Hello," I said. "Do you think you could let me in? I left my key inside."

"Yes," she answered, unlocking the door. I gave her a large tip, quickly entered the room and shut the door.

The large tip was a gamble. It was not something a guest at that hotel could be expected to do and might well raise her suspicions. On the other hand, I guessed she probably would be sufficiently eager to keep it to refrain from discussing the matter with anyone else at the hotel.

I waited to give her time to leave the area, then walked to the dresser and with some difficulty found the envelope that Terrell had hidden. I checked to be sure the photos were still there, then put the envelope in my pocket, closed the dresser drawer and started to leave the room.

Suddenly, I stopped. I realized that when Terrell found the photos missing, I would be the first person he would suspect. His reaction would be unpredictable. He might well initiate the scandal concerning Buck I was trying to prevent. I had to have at least a fig leaf to mask my theft of the envelope.

Leaving the door of Terrell's room ajar, I walked out into the corridor and looked for the chambermaid. I was lucky; she was still on the same floor.

"Miss," I said, "I wonder if you could do me another favor."

She smiled at me. The large tip I had given her for unlocking the door made her anticipate another generous one.

"I'd like you to pack my things." I said. "I'm checking out tomorrow."

I led her back to Terrell's room and watched her empty his dresser drawers and put the contents into his suitcases. She carefully took the suits that were in the closet and put them in. I took out a twenty dollar bill from my wallet and handed it to her.

You've done a great job," I said. When you finish, just lock the door behind you. I'll be back tomorrow to check out and to pick up my suitcases."

She smiled at the twenty. Apparently, it was more than she had expected.

"Thanks," she said. "Glad to help."

I descended the stairs and walked into the street. It was already dark. There were no taxis in sight and no traffic. I didn't fancy being alone after dark in that neighborhood and walked quickly in what I hoped was the right direction.

After a few blocks the neighborhood improved and I spotted a cab waiting for a traffic light. I ran and reached it before the light changed. The driver looked at me carefully before unlocking the door and allowing me to enter. Feeling relieved, I gave him the address of Terrell's home and relaxed in the rear seat.

We drove for about half an hour, leaving downtown Oklahoma City and heading into a residential area. The cab turned on to a tree-lined street of expensive colonial homes and stopped in front of one. It had been a beautiful home, but showed signs of neglect. Dead leaves and branches covered areas of the front yard and the front door and shutters needed repainting.

I paid the driver, walked to the door and knocked. After a short wait, the outdoor light was turned on and the door opened a crack. I could see it was still secured by a chain.

"Yes?"

"Are you Mrs. Terrell?" I asked.

'Yes." Her voice sounded suspicious.

"Good," I said. "My name is Melvin Shultz. I'm president of Lust Cosmetics. I'm here to talk to you about a job."

"At this time of night? Don't be ridiculous. If you don't scram, I'll call the police."

I took out my wallet, removed my driver's license, and showed it to her.

"This will confirm who I am. If you want to check further, you can call my hotel and they will confirm I'm staying there. Or you can call my home in Watsonville and speak to my wife."

Terrell's wife closed the door, and for a few seconds I thought I might have failed to convince her. Then the chain was unlatched and the door opened. She motioned me to enter. There was no doubt that Mrs. Terrell and the woman in the photo with Buck were one and the same person. However, the years had not been kind to her. She looked considerably older and more worn than she had in the photo.

Mrs. Terrell led me into the living room and asked me to sit down. I could not help but noticing the condition of the house.

Newspapers were scattered over the floor and a stack of unwashed dishes was visible in the kitchen.

"Mrs. Terrell," I said, "Let me be frank. I have offered your husband a good job doing market research for my firm. I think it will get him back on his feet. There's only one problem. You are suing him for divorce on grounds of adultery. I can't allow my firm to be involved in scandal. Unless you drop the suit, I can't give him the job!"

"To Hell with him!" she spat out bitterly.

I looked directly at her, shaking my head.

"You're an intelligent woman. Think of what will happen to you. I can't hire him if you accuse him publicly of adultery. With nothing to lose, he'll sue you for adultery. I understand his grounds. He showed me pictures…"

Her face flushed a brilliant red.

"That son of a bitch!" she said. " You get the Hell out of here!" She stood up, as though to throw me out.

"Hold on," I said, speaking as calmly as I could and choosing my words carefully. "There's a better way for both of you. We all make mistakes. There's no reason to let this one ruin your life. I know he's hurt you, but nothing will be served by hurting him back. It won't make you any better off. I can get a good job for you, too. Now please sit down for a minute and hear me out."

To my relief she sat back down.

"I know you don't have a job." I pointed to the open newspapers on the floor, many of them open to the employment ads. "Nobody is going to give you a job if George uses those pictures. And he will if you charge him with adultery or if I don't hire him. But if you really want a divorce, I can get both of you good lawyers. They can work out a fair divorce settlement so that neither of you is hurt. And I may be able to get you a job."

I was glad to see that she was listening to me carefully.

"What kind of a job?" she asked.

"I know you ran Porter's office when he was Governor," I said. "I was thinking of a job which would take advantage of your knowledge of state procedures and politics."

She nodded in agreement. "I always wanted to do something like that," she said.

"Let me spell out exactly what I'm offering. If you don't accuse George of adultery, I guarantee he won't accuse you or use those photos. If you wait till the end of the year and still want a divorce, I will hire a good lawyer for you to work out a fair divorce settlement on other grounds. Until then, I will insure that George pays off his IOUS's and covers the mortgage payments, so that you don't lose he house. That way, if you divorce him, you and he can divide the equity you haven the house."

"What about my job?" she asked suspiciously.

"George is really sorry he hurt you and wants to try and get together with you again. If you and he at least pretend to be living together for, say, a nine month trial period, I'll arrange for you to get a good job."

"You drive a hard bargain."

"But, I hope, a fair one," I said.

"All right, Mr. Shultz," she said. "I want that job. You can tell George to come here so we can talk things over."

"I'll take care of it," I said. "And of the job for you. I don't think you'll be disappointed."

I stood up. "I'll be going now, Mrs. Terrell," I said. "I wonder if you could call me a cab."

She got up, too, smiling.

"Glad to," she said. After she finished the call, she turned to me. Her housecoat slipped open, revealing she had nothing on underneath it. I wondered if she was trying to seduce me. If she was, she thought better of it, secured the housecoat, and offered to make some coffee for me while I waited for the cab to arrive.

I was in the kitchen happily sipping my coffee and chatting with Mrs. Terrell when the taxi arrived. I put down the coffee and rose. She came over and extended her hand.

"Thanks a lot, Mr. Shultz," she said. "You really have helped me out. I' very grateful. I'll really work with you."

I thanked her and left. As the cab drove me to my hotel, I thought back over the events of the day. I felt pleased over the possibility that I had helped the Terrell's get back on their feet. It helped cover my regrets for being obliged to steal the photos from Terrell.

When I paid the driver and entered my hotel, I was surprised to find Alan sitting in the lobby waiting for me. He had a frown on his face and looked worried.

"Melvin," he said, "We may have a problem. I got Terrell a room here and had dinner with him. The barbershop was closed, so I couldn't get him a haircut and shave, We started to go up to his room when he suddenly told me he had to go immediately to his old hotel to pick up his things. I couldn't talk him out of it."

"That's no problem," I said, trying to sound more confident than I felt. "I talked to Mrs. Terrell and convinced her to withdraw her divorce suit against him. She also agreed to consider a reconciliation. Now I want to thank you for all your help today, and for your good work here. You go back to your hotel and relax. I'll call you tomorrow before I take off for Illinois to let you know if there's anything happening."

Alan looked reluctant to leave, but said nothing more. I walked with him out of the hotel and waited till he got into a cab. I then ate a snack in the hotel coffee shop and went up to my room.

Turning on the TV, I was pleased to find a western movie to watch, put on my pajamas and settled into bed.

I had started to doze when there was a loud pounding at the door. I opened it and Terrell pushed his way into the room."

"Where's my fuckin photos?" he demanded. His face was flushed and he was literally shaking with anger.

"What photos?" I asked, trying to look innocent. Terrell repeatedly clenched and unclenched his fists. I thought he was about to hit me. With an obvious effort, he restrained himself.

"Those photos of my wife and Porter. If you don't given them back to me, I'll smash you into a bloody pulp."

I had no doubt he could do it. Unconsciously, I started to look at my bed, to make sure that the envelope containing the photos, which I had concealed under the mattress for safekeeping, was not visible.

I caught myself and said, trying to appear sincere, "Mr. Terrell, I don't have your photos. You took them and put them away yourself. Where did you leave them?"

"Don't fuck with me!" he roared. "You saw me put them in the dresser drawer. You went back to the room after I left and took them!"

"I did go back to your room," I said. "But only to have your things packed. I didn't have the key to your room and had to ask the chambermaid to unlock the door and let me in. Then, I had her do the packing. I didn't do it myself. I was never in the room alone," I lied. "If you don't believe me, ask her yourself. And if you like, please search my room."

Terrell made a half-hearted search of my room, opening my briefcase and going through my pockets. Fortunately, he gave up his search before looking under my mattress. He sat down in a chair, burying his face in his hands. I walked over and put my arm on his shoulder in a consoling gesture.

"Relax," I said. "I don't think the maid took the pictures. I was in the room while she packed and would have seen her if she took them. But she did ask me about some torn underwear and I told her to throw them out. It's possible she tossed out the photos with the underwear, if they were in the same drawer."

"Anyhow," I went on, "It doesn't make any difference. I went to see your wife tonight and persuaded her to drop the divorce suit against you. She is willing to talk to you about reconciliation. If it doesn't work out, she agreed to cooperate with you to reach a fair settlement, without any talk about adultery on either side. If the pictures somehow get out, that won't stop me from giving you the job. You are not connected with them in anyway. I doubt anyone would recognize your wife in them. All they would have would be photos showing Porter in bed with a naked woman, and that would have no impact on you, on Mrs. Terrell or on Lust Cosmetics."

Terrell looked up at me. He had the first cheerful smile I had seen on his face.

"Thank you," Mr. Shultz," he said. I'd give anything to have her back." Incongruously, he began weeping again.

"Cheer up, Mr. Terrell," I said, trying to be as consoling as possible. "If you play your cards right, I think there's a pretty good chance you will get her back."

I took him by the arm and gently urged him into a standing position. "Let me help you to your room," I said, walking him to the door. I was glad he did not resist. I steered him into the corridor and went with him to his room. Inside, the room was in a state of utter confusion. His suitcases were lying open on the floor, their contents spread on the floor in disarray. Clearly, he had conducted a frantic search for the photos.

I was glad that Alan had gotten a deluxe room for him. It was substantially nicer than the basic room I had taken for myself. I hoped that the luxurious surroundings would help convince him of the desirability of cooperating fully with me.

Terrell sat down in an arm chair. I thought of ordering him a drink to settle his nerves, and then discarded the idea. While a drink might help to relax him, there was too great a risk that he would return to his heavy drinking.

"Go to sleep, Mr. Terrell," I instructed him. "I've set up an appointment early tomorrow to introduce you to the president of the firm where you'll be working. You'll be working directly for me, of course, but they will provide you with the office and secretarial help you will need."

Saying goodnight, I returned to my room and got back into bed. I checked carefully before I did so and assured myself that the envelope with the photos was still safe under the mattress. I looked at my watch. It was past nine p.m. As I wondered whether to go to sleep or to try watching another movie on TV, the telephone rang.

I picked it up and was surprised to find the caller was a woman. Her voice was deliberate and cold.

"Mr. Shultz," she said, "This is Tammy Porter. I must see you at once. Please come to my office immediately!"

"Mrs. Porter," I replied, "Do you realize what time this is? I'll be glad to come to your office tomorrow."

"Not tomorrow," she said. "Now!"

Her voice was even colder than before and her assumption of authority more blatant. I have never liked being spoken to imperiously, and certainly not by anyone whose authority over me I saw no reason to accept. Our previous telephone conversation had been unpleasant and this was much more so. I was about to tell her to go to Hell, but reconsidered. It would be foolish of me to create an open breach with her without finding out what she wanted.

"All right, Mrs. Porter," I said. "I'll come to your office as soon as I can get dressed."

She gave me directions to her office. I hung up, put on my clothes and went down to the lobby and out onto the street. I was pleased to see a waiting taxi and climbed in. After a few minutes of driving through nearly deserted streets, the taxi deposited me in front of a modern high rise building in what appeared to be one of the city's best commercial neighborhoods.

I entered the building and was immediately hailed by the security guard at the reception desk. Identifying myself, I told him I had an appointment to see Mrs. Porter. He requested some identification with my photo on it and I complied, showing him my driver's license. After using his phone to call her office, he asked me to sign in and directed me to the bank of elevators behind him.

"Eighth floor," he said, with no hint of cordiality. I wondered if he was naturally unpleasant, or had been instructed to act so by Mrs. Porter.

The elevator reached the eighth floor and the door opened. I found myself facing an attractive woman of moderate height. Intelligence seemed stamped on her face. She was wearing a well-tailored suit. Her blond hair was so well coiffured that I was uncertain whether it had been dyed. I would have described her as beautiful except for her aggressive stance and the assertive expression on her face.

"Mr. Shultz," she said. It was a statement rather than a question. "Follow me." There was no hint of cordiality on her face and she made no effort to shake my hand. She turned and led me into her office. From the back, she was as attractive as from the front. I wondered what had ever attracted her to Buck. They appeared to be totally opposite in terms of their personality and intelligence.

Mrs. Porter's office was large and well-furnished. It reminded me of Prescott Cooper's law office in New York. Mrs. Porter sat down behind a large mahogany desk. It was covered with documents. She picked up a cardboard coffee container and sipped some coffee. I noticed a coffee-making machine in her office and waited for her to offer me a cup. She didn't bother. Neither did she invite me to sit.

I had been taught as a child by my mother never to sit down in someone's home or office until invited to do so. After standing awkwardly for a few minutes as Mrs. Porter drank her coffee in silence, I decided to ignore my mother's admonition. I didn't think that my mother, a flinty school teacher who helped my father run the newspaper, would have put up with any foolishness from Mrs. Porter either.

I sat down and returned Mrs. Porter's stare. When she finished her coffee, she put the cup down.

"Mr. Shultz," she said, her voice as cold as ice. "Why are you prying into my personal life?"

I wondered if she was referring to the investigation Alan Barnes was conducting. Trying to sound friendly, I said, "Mrs. Porter, you are aware of my deep involvement in helping your husband win the nomination and then the presidency. I have to know what dirt his opponents will try to use against him in order to prevent their doing so."

"And what did you find out?"

There was no note of softening in her voice. She sounded like a lawyer pressing a hostile witness. Despite my dislike of Mrs. Porter, I found myself enjoying sparring with her. She certainly was a worthy opponent.

Giving her a big smile, I said, "Mrs. Porter, we all do things which can be used by people who don't like us to make us seem very foolish. I'm no exception and neither is your husband. I didn't find out anything about him that you don't know."

"I'll be the judge of that." There was no give in her voice.

"I'm sorry, Mrs. Porter," I said. "I can't tell you any more than that."

"You don't have to," she said sarcastically. "I don't like you and I loathe those crazy things you've had my husband say in the campaign. You're through! I'm picking up this phone right now and telling my husband to remove you from the campaign. And he'll do it. Now get out!"

I sat back in the chair and smiled at her. By her behavior she had made what I was about to do fun.

"Mrs. Porter," I said. "I don't like you, but I have to respect you. You do have balls. And you do have intelligence. Out of respect for your intelligence, I'm going to speak frankly to you. You might very well be able to convince your husband to remove me from the campaign. That would make it impossible for him to win the nomination, but you might very well feel that was a price you were prepared to pay."

"Good," she said. "Since we agree that you're going to leave, please stop wasting my time and leave."

"Certainly," I said, making no move to get up from my chair. "However, you might be interested to learn what I found up about Buck. His sexual activities are really quite astounding. In fact, they would make a great porno film. If word of what he did got out, it would finish his political career permanently."

"Don't try to blackmail me," she said. "Take your filth and get out!"

"It's not just that I found out what he did," I continued calmly. "I also have the notarized statements describing his activities from the participants in great detail, as well as pictures of him in bed fornicating. If you fail to cooperate fully and enthusiastically with me, I won't just make the material public. I'll make damn sure that the media use it."

"Just think," I continued, ignoring her mounting fury. "Pictures of Buck in action appearing in every newspaper and magazine, newscasters discussing it on every new show. When I've finished, your husband will be a laughing stock. He would be lucky to get a job driving a cab again."

"And as for you," I said smiling, "Just how long do you think your very prim and proper law firm will keep you on as a partner? It's not just that they will courteously ask you to resign for the good of the firm. You won't be able to get a job in any respectable law firm in the country. As you chase ambulances and scramble to earn pennies doing wills and estates, you'll hear people snickering at you behind your back. I'm not joking, Mrs. Porter. I mean every word of it. Not that I'll enjoy destroying you and your husband. But I'll do it and do it thoroughly, just to make sure than people know I've done it and that nobody ever tries to cross me again."

Mrs. Porter's face had turned white. I could see bitter anger on her face, but also the realization that I could and would carry out my threat.

"All right," she said hoarsely. "I believe you. I will make no effort to remove you from the campaign."

"Thank you, Mrs. Porter," I answered. "It's always a pleasure dealing with an intelligent woman. Look at the good side of things. You might enjoy being First Lady. Of course, you won't be able to practice law while he is in the White House, but after your husband leaves office, you'll be inundated with offers from the most prestigious law firms in the country to become a partner. Or, if you prefer, you can head up some large non-profit organization like the Red Cross."

She nodded in agreement, but said nothing.

"Now the first thing you have to do," I went on, "Is to counter the stories in the press that you are opposed to your husband's candidacy. I don't expect you to give up your law practice or campaign at his side. A day or two on the stump with him would be sufficient. I'd like you to accompany me back to Illinois tomorrow. You can stay overnight at my house and then join him the next day. He will be campaigning in Ohio. You can make an appearance with him the following day and then fly back here. I'll call the airline and make the reservations for you."

I looked at Mrs. Porter, expecting an objection. To my surprise, there was none.

"I'll arrange to take the time off," she said calmly "and meet you at the airport."

She stood and escorted me to the door of her office. I told her the time and location I would meet her at the airport. This time she shook hands with me, a smile on her face. Her smile might have been convincing, except for the cold look of her eyes. I knew that whatever she might say, she remained determined to get her revenge for the way I had treated her, whenever the circumstances permitted.

The security guard in the lobby scrutinized me suspiciously as I called a taxi to pick me up and then for the next few minutes until it arrived. A short time later I was back in my hotel room. I checked to make sure the photos were still safe under the mattress where I had left them, and considered turning on the TV to see if I could find any movie to watch. I decided, however, it was too late and turned in.

The next morning, I was up early. I made several phone calls to Lust Cosmetics' distributors and suppliers, looking for an Oklahoma City firm that that provide the assistance in creating the jobs for the Terrell's. The company presidents I called were not happy about being disturbed so early in the morning at their homes. I persisted, however. By the time I knocked at George Terrell's room to take him to breakfast, I had been successful in making all of the necessary arrangements. In return for paying for his salary and expenses and a generous amount to cover a secretary and office, the president of a market research firm agreed to provide the necessary assistance to Terrell to carry out the work I would assign him. I made similar arrangements for Mrs. Terrell to be employed by a local public relations firm.

When Terrell opened his room door, I was pleased with his appearance. He had shaved and was wearing a good suit, shirt and tie. As we ate in the hotel dining room, I discussed the marketing data I wanted him to acquire and collate. None of it was essential to my company's planning, but it would be useful. It would, in part, justify the expenses I was incurring to provide him with a job.

After breakfast, I had him get a haircut. I then took him to the firm at which he would work and insured that he found his office acceptable. As we parted, I instructed him to lease a new car for his use at my company's expense. I didn't consider my generosity absolutely necessary, but thought it essential to insure the silence and cooperation of the Terrell's until after the presidential election.

Before checking out of my hotel, I called Mrs. Terrell and told her the arrangements I had made for her employment. She expressed her appreciation and said she was looking forward to hearing from her husband and hoped they might be reconciled.

My last call before leaving for the airport was to Alan Barnes. I told him about the jobs I had arranged for the Terrell's, omitting any details which I thought likely to trouble him. He was genuinely pleased when I informed him of the possibility the Terrell's might get together again. It was with reluctance that I instructed him to carefully monitor their activities to make certain they remained pleased with their jobs and were not about to do anything which might jeopardize Buck's candidacy.

Traffic to the airport was heavy, and I arrived there late. I looked for Mrs. Porter, but she was nowhere to be seen. For a few anxious minutes, I waited impatiently, fearing that had changed her mind about flying with me to Illinois and even that she might be stirring up trouble between me and her husband.

I was relieved to see her running toward me, a large suitcase in each hand and a worried expression on her face. She looked less hard and much prettier than she had appeared on our previous meeting. I felt some regret at having purchased a tourist class ticket for her to travel with me rather than having us both travel first class. She explained that her cab had been delayed by the same heavy traffic that had made me late. Her explanation was interrupted by the announcement that our flight was ready to board.

We passed through the gates and boarded the plane. When she realized that we were traveling tourist class, she looked at me curiously but did not complain. I gathered that her firm had its partners fly first class. I thought of explaining that that my habit of flying tourist class originated in my younger days, when I did not have the means to travel any other way. However, I decided to keep silent.

As a gesture of politeness, I helped her secure her suitcases in the luggage rack and offered her the choice of seats. We exchanged a few polite comments during the flight, as she busied herself with legal papers from her office. The plane arrived on time, and we took the airport shuttle to where I had parked the Buick. Mrs. Porter seemed as bemused by the car as she had been by our traveling tourist class, but again refrained from any comment.

I turned on the car radio to get the news, hoping to learn something about Buck's campaigning. I was not disappointed.

After what seemed like innumerable commercials, there was a brief summary of the candidates' activities, including a reference to Buck appearing at several well-attended rallies. I glanced at Mrs. Porter and noticed she was following the news of the campaign with interest.

"Your husband's campaign seems to be going well," I said. "When you join him tomorrow, it will give him an added boost."

She nodded, but said nothing. I wondered again if her apparent cooperation with me was no more than a ploy. For the life of me, I was at a loss to know how committed she really was to helping Buck win the presidency.

When we reached my house, I led Mrs. Porter to the door and knocked. The door was opened by Milly. She greeted me warmly and as we stepped inside told me that she had prepared pork chops for dinner. I thanked her and had started to introduce her to Mrs. Porter when Pergamon came downstairs. I introduced her to my wife and explained that she would be having dinner with us and spending the night. To my relief, Pergamon indicated no resentment at having an unexpected guest imposed on her. I then went back to the car and returned with Mrs. Porter's suitcases. I had thought of allowing Mrs. Porter carry them herself, but decided that this seeming lack of politeness would offend Pergamon.

It required two trips to bring both my suitcases and Mrs. Porter's into the house. Hers were extremely heavy. I was amazed that she had had the strength to carry both of them at the same time. With some effort, I carried her suitcases upstairs to our guest bedroom and returned downstairs to find Mrs. Porter and my wife in animated conversation.

They were already on a first name basis. I realized that I should not have been surprised they were getting along so well. Both Pergamon and Tammy Porter had been born and raised near

Boston. Both had attended Radcliff College, although Pergamon some twenty-five years earlier, and they knew or had heard of the same people.

The two continued to reminisce throughout dinner, with only an occasional comment to me. I would have been annoyed at being excluded except for the delicious dinner, which I thoroughly enjoyed after the quick and not very enjoyable meals I had eaten while in Oklahoma City.

After dinner, I excused myself and went into the kitchen to use the telephone. I was glad to reach Eric Baxter in Indianapolis and learn, as I expected, that the campaigning was going well.

"Buck's a natural campaigner," he said. "We are drawing good crowds and the response to his speeches is enthusiastic. I think we have a good chance of winning Indiana."

I told Baxter that Mrs. Porter had flown with me to Illinois and would be joining Buck for some campaign appearances tomorrow.

"That really will be helpful," he said. "There have been some snide comments in the press about her failure to campaign with him."

After making arrangements for Mrs. Porter to fly to Ohio to join Buck there, I went back into the living room and informed her of what I had done and the flight she would take. I was about to add that I would arrange for a car to take her to the airport when Pergamon interrupted to say that she would drive Mrs. Porter to the airport herself. I raised no objection, said goodnight, and went to my bedroom, where I relaxed in bed, watching a movie on TV.

The next few days went well. Mrs. Porter proved as skillful a campaigner as her husband, and Buck did well in the election returns, coming in first in Illinois, thanks to my political contacts in the state, and in Indiana. However, Senator Tobin came in first in Ohio and Governor Atwood first in Wisconsin.

By now, most of the delegates to the Republican convention had been selected. California, the state with the largest number of delegates, was next on the list. As Governor of California, Atwood was in a good position to win most if not all of that state's delegates. This made it virtually certain that no candidate would have the necessary number of delegates when the convention began, although Buck's total would probably still put him the lead.

I was optimistic that by using the three B's (bribery, bullying and blackmail) I would be able to win over enough delegates to gain Buck the nomination, particularly as I still had the vice-presidential nomination as trading material. Buck, Eric and the rest of the campaign staff were already hard at work in California and Tammy Porter had accepted with unexpected cordiality my suggestion that she spend a few days campaigning with Buck in the state.

My optimism was shattered by a phone call from Baxter. He informed me that Tobin had suddenly withdrawn from all campaigning in California on the grounds that it would not be proper for him to challenge Atwood in his home state. That this was only a pretext was obvious. Baxter picked up reliable information that Tobin's decision was part of a deal with Atwood to join forces at the convention to deny Buck's the nomination. With Buck out, they would slug it out between them, with the loser to receive the vice-presidential nomination.

I thanked Baxter and told him I would get back to him. A feeling of despair enveloped me. Buck's candidacy appeared doomed. Tobin and Atwood had come up with an excellent strategy, one that might very well be impossible for me to counter. Buck's hold over his delegates was weak, with most likely to desert him as soon as they could in exchange for favors for themselves or for their states.

For a moment, I even considered throwing in the towel, ending my involvement in politics and returning full time to running my company. However, I resisted the impulse to walk away. All my life, I had been successful in using my intelligence to solve problems. Surely, there had to be a solution to my present dilemma.

I carefully reviewed the background reports I had received on Tobin and Atwood. With Alan Barnes tied up in Oklahoma City, I had used other investigators. They were not as competent as Alan. Neither were they as ethical. Considering the type of information I was seeking, this was a distinct advantage.

The reports sent to me on Tobin and Atwood contained no indication that Buck's rivals were anything other than honest and honorable, at least by the standards used to judge contemporary politicians. As I went over them again, searching for something I might have overlooked, it struck me. The reports covered in detail their activities over the past few years, but had been very scanty in terms of the earlier period.

With Tobin, I didn't think this was important. As a career Marine Corps officer before his retirement and subsequently the victor in a hard-fought race for the Senate, any warts he had almost certainly have been revealed. If he had successfully concealed something, it would be exceedingly difficult for me to uncover it, since the military traditionally pride themselves in looking after their own.

Atwood, however, was a different case. He had been a career politician, serving in the California legislature before becoming Governor. Earlier, he had been a mayor and a city official in Fresno. Here, I thought, might be fertile ground in which to dig. I picked up my office telephone and called Baxter's hotel, leaving a message from him to get back to me as quickly as possible.

I left a similar message for Joe Devine, the investigator I was using in California. Devine had risen to be a Lieutenant in the Los

Angeles Police Department Vice Squad before being fired for wife abuse. I thought he might be just the person I required to obtain the information I needed on Atwood.

When Baxter returned my call, I told him to hire a bright political science graduate student and have him research the newspaper morgue in Fresno to see what he might learn about Atwood's political career there. Devine I sent to Fresno to interview anyone he might be able to locate who was in a position to know about Atwood's activities. With Devine I could be a little more honest, making it clear to him that there would be a generous bonus in store if he could come up with derogatory information on Atwood.

Surprisingly, the information I needed was provided not by Devine, but by the graduate student hired by Baxter. The first I heard about it was when my secretary informed me that there was a collect phone call for me from one Rodrigo Garcia in Fresno. The name didn't ring a bell, but I guessed that Garcia might be connected with the investigation I had ordered in Fresno and accepted the call. Garcia confirmed that he had been hired by Baxter and gave me the information on Atwood's career as a member of the California Legislature and Governor which was part of Atwood's official campaign biography and which I already knew.

I was about to hand up in disgust when Garcia added that while a city official, he had been investigated on charges of corruption. A subsequent investigation had cleared Atwood of any wrongdoing. Despite Atwood's exoneration, I was cheered by the information. Where there was smoke, I knew, it was always possible there was fire.

Concealing my elation, I thanked Garcia for his diligence and told him I would send him a generous bonus. Upon hanging up, I telephoned Joe Devine in Fresno, instructing him to drop everything else and concentrate his efforts on obtaining information about the corruption allegations directed against Atwood.

CHAPTER 5

Devine's eagerness to earn the bonus I had promised him for producing adverse information on Atwood was a strong motivating force. Within twenty-four hours, he called back to inform me about the results of his efforts. Atwood had been acquitted on charges of taking kickbacks from the Bulwark Construction Company for sewer line construction projects awarded to it by the city of Fresno. His acquittal had been based on testimony from one Daniel Pardoe, an official of the company, buttressed by one of his subordinates. Devine had interviewed Pardoe and gotten him to state that Atwood had been guilty regarding the kickbacks and that he had exonerated Atwood only to save his own skin.

I thought it better not to inquire as to how Devine had persuaded Pardoe to change his story. What sufficed was that he had done so, and in writing. Even better, Devine reported that the subordinate who had corroborated Atwood's innocence was a young woman who had subsequently become Atwood's wife. I congratulated Devine on his good work, telling him he would receive an even bigger bonus if he could obtain additional derogatory material on Atwood. I then arranged to meet him in Los Angeles, where Atwood was campaigning and where I intended to meet face to face with the California Governor.

The flight to Los Angeles was easy, but that was the only part of the trip that was. A meeting with Devine was disappointing. He had failed to obtain any additional evidence confirming Atwood's involvement in corruption. The best he was able to come up with was information that Atwood had once quashed a ticket for driving under the influence of alcohol while he was a member of the state legislature.

My attempts to meet with Atwood were equally frustrating. A call to Al MacDonald, his campaign manager, elicited the response that the Governor was too busy to see me. I had Baxter try to arrange a meeting, with a similar lack of success.

In desperation, I decided to use nastier tactics. I bought a large box of chocolates, wrapped it as a gift, and had it delivered to the hotel at which Atwood was staying. The package was addressed to the Governor's wife. Inside I placed a gift card reading "Best wishes from your friends at Bulwark Construction." The next day I sent a bouquet of flowers to the Governor's wife with a similar card accompanying the gift.

Atwood's response was not what I expected. I had just returned to my hotel room after dinner when there was a knock at the door. I opened it and two burly men pushed their way in. One informed me they were from the California State Police.

"Get your coat!" he ordered.

"What for?" I asked.

"Because the Captain wants to see you."

One of the men picked up my jacket and approached me. I gathered they were not about to give me the opportunity to decline. For the first time in years, I felt physical fear.

"Are you arresting me?" I asked, trying to hide my fear. "What's the charge?"

"No, we're not arresting you, but you're coming with us!"

"My name is Melvin Shultz," I said. "And I'm a very wealthy man. Either you show me a warrant or tell me where you want me to go. Otherwise, I'm calling my lawyer and suing you for false arrest. I promise you I will spend millions if necessary to get you personally. Not the State Police, but you two as individuals. If you touch me, I'll resist and then charge you with police brutality. Now why don't you tell me what this is all about? Who's your Captain?"

The state policeman with my jacket was not in the least fazed by my words. He grabbed me by the arm, twisted it so that I couldn't resist, and forced my arm into the jacket sleeve. The other, however, looked worried.

"It's Captain Miller," said. "The head of the Governor's security detail. He just wants to talk to you, so don't make any fuss!"

I looked hard at the officer. His demeanor indicated he was unsure of himself.

"Don't be a fool!" I said. "You don't want to get mixed up in something you know nothing about and end up holding the bag. I'm handling Governor Porter's presidential campaign. Some of Atwood's people are trying to lean on me to prevent me from criticizing Atwood at a press conference before the primary. First of all, I'm not after Atwood. I'm just trying to prevent his attacking Porter. Second, I've arranged to have strong anti-Atwood attacks appear automatically if I should be harassed or put away for a few days."

A brief glimpse at the officer revealed he was more than half convinced by my words.

"Before you do anything stupid," I went on, "Call your Captain Miller and let me talk to him. Or if you can, let me talk to someone close to the Governor, possibly Al MacDonald."

"Joe," said the state policeman to whom I addressed my comments, "I think we ought to do as he says. It won't hurt to check with MacDonald.

His partner, who had finished forcing me into my jacket, reluctantly agreed. He shoved me down into a chair and stood behind me, ready to grab me if I attempted anything he didn't like.

I waited, hoping my bluff would work. The state policeman to whom I had been addressing my words picked up the telephone. To my relief, I heard him ask for "Mr. MacDonald." This was far better than I had hoped. I had not expected my captors to have direct access to Atwood's campaign manager.

After further conversation in a tone so low that I could not catch all of the words, he handed me the phone.

"MacDonald's out," he said. "You can talk to his assistant."

"This is Melvin Shultz," I began. "I'm handling Governor Porter's campaign. Two of your men forced their way into my hotel room and are threatening to kidnap me. You had better tell Atwood that if he doesn't want a nasty scandal in the headlines tomorrow, he had better call them off and set up a meeting with me immediately. Warn him he doesn't have much time! If I don't stop what I have in the works in the next couple of hours, I won't be able to stop it at all! I'll stay here in my room until I hear from you."

Without waiting for a response, I handed the telephone back to the state policeman. He apparently received his instructions and hung up. I waited impatiently to see what would happen.

After almost an hour, the phone rang. I started to get it, but the officer called Joe motioned me to return to my chair and picked up the phone himself.

"OK," he said, hanging up the phone and turning to me.

"Governor Atwood will see you in his hotel."

Without waiting for my agreement, his partner handed me my jacket. I was under no illusion that he would accept a refusal to accompany them. As I left my room, one of the state policemen on either side, I was uncertain in my mind as to whether I was really being taken to see Atwood.

Walking through the crowded hotel lobby, I considered my options. I could create a disturbance, shouting that I was being kidnapped. Such a tactic would probably prevent their taking me to some secluded spot and murdering me or keeping me captive. On the other hand, it almost certainly would make it impossible for me to make a deal with Atwood, which was my objective. Weighing the various scenarios, I decided to avoid a fuss and hope that I was really being taken to meet with the Governor.

We walked out of the hotel to where their car was parked. Joe opened the rear door to allow me to enter and then climbed in next to me, while his partner got behind the wheel. The car started and after what seemed to be an interminable time, actually no more than a couple of minutes by my watch, I was relieved to see us arrive at Atwood's hotel.

We parked. The driver got out of the car, opened the rear door and waited for me to get out of the car. Then, sandwiched in as before between my two guardians, I entered the hotel and we took an elevator up.

The elevator door opened and we stepped out into the corridor. I realized that we were on the floor housing Atwood's temporary campaign headquarters. Several burly men, clearly members of his security detail, scrutinized us as we proceeded into a large room, which had been converted into a makeshift operations center.

There were several people in the room. I recognized Atwood at once from his campaign photos. He was seated in his shirtsleeves behind a desk, issuing orders to a pretty young woman. He stared at me, then cut short his conversation with her and motioned curtly to the woman to leave the room. Most of the others in the room also left and I found myself alone with Atwood and my two escorts.

"We have laws in this state against blackmail," he said coldly. "I was going to let the State Police inform you of that fact, but since you want to hear it directly from me, I have taken the time to do so myself. Do you see any reason why I shouldn't have you arrested?"

I returned his stare as calmly as I could. It has been rare in my life that I have taken an instant dislike of anyone, but Atwood claimed that distinction. I don't know which I found more distasteful, his tone of voice or the contemptuous manner with which he looked at me.

"I think it would be best if we discussed this alone," I said. "I don't think you want what I am going to say widely known."

Atwood looked hard at me, then motioned to my escorts to leave.

"All right," he said. "You a have a minute before I have you taken out and arrested."

I smiled at him.

"That will make a great story on TV and in the papers," I said. "Better than that about the deal you made with Tobin. Just think. 'Porter's campaign charges Atwood with corruption; Atwood arrests key Porter supporter for blackmail'."

"You don't think you can pull that bluff, do you?" he asked. His voice was even colder than before. "There is not and never will be a deal between me and Senator Tobin."

"It's not a bluff," I've arranged to have the story released about your corruption unless you and I come to an agreement."

"And what will you use as the basis for your corruption

allegations, Daniel Pardoe?"

"That's right," I said. "He provided a written statement saying that he had lied when he cleared you of taking kickbacks from the Bulwark Construction Company."

Atwood laughed. "I thought so," he said. "And did you know that he was convicted for lying to a grand jury?"

The way he said it made me believe Atwood was telling the truth. I realized that Joe Devine had either not found out about this crucial fact, or, more likely, had had deliberately withheld from me the information discrediting Pardoe's statement.

I looked at Atwood. He was enjoying my obvious disappointment. He stood up, went o the door and called the state policemen back into the room."Are you ready to go to the station now?" he asked, with a sneer in his voice.

"Don't fool yourself, Governor," I said evenly. "You had better have your goons leave, unless you want to be thoroughly embarrassed."

Atwood looked at me closely, then motioned the state policemen to stay outside and closed the door.

"Just what are you getting at?" he asked.

"For what it's worth, I'm inclined to believe you're telling the truth about Pardoe. But it doesn't make any difference if Pardoe is lying," I said, with more assurance than I felt. "If you don't reach an understanding with me, I'll make sure that every delegate to the convention receives a copy of Pardoe's statement along with the report of how you managed to quash that ticket for driving under the influence of alcohol."

Atwood's attitude of triumph evaporated. It was clear that he was much more concerned about the second charge than about Pardoe's statement.

"That won't stop me from keeping Porter from getting the

nomination!"

"You're right," I said. "You can block Porter from being nominated. But what will that do for you? If you shoot down Buck, the copies of Pardoe's statement that I'll give to every delegate and put on TV will make it certain you don't win the nomination either. It will go either to Tobin or to a dark horse."

"At least I'll have stopped Porter!"

"Don't be stupid," I said. "I can give you a better option."

He looked at me carefully. "What do you propose?" he asked.

"That before the ballots are tabulated in the round of voting, you have the California delegation announce that in the interests of party unity, you are withdrawing your name from consideration and calling upon all California delegates to support Porter. In return, Buck will name you as his running mate.

"I wouldn't lower myself to be vice-president under that buffoon!"

"It would delay your nomination as President for only four years," I said. "I can promise that Porter will not run for a second term. As Vice-President, you will have a great chance of moving into the White House at the end of Buck's first term. That's a better deal than you can get from serving as Tobin's Vice-President for eight years."

"You're crazy," he said suspiciously. "Porter wouldn't give up serving a second term. Did he authorize you to make that offer?"

Choosing my words carefully, I said "He has left it to my discretion to make any deal I think necessary to put him in the White House."

"Suppose he decides after he is President to renege on the offer? Will he put the deal in writing?"

"Don't be silly," I said. "Would you put that sort of thing in writing? But I give you my word of honor that he will serve only one term."

"Your word of honor!" Atwood said contemptuously. "How much value is there in that?" I smiled to myself. I could certainly see Atwood's point of view.

"Let me put it this way," I said. "For reasons of my own, I intend to make Porter President and then to allow him only one term. You know that I can be as ruthless as I have to be to get what I want. Porter will not have the option of rejecting my advice, even if he is so foolish as to think of it."

Atwood turned and stared out the window. He was silent for a long time and I could almost see his mind evaluating his choices.

"All right," he said at length. "It's a deal. I guess I can wait four years, even if I have to serve under an idiot."

I stuck out my hand to shake his. After a moment's hesitation, he took it with obvious disgust. I knew that while he had agreed to go along with me, I would always have him as an enemy.

Back in my hotel room, I felt elated. I wanted to share the good news with someone. I thought of calling Buck or Baxter, but decided against it. It would be foolish to give them information they might mishandle. I thought for moment, then called Pergamon in Watsonville. She answered the phone, sounding sleepy.

"Dear," I said, "How would you like to go with me on a vacation to Bermuda? Just for a few days. It would like a second honeymoon."

"I'm sorry." She said. "It would be fun. But I have a meeting I have to go to at St. Mark's."

"Do you really have to be there?" I asked."

"I agreed to host the luncheon," she said softly. "I can't disappoint them."

I stifled a nasty rejoinder. Even if I did succeed in pressuring her to go to go to Bermuda she would spend the entire time there bemoaning the fact she had not fulfilled her obligations at our church. My happy anticipation of the trip evaporated. I said goodnight and hung up. As I fell asleep, I reflected over the great love I had for my wife. Sometimes, I thought, it would have been useful for me to share what I had observed in so many of the men I dealt with, an ability to enjoy myself with the mistresses, call girls or one-night stands that seemed to satisfy them.

Rather than remain in California, I decided to return to Illinois and supervise Buck's campaign from there. If Atwood lived up to our deal, the outcome of the California primary would have little effect on Buck's winning the nomination. If the Governor double crossed me, which was quite possible, there was little I could do about it except carry out my threat to launch a campaign to demolish his reputation. The California primary went much as I had expected. Atwood won the lion's share of the delegates and Buck garnered less than thirty percent of the votes. It was not a bad showing for Buck, given the fact that he was challenging a powerful governor in his home state.

Tammy's campaign appearances with Buck for two days won us some votes, and Buck's promise to eliminate the federal income tax did well among the state's conservative Republicans. My decision to avoid heavy spending in California cost Buck some votes, as I knew it would. Baxter had argued against this. Not wanting to tell him my reason, I explained that I was saving our resources to use at the convention.

Meanwhile, I carefully monitored Atwood's public comments about Buck. I had told him to feel free to go on attacking Buck, so long as he said nothing that would make it awkward for Buck to name him as a running mate. Atwood's campaign attacks on Buck never went beyond that point, leaving me optimistic the California Governor intended to honor our deal.

The Republican Convention opened in the middle of August in Dallas, the first time it had been held that city since 1984. I arranged to meet there a few days before it opened with Baxter and Buck to insure that our preparations were complete. Unexpectedly, Pergamon brought up the subject of my attendance, suggesting that she accompany me. I was surprised until she told me she had been in touch with Tammy Porter and that they had arranged to spend time together during the convention.

We arrived in Dallas and checked into the hotel which housed Buck's campaign headquarters. Pergamon had volunteered to make our hotel reservations. It was a more expensive hotel than I normally would have used and also did not provide the complimentary breakfast buffet I always looked for. To my complaints, Pergamon answered that she had chosen it because I would find it more convenient to be staying at the same hotel as Buck and the campaign staff.

Rather than provoke a nasty argument with my wife, I dropped the subject and went off to meet with Baxter and Buck. Baxter briefed me on the preparations he had made and on the assignments he had given to campaign staffers to woo the few uncommitted delegates and to hold the loyalty of the delegates pledged to Buck. I considered telling them about the deal I had made with Atwood, but once again kept my silence. I saw nothing they could do to make it firmer and a lot they might do which could disrupt it.

On the evening the balloting began for the nomination, I ate alone. Pergamon had let a message for me saying she was spending the day with Tammy and would have dinner with her. I declined an invitation to eat with some of the campaign staff in the hotel and instead had a good dinner at a Chinese buffet restaurant. I then spent a pleasant hour walking through Dallas and arrived at the convention hall a bit before the nominating speeches were scheduled to start.

I had secured a seat which gave me a good view of the California delegation. To occupy my time until the actual voting started, I scanned a paperback novel. I happily put it down as the speeches started. To my relief, there were no surprises. When the first round of balloting ended, Buck commanded a plurality of about forty percent of the votes, followed by Tobin with some thirty-five percent and Atwood with twenty-five percent. I stared down at the California delegation, searching for signs Atwood would carry out our agreement and withdraw.

After a few anxious seconds, I was elated to see a spokesman for the California delegation ask for the floor and step up to the microphone. Following the script Atwood and I had agreed upon, he announced that Governor Atwood had asked that his name be withdrawn for consideration and that he was calling upon his delegates to back Buck.

There was a moment of shocked silence and then pandemonium broke out. Campaign aides from Buck's and Tobin's camp scurried furiously about the convention floor, trying to garner the delegates Atwood had unexpectedly released. I wondered if I had erred by not informing Baxter of the likelihood of this development. In any event, our staff was no more prepared than Tobin's.

There was still doubt about the effects of Atwood's sudden withdrawal, since his delegates were under no compulsion to follow his advice and switch their votes to Buck. To help create the impression of an unstopped bandwagon for Buck, I had maneuvered beforehand to have two delegations switch to him immediately upon Atwood's announcement.

My freedom of action was limited by my unwillingness to risk divulging word of Atwood's move prematurely and by the fact that I had already used up much of my trading material. I still had the

Treasury Secretary post unencumbered, but I felt I could only have it go to someone eminently qualified and respected in order to lessen Wall Street fears over Buck's likely unorthodox approach to finance.

To insure that I could contact delegates likely to accept my offers, I had Joe Devine come east from California to assist me. I did not trust him, but he was the best available person for the job. Devine did not disappoint me. Based on his investigative reports, I was successful in my approach to Rita Caruso, an insurance company executive and a power in the Massachusetts delegation. Her son had had some problems with the law, which she had concealed. In return for my promise that Buck would name her Secretary of Education, she had switched her support to him, carrying with her about half of the Massachusetts delegation.

A similar approach worked with Mike Forrester, one of the few union officials serving as a delegate to the Republican convention and a member of the Hawaii delegation. He agreed to come over to Buck with as many delegates as he could persuade to follow him, in exchange for the promise of appointment as Secretary of Labor.

I would have preferred making deals with leaders of the larger delegations, but decided that approaching them without a reasonable expectation they would accept would be too risky. Happily, the movement of only a handful of delegates to Buck did the trick. Other delegations frantically clamored for the microphone, anxious to join the winning side early enough to be able to claim favors in return.

Within an hour, Buck's delegate total reached the magic number needed for nomination. I left the convention hall, pushing my way through the crowds. It was easy to tell from the expressions on their faces those who had supported Buck from those who had backed his rivals.

Because it was late, I took a taxi back to my hotel rather than walk. When the elevator let me off on the floor housing our campaign headquarters, a fascinating scene met my eyes. It resembled what I imagine London must have looked like on the day in June 1945 when Germany surrendered. Empty champagne bottles littered the floor. Couples were embracing in jubilation. I was warmly kissed by two female staffers before I could free myself and motion Baxter and Buck to follow me into an office.

"Who would have thought it?" Buck said with a big smile. "Atwood pulling out of the race like that. God must really be on our side."

"God may be on our side," I said, "But Atwood pulled out of the race because I offered him the Vice-Presidency in exchange."

The smile vanished from Buck's face.

"I don't want Atwood as Vice President," he muttered. "Tammy and I have discussed it. She thinks it would be good for me to choose a woman as my running mate."

"That's a fine idea," I said, trying to sound sincere. "Unfortunately, you couldn't have gotten the nomination without Atwood's pulling out of the race. And Atwood wasn't about to pull out until I promised him the Vice-Presidency."

"No," Buck said petulantly. "I won't have Atwood!"

"Buck," I answered as calmly as I could, "It's the price you have to pay to be President. The nomination will be worthless if the party is split, particularly with Atwood spreading the word that you reneged on the deal. You tell Tammy that you will name women to the Cabinet. One will be Rita Caruso. I promised her she will be Secretary of Education in return for the votes we needed in the Massachusetts delegation.

My words had the effect I had hoped for. Buck's smile returned.

I turned to Baxter. He was another story. The sulky attitude he had assumed upon learning of my deal with Atwood was unchanged. He apparently resented the fact that I was not giving weight to the adverse information he had secured about Atwood.

The limited patience I possess ran out.

"Eric," I said, using the tone once directed against me by an irate general when I was a private first class in the Pentagon public relations office. "Please get in touch with Al MacDonald and set up a meeting tomorrow between Buck and Atwood. It will be necessary to make preparations for Buck to publicly select him."

My tone had the desired effect of reminding Baxter who was running the show.

"Yes," he said, in much the same way I had answered the general.

I looked at my watch. It was late and I was feeling tired. I said good night and left the room. The crowd in the outer office had thinned. I assumed some of the celebrants had tired and gone to bed to go to sleep, with the others gone to bed to make love.

I entered my room and found that Pergamon was still out. Disappointed that I could not share my happiness with her, I made some instant cocoa and turned in.

The remaining days of the convention went by rapidly. I sat in on the meeting between Buck and Atwood to make sure things went well. It was fortunate I did so. Atwood suggested that Al MacDonald take over as campaign manager. Buck started to object when I intervened. I realized it would be a poor idea for us to flatly reject Atwood's suggestion. MacDonald has the reputation of being a skilled campaign director and I certainly didn't want Buck making decisions on his own.

I modified Atwood's suggestion to insure that my control over the campaign would not be threatened, while mollifying him and obtaining MacDonald's expertise. I suggested and won agreement to the establishment of a triumvirate of MacDonald, Baxter and myself to jointly direct the campaign. I calculated, correctly as it turned out, that Baxter and MacDonald would regard each other as rivals, permitting me to play one against the other when it suited my interests.

I wrote most of the initial draft and then carefully edited the final version of Buck's acceptance speech at the convention. I had to admit as I watched him deliver it that he was indeed a superb politician, almost making me believe that he knew what he was talking about.

On the flight back to Illinois the day after the convention ended, Pergamon remarked to me that Tammy Porter had seemed surprised about the choice of Atwood as Buck's running mate. I had not told my wife the details of my involvement in Buck's campaign and even less since she had become friendly with Tammy. When Pergamon asked me directly if I had played any role in Atwood's selection, I said only that I thought it was a good choice.

"That's funny," she observed. "Tammy seems to think it was all your idea. I don't think she likes it."

I looked at my wife carefully. She didn't seem to have intended any hidden meaning, but I wasn't certain. It seemed clear, however, that I was correct to consider Tammy a threat.

Buck's nomination as the Republican Party's candidate significantly changed the complexion of my association with the campaign. The party organization and fund-raising apparatus went into high gear to support him. I moved back from day-to-day supervision of the campaign, allowing MacDonald, Baxter and the other professionals to direct the work, subject to my overall supervision. Similarly, I reduced my financial support to what was legal, without employing the complex mechanisms Sol Sugarman had created to take advantage of loopholes in the election law.

My major contribution in the months leading up to the general election was to insure that the party was united behind Buck. Atwood's supporters were toiling as actively as Buck's, but it was vital to bring in Tobin's disgruntled backers. I accomplished this by offering him the post of National Security Adviser to the President, which I knew he would not accept, and by promising it to the highly qualified foreign affairs expert he suggested as an alternative. I also told two of his most influential political allies that Buck would name them to the Cabinet.

Buck put forth one of the most skillful campaigns in recent years, confounding those of us who regarded him as little more than a likeable buffoon. He was aided by Tammy. To my surprise, she threw herself into the effort, sharing the campaign spotlight with him and acting as the perfect political wife.

The only difficulty I had with her in this period concerned my suggestion that to attract the votes of pet lovers, she and Buck publicly adopt a dog about to be put to sleep. Tammy adamantly refused, arguing fiercely that she disliked dogs. If she had to adopt any animal, it would be a cat. Fortunately, Al MacDonald successfully convinced her that here were far more dog lovers among the voters than cat fanciers. She went along with the dog idea, but MacDonald had to assign one of the campaign aides to taking care of the dog, bringing it out only for media events.

At Pergamon's suggestion, we flew to Oklahoma City to spend election night with the Porters at Buck's campaign headquarters there. Dinner with the Porters was at seven p.m., a fashionable time according to Pergamon, but late for me. As usual, I found Buck's company tedious. Tammy surprised me by going out of her way to be cordial. Atwood and his wife, on the other hand, treated me with barely veiled hostility. It was clear he still harbored resentment over the tactics I had employed to get him to support Buck.

Buck was his usual ebullient self, exuding confidence that he would be elected. Atwood said little. I became increasingly concerned as to whether California's massive electoral vote could be counted upon.

Fortunately, I need not have worried. With President Cartwright unable to run for a third term, the Democrats had chosen as their candidate the incumbent Vice-President. His campaign had been marred by indecisiveness and by a temporary slowdown in the economy. This made Buck's call for an end to the federal income tax more popular. Although Buck lost New York State, a casualty of his behavior during the assassination attempt, he reached the level of electoral votes needed to make him President once the California votes had been counted.

When the TV networks declared Buck the winner, he jumped up from the sofa and embraced Tammy. He then shook hands with the Atwoods, with Pergamon and me, and with Baxter and MacDonald, who had joined us. For once, I did not regard his big grin as misplaced. He certainly deserved to feel good over his success.

As Buck went downstairs to say a few words to his campaign supporters, gathered in the ballroom beneath us, I took the opportunity to excuse myself and go to my room. As I undressed and got into bed, I felt moderately pleased about Buck's victory, but not as elated as I should have been. I had spent a considerable sum of my own money to elect him and gone through a great deal of effort, including doing some unsavory things, of which I was not proud.

I wondered if I had been foolish to do so. I had done it almost as a whim, to see whether my theories about advertizing were correct. Now I wondered if I might have inflicted on the country a President who would prove to be a disaster. I comforted myself that he probably would be no worse than any of the mediocrities who had occupied the White House in recent years.

Between the time of Buck's election and inauguration day, I distanced myself from the preparations for the change in administrations. My only involvement was in making certain that Buck honored the commitments I had made to people for posts in the administration in exchange for their support during the campaign.

I had no interest in serving in the new administration, myself. I desired only to return to running Lust Cosmetics. I felt certain that I possessed sufficient derogatory information on Buck to prevent him and the government from acting unfairly against me or significantly harming the United States by his actions. I certainly had no intention of asking him to violate the law on my behalf.

Momentarily, I considered asking him to name some of my friends to government positions. Sol Sugarman would have been a good appointee to a senior position in the Justice Department. However, I shied away from placing Sol in a position where he might feel compelled to take action against my firm.

Back in Watsonville, I happily reverted to my daily routine running my company. It was during the Christmas holidays, when the pervasive holiday spirit had left me feeling uncharacteristically mellow, that Pergamon broached the idea of our attending Buck's inaugural. It seemed to mean a lot to her. She had been unusually agreeable that day and I found myself agreeing to what seemed to be a spur of the moment idea on her part.

Only later, when I overheard her on the phone speaking with Tammy, did I realized it was part of a long-term plan. She was discussing the gown she had previously ordered from the same high-priced couturier dressmaker who was supplying Tammy's gown, so that the two of them would make a stunning impression at the inaugural balls.

CHAPTER 6

A loud blast of a horn shook me out of my reverie. I realized that I was almost at my hotel. The walk from Buck's hotel and taken longer than I expected. Pergamon would most likely berate me for my late arrival, complaining that we would be late for the inaugural balls. Shrugging my shoulders, I entered the hotel and took the elevator to our room.

Entering our hotel room, I found Pergamon standing in front of the full length mirror on the bathroom door, putting on her makeup.

"You're late," she said, "We have to hurry to get to dinner on time."

She was wearing a bra that revealed much of her cleavage. I know little about such things, but assumed it had been purchased from the couturier to go along with the low cut gown she had bought to wear to the inaugural balls.

Pergamon and I had been married almost forty years, and she was the same age as I am, sixty-four. Despite her age, she had kept her figure remarkably well. As always when I looked at her undressed, I felt passion rising within me. I walked to her and kissed her gently on the back of her neck. She laughed a bit.

"Pergamon," I said. "Let's make love."

She shook her head. "We don't have time. We have less than thirty minutes to get to dinner."

"We can come late," I persisted. "We won't miss anything."

"Don't be silly," she said. "Anyway, it would mess up my makeup."

Disappointed, I took off my jacket and shirt and prepared to shave.

"How did your meeting with the President go?" she asked.

"Fine," I said. I started to apply lather to my face. "Oh," I added as an afterthought. "He did ask me to take the job of Director of CIA."

"What did you tell him?"

I turned around in surprise. "Naturally, I said no. I have no experience in intelligence and I don't want to be part of the administration."

"But you helped put him in office."

"That's right," I said, "I hope it wasn't a mistake."

"Melvin, "she persisted. "It would be fun living in Washington. And you can do the job. Besides, don't you have a responsibility to stay on and help keep him from making mistakes?"

"No," I said firmly. "It's foolish. We're going back to Watsonville tomorrow, and that will be the end of my association with Buck."

I finished shaving, and walked out of the bathroom. I had expected to find Pergamon dressed, waiting impatiently for me to get ready. Instead, she was unhooking her bra, her beautiful breasts now naked.

"Let's make love," she said in a husky voice, removing the rest of her clothing. She lay down provocatively on the bed.

I tore off my clothes and joined her on the bed, embracing her tightly. She kissed me passionately on the lips. I started to return the kiss when she whispered, "Be careful, don't ruin my makeup."

I didn't let this comment lessen my ardor. As always, our love making was exquisite. Even her urging me not to take too long did not quell my passion. After our love making ended, Pergamon waited a few brief minutes and then disengaged herself from me. "We'll really have to hurry now, "she said.

I waited until Pergamon washed, then did so myself and dressed in the formal garb I would have to wear to the inaugural balls. I then turned to stare at my wife. The dark blue gown she was wearing made her look even more beautiful than ever. It obviously was extremely expensive. I didn't ask her how much it cost, fearing that if I found out it would mar my enjoyment in seeing her in it. Whatever it cost, it made her look so good it was probably worth it.

"Pergamon," I said, only half joking, "You're the most beautiful woman I've ever seen. Let's make love again."

She smiled appreciatively and motioned me to rise. She adjusted my tie to make it look better, then told me to rush. We took the elevator down to the lobby and walking outside, took a taxi to Buck's hotel.

As we looked at the passing scenery, Pergamon turned to me. "Washington is such a beautiful city," she said. "It would be fun to live here for a year or so. Couldn't we?"

I smiled, but said nothing. Nonetheless, her words impressed me. Possibly I was still enjoying the afterglow from our lovemaking, but it seemed as I thought it over she might be right. I had no doubt in my mind that, inexperienced though I might be in intelligence matters, I could do a better job than the recent directors in running CIA. Pergamon had also touched a raw nerve when she suggested that I had a responsibility to take part in the administration to make certain that as President, Buck committed no grievous mistake.

Having dinner with Buck that night convinced me that I had no choice but to stay on in Washington. Most of the party was made up of Buck's friends from Oklahoma City. Listening to them converse, I was appalled by their shallowness, cupidity and lack of intelligence. God help the United States, I thought, with this lot in charge of the government.

When we left the table, I tapped Buck on the shoulder and drew him aside for a private conversation.

"Buck," I said, "I've decided to take the CIA job."

He gave me a big grin. ""I'm very glad you reconsidered," he said. "I want you in this administration."I stood there wondering what advantage he could possibly see in having me as CIA Director.

As had become the custom in recent years, numerous inaugural balls were held that night to commemorate the start of Buck's presidency. Pergamon and I were invited to the ball considered to be the most prestigious. As I expected, I found it tedious. I am not a good dancer, and am able to be an adequate one only when doing the waltz. The band played one waltz early in the evening, which I danced with Pergamon. Then the music became increasingly louder and faster.

Pergamon became increasingly testy as she sat out the succeeding dances, particularly after Buck and Tammy departed to make appearances at the other balls. I obtained a brief moment of relief when I arranged for one of the young military officers invited to the ball for such purposes to dance with Pergamon. However, her annoyance returned as soon as the dance was over and the officer gone.

By midnight, my patience was exhausted and I told Pergamon that I was going back to our hotel. She accompanied me, but in the taxi back her anger was apparent. In order to avoid a nasty fight, I decided to tell her that I had reconsidered and would take the CIA job. When she heard this, she enthusiastically grabbed and loudly kissed me, to the amusement of our cab driver.

Back in our hotel room, Pergamon began bubbling about what a fine time we would have in Washington, including purchasing a fourteen room mansion she had seen in the prestigious upper northwest part of the city. It had, she informed me, outdoor and indoor swimming pools as well as a tennis court.

The next weeks were busy ones. After considerable argument, I was able to persuade Pergamon that it would be foolish to buy a home in Washington if we might not be staying there more than a year or two. With her reluctant acquiescence, I then rented a furnished luxury two-bedroom apartment in nearby Virginia. Its most important asset, as far as I was concerned, was that it had a beautiful panoramic view of the Potomac River.

The eagerness with which Pergamon planned our move to Washington saddened me, although I could understand it. After years of living in small town Watsonville, she looked forward toward becoming a leading member of Washington society. However, her obvious pleasure at leaving our home bothered me when I contrasted it in my mind with the enthusiasm she had displayed when I first met started dating her.

A twenty-two year old graduate of Radcliffe, she had come to Watsonville to research and write a biography of General Thomas Watson, the Civil War hero for whom the town was named. She was the only child of an Episcopal minister who had had a small church near Boston. Both of her parents were dead, and I gathered the small stipend her college adviser had secured for her to cover her expenses while writing the biography was primarily an act of charity.

Pergamon and I had met while attending services at St. Marks, the only Episcopal church in Watsonville. It was her first Sunday in town. She told me later that she had heard the church bells in her nearby room at the dorm for graduate students and had decided to attend the services. I had only recently returned to Watsonville myself, having reluctantly given up my reporter's job at the "Washington Star" to take over our paper after my father's death.

When I saw Pergamon in the church, I thought she was the prettiest woman I had ever seen. It was not only that she was attractive. The clothing she was wearing she had bought in Boston. It was more stylish than that that worn by the young women of Watsonville and showed her superb figure to best advantage.

Most of the young people my age had left Watsonville to live and work in Chicago or other large cities. Pergamon and I were virtually the people our age at St. Marks. It was only natural that I started taking her out. I loved the warm way she called me by my nickname Scoop and the enthusiasm she showed as she discussed the material she had uncovered about General Watson. The life of the General had been covered in detail in my classes at the Watsonville Elementary School, but it was all fresh to her, including his resigning as Rector of St. Marks at the outbreak of the Civil War to lead the local contingent of volunteers to join the Union Army.

While I very much enjoyed Pergamon's company, I had not started to think seriously of getting married. The turning point in our relationship came one warm summer Sunday after church, when we were having a picnic in a deserted meadow. We had embraced, and before I had thought about what I was doing, we were both undressed and making love.

I had made love previously with other women and did not

regard doing so with Pergamon as committing myself to anything. I told her as we dressed how much I had enjoyed it. He looked embarrassed, but said nothing, till I dropped her off at her dorm. She embraced me warmly and told me that she loved me. I felt it only polite to say I loved her, too. The next day, she invited me over to her room for dinner, actually to take her to a nearby pizza restaurant.

After dinner, she asked me shyly what date would be best for our wedding. Concealing my surprise at the idea we would be married, I thought it over. She was beautiful, intelligent and fun to be with. It was unlikely that I could do better. Casting aside my doubts that I was ready to take on the responsibilities of marriage, I told her that I would leave the date to her, hoping I sounded more enthusiastic than I felt.

In the years following our wedding, I never seriously regretted marrying Pergamon. More than once, however, I wished she had remained the warm, agreeable person I had married. Our interests increasingly differed. Whereas she had abandoned her research on General Watson after the wedding to assist me in running the paper, after a few years she began to urge me to sell it and move to Chicago. Her attitude became worse following my acquisition of Lust Cosmetics. At best it was marked by indifference. More often, it was a barely disguised contempt.

The growing divergence with which we looked at things was reflected in her reaction when Milly declined Pergamon's invitation to move to Washington with us. Pergamon thereupon proposed that we give Milly two months' pay and terminate her work for us permanently. I absolutely refused to consider such a thing. Not only was I fond of Milly, but I feared at her age she would be unable to get another job. It was not in my character to behave so cruelly to someone who had been loyal to me. I asked her to stay on at our house and act as caretaker at her regular salary, an offer she gratefully accepted.

Our move to Washington was facilitated by the fact that the apartment I rented there was fully furnished. I spent a few weeks in Watsonville arranging with Sol Sugarman's assistance the procedures under which I could temporarily divest myself of control of Lust Cosmetics during the period I served as CIA Director, while retaining ownership of the company. Pergamon and I then had packed for shipment to Washington those few things we desired there. I bid goodbye to Milly, pleased by the prospect that she would carefully look after our home while we were gone.

My relations with Pergamon were pleasant during this period. She was buoyed by our move to Washington. Our only argument occurred when she learned I had arranged for my 1980 Buick to be shipped to Washington. She had erupted, arguing that since I would have the use of a chauffeur-driven car as CIA Director and that she would be taking her BMW, I had no need for the Buick.

"It's not only not necessary" she exploded, "But it's ridiculous! Who ever heard of a Cabinet member driving a wreck like that?"

I had to admit that her arguments made sense. Still, one of the advantages about being rich was that I could afford to appear eccentric if I chose. I changed the subject. Subsequently, I went ahead with the arrangements to have my car transported to Washington for me to use. As I did so, I thought to myself that while I was usually frugal, it was nice to have enough money to be able to do the things that were dear to me.

We could have flown to Washington, but I opted instead to have us drive there in Pergamon's BMW. The road trip was pleasant, like a mini-vacation. We checked into a motel there for a few days, then moved into our rented apartment with little effort. Pergamon engaged a housekeeper to cook and supervise the elaborate dinners she planned to hold as a budding Washington hostess. I took an immediate dislike to the housekeeper, a tall, thin woman, who told me pointedly that she wished to be addressed as "Miss Pritchard."

After getting settled in our new apartment, I contacted the White House Personnel Office to inform them I was ready to begin the steps necessary for my Senate confirmation. I had naively assumed it would be a simple procedure once Buck announced his choice for the post. What followed strengthened my growing fear that Buck's administration would be totally inept.

The White House staffer I spoke to assured me that everything was on track. A few minutes later, I received a phone call from a pompous sounding individual who introduced himself as Walter Tilden. He told me he had been assigned by the acting Director to serve as my aide and to assist me in going through the confirmation process.

Promptly at 9 a.m. the next morning, Tilden arrived at my apartment to escort me in a chauffeur-driven limousine to the Executive Office Building, or EOB as he referred to it. He introduced himself to me and I found myself disliking Tilden in person as much as I had on the phone. He was short, plump and, I thought unctuous. If this was the type of officer CIA senior officials thought provided the proper impression of the Agency to its new Director, I feared I might have some problems in dealing with them.

When we arrived at the Executive Office Building, it revived old memories. I had visited occasionally during my stint as a reporter in Washington. Tilden led me to an office which issued me a temporary badge to enter the building and a parking space for me to use on the street south of the EOB. He then escorted me to a small office, furnished with a wooden desk and chair and three large combination safes. This office, he told me, would be for me to use during my confirmation hearings. I looked around and realized it was certainly not one of the building's luxury offices, hardly suited for a proscriptive Cabinet member.

"Do I really need three combination safes?" I asked.

Tilden looked very serious and lowered his voice to a whisper. "Most assuredly," he said. "Everything we will send you will be highly classified."

In the same serious manner, Tilden showed me how the safes were opened and closed. He then had me practice locking and unlocking them several times.

"Don't I have a secretary who will do that for me?" I asked.

He mumbled a non-answer and changed the subject. I decided not to press the issue and breathed s sigh of relief when he left, informing me that the briefing books would be delivered to me on the next day. I fervently hoped he was not typical of Agency personnel.

I looked around the office. Other than stare out the window at the passing traffic, I had nothing to do. I walked out of the office and asked the first person I saw, a woman seated at a desk, if she had a newspaper I could read. She looked up from her work and asked me pointedly, "Who are you?"

"Melvin Shultz," I told her. "The nominee to be Director of CIA."

"Oh," she said, a trifle abashed, and handed me copies of that day's "Washington Post" and "New York Times" to read.

Reading them took me an hour or so. After doing the crossword puzzle in the "New York Times," the first occasion I had taken the time to do so in many years, I got up from my desk and stared out the window. I could think of nothing more to do there. I left the office, walked to an exit, and out into the street. I thought of taking a taxi home, but decided instead to walk. It was a beautiful day, and I enjoyed walking along Pennsylvania Avenue and then down to Constitution Avenue. I neared the Lincoln Memorial when it occurred to me that walking all the way to my apartment would be too far a walk, even for me. I managed to hail a cab and had the driver take me to my apartment in Old Town, Alexandria.

Miss Pritchard met me as I opened the door. She informed me that Pergamon had gone to a reception for the wives of the incoming Cabinet members. Her attitude was officious, very different from Milly's warmth. I felt disinclined to ask her to make me lunch. Instead, I went into the kitchen and fixed a sandwich for myself. I then spent the rest of the afternoon unpacking my books and arranging them in the bookcase I had shipped from home.

The next morning, I made myself an early breakfast and waited for Tilden to pick me up. By 9:30 a.m., neither Tilden nor the limousine had arrived. I called his number and his secretary told me that no arrangements had been made for my transportation to the Executive Office Building. It suddenly became very clear to me why Tilden had pointedly told me that he had obtained an on-street parking space for me.

Overcoming my initial inclination to bawl out the person with whom I was speaking and order a car to pick me up immediately, I said goodbye politely and hung up. I promised myself tht as soon as I was Director, I would take corrective action against the incompetents with whom I was dealing.

I considered taking a taxi to the EOB. However, my 1980 Buick Skylark had been delivered the day before, and I decided to drive there instead. Pergamon had raised a storm when she saw it in the building garage, informing me among other things that "I would disgrace the entire administration" if I were seen in it. It had been hard, but I had manfully resisted telling her that in my mind, the administration would probably be a disgrace in a lot more important ways.

I parked the Buick in the area south of White House in one of the spaces reserved for White House personnel. Looking at the other cars parked there, I had to admit that my car was the most dilapidated.

The guard at the Executive Office Building examined my identification pass and then permitted me to enter. On the way to my office, I stopped by the same woman who had provided me with the newspapers on the previous day. Her reception was slightly more cordial when I again asked for the daily papers. Armed with reading material, I entered my small office and prepared to occupy myself with the papers.

My reading was interrupted in mid-morning by Tilden, accompanied by an assistant. Each of them carried a metal box secured by a combination lock. With great fanfare, Tilden opened the miniature safes. From each, he extracted a large, loose-leaf binder.

He told me in a hushed voice, presumably to convey the gravity of his words, that they contained the most sensitive, highly classified CIA Material. The material in the books was so secret, he stressed, that they had to be kept in the safes at all times, except when I actually was reading one. Not only was I never to utter a word about what they contained to anyone not expressly authorized by the Agency to receive such information, but I was never even to mention my having the books.

"Exactly what do you want me to do with them?" I asked him, "Burn them before reading?"

His displeasure at my joke was obvious in the disapproving look he gave me.

"It is essential," he said, "For you to read and memorize all of the information. You almost certainly will be asked questions based on this during your confirmation hearings."

I thanked Tilden, signed my name on the receipt he presented to me for the books, and watched with relief as he and his associate left. I manfully resisted asking him how the Senators at my confirmation hearings could ask me questions about the material in the books unless they also had been given access to them. Judging from the size of the books, they must have contained every secret the United States had ever acquired since the original thirteen colonies gained their independence from Great Britain.

It was with no little curiosity that I opened the first briefing book. The pages were tightly crammed with information. Many of them described conditions in foreign nations and problems the United States was facing in dealing with them. I have always loved reading about history and international relations and was enjoying the information when I suddenly realized that most of what I was reading had been better reported in the newspapers I read daily. Other issues were so arcane that I doubted most members of the Senate were aware of them, let alone prepared to frame questions about them during the confirmation hearings.

I turned hopefully to the second briefing book. It contained information about individual Agency operations. I was amused to find that each section described a seemingly important achievement, such as convincing an important official in a specific country to act as a CIA spy. This effort to obtain dramatic effect was undercut by the lack of such specific detail as the name of the recruited agent, which was understandable, but also his position or the information he was providing. After reading several of the sections I concluded they were useless for my purposes. If I had been a Senator and the nominee for CIA Director possessed no more than the information contained in the briefing book, I would have despaired of his common sense and voted against the nomination on general principles.

Feeling both disappointed and disgusted, I stowed the books in one of the combination safes, locked it and left my office. I walked directly to the White House Personnel Office. Ignoring the efforts of the first secretary I encountered to stop me, I found someone who looked like a senior official, and demanded to know the location of Walter Hanke, the official in charge. Hanke had played a leading role in Buck's campaign effort. He was from Oklahoma City and had come to the campaign with Tammy's strong endorsement. I would have preferred to veto him, but had finally decided to go along with his appointment when Buck had strongly urged it.

To Hanke's credit, he jumped up from his desk as soon as he saw who it was and walked toward me with a big smile on his face. Extending his hand he said, "Mr. Shultz, what can I do for you?"

"How is my confirmation going?" I asked.

His answer, "Very well," did nothing to reassure me.

"Shouldn't I be calling on key Senators?" I pressed on.

"There's no need of that. The President has spoken to the Chairman and ranking minority member of the Intelligence Committee. It's all taken care of."

I thanked him and left. It was clear to me that my nomination was in jeopardy. If I wanted the job, I would have to take charge of the effort myself. Back in my office, I decided to refrain from using the phone there in case my activities were being scrutinized. I carefully checked the combination safes to insure that they were securely locked, with no classified material out anywhere else in my office. I then walked out to my car and drove home.

When I arrived there, Mss Pritchard gave me a frosty welcome, informing me that Pergamon was attending a charity function with the first lady. I went into the kitchen to make a sandwich for lunch. As I opened the refrigerator, I stopped. The woman worked for me, I told myself. There was no reason for me to tiptoe around her.

"Pritchard," I called out crisply, "Please come here."

She arrived, an expression of anger, mixed with surprise on her face.

"I'm hungry," I told her. "Make me a hamburger for lunch. Please grill it on the stove-top grill and make it medium rare."

"We don't have any hamburger," she said, as though the thought of making such an ordinary dish was an insult.

"Then go out and buy some now!" I barked, "And get some relish, too."

She looked at me. For a moment, I thought she was about to quit. Then she quietly said, "Yes, sir."

After she left, I felt slightly embarrassed that I had humiliated her. Still, I thought, it had been necessary. Otherwise I would have had to endure her obvious contempt for me, which I found unacceptable.

I picked up the phone and called a firm in Chicago I had used on several occasions to collect information I needed to prepare advertising campaigns for Lust Cosmetics. I instructed them to gather information and newspaper clippings on CIA operations going back for the past five years and on the confirmation hearings of the previous three Agency directors. Particular attention, I added, should be given to items in the British, French and Russian newspapers, since I had found the foreign press frequently reported useful news not carried in American publications.

While I waited for Pritchard to return and make my lunch, I relaxed watching the cable new n TV. She returned quicker than I expected, made my lunch, and served it in the dining room. The hamburger was delicious. When I had finished, I called her to come.

"That was a damn good hamburger," I said. "Thank you."

She smiled and said "Yes, sir," in a non-committal way.

"Pritchard seems a strange way to address you," I remarked. "What's your first name?"

"Agnes, but I don't care for it."

"What do your friends call you?"

She thought for a moment. Then, in a low voice she said, "My brother used to call me Fred. My middle name is Fredericka. He was a flier in Korea and was killed there. Nobody has called me that since."

"I'm sorry," I said. "Would you prefer Fred to Pritchard?"

She gave me a hesitant smile. "Yes," she said. "That would be nice."

Feeling pleased, I went back to the hall. I was about to read a news magazine when I suddenly thought of Bob DePorte. I had met him years before, when he was serving as a corporal in the same Pentagon public relations office to which I had been assigned after being drafted and completing my basic training. Like me, Bob was from the Mid West and unmarried. He had befriended me and shown me the ropes. We became good friends and occasionally went out on double dates. On a few Sundays we had gone to Griffith Stadium to watch the old Washington Senators team play baseball.

Bob finished his tour of military service and was discharged a few months before I was. He had been fortunate enough to find as job as reporter on the old "Washington Star," the capital's evening newspaper. Shortly before my discharge, he offered to help me get a job at the paper, a suggestion I eagerly accepted. I was far more interested in working as a reporter for a big city daily than in returning to Watsonville to help my father run the printing shop and our small town paper.

Bob's recommendation helped me get an interview with the "Star's" City Editor, who agreed to give me a trial as a reporter covering local news. It was not the glamorous coverage of the White House, Congress or the State Department that I had hoped for, but I found the work and living in Washington enjoyable. Bob and I shared a small apartment in Georgetown and had a great social life with the numerous attractive government women sharing apartments in the same area.

My idyllic existence ended suddenly when I received word that my father had died. My mother had passed away several years earlier. I had always felt close to my father, even when living and working in Washington, and we had called each other frequently to keep in close touch. Rather than see my father's paper closed, I regretfully resigned from my job, said goodbye to Bob, and returned to Watsonville to run the paper and live in my parents' old home.

After returning to Watsonville, I had lost touch with Bob. Running a struggling small town weekly paper left me little time for anything else. Then I met Pergamon and soon began spending what free time I had with her. The last note I received from Bob had informed me he was leaving the "Star" to take a better job at a Los Angeles newspaper. Years later, I had heard he was Washington Bureau Chief for a chain of West Coast papers. I planned to look him up on one of my occasional trips to Washington, but had never quite gotten around to doing so.

Bob, I thought, would be the perfect person to talk to in order to obtain an insider's viewpoint of the status of my confirmation. He came on the phone almost as soon as I gave my name to his secretary.

"Mel," he said as soon as he came on the phone. "It's great to speak to you. I was hoping you would get I touch with me when you got settled. How is everything going?"

"It's too early to say yet," I answered. "Washington looks very different from this perspective than it did when we worked on the 'Star'. I was hoping we could get together for lunch. I'm temporarily using an office at the EOB."

"That's a great idea! Are you free tomorrow? I know a couple of good restaurants near here. My office, you know, is at the National Press Club Building."

"Tomorrow's fine," I replied. How about noon at the Press Club?"

"It's a date. I'll meet you at the front desk there."

"Let's make it in the library there," I suggested. "I'm still a club member, you know, so I'll have no difficulty going up to the library."

The next morning, I got up and dressed early as usual and drove to the EOB. There was no reason why I couldn't read a news magazine more comfortably at home as at my temporary office. However, I thought it better to conceal my actions by going through the motions of following Tilden's instructions for preparing for the nomination hearings.

About 11 a.m., I left my office and walked along Pennsylvania Avenue past the White House and Treasury Department to 14th Street and then down to the National Press Club. I was enjoying myself in the club library scanning the out-of-town newspapers, when I felt a tap on my shoulder. I turned around and it was Bob. He looked older and heavier than when I had last seen him, but so did I. We shook hands warmly. He suggested that we eat lunch in the prestigious club restaurant used primarily by lobbyists and seemed amused when I proposed instead that we go to the informal club restaurant on the club's 14th floor used by working reporters.

We sat down by at a table near the bar and a waiter approached and asked Bob for his club number. Before Bob could respond, I quickly gave the waiter mine.

"I didn't realize you were a club member," Bob said.

"Oh, yes," I replied smiling. "I joined as an out-of-town member back in Watsonville after I started having a bit of extra money. I still officially am editor of my dad's old weekly, which qualifies me as a working journalist."

"So you never were able to carry out your plans to turn it into a daily paper?" he asked.

"No, Watsonville is too close to Chicago to compete with the Chicago papers."

The waiter brought the hamburgers and beers we had ordered for lunch and we chatted a bit about old times. Then, during a lull in the conversation, Bob changed the subject.

"Do you have any thoughts about how you will run CIA?" he asked.

"Bob," I said, shaking my head. "I don't think I can discuss the Agency with you, even off the record. I might well inadvertently mention something I shouldn't."

The look of annoyance that crossed his face bothered me. As a reporter he must have heard that excuse many times. He naturally had found it irritating, coming from an old friend.

"However," I added, "I would be happy to discuss anything other than the CIA with you, off the record."

He relaxed. "All right," he said. "That sounds fair. How did you get involved with Porter? It doesn't seem to be anything you'd be interested in?"

"It was purely accidental. I bumped into him in a bar in New Hampshire shortly before the primary last year. His campaign was in a pitiful state. I began aiding him with advice because I felt sorry for him, then continued on as a whim and, I guess, to see if I could get him elected President."

"Do you think he will make a good President?"

"Frankly no. I think I made a serious mistake. All this is off the record, but I think this may be the worst administration since Grant's."

"Didn't you have a major role in suggesting key appointees?"

"Only during the primaries," I said, "when it was necessary to swap positions for votes. I had been confident that Cairns would do a good job as Secretary of State. He certainly had the expertise. Unfortunately, after his heart attack, his doctors talked him out of taking the post."

"Then why are you willing to take the CIA job?" Bob asked. "Aren't you risking being tarred by this administration?"

"Yes, there is a good risk of that. Lord knows, I didn't want any government position. I tried to refuse it when Porter sprang it on me. However, my wife convinced me that I had an obligation to make sure he doesn't do any serious damage. As CIA Director, I will be on hand to stop him if he goes too far."

"Can you do that?" Bob asked, surprised.

"I think I'll have enough of a say to keep him from going too far astray," I answered, thinking of the photos of Buck I had taken from Terrell.

"Tell me," I said, changing the subject, "What have you heard of the status of my confirmation?"

Bob looked embarrassed. "I'm afraid it doesn't look good," he said. "Senator Manley is dead set against confirming you. As Chairman of the Intelligence Committee, he carries a lot of weight. He thinks you're unqualified for the CIA post. Even though he's a Republican, he doesn't like Porter and sees no problem with blocking your nomination, even if it's pushed by of a President from his own party."

"And the rest of the committee?"

"You don't have any friends on the committee. The other members are all opposed to you or, at best, undecided. Unless you give them a strong reason to oppose Manley, they'll follow his lead. About the only thing that could change that is if the President goes all out to push for your confirmation. And I have to say, the White House seems to be doing nothing to support it."

"Thanks for your honesty," I said. "I've come to the same conclusion, myself."

"What are you going to do about it?"

"Oh," I answered, smiling. "I think I can persuade the committee to confirm me. But please keep that off the record, too. I'll alert you if the situation changes."

Bob said nothing. I gathered from his expression he thought I was crazy, both for agreeing to take the CIA post and because I still thought I had a chance to be confirmed. After lunch, he proudly showed me through his office in the Press Club Building. We then said goodbye and exchanged home telephone numbers so that we could keep in touch.

As I walked back along Pennsylvania Avenue, I reviewed what Bob and told me. There was no doubt in my mind that I faced a hard fight if I wanted to be confirmed as CIA Director. Unless I wanted to give up or face a public humiliation, I had to take charge of it myself.

Rather than return to my EOB office, I continued to where I had parked the Buick and drove home. Fred greeted me in a friendly fashion, informing me that Pergamon was out. She offered to make me lunch, which I politely refused. Going to the telephone, I called Alan Barnes in Chicago. I had not spoken to him since I had taken him out to lunch before leaving Watsonville for Washington. We had parted on good terms, Alan expressing his gratitude at the bonus I had given him as a reward for his work in Oklahoma City.

"Alan," I said, after we had chatted amicably for a few, "I have another important job for you. I want you to go to South Carolina and do a thorough investigation on Senator Manley, Chairman of the Senate Intelligence Committee. You know," I added, "The same sort of job you did for me on Porter."

"Yes, sir," he replied, then added something which caused me some apprehension, "I hope it won't involve the same sort of things I had to do about the Terrells."

"I don't think it will," I said, hoping I was dead wrong. But if it does, I do need it."

To ease his concerns, I reminded him that I had arranged for good jobs for the Terrells and that they were doing well. After hanging up, I thought for a minute and then called Joe Devine. If Alan's scruples got in the way of his collecting the sort of information on Manley that I was seeking, I was confident Devine's would not. Devine's gratitude at getting another assignment from me was overwhelming. I was sure he would provide what I needed, even if he had to fabricate it himself.

Over the next weeks, the reports I had requested from the firm in Chicago began arriving almost daily. I found them detailed and very useful. I carefully read them and made notes, memorizing the most important material. Periodically, I called the White House Personnel Office. Each time, Hanke assured me that the arrangements for my confirmation by the Senate were progressing well. I was certain the contrary was true, but did not reveal my opinion.

The press reported almost daily about the other nominees for Cabinet posts paying courtesy calls on key Senators. The anomaly of my situation struck Pergamon, who asked me why I hadn't mentioned to her my calling on Senators. Fearful that her friendship with Tammy might lead my wife to pass on anything I might tell her, I answered only that I had been assured the President had taken the steps necessary to obtain my confirmation.

"I certainly hope so," she replied. "The papers and magazines are saying horrible things about you. The wives of the other Cabinet nominees are starting to avoid me. If only you hadn't gotten mixed up with that awful Lust Cosmetics. I told you it was a mistake."

I was tempted but did not remind Pergamon that it was the profits from Lust Cosmetics that had made us rich. Instead, I smiled and changed the subject. But actually I had to admit that my wife was correct about the treatment I was receiving in the press. Almost every day, there was a critical piece about me as though part of an orchestrated campaign.

The only indications of action on my nomination came from Walter Tilden. He periodically arrived at my EOB office accompanied by an aide with a locked briefcase secured to his wrist by a chain. With great ceremony, he would open the briefcase and extract from it documents which he officiously assured me contained the latest briefing materials essential for my confirmation hearings.

Striving to keep a serious face, I would gravely tell him I would study the documents, safeguarding them with the appropriate level of security. Upon his departure, I would glance at them, confirm that they were as useless as the documents previously inserted in the briefing books, and lock them in my office safe.

I would also ask Tilden about the preparations for my confirmation hearings. "All is going well," he would say, stressing that I should devote myself to becoming thoroughly familiar with the briefing materials he had provided.

Just about the time I had begun to think the Senate Intelligence Committee would never act on my nomination, I received a call from Walter Hanke informing me that my hearing had been scheduled for 9 a.m. on the following day. I did not bother asking why I had received so little advance note and instead inquired how things looked. He answered that the President had stressed his interest in my nomination to Senator Manley and other members of the committee and that everything "was on course."

No sooner had I hung up an Hanke when Walter Tilden called to tell me that he would pick me up at 9 a.m. the following day to escort me to the hearing. Continuing the charade, I asked him how things looked. He was as optimistic as Hanke, telling me that the Senate Committee's questions would be "pro forma" and that my confirmation was assured.

I might have been led to think that my own suspicions were groundless, if it were not for Bob DePorte. He called me at home that evening.

"I see you're still going ahead on the nomination," he said. "I must say you've got guts."

"You think I'll have a tough time tomorrow?" I asked.

"I'd bet on it," he said. "They're giving odds of six to one that your nomination won't even get out of committee. I think Manley plans to humiliate you tomorrow at the hearing. If I were you, I'd develop a sudden diplomatic illness and skip it."

"Thanks for the tip," I replied. "But I'll be there. And I suggest you come, too. It should be interesting."

"Oh, I wouldn't miss it for the world. I just hate to think of an old friend voluntarily putting himself in a spot like that. But if I can't talk you out of attending, good luck!"

I was touched by Bob's obvious sincerity. "Thanks," I said, and hung up.

The following morning, I got up early. As I shaved, I went over in my mind what I planned to say at the hearing. I had received nothing I could use from Alan or Devine, so I was on my own. At breakfast, I was joined by Pergamon, who surprised me by saying that she planned to attend the hearing.

"Would you like to drive over with me?" I asked. "The Agency is sending me a car to take me over."

"No, thanks," she answered. I'll be going with Dorothy Everett."

I had not realized that Pergamon had become friendly with Mrs. Everett. She was the wife of Joshua Everett, who had just been confirmed as Treasury Secretary. I knew little about Everett and had no idea why Buck had named him to head the Treasury Department, a key post in any administration. Everett had been president of a prominent Boston investment banking firm and, as far as I knew, had no powerful political support.

Dismissing Everett from my mind, I said "I'll see you at the hearing."

I arose from the table and went into the bedroom to dress. Pergamon followed me.

"Please behave yourself with the committee, Melvin," she urged. "For God's sake, don't embarrass me or yourself! And don't embarrass the President!" she added, "Remember all he's done for you."

With great difficulty, I choked back reply about all I had one for the President. It would be silly to get into a fight with my wife at that moment

Tilden arrived early and escorted me downstairs to where the chauffeur-driven limousine was waiting. I was surprised to see another man in the car. Tilden introduced him as a representative of the CIA Congressional Relations Office who would accompany me to the hearing. As the limo started off, Tilden told me that we would stop of at the EOB to pick up the briefing books.

I had expected that during the trip to the hearing, Tilden would brief me on any last-minute developments. Instead, he contented himself with some inane comments on the weather, as did his colleague from the Congressional Relations Office.

Despairing of any assistance from my companions, I allowed the conversation to lapse and thought about my nomination and the reasons why I was being set up for humiliation at the committee hearing. I wondered if the person responsible was Tammy, Buck, or possibly some senior official at the White House or CIA. At one time, I would have thought Buck too inept to pull such a thing off. However, I had come to realize that he was capable of flashes of brilliance. It was not impossible that he had deliberately pressed me to accept the CIA post in order to see me publicly embarrassed as repayment for my lack of respect for him.

After stopping at the EOB to pick up the briefing books, the limousine deposited us at the Senate Office Building a few minutes before 10 a.m. The committee room in which the hearing was to be held was a large one. It was already packed to capacity. I was pleased to see many TV cameras there to cover the hearing.

News photographers hurriedly photographed me as I walked to the front of the chamber and took a chair at the witness table. Looking around, I saw Pergamon sitting with Mrs. Everett and waved to her. She looked annoyed at my wave and barely nodded her head in response.

There were two tables for reporters covering the hearing. Bob DePorte was sitting at one. I smiled at him and he gave me a thumb's up gesture. Tilden and his companion, sitting at either side of me, opened those infernal briefing books. I ignored them, awaiting the start of the hearing.

A few minutes after 10 a.m., the committee staffers began to filter into the hearing room, followed by the Senators. I was surprised to see that virtually all of the committee's fifteen members were present. The last to enter was the Chairman, Senator Manley. He was a relatively short man, but walked so erect that he gave the impression of being much taller. The deference accorded him by the other committee members reflected his prestige on the committee and in the Senate at large.

Manley gaveled the committee to order and launched into an introductory statement describing the importance of CIA to America's national defense.

"The committee's role in approving the individual nominated by the President to serve as CIA Director," he stressed, "Is one of the most important responsibilities of the Senate Intelligence Committee."

The Chairman's voice was rich and melodic, and he looked every inch a statesman. It would be extremely difficult, I realized, to challenge his hold over the committee. Manley finished, then directed his glance at me.

"Mr. Shultz," he said with a slight smile, "Do you have a written statement you would care to submit to the Committee, or perhaps you have a few introductory remarks?"

"No, Senator," I said, smiling in return. "My career has been widely described in the media and should be familiar to all of you. I think it would be most efficient for the Committee members to utilize the limited time available to question me at length about my background."

Manley's smile grew broader. "Then, Mr. Shultz," he said, with elaborate courtesy, "Perhaps you would care to inform the members of this committee why you are qualified for the important post of CIA Director."

"I presume, Senator" I replied, "That you are referring to the critical comments that have appeared about me in the press. For example, I have been described as 'the sinister presence lurking in the White House,' and the individual who 'manipulated the primaries and the presidential election to achieve President Porter's victory.'"

"Or perhaps," I continued, "You Are referring to those reports which have described me as 'totally lacking any qualifications to be CIA Director.' Again, you may have found relevant the article that charged I had used my 'ill-gotten wealth acquired by selling cheap cosmetics to gullible women using pornographic advertising.'"

"I hope," I went on, "That I have not shocked you or those watching this hearing on television by repeating some of the garbage printed about me. I mean no disrespect. However, apparently unlike some people in the media, I believe the American people deserve to be told the truth, not deceived by half-truths and fairy tales. The vital need for someone qualified to head the CIA requires me to speak frankly."

I was fully conscious as I made these remarks of the risk I was taking, of their probable effect on the committee members. I also knew, I had no other real alternative. My hope of receiving some bit of information from Alan or Joe Devine that I might use had so far not materialized.

"It is true," I went on, ignoring the warning signs I was receiving from Bob and the frantic notes Tilden was passing me, imploring me to stop, "That I am the President and sole owner of Lust Cosmetics. I should add that I did not give the company its name. The company name goes back to 1884, when it was named after its founder, Sadie Lust, a distinguished Illinois school teacher."

"As for my qualifications to be CIA Director," I asked pointedly, "Is it not true that this committee has appointed three different individuals to be CIA Director in the past five years?"

I paused for an instant, as though giving Manley time to

answer, but went on quickly enough to effectively deny him the opportunity. I wanted to create the impression that I was in charge of the hearing and not the Chairman.

"It is unfortunate that my parents never had enough money to send me to college or graduate school. It is also true that my three predecessors as Director all were not only college graduates but, at the time of their appointment, had considerable experience in other senior government posts?"

This time, I gave Manley time to respond.

"Exactly so," He said. "What is your point, Mr. Shultz? That lack of qualifications entitles you to the job?"

"No, Senator," I thundered back, trying to make my voice sound as commanding as Manley's. "I wouldn't presume to waste the committee's time or that of the American people by uttering such nonsense. What I am stating, in plan, simple English, is that the criteria used to select CIA directors in the past are no longer valid, if they ever were. As a result, over the past five years, the Agency has turned in one of the sorriest records of any government agency."

Once again, I gave Manley no time to interrupt me.

"CIA over this period has failed to warn the U.S. Government of the major developments that have occurred, including changes in the Russian government and the former East European satellites, the growing economic power of China, or the rise of Islamic extremism in the Middle East. The Agency has compounded these failures," I went on, "By its sorry record whenever it attempted to influence events in foreign countries. And all this, mind you, at the same time it successfully request large budget cuts each year. In short, Senator, never has so much money been spent for so little value. The United States government and the American taxpayers would have been far better served, as a direct result of the faulty criteria used to select the Directors of CIA, if the Agency had been abolished and the President and the American government told to obtain their intelligence on international developments from the media in those countries."

"As for my qualifications to be CIA Director," I stated, "I took over a bankrupt cosmetics company and in the space of twelve years turned it into a multi-billion dollar industry leader, creating hundreds of new jobs in Watsonville in the process. I suggest that shows a certain level of executive ability on my part. Along the way, I successfully negotiated with foreign governments to establish major plants abroad and to gain access for my company's advertizing on state cable and television."

"Although I have no government experience other than that of a private first class in the army," I said, "I would point out that my business, selling cosmetics, requires a thorough knowledge of human psychology. I have been successful enough in analyzing the emotions and aspirations of consumers in Latin America, East Asia and Europe to motivate them to buy hundreds of millions of dollars of my products each year."

"Finally, President Porter was put in the White House by the American voters and not because of any sinister machinations on my part. But if I was one of his key advisers, and I was, I think the American people would prefer as CIA Director someone who knows how elections are run and not some bureaucrat who can't find his way into a voting booth."

"Let me make this promise to you and to the American people," I declared. "If I am confirmed as Director of CIA, I will present myself here to you one year to the day after taking the job. I will submit a list of my accomplishments. I will provide you with all the details you require concerning those foreign affairs problems about which the Agency has provided advance warning. I will give you a detailed accounting in a closed session about those instances in which the Agency has successfully influenced developments abroad in pursuit of American foreign policy. If you determine after you receive my report that I have not done a superior job as CIA Director, I will immediately submit my resignation. And I will run CIA without the increased budget for next year which the Agency has requested, but with the same funding as last year. I have never failed in any job I have ever held. I swear to you and to the American people that if confirmed, I will not fail now."

As I finished, there were a few cheers from the rear of the room, where members of the public were seated. I looked at the faces of the committee members. Most seemed shocked. On a few faces, I detected what appeared to be expressions of interest in my offer. On the face of the Chairman, however, there was only fury. He angrily banged his gavel down.

"This hearing is adjourned!" he said in a cold voice. Then, ignoring the other Senators, who seemed perplexed by his action, he stood and stalked out of the hearing room, followed by the members of his staff.

Manley's departure launched a wave of noisy confusion in the chamber as the rest of the attendees stood and headed for the exits. I rose too, turned to my two companions and gravely thanked them for their assistance. Neither could look me in the eye. I instructed them to take charge of the briefing books, adding that they could take the limo as I would provide my own transportation home.

The crowd around the reporters' tables was so great that I decided to delay trying to talk to Bob until later. Instead, I headed over to where Pergamon had been sitting and was successful in catching up with her. She glowered at me, her anger obvious in her face. I turned to Mrs. Everett and introduced myself. She shook hands with me, a polite smile on her face. I then turned back to

Pergamon.

"How could you embarrass yourself like that?" she hissed. "How could you embarrass me that way?"

Her face was burning; her eyes flashing. I had never seen her so upset. I thought of trying to jolly her out of it, but decided it would only increase her anger.

"Would you like to ride back with me in a cab?" I asked, smiling at Mrs. Everett to include her in my offer.

Pergamon shook her head. "We'll go home ourselves, thank you."

I said goodbye and left the hearing room. Several reporters came up to interview me. I politely refused, telling them that I had nothing to add to the comments I had made to the committee.

When I arrived home, Fred rushed to greet me. "I watched the hearing on TV," she said. "I thought you did a great job."

"Thanks," I replied. "I can't tell you how happy you've made me."

I gratefully accepted her offer to make lunch for me. As I waited for the hamburger to be ready, the phone rang. It was Bob.

"Sorry I wasn't able to get to you when the hearing was over," I said. "I thought I'd better talk to my wife as soon as I could."

"Don't worry about that," he replied. "I had to rush off and file my story."

"It sure was an experience for me appearing before a Senate committee."

"It was quite an experience for me, too." He said with a chuckle. "I've never seen anything like it. And I don't think I'll ever see another one to match."

"How do you think it went?"

"Frankly," Bob said, "On a scale of one to ten, I'd have to give you a ten for bluntness and forcefulness and a zero in political acumen. Before the hearing, I didn't think you had much of a chance to be confirmed. Now I think you have none at all. I hope you won't mind, but I said as much in my report on the meeting."

"Of course I don't mind," I replied. "You had no other choice. Still, it was fun and the things I said about CIA doing a poor job had to be told."

"Do you have anything you can say for attribution?" he asked.

"Certainly. You can quote me a saying that I appreciate the kindness of the committee in giving me the opportunity to appear before it and I am confident that the American public will appreciate the accuracy of my criticism of the Agency's performance. I am looking forward, after my confirmation to working closely with President Porter to improve CIA and give this nation the superb intelligence capability it needs and deserves."

"That's quite a statement," he said. "Did you work it out with the White House?"

"Off the record, they had nothing to do with it. They're probably shell-shocked by my testimony."

"I hope I'm wrong about my assessment," Bob said. He hung up with a cheery goodbye.

Pergamon did not come home until it was almost time for dinner. "I was worried you were so late," I said, as I walked up and kissed her lightly. She pulled away from me, but seemed less angry than she had at the hearing.

"Melvin," she said, "I don't want to leave Washington. I'm having too much fun here. I won't go back to Watsonville."

I wondered if she was telling me she was leaving me. Trying to sound normal, I said, "I don't want to leave Washington now either. And I don't plan to."

"Oh Melvin," she replied, and for the first time her voice was close to normal. "Is there a chance? Has the President said he will fight for you?"

Choosing my words carefully, I said, "When he asked me to take the CIA job, he was aware there might be some opposition. He has all the powers of the presidency at his disposal. I think there's a good chance I will be confirmed."

"Thank God!" she declared. It was clear she really meant it. We had a pleasant dinner, carefully avoiding the subject of my nomination. Her cheerfulness lasted through the meal and breakfast the next day.

After breakfast, she went off to a charity lunch at which Tammy and some of the other Cabinet wives had been invited. I took a walk and then read in the apartment until Fred made me lunch.

I was eating as Pergamon returned.

"You're home early, dear," I said, finishing my hamburger. Did you have a good time?

She did not answer, but rushed straight into the bedroom and slammed the door. Slowly, I got to my feet and followed her. I knew I was in for a nasty scene.

I found her lying across the bed, sobbing. "What's wrong?" I asked.

"It was awful," she answered. "I could see them smirking at me. When I tried to talk to someone, the others just stared at me. It's all your fault."

I tried to hug her, but she just moved away.

"Can I get you something to eat?" I asked.

"No."

"Was Tammy there? Was she nasty, too?"

"No, she was the only one who acted friendly. We talked for a few minutes. Then she had to run off. I was left all alone."

It took me a couple of hours, but I was eventually able to calm Pergamon and get her to eat something. I took her out for dinner to an expensive restaurant she had been urging us to try since we came to Washington. By the next day, she was reasonably normal, although she adamantly refused ro leave the house to attend any social events by herself.

Feeling responsible for the way she had been treated, I spent a lot of time keeping her occupied. We visited some of Washington's museums and art galleries. It was fun.

Meanwhile, there was no movement on my nomination. The press reported Senator Manley had no plans to call another hearing and that my nomination was dead. When asked whether the White House still believed I should be confirmed, Buck's White House Press Secretary said only that the President had no plans to withdraw the nomination at this time. It was obvious that if I were to secure the CIA position, it would have to be as a result of my own endeavor.

The days passed, and I was beginning to think I would not be successful. Then I received the break I needed. Alan called from Charleston elated. He had learned that Manley had had an affair with one of his teenage campaign workers during a period in which he was having marital problems with his wife. The young woman in question, one Pamela Marshal, had refused to talk to Alan. However, Alan had located the owner of a motel in Columbia who had positively identified photos of the Senator and of the campaign worker as individuals who had shared a room at his motel on several occasions. Alan had then secured a written statement to that effect.

I thanked Alan and asked him to forward the photos and the statement to me as quickly as possible. However, I was not enthusiastic that what he had acquired would be useful. It was unlikely by itself for me to successfully press Manley to drop his opposition to my nomination. He was too strong a personality and had too much prestige to be vulnerable to this type of pressure. Moreover, the teenager was over eighteen, thus not a minor, and had flatly refused to provide any supporting evidence.

A few days later, I received a call from Joe Devine. He was sending documented proof, he informed me, that while he was a scoutmaster, Manley had sexually molested a boy in his scout troop. The boy, one Jimmy Hunter, was now in his twenties. He and his mother had both signed sworn statement repeating their accusations. They had also furnished a photo of Manley with his arm around the boy, both of them facing the camera.

I congratulated Devine and assured him he would be amply rewarded if the material was as good as he had depicted. When it arrived the next day, I opened the package from Devine and examined the statements carefully. They were what I expected, almost certainly spurious and motivated by the Hunters' desire to extort money from Manley. Still, in conjunction with the information Alan had obtained, they might be enough to persuade Manley to drop his opposition to my confirmation.

Having obtained the derogatory information on the Senator, I now attempted to use it. I found this to be more difficult than I had expected. Manley rebuffed all my efforts to see him. His office responded to my phone calls that he was not available. I even went so far as to call at his Senate office and attempt to force my way in, only to be told that I would be arrested by the Capitol Police if I did not leave.

Finally, in desperation, I called Bob Deporte and asked if he could help me see Manley. He promised to do what he could.

The next day, he called back to tell me he had been successful. Manley was scheduled to attend a dinner party given by Millicent Tyler-Harrison, a prominent Washington hostess.

"I have arranged," he said, "For you to receive an invitation.

It will be a large party, but hopefully you will have a chance to talk to Manley."

"I can't tell you how grateful I am," I said. "I owe you one."

"Always glad to help out an old friend," he answered. "Incidentally, the invitation didn't come cheap. I had to promise the fellow who provided it, he's in charge of public relations for one of her pet charities, that you will give the charity a healthy donation."

"Will you be there? I asked.

"No, I have another party I have to attend. But do let me know how it comes out. And best of luck!"

The invitation was delivered to my door by a messenger two days later, the day of the party. I looked at it and saw my donation would have to be a large one as the invitation included Pergamon.

My wife had been pathetically grateful when I informed her we had been invited to dinner at Millicent Tyler-Harrison's that night. Since my appearance at the hearing, she had avoided most social events and had stayed in our apartment unless I took her out.

"Oh Melvin," she enthused. "How wonderful! Millicent Tyler-Harrison is the leading Washington hostess. Did Tammy arrange it?"

I decided it would be better not to tell her the truth. "She may have played a part in it," I said. "Anyhow, the important thing is that we're going."

"Please, Melvin," she begged. "Behave yourself! Don't sulk in a corner as you always do! Circulate! Make friends!"

"Yes, dear," I replied, smiling. For once, I thought, Pergamon didn't have to worry about my not speaking to anyone at the party. I intended to talk to Manley at any cost.

Pergamon began preparing to go to the dinner party in the early afternoon. She went to the beauty parlor and took a long bath when she got home. Although the invitation gave an 8 p.m. time for the guests to arrive, Pergamon began dressing three hours earlier. She carefully took out a new gown, one of the several she had purchased after we arrived in Washington in preparation for an expected heavy social schedule.

I prepared in my own way for the party. In Watsonville, I normally ate dinner at 6 p.m. If I haven't eaten by 7 p.m., I lose my appetite and am no longer interested in eating anything other than desert. Based on our 8 p.m. arrival time, I didn't anticipate sitting down to dinner until 9 p.m., by which time I am normally in bed. Accordingly, I had Fred make a hamburger for me to eat.

Pergamon came into the kitchen to show me the gown she was wearing to the party and caught me eating my hamburger.

"Oh, Melvin," she said with obvious disgust, "How can you eat that when we're going out to a party?" Mrs. Tyler-Harrison has the best cook in Washington."

"I know," I said. "But I want to be able to talk to people at the party. If I didn't eat here, I'd be giving all my attention to getting something to eat there. You know," I added, seeking to change the subject, "You look beautiful in that dress."

Rather than going to the expense of taking a taxi to the party, I elected to drive. I felt sure I could find a parking space close to Mrs. Tyler-Harrison's home in Georgetown. In deference to Pergamon, we did not go in my old Buick but in her BMW.

Parking space in Georgetown was not as easy to find as I had supposed. After driving around for some time, I had to park some blocks away from our destination. Pergamon complained loudly about having to walk so far in her good shoes. By the time we arrived she was in a nasty mood.

Because I wanted to make certain of getting to the party before Senator Manley, we had left early. Pergamon was unhappy about this, objecting that it was not polite to arrive less than fifteen minutes before a party's scheduled starting time and that the really important guests would not be there until at least fifteen minutes after that. By ignoring her objections, we arrived at our hostess' door precisely at 8 p.m.

Mrs. Tyler-Harrison lived in a beautiful home, one of the largest mansions in Georgetown. I rang the doorbell, ignoring Pergamon's complaint that we were far too early. The door was opened by a butler who examined our invitations, took our coats and led us into a large parlor. A quick look around the empty room revealed we were the first guests to arrive.

Our hostess, a rather stout, elaborately dressed woman of about fifty, approached to greet us. She was not at all flustered by our early arrival. I gave her our name, and was amused to see she had not the slightest notion who we were. After making a few obligatory polite remarks, I moved off to where a bartender was preparing to serve drinks. Pergamon stayed behind, talking in an animated fashion to our hostess. I assumed my wife thought that in this way, she might impress Mrs. Tyler-Harrison and assure herself of further invitations to similar Washington parties. I wondered whether our hostess was interested, amused or irritated by Pergamon's comments.

I really felt like asking the bar tender for a beer. However, I complied with Pergamon's request not to embarrass her by ordering a beer at the party and instead asked for tomato juice. I don't like hard liquor, and I hoped the other guests would assume that my tomato juice was really a Bloody Mary. With my drink in hand, I wondered over to a buffet table, filled with so many hors d'oeuvres that I found it hard to believe to think that a sit-down dinner would follow.

As I stood by the buffet table watching the other guests arrive,

I got into a conversation with an elderly Oriental man. Normally, I dislike what passes for bright repartee at cocktail parties, and I was surprised to find myself interested in what he had to say. He explained in excellent English that he was the Commercial Counselor at the Chinese Embassy in Washington, I took advantage of this opportunity to ask him about the market for Western style cosmetics in China and in a few minutes learned a wealth of information.

Seeing Manley enter the room, I quickly excused myself from the Chinese diplomat and headed directly for the Senator.

"Good evening, Senator," I said pleasantly, catching his arm to prevent him from escaping.

Manley politely responded, "Good evening" before realizing who I was. Then he deftly extracted his arm.

"Please excuse me," he said with menace in his voice, "There is someone there I must speak with."

I did not like what I was about to do, but had no choice. I was desperate.

"I wouldn't advise that," I said. "Not until I pass on what I learned from the Hunters. It seems they're accusing you of sexually molesting little Jimmy when he was a member of your Boy Scout troop. The story could cause you considerable embarrassment, even the loss of your Senate seat."

Manley's face darkened perceptively. I thought he was about to strangle me.

"You contemptible bastard!" he spat out, his South Carolina accent more pronounced. "If you think you're going to blackmail me by repeating that garbage, you're wrong. Betty Jo Hunter tried to extort money from me before with that story. I warned her and her son that I'd put them in jail if they ever tried it again. I intend to do just that. It will give me the greatest pleasure to put you in jail with them."

"The Hunters did supply proof," I persevered, seeing no option but to do so. "To back up their sworn statements, they furnished a photo of you with your arm around Jimmy. He's wearing a Boy Scout uniform. On the back of the photo in what they say is your handwriting is the inscription 'to my good friend' and your first name. If I have to, I'll put that photo on billboards around the state and make certain that the press and TV carry the Hunters' accusations. I'm pretty sure you'll lose your Senate seat."

"That's all garbage!" Manley declared emphatically. "Betty Jo Hunter is a small-town crook who has convictions for prostitution and attempted blackmail. Her son is mentally retarded. He will repeat anything she tells him to say. I posed for pictures with every boy in my Boy Scout troop and wrote the same thing on every photo. I've never done anything to be ashamed of. Do your damnedest!"

"Have you forgotten Pamela Marshal?" I asked. "Or do you think having trysts with a young campaign worker is something a married man your age and a Senator should be proud of?"

The expression on Manley's face changed dramatically. I could tell I had gotten to him and that the story about Pamela Marshal was true.

As I spoke, I noticed several of the other guests staring at us with curiosity. "Senator," I said softly. "I think it might be better if we continued this conversation in private."

I motioned toward an adjacent room, turned, and headed toward it. I knew I was taking a risk, but it worked. He followed me. I found myself in a large room fitted out as a library, with beautiful book cases lining most of the wall space. I shut the door and turned back to Manley.

"I made a grave mistake," he said in a low voice, as much to himself as to me, "And it's come back to haunt me. But I'd rather spend an eternity in Hell than see a man like you named head of CIA."

I stared at Manley and realized I had completely misjudged him. He was a rare commodity in Washington, a man of integrity. He really was prepared to give up his Senate seat to prevent someone he considered unacceptable from taking over as Director of the Agency.

"It's ironic, sir," I told him. "You will give up your position as one of the most powerful men in the Senate rather than see me confirmed. You think I am unqualified. If you act in this way, I will destroy you politically. And most unhappily. Because you are a man of principle and the country can ill afford someone like you leaving the Senate." I looked at Manley and saw he was listening to me intently. "And the sad part about all this is that I really am the best choice to head the Agency."

"Don't be foolish," he said.

"No." I replied. "I really am. All those things I said at the hearing about the Agency having turned in a pitiful job over the past five years are correct. CIA needs someone like me to direct it. The individuals who have served as Director have lacked the necessary qualifications, regardless of their distinguished service in the government and their academic training.

"And you are qualified?"

"Yes, I am. Remember, I'm the person who manipulated the political processes to put Porter in the White House. The techniques I used to accomplish that are just what are needed to run the sort of intelligence agency the country needs."

Manley was silent for a minute before answering. "You know, Mr. Shultz, I really have misjudged you. I thought you were incompetent. You are competent. In fact, too much so. And far too ruthless. I would never allow someone as unscrupulous as you to run CIA. It would be far too dangerous for the country."

"No, Senator," I replied, trying as hard as I could to convince him of my sincerity. "This is the United States. Do you really think I would try to assassinate the President or lead a military coup? All I would do is attempt to convince Porter he was wrong. If he failed to listen to me, I would resign and oppose him publicly."

"It would be far more dangerous for the country," I went on. "If I am not appointed. I decided to support Porter for the presidency on a whim, to see if I could do it, not because I am ambitious or wanted a government post. You can check yourself. He pressed me to accept the CIA job. I did not seek it. I would prefer to go back home to Watsonville to run my company. I agreed to serves as CIA Director because I now realize I made a horrible mistake. Porter is too incompetent to be President. He can really harm the country, if he is not prevented from doing so. And I am the only one who can control him."

"That isn't much of a safeguard."

"No, Senator, it isn't. But it's all we've got. Can you control Porter? Can you organize enough strength in the Senate to block him?"

"No, he said, after a minute. I can't." after what seemed like an eternity, he added, "You may be telling me the truth. I will investigate whether naming you to the CIA job was Porter's idea. If it turns out that is what happened, I will reopen the hearings and give you a chance to show you are qualified for the job. I do not like or trust you. But confirming you as CIA Director may be the lesser of two evils"

In response to Manley's words, I smiled and extended my hand to shake his. He looked at me coldly, ignored my outstretched hand and left the room. Through the open door, I could see that more guests had arrived and that the party was in full swing.

I felt no desire to join the other guests. The exchange with the Senator had drained me completely. Not only was I exhausted, but my head ached. I sat down in an armchair in the library and closed my eyes, trying to ignore the noise of the party in the next room.

Suddenly, I realized that he noise had ceased. I stood up and left the library. The parlor was empty. All of the guests had gone into the dining room and were seated at a long table. The first course had been served and the guests had started to eat. Feeling conspicuous, I walked into the room and sat down at the only vacant spot. I could sense that everyone was staring at me.

I turned to the woman on my right and introduced myself. She turned out to be the wife of a Supreme Court Justice. The younger woman on my left was strikingly attractive. When she identified herself, I realized she was Buck's new nominee for a post on the Federal Communications Commission. I wondered if she owed her nomination to her professional expertise or to the fact that she was also from Oklahoma City. More probably, Buck had named her because she was sleeping with him.

Across the table, I saw Pergamon. She was staring at me with an angry expression on her face, clearly embarrassed by my late arrival and by the fact that I was ignoring the food on my plate. It was well past 9 p.m. and my desire to eat had long since evaporated. I tried to stir the food around my plate with my fork to give the appearance of eating, but I did not do a very satisfactory job. The waiter, as he picked up each succeeding course, all of them uneaten, looked at me curiously. So did the other guests who noticed it.

Despite my headache and tiredness, I tried to make polite conversation with the people seated near me. My lack of enthusiasm must have been obvious. Gradually, the people near me turned to others to converse, leaving me to enjoy my solitude and to pray silently for the evening to be over as rapidly as possible.

After what seemed like an eternity, the hostess arose and we returned to the parlor.

Coffee and sweets were served. I sat silently in an arm chair off to one corner, watching Pergamon in animated conversation with a cluster of other guests. At the earliest possible moment politeness permitted, I stood and walked to her. Interrupting the conversation more brusquely than I intended, I told her that it was time for us to leave.

Pergamon's face clouded over, and I thought there would be a nasty scene. I was grateful when she slowly stood and said goodbye to the people with whom she had been chatting. After saying goodnight to the hostess, we gathered our coats and went out into the night.

No sooner had the door closed behind us than Pergamon stopped in her tracks and turned to me.

"How dare you treat m like that!" she shouted. "I'm sorry I ever married you!" You stay at home, refusing to go out! And when we finally do go to a party, you act like a lout and won't eat or talk to anyone!"

I started to walk on by myself. Pergamon ran after me, repeating her complaints. I allowed her some time to vent her anger, then turned to her.

"Pergamon," I said, as sweetly as I could. "I just couldn't wait to tell you some good news. I had the opportunity to talk to Senator Manley. There's a good chance he will reopen the hearings and that the Senate will confirm me. That means we'll be able to stay in Washington."

My words caused an instantaneous change in Pergamon. She grabbed my arm, a big smile on her face.

"Oh Melvin," she said, "How wonderful! You should have told

me at once."

We walked back to where I had parked the car. On the drive home, Pergamon bubbled over, chattering about how we would enjoy life in Washington and what an active social life we would have. I decided it would be foolish to discourage her and limited my responses to monosyllabic grunts that she interpreted as confirmation.

Back at our apartment, I hurriedly undressed and got in to bed, hoping that sleep would ease the discomfort of my headache. I had almost drifted off, when I started to feel something strange on my face. I opened my eyes and was startled to find Pergamon kneeling above me, stark naked and gently rubbing a hardened nipple on my lips.

"Let's make love," she said, her voice husky.

I was about to refuse when I felt desire surging over me. No matter how I felt or what disagreements I might be having with my wife, I was always eager to have sex with her. I rolled over, threw off my pajamas and embraced her. As always, I found our love making grand.

The next morning, I called Bob DePorte to thank him again for arranging the invitation to Mrs. Tyler-Harrison's party. I added that I was fairly confident that I had persuaded Manley to reopen the confirmation hearings.

"You must be a magician," he said. "How did you accomplish that?"

"I was able to convince him that I am competent to head CIA," I said. "Also, off the record, I told him that if he didn't drop his opposition to me, I would do everything I could to insure that he lost his Senate seat. I must say, though, that the latter argument didn't seem to carry any weight with him. He's one of the few people in Washington, possibly the only one, who is willing to give up his political career for a matter of principle."

"He does have that reputation," Bob replied."It sure must have been some conversation you had with him. I wish I had been there to hear it."

"Some day, I'll give you a verbatim play-by-play. That's when you and I are both retired and writing our memoirs."

I said goodbye to him and was about to hang up when Bob interrupted me.

"Mel," he said. "I've picked up something I can't use but which you should know. One of my friends with good White House contacts told me that Mrs. Porter let slip something about you. She said she was very glad your nomination was dead and that she had done everything she could to keep you out of the CIA post,"

"Thanks," I said, "It confirms my suspicions. I didn't think that without direction even the current White House staff could have done such a miserable job in handling my nomination."

When I hung up, I wondered if Tammy had been acting on her own or with Buck's knowledge. Whichever the case, it made little difference. My dealings with the two of them left me convinced she could manipulate him whenever she chose to do so.

Two days later, I received a call from Walter Hanke, informing me that Senator Manley had scheduled a follow-up hearing on my nomination. A few minutes later, Tilden called to give me the time set for the hearing and to arrange for the limo to take me to it.

On the scheduled day, I was escorted by Tilden to the hearing, the limo stopping as before to pick up the briefing books. When I entered the chamber, I saw it was as crowded as before. This was no doubt due to the widespread coverage the re-convening of the committee hearings had received in the media. Most of the commentary suggested that my chances of being confirmed by the committee were still nil and the occasion would only give me another opportunity to make a fool of myself.

Senator Manley gaveled the hearing to order, but made no opening statement other than to invite the other committee members to ask whatever questions they might wish. The first question concerned the situation in Algeria. I gave a detailed answer, based on the material in the briefing books. The Senator who had asked the question looked surprised that I had given so detailed and, in his mind, correct an answer. I then looked direct at him and said that my answer was based solely on the briefing materials supplied to me by the Agency.

"All that shows," I went on, "Is that I have a photographic memory and can parrot what I am told. It indicates nothing about my ability to serve as Agency head. In fact, the information is either incorrect or too unspecific to assist policy makers to implement an effective international security policy. The actual situation in Algeria, based on the information I have secured from unclassified sources and which I would have provided if I had been Agency Director, is quite different."

I went on to give my own appraisal of the situation in Algeria, as Senators on the committee stared at me, their jaws hanging open. Several posed follow-up questions or attempted to refute me. In each case, I effectively demolished their arguments. Subsequent questions concerning other foreign policy matters took the same course.

When no Senator indicated a desire for further questions, Senator Manley closed the meeting, making no personal comment about the proceedings. I avoided any discussion with Tilden about the hearing, dodged questions from reporters, and took a taxi home. When Bob called, I asked him how he thought I had done.

"God knows," he said. "I have no idea whether you put the final nail on the coffin lid burying your nomination or changed the Senators' opinion of you. I do know, nothing like that has ever occurred in Washington before."

I waited nervously to see what the outcome would be. Once again, I had knowingly taken a terrible risk, simply because I saw no other alternative. Two days later, I learned my gamble had paid off. The committee had approved by a very narrow margin recommending my nomination to the Senate. Senator Manley, it was reported, had abstained from the vote. It was clear to me, that he could easily have led the other Senators to reject my nomination if he had wished. The final vote in the full Senate was similar. Once again, it was approved by a narrow margin, with Senator Manley abstaining.

CHAPTER 7

My swearing in as CIA Director was held in the Rose Garden of the White House. Those present included Buck, Pergamon, and several of the President's national security team. Tammy was not present, which I did not find at all surprising.

I might have taken the fact that it was held in the Rose Garden, with the President in attendance, as an indication of Buck's friendly attitude toward me. However, he made no public statement welcoming me to his administration. When the ceremony was over, he asked me to appoint a "good friend" of Tammy's to a top Agency post. I put him off with a vague, and non-committal reply. When it came to Agency appointments, I intended to be even more scrupulous than Senator Manley in filling posts based exclusively on competence.

On the day following my swearing-in, the CIA limo assigned to the Director arrived at my apartment sharply at 8 a.m. to take me to the Agency. I had wanted to be picked up about 6:30 a.m., the time I usually left my home for Lust Cosmetics, but had reluctantly yielded to the urging of Walter Tilden that there would be no one at the Agency at that hour to receive me.

I was glad that I was alone in the car with only the driver, so I was spared the feeling of having to make conversation. The ride along the George Washington Parkway was beautiful, and I enjoyed the occasional glimpses I got of the Potomac River. The limo turned into the CIA compound, stopped briefly to be passed by the guards, and entered a garage underneath the building. It stopped at the parking space reserved for the Director's car and Tilden stepped from behind a pillar to open the car door.

"Good morning, sir." He said. "The Director's personal elevator is this way."

He led me to the elevator. As we ascended, I looked around and concluded it was in no way different from the scores of other elevators I had seen in other government buildings. I laughed to myself, wondering what I had expected. The doors opened and I found myself in an inner corridor.

We approached a large office, as a group of some dozen individuals left the office and passed us. From their dress and demeanor, I thought they had to be senior Agency officials. I glanced questioningly at Tilden.

"A meeting of some kind?" I inquired.

"Yes, sir," he answered reluctantly, speeding up his pace to lead me swiftly by the group. Several of them eyed me with curiosity. We entered the office and I looked around. It was a large office with dark wood paneling and several oil paintings of landscapes on the walls. There were two wooden desks facing each other at the end of the room. At each sat a woman.

"This is the Director's suite," he said, unnecessarily, leading me to the nearest desk. The woman seated there stood as we approached. "This is your secretary," Tilden said, "Ann Welch."

The woman gave me a warm smile as we shook hands. She was

about forty, reasonably attractive, with a pleasant face. "Can I get you some coffee" she asked.

"Yes, please," I replied, making a mental note to bring some instant cocoa to keep in the office in case I had to work late.

"Your office is in there," Tilden said, pointing through an open door behind Ann Welch's desk. He then led me to the desk opposite. "This is Mona Peterson," he said, introducing us. "She is Mr. Brewer's secretary. Mona gave me a half smile and remained seated as we shook hands.

Fleming Brewer, I knew from my study of the Agency, was Deputy Director and Acting Director.

"Is that Mr. Brewer's office in there?" I asked, pointing to the close door behind Mona Peterson's desk.

"Yes sir." Tilden replied. "And that's my office next to his. "I act as executive assistant to both you and Mr. Brewer."

It struck me as odd that the Deputy Director's office occupied the corner of the building and had to have windows along two walls, whereas my office was smaller and had windows only along one wall. I walked into my office and Tilden followed me.

The office was a pleasant one. It had wood paneling similar to that of the outer office. A small Oriental carpet lay on the floor in front of a large executive wooden desk, which faced the door. An upholstered sofa and several comfortable looking upholstered arm chairs lined the walls.

I sat down behind the desk and looked around me. Tilden stood by my desk, a broad smile on his face. I smiled back at him, concealing my curiosity.

"I'll go and tell Mr. Brewer you're here," he said. I nodded my ascent. As he left, Ann Welch entered with my cup of coffee.

As she handed it to me, I said in a low voice, "Ann, was there a meeting here this morning?"

"Yes, sir," she answered calmly. "The regular morning staff meeting. We have one almost every day at 8 a.m."

"Thanks," I said.

Tilden and another man entered the office, Tilden standing back deferentially to allow him to enter first. As Ann Welch left, I stood up.

"I'm glad to meet you, Mr. Brewer," I said to him, shaking his hand.

Brewer was about fifty, slightly taller than I am and rather plump. A dark thatch of hair accentuated the pasty whiteness of his round face.

"Please call me Fleming," he said. "Since we're going to be working closely together, we ought to be on a first name basis."

I don't know if I was more irritated by the prospect of having him call me Melvin or by his strong English accent, which I assumed must be an affectation. It seemed out of place for someone whom I knew had been born in Iowa and educated in the Middle West.

He and Tilden sat down on the sofa. Brewer pointed to an oil painting hanging on the wall behind me. I considered the painting to be a singularly innocuous still-life.

"That's considered to be a remarkably fine painting. Of course, the Agency decorator can bring you a book showing the various paintings that are available in case you'd like to change it."

No, thanks," I said. "This office looks fine to me." I noticed Brewer and Tilden exchange glances. "Of course," Brewer added, "This is not nearly as nice as your office in the EOB."

"Is that the one I used while I was preparing for my confirmation hearings?" I asked, thinking of the small, rather mean office I had used.

"Not at all," Brewer replied. "The Director's office is one of the finest in the EOB. It's been outfitted especially well because it's where Directors usually spend their time. It's close to the President and other senior officials and saves the Director the time of traveling between the White House and Langley."

Brewer rose and handed me a folder. "These, Melvin, are the materials we've prepared for you to use at the Cabinet meeting today."

"Do I gather," I asked innocently, "That the Director usually works out of the EOB, with the Deputy Director running the Agency on a day-to-day basis?"

"Generally, that's the breakdown of the work," Brewer answered.

"It seems like a logical division of responsibilities," I said, noticing Brewer and Tilden exchange brief smiles of triumph. "However, I added, handing Brewer back the folder, "I think today I'll ask you to represent the Agency at the Cabinet meeting. I don't think it wise to go myself until I feel I have a better grab of the job."

My tone was crisp. I wanted to leave Brewer no room for argument. The Deputy Director apparently thought otherwise. As he reluctantly took back the folder he said, "Certainly, Melvin, if you think it's wise to miss the first Cabinet meeting after your confirmation. The President may want to give you some personal instructions on what he'd like you to do."

"That's all right, Fleming," I answered. "I'm sure you will pass them on to me correctly. Now you'd better go and get ready!"

Fleming's mouth opened, but he couldn't think of anything to say. Finally he said, "Yes, Melvin," in a low voice, turned and left.

Tilden had watched the byplay between Brewer and me silently from his vantage point on the sofa. He now arose and walked to my desk.

"Sir," he said, "Since you're staying here this morning,

would you like to take advantage of the opportunity to tour the principal parts of the Agency, possibly the DDO? You know, that's the Directorate for Operations, the part that handles foreign clandestine operations."

I nodded, as though it was all new to me. Actually, I had read every scrap of information the Chicago clipping firm had sent me on the DDO, including some very detailed critiques translated from the Russian media.

I waited as moment, as though considering his offer, then said, "No, that won't be necessary."

Tilden waited, but I said nothing more. Finally, he left the office, leaving me alone. As I pondered my next step, there was a knock at the door and Ann Welch entered.

"May I speak with you, sir?" she asked in a soft, pleasant voice.

"Certainly," I answered, motioning her to sit down.

She sat and looked at me. I could see she was trying to summon up her courage to speak.

"Sir," she finally asked. "How long do you want me here?"

"What do you mean?" I asked, not understanding the question.

"I hate to bother you on your first day here," the words came tumbling out, revealing the depth of her concern, "But I really need my job. It's not just me. I also have to take care of my seventeen year old son. Directors always bring their own secretary with them. I have to be able to arrange for a good job when you won't need me anymore."

At last I grasped the meaning of her words. "What you are saying, is that you are not permanently assigned here? How long have you been here?"

"I came back from overseas three months ago. They wouldn't let me stay in government housing there after my husband left me." She was clearly embarrassed to have to describe her predicament.

"They assigned me temporarily up here to fill in when the old Director resigned until you came on board and brought in your own secretary."

"So you've been working here just three months?"

"Yes, sir," she said. "This time. Before I went overseas with my husband they used to have me fill in here whenever the Director or Deputy Director's secretary went on leave.

"Let me think about it," I said. "I'll give you an answer today. But first, I have a question. Wasn't this office previously used by the Deputy Director and the one Brewer is using by the Director?"

"Yes, sir," came the answer. I relaxed, glad there had been no subterfuge on her part. It's rare that you have an opportunity to be kind to someone else while doing yourself a favor. Ann Welch's prior experience in the Director's office was something I could use to my advantage.

"Ann," I said. I haven't planned to bring my secretary with me. As long as you do good work, the Director's secretary job is yours. I am a tough boss, but I try to be a fair one. And I reward people who do their work well and are loyal to me. Do I make myself clear?"

She smiled with relief. "Yes, sir," she said. "I'll do my best to make sure you're not disappointed."

"Good," I said. "First thing. I want all traffic that has gone to Mr. Brewer to come to me first."

Her smile disappeared. "That may be a problem, sir. Mona Peterson is a GS-12. I am only a GS-10. When I applied for my old job back, they couldn't take me in at anything higher. I needed the job, so I took it. Mona's very close to Mr. Brewer and I will have a hard time making sure she's giving you all the traffic you want. Possibly you ought to get a secretary who is more senior."

"There won't be any trouble," I said. "Who handles the

personnel work around her?"

"That's Mr. Fisher. He's Director of Personnel."

"Please get him on the phone. Tell him I wish to speak to him immediately. Then come back here yourself."

She left and returned in a minute. "Mr. Fisher is on the phone for you."

I picked the phone. "Mr. Fisher," I said, in response to his greeting. "Ann Welch has been assigned to fill in as Director's secretary. I wish that assignment made permanent. She informs me she is only a GS-10. What grade does the position call for?"

"Normally, the Director's Secretary is a GS-12, although the grade can be raised if the position is changed to be that of an administrative assistant."

"Please change the slot title to that of administrative assistant and promote Ann Welch to the grade of GS-12 immediately. I'd like her to know there was headroom for her to be promoted."

There was a moment of silence. Then he replied. "I'm afraid that's impossible."

"Why, is it against the law?"

"Not against the law. It violates Agency policy."

"Who determines Agency policy?"

"The Director."

"Fine, as Director I have just set the policy."

"But you just can't do that," he protested.

"Mr. Fisher," I said, as coldly and forcefully as I could, "You are the Director of Personnel. If you find yourself unable to carry out my direct order, I will replace you with someone who can. Do I make myself clear? I want the papers promoting Ann Welch to GS-12 and making her an administrative assistant to the Director on my desk before close of business today or else you can move out of your office!"

"Yes, sir," he said.

"They will be there."

I hung up and turned to Ann Welch. Her face expressed both astonishment and gratitude at what I had just done. She started to thank me, but it embarrassed me and I interrupted her.

"Has Mr. Brewer left for the Cabinet meeting?"

"Yes, sir."

"Then please come with me."

I walked out of my office through the secretary's area, followed by Ann. Mona Peterson looked up from her work.

"Mr. Brewer is out," she said.

"I know," I answered, walking past her into the office. She started to stand up to block me, then reconsidered and sat down. As I had expected, it was about twice as large as the one I was currently using and far more attractive. The windows on the two corner walls overlooked the beautiful Virginia countryside. Almost all of the floor area was covered by a magnificent Oriental carpet. On another wall hung an impressive life-size oil painting of George Washington. Mounted on the fourth wall were several jeweled scimitars.

I turned to Ann. "Are any of the things in the office Mr. Brewer's personal possessions?"

"I believe those scimitars on the wall belong to him. I think I once heard him say he had received them as a gift when he was stationed in Iran. The rest of the furnishings belong to the Agency."

I left the office and stopped at Mona Peterson's desk. "I'm exchanging offices with Mr. Brewer," I said. You had better exchange desks with Ann for convenience. It will be easier if her desk is closer to my office"

She stated to raise an objection, but I cut her short. Turning to Ann, I said, "Please arrange for the handymen to move any personnel belongings of Mr. Brewer's to his new office immediately. The materials in the safes will remain there. If he has anything personal in the safes, he can remove it later."

Ann turned away to implement my instructions. Mona stood, staring at me, an angry expression on her face. "You can't do that!" she said flatly.

"Oh yes I can," I answered. "I just did."

I left her standing speechless and returned to my office. A few minutes later, there was a knock at my door and Tilden entered. "Don't you think you ought to wait until Mr. Brewer returns to discuss the change of offices with him?"

"I don't see any need for that," I said. "As Director, I need the best office to carry out my job. And, as Mr. Brewer told me, the Director's office at the EOB is one of the finest in Washington. Since he will frequently represent me at the Cabinet meetings, he can use that office as his primary one."

I deliberately spoke in a decisive tone to make it clear I wished no further discussion with Tilden on the matter. He started to reply, reconsidered, and left the office without a word.

It was now close to noon and I was getting hungry. I walked out of my office and stopped at Ann's desk. I was glad to see through the open door of Brewer's office that two handymen were carefully removing the scimitars from his wall. "Is there an Agency cafeteria?" I asked.

"Yes, sir," she replied. "On the ground floor. Most of the senior officials eat at the Executive Dining Room on the second floor. I've never eaten there, but I believe the food is considered to be better and there is also waiter service. And, as Director, you have the Director' Dining room. It's used primarily to entertain important visitors, but it has a first class chef always on duty.

"Thanks," I answered. "I think I'll try the general cafeteria."

Taking the elevator down to the ground floor, it was easy to find the cafeteria by following the groups of Agency personnel walking there. I was pleased to see it served hamburgers and ordered one. I noticed that the food prices were somewhat higher for the Agency cafeteria than those charged at the Cafeteria I had set up in the Lust Cosmetics plant in Watsonville, probably because I had provided it with a more generous subsidy.

I paid for my hamburger and coffee at the cashier and sat down at a table. As I ate, I took the opportunity to observe the Agency personnel seated near me. From what I could tell, morale was good. The employees appeared happy. Those snatches of conversation I could overhear contained no complaints. I noticed that the average age was lower and the people better dressed than at Lust Cosmetics. That was to be expected, given the government's efforts to recruit younger people and the higher percentage of white collar employees than in the Lust Cosmetics work force.

When I finished, I retraced my steps and was pleased to find my way back to my seventh floor office without getting lost. Ann was now seated at the desk previously used by Mona Peterson. Mona was nowhere to be seen.

"Good lunch, sir?" Ann inquired politely. "While you were gone, the handymen moved Mr. Brewer' s things out of the office. I left the traffic that used to go to Mr. Brewer on your desk, as you requested."

I saw that she was eating her lunch at her desk. The sandwich and coffee had been obtained from one of the vending machines in the corridor rather than from the cafeteria.

"Didn't you have a chance to go out for lunch?" I asked. "There's no need for you to eat at your desk unless there's a crisis. Why don't you go out for a bit? Have the mailroom send up someone to sit at your desk and answer the phone until you get back."

"Thanks," she replied. "Normally I do that. Today I thought I ought to stay here in case Mona tried to take something out of Mr. Brewer's office that belongs there."

I smiled, but said nothing more as I entered my new office and sat down at the desk. I decided I had made a wise choice in selecting Ann to act as my permanent secretary. Looking around, my office seemed even finer than I had thought at first sight. The oil painting on the wall of George Washington with its gilt-plated antique frame was particularly impressive. I noticed for the first time a small table on which had been placed a polished metal carafe and several crystal glasses. Opening the carafe, I found it was a thermos of sorts, filled with ice water. A beautiful small wooden cabinet turned out to conceal a refrigerator. Opening it, I saw a large container of Iranian caviar. My old office at Lust Cosmetics, of which I had been so proud, paled in comparison. I decided I would have to find a similar painting and small refrigerator to put into my office when I left CIA and returned to Lust Cosmetics.

I looked at the in box on my desk. Ann and placed in it my traffic. Most of the papers turned out to be information copies sent to keep the Director informed of actions Agency components were taking or of developments in foreign countries. I initialed the documents to indicate I had read them and transferred them to the out box on my desk. Those few documents sent to me for approval I put aside, planning to contact the drafter listed to obtain background information.

I started to pick up the phone and call about the first document in my pile, then stopped to reconsider. It might unnecessarily ruffle the feathers of my senior deputies if I directly contacted their subordinates without at least meeting the senior deputies first.

Most of the documents that required my approval had originated to the DO, as the Operations Directorate was referred to in the

Agency. This was the part of the Agency that was responsible for clandestine activities abroad, the charter of the Agency barring it from clandestine activities in the United States. I decided my first step would be to ask Ann to call William Churchill, the Deputy Director in charge of the DO, and have him come to my office to meet me.

Churchill had spent his entire career under cover in the DO, so that there was no information about this phase of his life in the American press. However, the clipping firm in Chicago, by dint of excellent research, had collected some reports about him originating in the American and foreign media. He had been described as "the pride" of the CIA and as almost certain to be one day named its Director. His credentials were impressive. He was a graduate of Choate and of Yale, Captain of the Yale football team, and a Rhodes Scholar.

Returning to the United States from his studies in Britain, he had joined the Army as Second Lieutenant. He had been promoted to Captain while serving as a member of the Special Forces in Vietnam. His military service was highlighted by his being awarded the Distinguished Service Cross for carrying a wounded comrade on his back several days through the jungle from deep behind enemy lines to reach safety. Of his activities after joining the Agency, there was only a report from the Russian press that referred cryptically to the intelligence coups he had scored in the Middle East.

In a few minutes there was a knock at my door and Churchill entered. He was tall, handsome, well-built and moved with the grace of an athlete. His dark hair had begun to gray at the temples, making him look both youthful and distinguished at the same time. If I had been a movie director, Churchill would have been my first choice to play the President of the United States.

I stood to shake hands with him, feeling pleased to have such an individual as a key subordinate. "I'm very glad to meet you," I said. "I would appreciate it if you would explain to me what the DO does."

As I uttered these words, I realized just how naive they made me sound. "The Directorate of Operations," Churchill began, "Is responsible for the secret side of Agency operations, basically the spying." He then went on to explain his work in language so general and simple that I would have felt embarrassed using it in a talk to a gathering of high school students.

The meeting was going poorly. He glanced at his watch, indicating he had more important things to do. I decided to try another tack.

"Mr. Churchill," I said, "I would like you to give me a briefing of the problems facing the Agency that you think are most important from your vantage point as Deputy Director for Operations."

"Yes, sir," he said. "I'll have the briefing books prepared."

I almost exploded in reply, then curtailed my anger. "Mr. Churchill," I answered. "I have had enough bull shit given me in the last few months to last me a lifetime. What I would like is a succinct, oral briefing. There is no need to put the problems in order of importance."

A look of astonishment crossed his face, but he quickly concealed it. He thought for a minute and then began. "The growth of Islamic fundamentalism in the Middle East is probably the most important problem. It threatens the stability of the nations in the area, some of whom are American allies, the strategic interests of the United States, a growth of terrorist groups and the access of this country and the rest of the world to the vital Middle East oil. Unfortunately, we have very limited ability to obtain information about the secret intentions of the Islamic fundamentalists or to influence their behavior."

I nodded when he had finished his comments. "The second major problem," he continued, "Is the great growth in power of China. Not only has China transformed itself into a major economic force, with the largest foreign exchange holdings in the world, but it is using its financial leverage to buy up reserves of many of the key commodities in the world. Its holdings of United States Treasury bonds permit it to strongly affect American financial policy. Moreover, it is building up its military forces with the acquisition of modern naval vessels and aircraft. In a matter of a few years, it will be in a position to challenge American naval control of the Western Pacific. As with Islamic fundamentalism, the Agency has few good clandestine sources of information or ability to influence events in China."

Again, he stopped to allow me to raise any questions, and then went on to discuss the growing authoritarian control in Russia. "Our hopes for a democratic evolution in Russia have evaporated," he said. Moscow is re-establishing its influence in many of the former Soviet states which obtained their independence. They are not helping us with regard to establishing stability in the Middle East and are cooperating more with China than in previous decades. We have some clandestine coverage in Russia," but not nearly enough."

"Finally," he said, "There is Project Venus. It concerns a large, covert operation in Africa."

The phrase "Project Venus" was not new to me. It had been referred to in some of the operational traffic Ann had put in my in box.

"Could you fill me in on Project Venus," I said.

To my surprise, he shook his head. "I can't, he answered. That information is available on a strict need-to-know basis. Your name is not on the approved list."

I stared at him in amazement. "Are you serious?" I asked him. "Are you stating you can't tell the Agency Director about Project Venus?"

"Yes sir."

"Do you know about it?"

"Of course, I'm supervising all the detailed planning."

"Does Fleming Brewer know about it?"

"Yes sir." He answered. "As Acting Director, his approval was necessary for the project. He was fully briefed on it."

"All told, about how many people in the Agency are aware of the project?"

"About forty," he answered. "That includes the people in Finance, who have to move the funds, the logistics people handling that aspect, and the operations people."

"Is anyone outside the Agency knowledgeable?" I pressed on.

"Yes sir. Secretary of State Ashby, the President's National Security Adviser and," he added, "I believe the President is aware of the operation in general terms."

All of this was ridiculous to me, but the fact that Buck was aware of it and I was not struck me as the height of absurdity. I shook my head. "I'm afraid that isn't satisfactory," I said.

"Perhaps it is," he said slowly, "But there is nothing I can do about it."

"Tell me," I said, "Who makes up the list of cleared personnel?"

"Why, ultimately, the Director." I was about to tell him that as Director, I was about to modify the list to add my own name, when another thought crossed my mind. There was no reason to challenge him, if I could avoid doing so.

"You said, the project involves a large covet action in Africa," I began. "There is only one thing that could be. It has to involve a coup to overthrow President Ngola."

Now Churchill looked me in amazement. "How did you know?" he asked before he realized he had confirmed my suspicion.

"It's a no-brainer," I answered. "The world press has been filled for weeks with reports about the human rights violations in his country. Lately, the American media have featured accounts every day of the inhabitants of Bokasa being killed, imprisoned or simply disappearing. Editorials have urged the United States to take the lead in ousting General Ngola from power. When the Bokasa President had his army fire on the protesters in the capital, Ashby denounced the Ngola regime and stated at his press conference it was time for the Ngola to give up power."

Churchill looked crestfallen, that it had all been so easy for me to decipher.

"Why don't we just stop this nonsense and have you fill me in on anything I've missed?" I said.

He thought for a minute and then did so. When he finished, I asked him, "What do you think of the coup plan?"

"It's not bad. I think it might work."

"Yes, but the coup group will have no air cover. The Bokasa air force is under command of the President's nephew and the pilots are virtually all from his tribe. It will remain loyal to Ngola. Any coup force we can organize will be heavily attacked by the air force. It's likely to be the Bay of Pigs all over again."

Churchill seemed surprised by the extent of my knowledge of the situation on the ground in Bokasa. "The coup force we will organize will be backed by a small group of South African mercenaries. They should stiffen our Bokasa forces long enough for them to seize the radio and TV stations and call on the population to rally to the coup. And we're betting that the air force will not obey orders to bomb the TV and radio stations to know them off the air."

"The police chief," Churchill added, "Has agreed to support the coup if it looks like it has a chance."

"That's nice." I said, "But the President's Guard and the armored regiment in the capital are both under the command of other Ngola family members and made up of people from his tribe. If I had to bet, I'd wager that the chances of this coup succeeding are less than twenty percent."

"You may be right," Churchill admitted, "But the Agency has been under heavy pressure to organize a coup."

"All right," I said. "Continue with the planning. But keep me fully informed."

As he left, I thanked him. I started to go through the papers on my desk when I heard a noise outside my office and stood up to investigate. In the outer office I saw Brewer, Tilden and Mona discussing something in animated fashion. As soon as they caught sight of me, they stopped, strengthening my suspicion that they had been discussing me.

"Oh Fleming," I said, "How did the Cabinet meeting go? Come into my office and tell me about it."

Without pausing, I turned and entered my office. I glanced behind and saw he was following me with a sullen expression on his face. I sat down behind my desk and motioned him to sit down.

"I hope you don't mind my exchanging offices with you," I said. "I decided that since I'm going to run the Agency, it was more efficient for me to use the Director's office. I've decided to have you represent CIA at most Cabinet meetings, so you can operate out of the Director's office at the EOB."

"I don't think that's wise," he began, but I cut him off.

"We'll try it for a bit and see how it works out. If it seems advisable, we can revise our responsibilities then. Now, what happened at the Cabinet meeting?"

"Yes sir."

I listened as Brewer reluctantly began his report on the Cabinet session. It became apparent to me that I had made a serious mistake in not attending myself. Many of the planned domestic policy initiatives brought up by Buck and some of the other Cabinet members seemed questionable, a few downright dangerous. I had foolishly put Buck into the White House. My most important responsibility now was preventing Buck's administration from doing serious harm to the country. To do that, I would have to attend Cabinet meetings personally and intervene when I judged vital.

When he finished, I saw that Brewer was mustering up his courage to press me again to return his former office and responsibilities to him. To cut him short, I said, "That was an excellent report Fleming. Let me think over our division of work and get back to you on it." I then picked up some papers from my in box and began to read them in a clear sign to Brewer that our meeting was over. As I did so, I could not help thinking of my mother. She would have punished me for being so impolite to anyone.

My tactic worked. Brewer arose without speaking further and left my office. I picked up the first paper requiring my attention and saw it was from Fisher, the Director of Personnel, implementing my order to promote Ann. I signed the approval line formally promoting her two grades and buzzed her to come in.

"Congratulations, Ann," I said with a smile. You are now officially a GS-12 and administrative assistant."

"I can't begin to thank you, sir," she said earnestly. "It means a lot to me."

Embarrassed by her emotion, I changed the subject. "How are things out there?" I asked, motioning toward the outer office.

Choosing her words carefully, Ann said, "Mr. Brewer, Mr. Tilden and Mona don't seem very pleased by the new working arrangements."

"I wouldn't worry about that," I answered dryly and went on, "When you filled in here before you went overseas, was Mr. Tilden the Executive Assistant to the Director?"

"No sir. He was the Executive Assistant to Mr. Brewer, who was the Deputy Director. Mr. Frazier had his own Executive Assistant. When he resigned as Director, Mr. Collins, his Executive Assistant, went downstairs to work in the Russian Division."

"Thanks," I said. "Could you please get Mr. Fisher on the phone for me."

A few minutes later my phone buzzed and I picked it up. It was Fisher. I was amused at the apprehension in his voice.

"I've just signed off on Ann Welch's promotion papers," I said. "I wanted to tell you I'm pleased at the speed with which you got the job done."

"Thank you sir," he said his relief obvious.

I hung up and carefully considered my next move. If I had to spend time at Cabinet meetings I clearly required an able Deputy Director to help me administer the Agency. I doubted Brewer's competence and even more his loyalty to me. The effort he had made to push me aside as Director was something only a fool would risk being repeated. Brewer had to go. I picked up the phone and buzzed Ann. "Please ask Mr. Churchill come here as soon as possible," I said.

A few minutes later there was a knock at the door and Churchill entered. I motioned for him to take a seat. As he did, I noticed him surreptitiously look at his watch. I could well understand it. In his place, I would have been irritated at being summoned back in so short a time for a second meeting with the Director. I would have wondered "What the Hell did that damn fool want that he couldn't ask me about a few hours ago?"

"Mr. Churchill," I began. "I've decided to appoint you Deputy Director of the Agency. Please designate someone good to act temporarily as your replacement and report back here within an hour. You will use the Deputy Director's office and start work immediately."

Churchill stared me, amazed. "But you just can't do that," he finally managed to say.

"Oh yes I can," I said. Under current law appointment of the Deputy Director no longer requires Senate confirmation. It's completely at my discretion."

"What about Mr. Brewer?" he asked. "Has he retired?"

"No," I answered. "Your first job upon taking over will be to find him a suitable position. Is there any overseas Agency Station where he can't do any harm?"

"I don't think that would work," he answered. "I would him expect him to resign. He has a lot of powerful friends here in Washington. He is very likely to make as much trouble for you as possible, and there will be many people here and probably some now in the Agency who would help him."

"You're right," I said. "It doesn't pay to create enemies if it can be avoided." I carefully reviewed all of my options.

"I've got it," I said. "I'll appoint him to some sort of intelligence commission. What do we have available?"

"We do have some," Churchill replied thoughtfully. "But all of them do important work."

Again, I reviewed possible scenarios. Then the right one struck me. "Of course," I said.

"He will be named Co-Chair of a Presidential Blue Ribbon Panel to recommend improvements in the national intelligence effort. The other Co-Chair will be a highly respected former Senator. That way, Brewer can keep the same grade he has now as Acting Director. We'll rent luxurious quarters for the panel and its own limo. Other members can be former Senators, possible a university president and a few distinguished leaders from the private sector. Of course, I can't do it myself as Director. I'll raise it at the next Cabinet meeting and have the President endorse it.

"What exactly will the Blue Ribbon Panel do?" Churchill inquired.

"Actually, nothing. I doubt it will ever meet. If we have to have a meeting, we will provide it with a list of general problems and ask them to work on it. They can organize some groups to each study an individual topic. Even the organizing phase will take months. Really, it's a lot of busy work to keep incompetents so active they can't cause any real problems."

"I'll inform Brewer of his promotion myself. One more thing. I don't think it wise to keep Tilden on as Executive Assistant. Bring up somebody you know to be very competent and loyal to serve as your Executive Assistant. I will get someone to serve as my Executive Assistant. I think it's more efficient for each of us to have one. As for your secretary, you can keep Mona if you wish. My personal advice would be to bring up someone you feel comfortable working with and whom you can trust."

I thought for a minute and then added, "About our areas of responsibility. We will work very closely together. We each will receive the same traffic. I want you to see everything I do. You will act for me when I am not here. I will expect and rely on your advice for anything significant. Feel free to tell me if you think I am making a mistake. I don't promise to always follow your advice, but you may be assured that I will always consider it very carefully and explain to you why I am acting otherwise, if I do."

"I certainly can't ask for more than that," he said. He stood up and I shook hands with him. "I'll make the arrangements downstairs and be back here within an hour."

When he had left, I buzzed Ann and asked her to have Brewer come to my office. He entered and I shook hands with him, to his obvious consternation.

"Congratulations, Fleming," I said, "On your promotion. You'll take over as Co-Chair of the President's new Blue Ribbon Panel to review the national Intelligence effort. The President hasn't yet selected the other members, so you will in effect be acting as the panel's head for the foreseeable future. Naturally, you will have the same grade and salary as you have now. Tomorrow, you will check out the various locations on K Street to get an idea of what premises are available. They will have to be sufficiently large to accommodate the functioning of the panel and suitably luxurious to demonstrate its importance. We want the Senators and Congressmen to accept and implement the recommendations to the extent necessary."

Brewer seemed ready to argue, so I hurriedly continued to give him no opportunity to do so. "If you wish you can take Walter and Mona with you." I said. "Oh yes, I almost forgot. You get your own limo with the job. Take the rest of the day off. Tomorrow, I'll have a limo pick you up at your house and take you to look at those K street offices."

I then ushered him out of my office, as politely as I could while giving him no opportunity to object. I felt like the bouncer of a cheap bar, but it worked. I then buzzed Ann. Do you remember the name of the old Executive Assistant to the Director?"

"Collins," she said. "Don Collins. After Mr. Frazier resigned, Don went back to the Russian Division."

"Could you please ask him to come upstairs to see me."

A few minutes later there was a knock on my door and a young man in his mid-thirties entered. "You sent for me sir," he said. "I'm Donald Collins."

"Sit down please," I replied. "I understand you served as Executive Assistant to the previous Director, Mr. Frazier."

"Yes sir."

"You're now working in the Russian Division? How do you like it?"

"Very much sir. The work is fascinating and it's in line with my graduate training. I have a master's degree in modern East European History from Columbia University."

Collins demeanor impressed me favorably. "Would you be interested," I asked him, In coming back to this office to serve as my Executive Assistant?"

"May I be frank sir?"

"Of course."

"Serving as Executive Assistant to the Director is a great honor. The trouble is, it removes you from the mainstream of the Division in which you have served. When the Director leaves, you have a difficult time returning to your old division. I was very fortunate in being able to get the job I have now in the Russian Division. I doubt I would be so lucky a second time. I would therefore prefer to remain where I am."

"I can certainly appreciate your reasoning," I said. "Relax! I will not ask you to return here if that is your choice. However, I would like very much for you to consider doing so. Mr. Brewer and Mr. Tilden are being reassigned. Mr. Churchill is coming up here to serve as Deputy Director. He will bring along his own Executive Assistant. What I would like you to do is to serve as mine for no more than three months to assist me to do the work of Director and to help break in your replacement."

"I will insure," I continued, "that the head of the Russian Division is aware of the fact that you are performing a valuable service to the Agency and to me personally as Director and can return in three months to your current position. I will also place a letter in your file stating this and requesting the promotion panel to give the fullest weight to your willingness to so serve. At the same time, if you wish, I will see that you are assigned as Chief of Station to one of the former Soviet satellites. I believe you have sufficient grade to serve as COS in one of the smaller countries."

The smile on Collins' face was a joy to behold. "Under those circumstances," he said, "I'd be most please to serve as your Executive Assistant."

"Please pick up your personal things and install yourself in your old office," I said. When he left, I congratulated myself on my decision to choose Collins. I was impressed by his behavior and realized that when I selected my own Executive Assistant, I would be fortunate to find someone as competent.

I thought of asking Tilden to come into my office to inform him of his replacement as Executive Assistant, but decided against it. Brewer, I thought, had probably already invited Tilden to go with him to help in setting up the new Blue Ribbon Presidential Panel. Whatever the case, Tilden and Mona would no longer be part of the Director's office staff and, if I had anything to do with it, be assigned as far away from this office as possible.

With my inbox now empty, I decided it was time for me to make the acquaintance of Dr. Thomas Cousins, the Deputy Director for Intelligence. The Intelligence Directorate, or DI as it was called, was that part of the Agency responsible for analyzing foreign information collected by the DO, the State Department, the various military intelligence agencies and other elements of the far-flung American intelligence community and for preparing finished intelligence reports for use of the President and other senior Washington officials.

Unlike the DO, the DI's functions were largely a matter of public record and its personnel did not keep their affiliation with the Agency secret. Dr. Cousins frequently addressed scholarly meetings and foreign affairs groups in his official capacity.

I asked Ann to call Cousins and have him come up to see me at his convenience. Within a few minutes, there was a knock at my door and Cousins entered. When I saw him, It was hard to keep a straight face. He was tall and slightly stooped. His narrow shoulders accentuated his leanness. With his thick glasses, wearing a tweed sports jacket with leather patches at the sleeves, wrinkled gray flannel slacks and loafers, he exactly fit my mental image of a Harvard University professor. In fact, he had been a member of the Harvard University faculty before joining the Agency.

"Dr. Cousins," I said, standing and shaking his hand. "I hope I haven't disturbed you."

With Cousins, I had no intention of repeating the mistake I had made with Churchill, of attempting to seem uninformed about his activities. Cousins was widely regarded as one of the most brilliant senior career officials in the federal government.

"I very much enjoyed your book on the historical Jesus," I said. The book had been recommended to me by our rector at St. Mark's Church in Watsonville.

Cousins smiled. "I'm working on a revised version," he said with pride. "I'll send you a copy of the draft when it's completed."

"I'd appreciate that very much. Are you referring in it to that new German analysis of the manuscripts found in the Syrian monastery?"

Cousins looked at me sharply. I didn't know you were a Biblical scholar. The Syrian manuscripts are the reason for my revisions."

"I'm not an expert on the subject," I said. "But I am very interested in Biblical history. I read some lengthy articles about the manuscripts in the French newspapers."

Cousins looked impressed, as had been my goal. "Dr. Cousins," I said, "I am generally familiar with the organization and mission of the Intelligence Directorate. I would be grateful for your views on the DI's activities."

Cousins proceeded to give me a well-organized, detailed presentation, which I found extremely interesting and useful. The man was clearly a brilliant teacher.

When he finished, he opened up the briefcase he carried with him and extracted two publications, which resembled small news magazines. "These two," he said as he handed the first to me for my inspection, "are our most important publications."

I thumbed through the publication. It was about thirty pages in length and contained articles of various length on foreign affairs subjects. Many of the articles were several pages in length. The writing styles similar to that found in the "New York Times."

"This publication," he informed me, "Is intended for senior government officials, including members of the Cabinet."

After I looked through the publication more carefully and voiced my satisfaction, Cousins handed me the second publication with a show of pride. "This one," he said, "Is the most important document the DI produces. It is intended only for the President. It contains the most sensitive and highly classified intelligence available to the American government."

I read it carefully. Other than the multitude of warnings on it concerning the need to keep the contents from being seen by anyone other than the President, its contents seemed identical to the first publication Cousins had shown me.

"I'm afraid this won't do," I said.

Cousins appeared stupefied that anyone could question the value of his prized publication.

"I beg your pardon."

"It won't do," I repeated."

"Perhaps it could use some tightening up," he admitted.

"No, you don't understand," I said. "It has to be thrown out and replaced by a completely different publication."

"But every President I've worked for has praised it."

"Let me explain, Dr. Cousins." I answered. "I mean no reflection on your publication. The problem is the President."

Cousins looked at me strangely, trying to grasp my meaning.

"President Porter may be shrewd politically," I explained. "Unfortunately, he doesn't like to read anything more challenging than the sports section."

"You must be joking," Cousins said gravely. "I can't believe the American people would elect someone like that President. Why you backed him yourself."

"I did," I admitted.

There was no point in being frank with Cousins as to my reasons. In addition to Buck's inability to understand the finer points of foreign affairs or use the intelligence collected by the Agency effectively, controlling the flow of material to him could be essential to me if I wanted to prevent him from doing anything that might harm the United States.

Wording my answer to make it most agreeable to Cousins, I said, "Of course, no President is perfect. We have to change our procedures to make them compatible with President Porter's interests and preferences. The publication for the President's own use will henceforth consist of no more than six short pieces, each of no more than three sentences. The content and writing style will be that of a supermarket tabloid. The pieces will concentrate on such subjects as the sex life of foreign heads of state, financial scandals and the like. If you find something about Elvis Presley being seen in the Kremlin, print it!"

"But how do we carry out our mission of informing the President about serious foreign problems?" Cousins said. "Suppose we get word, for example, of a plot to overthrow the Egyptian government?"

"We alert the Secretary of State and other senior officials, some of whom hopefully will have the intelligence to recognize the important of the information and act on it effectively. If it is necessary to inform the President, you will brief me and I will personally make certain he grasps the importance of the threat. Henceforth, this publication and anything else addressed to the President will be sent to me first in draft for my prior approval. Is that clear?"

Cousins nodded. "Yes sir," he said soberly. As he left, I wondered if he believed me.

The rest of the afternoon passed quickly. Thomas Churchill occupied his office as Deputy Director. Don Collins came up and began functioning as my Executive Assistant. He periodically screened and brought the traffic for me, explaining which items he thought I should approve, which conflicted with previous decisions of the Director or with Agency policy, and which papers sent to me for my information were of special importance. I also read the documents that came to me via Churchill, in many cases the same documents. I recognized there was a lot of unnecessary duplication of effort, but I wanted to get both Churchill's and Collins' opinions on sensitive items.

I thanked Collins and when he had left carefully read each of the documents identified by him as important. In most cases, Churchill and Collins both came to the same conclusion. Where they differed, or where I disagreed, I saved the documents to discuss with the drafters.

About 5:30, I looked at my watch and suddenly realized what time it was. I walked out to Ann's desk and asked her if there was anything else that was time sensitive, as I was planning to go home.

"No sir, she said. "In any case, if there is anything urgent we can call you on your pager and have you contact the Agency Senior Duty Officer."

"Pager," I answered. "I don't have any pager."

She looked shocked. "Didn't Mr. Tilden or Mr. Brewer give you one?"

"No, they never mentioned it." Once again it flashed through my mind has smart I had been in removing both of them from the Director's office.

Ann stood, "I believe there is an extra pager in the safe," she said. She unlocked one of the safes, took out a pager, fiddled with it, and handed it to me. ""it will do the job," she stated.

I thanked her, asked her to inform Churchill and Collins that I was about to leave for the day and after she had checked with them requested her to have my limo ready to take me home.

"Yes sir," she said, "At what time would you like them to pick you up in the morning?"

"Would 6:15 be possible? Do they work that early?"

"You can have a car and driver at any time of the day or night, but most of the other senior officials don't arrive till shortly after 8 a.m. at the earliest. Do you want me to pass the word to have them here earlier?"

"That won't be necessary," I said. "I'm just used to coming in early. There's no reason for you to come in any earlier than usual, but please arrange for one of the night staff to bring me my traffic when I get here along with the daily newspapers."

"I'll take care of it," she said smiling. I gathered she was relieved that she wouldn't have to be in as early as I was.

Saying goodnight, I took the elevator to the garage and found my chauffeur and limo waiting. Traffic at that time of night on the George Washington Parkway was heavier than it had been in the morning. I savored the pleasure of relinquishing the care of driving to the chauffeur while I relaxed, looking at the beautiful scenery.

Pergamon was not home when I entered the apartment. She arrived a few minutes later from a charity auction presided over by Tammy and attended by several of the other Cabinet wives. Pergamon's social life had returned to its previous level after my confirmation as CIA Director. As far as I could determine, her relations with Tammy were as cordial as before. Accordingly, I answered in generalities when she asked me over dinner how my day had gone, uncertain whether she might repeat to Tammy anything I told her.

The next weeks passed quickly. I found myself busier than I had ever been before as I immersed myself fully in the running the day-to-day activities of the Agency and in attending the Cabinet meetings. Churchill and Collins were of great assistance to me with regard to the CIA operations. With regard to the Cabinet work, there was no one with whom I felt I could discuss the subject frankly. Normally, I remained silent during the Cabinet sessions, since foreign affairs matters were rarely raised. I did obtain the President's approval of the Blue Ribbon Panel intended to occupy Brewer's time. More importantly, I was able to raise procedural roadblocks to delay or stop some of the domestic programs favored by Buck which I viewed as likely to be fundamentally harmful to the country if actually implemented.

Meeting with the other senior Agency officials, I found few

pleased to accept me as the new Director. Fortunately, I saw no need to challenge their concept of CIA operations, as I had with Churchill and Cousins. My confidence grew that I would be successful in improving the Agency's performance to fulfill the promise I had given the Senate Intelligence Committee.

I also had the minor problem of some Agency components sending me documents in the late afternoon requiring my urgent attention just as I was getting ready to go home. This was certainly understandable in the case of fast-breaking events. However, after delaying my departure several times for matters which I determined subsequently could easily have been sent to me early in the day, I determined to stop the practice. I notified all elements that I planned to leave promptly at 5:30 each afternoon. "Any official unable to comply with this schedule," my memo stated, "If found to have unnecessarily delayed action on a problem requiring the Director's attention, will be transferred to a less demanding position."

CHAPTER 8

Shortly before 5:30 one afternoon as I was getting ready to leave, Ann buzzed to tell me that Churchill had to see me urgently. A minute or so later he entered my office accompanied by Phil Jackson, the Chief of the Africa Division and Ed Barnes, one of the Africa Division officers. My first thought was that Jackson was deliberately flouting my orders by bringing me a matter so late in the day. This was surprising to me; I had spoken to Jackson several times and been favorably impressed by his obvious competence.

Churchill must have read my mind. He apologized for coming in so late in the afternoon, explaining that the matter had just become critical. Placing a thick folder in front of me, he said, "You instructed me to inform you immediately before we implement Project Venus. The Secretary of State called me a few minutes ago on the secure line to notify me the President has authorized Project Venus to begin. The Secretary expects it to start this week. He said that the President shares this view. The final orders are here for you to sign."

I was startled by the news. Project Venus was far too sensitive to be discussed at a regular Cabinet meeting. But there had been no meeting of the National Security Council to discuss it. I couldn't understand how it had gone this far without Buck or the Secretary of State raising it with me privately. And how had the two of them decided to push it?

I opened the folder and read the top document carefully. At the bottom of the sheet was the signature line for me to indicate my approval.

"The President wants it to begin this week," Churchill repeated. I gathered he expected me to sign the approval line immediately on the basis of the President's express order.

"Tom," I said, using his first name as I had begun to do because of the growing friendship between us, "I don't care what the President wants. I will not commit the Agency to this plan until I know what it entails and what the risks are. I owe it to CIA, to the country and to the President to do no less."

"Yes sir," he said abashed. "As Bokasa Desk Chief, Ed Barnes io the most knowledgeable about project Venus. He can best answer any questions you may have."

Reading the details of the operation increased my doubts about its wisdom. "I gather," I said, "That in addition to the Presidency, General Ngola also is the Minister of Defense and Commander of the Armed Forces."

Barnes nodded in agreement. "Yes sir. There have been several unsuccessful coup attempts against General Ngola in recent years, involving units of the armed forces. He took over the top military posts to prevent the incumbents from using them to organize another coup against him."

"He seems like a cautious and intelligent man," I said.

"He is that," Barnes agreed.

"Then who is there to lead a military coup against him?" I

inquired.

Barnes looked at Churchill and Jackson to see if they wanted him to answer. When they remained silent he said, "General Buta, the Army Commander."

"Buta," I said, "Isn't he a Protestant and a member of a minority tribe? Isn't a majority of the armed forces made up of General Ngola's tribe and aren't most of them Roman Catholics. How likely are they to follow Buta in a coup against Ngola?"

"Buta told us he can count on the loyalty of his key subordinates," Jackson said.

"What troop units does Buta actually control?" I pressed on. "Does he have the support of Ngola's personal detachment of bodyguards? I believe they constitute an armored battalion and are equipped with heavy tanks."

"No sir," Barnes admitted. "The bodyguard detachment remains loyal to Ngola. Buta will use the paratroop regiment stationed at the airport to spearhead the coup."

"How far is the airport from the presidential palace?"

Churchill and Jackson looked inquiringly at each other. Barnes said after a minute, "About eight miles. But it's a paved highway."

"You know," I said, recalling something from the dredges of my mind. "I seem to recall in an attaché report that all orders for troop deployment have to be counter-signed by the Army Chief of Staff, Colonel Lumbuda. Isn't he a member of General Ngola's tribe? What about that?"

Churchill and Jackson looked at Barnes. The latter was silent. Finally, he said, "I don't know sir. We've been so busy with the coup plans, I've fallen behind on reading some of the traffic."

"Gentlemen," I said. I can't give my approval to launching Project Venus at this time."

"But the President and Secretary of State want us to act

immediately," Churchill answered, a desperate look on his face."

"It's odd," I said, "He never raised the subject with me."

Churchill looked at me. "Off the record, I understand the First Lady is pushing it."

"That explains it," I said. "She exercises a great deal of influence over the President in all areas."

"Please inform the Secretary of State that I am going out to Bokasa to check conditions on the spot myself. Add that a delay in any case is required because we have to make sure the weather when the coup starts is sufficiently bad to prevent Ngola's air force from intervening to put it down."

"Do you have any specific indication of the weather forecast for Bokasa?" Churchill asked.

"None in the least. But you can always look at a weather forecast and find things about it to question. Tom" I went on, "Please make arrangements for me to fly immediately to Bokasa. I'll take Ed and Don Collins with me. I'd like you to hold the fort here. Phil," I said, turning to Jackson. "I'd like you to come too, unless there are more important things for you to do here."

"I'll come with you," Jackson answered.

"Great," I said, pleased that I would have the benefit of Jackson's expertise readily available for what promised to be a challenging mission."

"You could take the Agency plane normally used by the Director," Tom put in. "That way you would travel most comfortably and most securely. However, I wouldn't recommend that. It would tip off General Ngola that something was going on for you to travel there. They're not very sophisticated in Bokasa, but they'll recognize your name and the plane identification."

"I don't plan to fly there under my own name or in the Agency plane," I said. "Make arrangements for us to fly there in alias via commercial means."

Churchill looked at me closely, a look of respect on his face. "We can do that," he said. "But I have to warn you that travel to Bokasa by commercial means is a long and arduous business, especially for someone of your age."

"I'll chance that," I answered "Please take care of it."

Some forty-eight hours later, Barnes, Jackson and I were among the passengers on an Air France plane from Dakar about to land at St. Henri, Bokasa's capital. Churchill had been correct. The trip from Washington had been long and arduous. My arms ached from the inoculations the Agency doctors had made me take as standard precaution for anyone traveling to Bokasa. In one respect, though, the shots had been helpful. The slight fever I had been left with had helped me doze on each leg of the flight, from Washington to New York, from New York to Paris, from Paris to Dakar and from Dakar to St. Henri.

When we boarded the plane in Dakar, it had been very early in the morning and I had been so tired I had taken no notice of my fellow passengers. Now, as the plane began its descent, I looked around me. I was sitting next to Jackson. Barnes was seated several rows behind us. Because Barnes and Jackson had visited Bokasa several times before and might be recognized, they were using modest disguises suggested by Agency technician, including changed hair styles, a false mustache in Barnes' case and wads of plastic in Jackson's mouth to make his face appear rounder.

The cabin was only half full, reflecting the depressed and underdeveloped state of Bokasa's economy. Jackson, Barnes and I were almost the only Westerners. The other two were a French priest and a French journalist with whom Jackson had struck up a conversation at the Dakar airport.

The plane landed with a jolt, causing me to grab my arm rest hard. We then taxied at what seemed an excessive speed toward the terminal. Jackson closed the novel he had been reading and looked at me.

"I wonder if they train those Air France pilots with the same book they use for airline pilots in the United States," he remarked with a smile. He had become increasingly friendly as our trip from Washington proceeded, particularly after I had ordered a meal at the Paris Airport restaurant in French. My linguistic ability is limited, but I had studied French prior to taking a vacation trip to Paris with Pergamon a few years before and still retained some fluency in the language.

"If they do," I answered Jackson, Remind me to travel back to Washington by train."

I pointed across him out the window at the wreckage of an airplane that had been pushed over beyond the runway, but not removed. "Is that another Air France plane?" I asked.

"No," he said. "It belonged to a local airline. Their safety record is questionable. That's why we took a bit longer to travel here on Air France."

The plane stopped taxiing and I stood up to retrieve my luggage from the overhead rack. My single suitcase followed Jackson's advice to limit myself to what I could place in the overhead rack. He had warned me that his experience in traveling to West Africa was that suitcases were often stolen.

The plane doors opened and the passengers exited the aircraft. We descended a rickety mobile staircase and walked across the tarmac to the terminal. Although it was still early in the morning, the temperature and humidity were uncomfortably high

The terminal building looked as though it had been built in the 1950's, during Bukasa's brief period of oil boom. It was now in an advanced state of decay, with the glazed windows broken, paint peeling from the walls, and gaps in the ceiling from which the tiles had fallen and were now littering the floor.

At the terminal doors and scattered throughout the terminal building I saw military policemen, armed with automatic rifles.

"Is the security always this tight?" I asked Jackson.

"It was the last time I was here, about six months ago," he answered. "Ngola is aware of the possibility of a military coup attempt against him."

This was the latest indication I had received during our trip that Jackson was less sanguine about the prospects for organizing a successful coup against Nogola than he had seemed in Washington. I suspected that his support for Project Venus had stemmed from the pressure exerted on the Agency by the President and the Secretary of State to launch it immediately.

We carried our suitcases to the immigration control officers, who carefully examined our passports, and then proceeded to the customs inspection area of the terminal. To maintain our cover as representatives of an oil company, Churchill had instructed the Embassy and the Station not to meet us. I waited as the customs official opened my suitcase and carefully examined the contents. He closed it, then demanded to see my watch. I removed it from my wrist and handed it to him.

"This is a new watch," he said in French. "You must pay a customs fee of fifty dollars to bring it into Bokasa."

"That's ridiculous," I replied. "It's an old watch and didn't cost forty dollars when I bought it new."

"Pay him!" Jackson whispered to me. "They frequently shake down businessmen. We don't want to attract attention!"

The customs official called over another official who scowled at me and put his hand on his holstered pistol in a menacing gesture."You must pay the fifty dollars or you will be arrested!"

"I will not give you any money to bring a used watch into your country," I heard myself saying. "But I will give you twenty dollars to have a drink in my honor."

The two customs officers seemed amused at my offer and spoke to each other in a native dialect. Then the one holding the watch said, "Drinks are expensive in Bokasa. You must give us thirty dollars."

"Agreed," I replied, taking thirty dollars from my wallet and handing it to him in return for my watch. I picked up my suitcase and Jackson, Barnes and I walked out of the terminal. Jackson turned to me. "You really gave me a scare," he said with a smile.

"I was a bit nervous myself," I admitted. "But that trick worked once before for me in the Far East when Indonesian customs officials tried to hold me up. I thought it should work again."

Just outside the terminal doors, several decrepit taxis were parked. Jackson bargained for several minutes with one of the drivers. He then told us the driver had agreed to take us to the Embassy for the standard price. We climbed into an ancient Citroen, which looked like it was held together with baling wire. The taxi started off in a cloud of exhaust smoke.

As the cab turned onto the highway leading from the airport to the capital, we passed a large military encampment.

"That's where the paratroop regiment is stationed," Barnes told us.

I wanted to ask him more questions about the military unit that was set to play the lead part in launching Project Venus. However, there was too much danger the driver might overhear us. I contented myself with trying to gauge the state of readiness of the regiment as we drove by the encampment. I was not impressed. The few buildings I could see appeared dilapidated and ill-cared for.

The airport highway was not heavily trafficked. This enabled the driver to avoid the numerous ruts and deep potholes in the pavement. From time to time we passed abandoned factories. Barnes informed us that they had been built in the 1950's by Bokasa's one-time large French community, now almost all gone by emigration back to France.

After what seemed like an eternity because of the heat, the taxi's slow speed and the bumpy nature of the ride, we reached the outskirts of St. Henri. I noticed several armored vehicles parked at the one location, apparently ready to close the road at a moment's notice. We turned off the airport road into a residential neighborhood.

"This is the so-called 'New Quarter' of St. Henri," Barnes told us. "Most of the foreign embassies are located here as well as the residences of most of the foreign community."

The 'New Quarter' belied its name. Most of the residences dated back before the First World War. The majority of homes were located in the midst of large compounds, each of which was encircled by a high stucco wall. The walls had at one time been painted in pastel colors which had faded into a dismal gray. Here and there a compound sported a well-manicured lawn along the walls that was at sharp variance with the overgrown grass and weeds that flourished in the broad median strip of the boulevard. We passed a nineteenth century French Catholic Church in fair condition and turned onto the street which housed the American Embassy.

We passed several foreign embassies, which I recognized by the national flags on or in front of the buildings. My expectation that the American Embassy would resemble the two story buildings occupied by most of the other foreign embassies was mistaken. It was the tallest building in the 'New Quarter.'" Its ultra-modern stainless steel facade and large plate glass windows clashed with its surroundings. I could only wonder how the unfortunate embassy officer charged with protecting the building from possible rioters and terrorists could handle the problem.

The taxi turned onto the embassy driveway and we were stopped at the embassy compound gates by a pair of Bokasa military police. They gestured threateningly with their automatic rifles in our direction until we pulled to a complete stop, then demanded to see our passports. Only when they were convinced we were American citizens, did they wave us on.

Jackson paid the driver. As the cab pulled away, I turned to Jackson. "It must be very difficult for our people to operate here," I said. "Those military police control who enters and leaves the embassy."

"It's even worse than that," he replied. "Bokasa has a first rate secret police, which was trained by the Soviets. Those food stalls on the street across from the embassy and the trucks parked next to them all belong to the secret police. They follow any embassy officer or embassy vehicle to see where it is going and with whom embassy personnel meet."

I inwardly shuddered. If I were a betting man, I thought, I'd lay odds that the details of Project Venus were already known to the Bokasa secret police.

Still carrying our suitcases, we entered the embassy, where we were carefully scrutinized by the armed American Marine guard. As I waited by our bags with Jackson, Barnes approached the desk of the receptionist and said in English, "Please tell me Mr. Hardesty that Mr. Peterson, Mr. Lockwood and Mr. Smith are here to see him. "

The receptionist, clearly a native of Bokasa, picked up the phone and repeated in colloquial American English what Barnes had told her. Barnes noted my amazement. "She was educated by American missionaries," he explained.

Before I could reply, a man in his mid thirties descended the staircase to the lobby and approached us. Shaking first my hand, and then Jackson's and Barnes', he said, "I hope you had no difficulty in reaching the embassy. Please follow me."

Reaching the second floor, he turned to me and said," I hope you don't mind sir. Our offices are on the third floor. That way, we can control our access better. Can I help you with your suitcase?"

"Thanks, no." I replied. "The exercise is welcome after our flight."

Reaching the third floor, the man led us to a heavy metal door. Pressing a series of numbered keys on a combination lock, he opened it and we entered a large room, dominated by a mahogany conference table. He carefully closed the metal door, then turned to us.

"Please make yourselves comfortable," he said. "Can I get you something to eat or drink?"

We sat down at the table and Jackson turned to me. "This is Paul Hardesty," he said. "Our Station Chief in St. Henri." Turning to Hardesty, he said, "This is the Director."

Hardesty shook hands with me again. "I apologize for not introducing myself to you in the lobby," he explained. "The receptionist works for the secret police, and I didn't want her to get wind of your identity."

"That's quite all right," I answered, smiling. I was favorably impressed by Hardesty's quickness of mind. I could understand how, despite his relative youth, he had been assigned as Chief of Station in St. Henri.

Jackson accepted Hardesty's offer of a cup of coffee and I did the same. Jackson said, "I didn't know the receptionist worked for the secret police. When did you find out?"

"About two months ago, since your last visit. Fortunately, I don't think we ever mentioned anything about Project Venus in her presence."

Jackson and Barnes visibly relaxed. "That's a relief," Jackson said. He turned to me. "Paul's one of the sharpest officers we have in the DO."

"I can see that," I replied.

Hardesty looked pleased. "Would you like me to brief you on the status of Project Venus?"

"In a few minutes, I answered. "First, have you received any messages addressed to me which are time sensitive?"

"We have two addressed to you. Neither has a priority classification."

Hardesty's reply left me relieved. I had harbored a deep fear that despite my strict instructions, Churchill might have found himself unable to resist a direct order from the President to launch Project Venus. Apparently at the Washington end Project Venus was still in the deep limbo I had placed it.

"Good," I said. "Paul, please go ahead with your briefing."

Hardesty's presentation generally adhered to what Churchill had told me back in Washington. The only significant change was that Colonel Tsombi, the Air Force Commander had agreed to back General Buta's coup group.

"Does that mean" I asked him, "That we can count on the Air Force to knock out the tanks belonging to Ngola's bodyguard battalion?"

"I'm afraid not, Hardesty answered. "Tsombi does not have access to the Air Force ammunition or bombs. They are controlled by the Air Force Chief of Staff, who is loyal to Ngola. The planes can buzz targets on the ground, but not attack them. Their involvement would be purely psychological."

"Paul," I said. "What would you say realistically, are the chances that Project Venus will be successful?"

"I think there's a reasonably chance it will work."

"Can you make a quantitative judgment?"

He thought for a moment. "I would say it's close to a fifty-fifty proposition."

"In other words, there is about a fifty percent chance that it will fail?"

"Yes sir," he admitted.

"Let me put it this way," I said. "If Project Venus is successful, I will promote you on the spot. If it fails, I wil immediately fire you. If you recommend it be delayed, it will have no impact on your career, either negatively or positively. Shall we go ahead with it?"

Hardesty, Jackson and Barnes stared at me in amazement. Hardesty swallowed hard. An embarrassing silence followed. Hardesty looked desperately at Jackson for guidance.

Before he could answer, I said, "Relax, Paul. That was an unfair question. The responsibility for deciding to go ahead with Project Venus is mine alone. I have no intention of risking CIA's reputation, not to say the effectiveness of United States foreign policy around the world on any such venture when there is such a significant chance of failure."

Hardesty smiled with relief. Then his smile faded. "You know, sir," he said, Ambassador Summerville is a strong supporter of Project Venus. He threw me out of his office when I tried to explain to him that we couldn't guarantee success."

"Thanks for telling me," I said. I had worried about having trouble with Summerville. He was a career diplomat, reportedly one of the best. Studying everything I could find about the man and his career, I had been surprised that someone of his ability had been assigned to the relatively unimportant embassy in Bokasa. Reading between the lines, I suspected he must have angered someone powerful in the upper levels of the State Department.

"Can you arrange for me to meet with General Ngola?" I asked Hardesty.

"I'm sorry sir. Ambassador Summerville personally handles all contacts with the President. He cut off my contacts about six months ago, when the criticism of Ngola in the US started. I could try, but I don't think I would be successful. If the Ambassador learned I had flouted his order, he would probably order me home."

"I understand," I said. "Please tell the Ambassador I want to see him."

Hardesty pick up a phone and dialed the Ambassador's extension. "Mr. Ambassador," he said after he had identified himself, "There's something new on Project Venus. Could you meet me in the vault, please."

When hardest hung up, I asked him how long he had been assigned to the Station. "About twenty-six months, sir" he answered. "My two-year tour was up two months ago, but I was asked to stay on to handle Project Venus."

Jackson inquired about Hardesty's wife and children. I gathered from Hardesty's response that they had not accompanied him on his Bokasa assignment, remaining in the US because there was no adequate schooling for his children in St. Henri.

I was about to inquire further about the morale of the Agency personnel in Bokasa when the vault door swung open and two men entered. I recognized the first as Ambassador Summerville. I stood up and extended my hand.

"Mr. Ambassador," I said. "I am Mel Shultz, Director of CIA. This is Phil Jackson, the Chief of our Africa Division and

Ed Barnes, our Bokasa Desk Chief" I added, introducing my companions. I am here to convey an urgent message from the President to General Ngola. Can you please arrange for me to see him immediately."

"I'm afraid that is quite impossible," he said. "It is against the policy of the United States to meet with President Ngola. You should know why."

"I'm carrying an urgent message from President Porter to General Ngola. That supersedes whatever the policy may or may not be."

"I can't do that," Summerville said "Without getting the prior approval of the Secretary of State.

I knew the Ambassador to be an intelligent man. I was confident I could reason with him, but that would take time, and time was running out.

"Ambassador Summerville," I said, making my voice as hard as I could. "What the Secretary of State thinks is immaterial to me. You probably have heard me described as the man who put President Porter into the White House. That's true. The reason the Secretary of State is in his office is that when the President asked me whom I wanted to put in, I told him that none of my friends was interested in the job."

Summerville stared at me. "If you feel you want to call the Secretary for his permission," I continued, "Please do so. I will call the White House and tell the President that his personal message to President Ngola is being delayed by you and that I strongly recommend you be replaced. Do I make myself clear?"

Jackson, Barnes, Hardesty and the man who had accompanied the Ambassador all stared at me. Summerville flushed crimson, swallowed and said, "Mr. Shultz, of course I have no wish to delay the President's message reaching President Ngola. "Frank," he said, turning to the man who had accompanied him, please make the arrangements for Mr. Shultz to see President Ngola at once. Please excuse me," he added, standing and leaving the vault.

Hardesty turned to me. "This is Frank Wilson," he said, introducing me to the man who had accompanied the Ambassador. "He is the Political Counselor."

"Mr. Wilson," I said, shaking hands with him. "I would be grateful if you could arrange for me to see General Ngola as soon as possible. Tell him that Mr. Smith is here to see him with an urgent message from the President of the United States. Use those exact words!"

Wilson picked up the phone and dialed the number. He spoke first in French, then in a native dialect, before hanging up. General Ngola's not at the Presidential Palace," he said. "They suggested I try to reach him at the Defense Ministry."

Wilson's second call was more successful. When he hung up, Wilson told me, "President Ngola has agreed to see you in three hours at the Defense Ministry. Would you like me to arrange for an embassy driver to take you?"

"I would appreciate that," I said.

"Jackson, Barnes, Hardesty and I left the vault. I turned to Hardesty and said in a low voice so that only he and Jackson could hear, "I think you two ought to stay here to handle things from this end. Remember, no action on Project Venus of any kind until I return!"

"I understand sir," Hardesty said. "I'll do my best to carry out your orders. However, I may not be able to stop the Ambassador."

"If you can't stop it, do what you can to delay it!" I said. I shook hands with Hardesty, who left. Before accompanying him, Jackson approached me and said in the same low voice I had used, "Paul will do his best. If he can't stop the Ambassador, no one can."

"I'm sure of that."

"Mr. Shultz," he added, "I didn't realize that you were carrying a message from the President to Ngola."

"I'm not," I relied. "It was the only pretext I could think of that would persuade the Ambassador to arrange for me to meet with General Ngola."

"Wasn't that awfully risky? Suppose Ambassador Summerville had called your bluff?"

"I didn't think he would. Besides, if he had, I thought I could persuade the President to say he had. In any event, there was no other way. I had to take the risk."

Jackson said, "I would like to go along with you for the ride. You've certainly got balls. I never thought I'd say it, but I think you were the best choice to take over the Agency."

"Thanks, Phil, "I said. "I appreciate that. But there's too much chance I'll go down in flames. I don't want that to happen to you. I'll fill you in on all the gory details when I get back."

Jackson, Barnes and I went into the embassy snack bar. We had not had a real breakfast or lunch And God knew when I might get dinner. I ordered a hamburger and was glad to see I could also get a beer. After lunch, I got a brilliant thought and went upstairs to the Ambassador's office. I told his secretary I wished to speak with the Ambassador and was promptly admitted.

"Mr. Ambassador," I said. "I think it would be a good idea for the two of us to have a little talk. Can I invite you to join me for a walk around the Embassy compound?" He thought for a minute, then nodded his agreement. He removed his suit jacket, put on a hat with a large brim to shield his face from the sun, and we went outside."

Fortunately, large trees shaded much of the compound,

shielding us from the sun. Under the shade of one particularly large tree, I stopped and turned to Summerville. "Mr. Ambassador," I said. "May I ask you a blunt question?"

He stared at me. "Shoot." He said. It seemed most uncharacteristic from someone whom I had taken to be a starchy Ambassador.

"Do you think we ought to launch the coup against Ngola?"

He thought for a minute, then smiled. "You know," he said, "That's the first time anyone has ever asked me that question."

It was my turn to look surprised. He continued, "I am a career diplomat. It's my job to loyally serve whatever administration is in office in Washington. Before this assignment, I made the mistake of volunteering to the State Department that I thought the policy they were following was wrong. As you can imagine, you don't make friends as an ambassador telling the State Department they are wrong. It's even worse when it turns out that you were right and they were wrong. It's something that kills your career every time. I was very fortunate to be able to get this assignment to Bokasa after that, even though Bokasa is a far less important post than my last one. Naturally, I have not volunteered my thoughts to anyone about the wisdom of Project Venus."

"Whatever you say, stops with me," I said. "What do you really think?"

"President Ngola has a dismal record in the area of human rights," he declared thoughtfully. "I can understand the pressures that have built up in Washington to remove him and why the State Department is anxious for the US to take the lead. He's killed hundreds of political opponents; thousands of others have either disappeared or are imprisoned in really awful prisons. There basically are no human rights in Bokasa. Any sign of potential opposition is ruthlessly surpressed by the secret police."

"How is his behavior in other areas?" I asked. "What is his basic attitude toward the US?"

"He is not hostile to the US," Summerville said, "except insofar as he suspects we may be involved in plotting against him. Before we started criticizing him in Washington, he was most cooperative in supporting American policy with regard to Russia, China, and the Middle East. Ngola, in fact, studied at a U.S. Military staff college for a year and the old military attaché reports describe him as pro-American. The regime also gets along well with the large American mining complex in the northern part of Bokasa."

"What do you think the chances are for Project Venus to be successful?" I pressed on.

"That's really more your area of expertise than mine," the Ambassador stated. "But if we try it and it fails, I can predict with absolute certainty what his reaction will be. He will do anything and everything he can to hurt the United States for as long as he is in power. We will have created a very dangerous and very shrewd enemy in this part of the world."

"May I now ask you a question?" he asked. "Can you give me some inkling of the contents of the message the President wishes you to convey to Ngola?"

"I looked at him. "There is no message."

He stared at me. "No message?"

"None,"

"But what then are you doing?"

"Mr. Ambassador," I said. "Let me be as honest with you as you have been with me. Everything I said about my putting Porter into the White House is true. I did it, and now realize I made a horrible mistake. He is so incompetent that he can cause immeasurable harm to the US. And all the damage he does will be entirely my fault. I have to prevent it from happening."

"But what will you tell Ngola?"

"Simple. I will tell him whatever I have to in order to kill Project Venus once and for all. I believe I can convince him to ease up in the human rights area to the extent necessary to prevent the coup.

Summerville looked stunned. "What you are doing sounds illegal. You could very well end up serving time in a federal penitentiary."

"I've tried to avoid doing anything actually illegal," I said. "Of course, I'm no lawyer. But I have no choice. I have to do it. I've always been lucky all my life. I keep in mind what a close friend told me years ago, when I was a young cub reporter in Washington. He said God looks after fools, idiots and Mel Shultz. I can only hope God still feels that some way toward me."

"Mr. Ambassador," I went on. "I'd like you to accompany me to the Defense Ministry and introduce me to Ngola as 'Mr. Smith,' the barer of a private message to him from President Porter. I will then state that it is for Ngolas's ears alone and ask you all to leave. I am hoping that when you and Hardesty do, he will agree to all his people leaving too. That way, hopefully, no one but me will be hurt if this all ends in disaster."

"Are you certain you really want to do this?"

"I don't want to, but I have to," I replied. "My own analysis is that Project Venus has a less than forty percent chance of succeeding. When we are heading back in the car, I will fill you in on everything that went on in my meeting with Ngola. But you can't be with me when I deliver my message, for your own good. If I succeed in killing the coup, I will have brought down on myself the eternal enmity of the President of the United States. If I fail, it will be much worse. You, yourself, gave an excellent analysis of what Ngola will do if the coup is attempted and fails."

Summerville said no more. We walked together silently back

into the embassy and to his office. I read some late copies of the "New York Times" in his outer office as he returned to his official work. When the time came for us to depart, the Ambassador, Hardesty and I left the embassy and got into the Ambassador's limo. The air conditioning made the interior quite pleasant and the seats were quite comfortable. The Ambassador and I sat in the rear, Hardesty in front with the driver.

"You are going to the Defense Ministry?" the driver said in passably good English.

I gathered he assumed it was a rhetorical question as he drove off without waiting for a reply. We passed through the embassy gate. The military police on duty scrutinized our departure but did not order the car to stop, either because of the diplomatic license plates or because they recognized it as the Ambassador's official vehicle. We turned on to a broad boulevard different from the one our taxi had taken to the embassy and drove into a newer section of town.

Here and there we passed some modern buildings, some as high as six stories. Noticing me looking at them, the Ambassador said, "Those buildings are deserted. The elevators don't work and you have to walk up the stairs."

The one relatively recent movie theater we passed was showing an American film more than a dozen years old. Next to it were several modern stores, closed and shuttered. The only indications of economic vitality I saw were the street stalls piled high with a wide range of delicious looking tropical fruits. Despite their other ills, St. Henri's residents appeared in little danger of suffering from a lack of food.

After almost ten minutes, the limo turned onto a smaller road lined with stucco buildings similar to those I had seen in the 'New Quarter.' At the end of the street was a large walled compounded, guarded by military police. "That's the Defense Ministry," the driver said, pointing to it.

The military police stopped our car and carefully checked my passport and Hardesty's. They then peered into the interior of the car, although they did not require the Ambassador to show his identification, apparently recognizing him. After requiring the driver to open the trunk of the limo for inspection, they waved us into the compound.

Inside was a large, two story building, with covered porches running the length of both floors. The approach to the entrance was guarded by two heavy tanks, their gun barrels pointing in the direction of the gate we had just entered. It was clear that Ngola was taking no chances of any unwelcome visitors getting close to the building.

The limo passed the tanks and stopped at the entrance under a large portico. As we got out of the vehicle, a young army officer stepped forward and saluted. The other Bokasa military personnel I had seen had been dressed in floppy fatigues. This officer, however, was wearing a sharply tailored, pressed summer dress uniform.

"How do you do, your Excellency," he said in good English. "Please follow me." I am Colonel Mubaki, General Ngola's aide."

The Colonel led us into the building. As we entered, the military police on each side snapped to attention.

The interior of the Defense Ministry had been decorated in late Victorian style. The ceiling was high, with large fans circulating. We ascended an ornate marble staircase to the second floor, passing several well-dressed officers, and into a large office. Seated behind an impressive wooden desk was General Ngola, President of Bokasa.

Colonel Mubaki snapped to attention and saluted the General. I was surprised to see that Ngola was wearing jungle-colored fatigues rather than the summer dress uniform of the other officers I had seen in the Defense Ministry. He looked like someone who had interrupted himself from a long day's arduous work to handle an emergency situation. Seated slightly behind him were two other officials. Summerville whispered to me that one was the Foreign Minister and the other the Minister of Internal Affairs.

Ngola returned the Colonel's salute and invited us to sit. As we did so he looked at the Ambassador.

"To what do I owe the honor of your visit?" he asked the Ambassador. He spoke in French, but so slowly and distinctly, I could understand his words."

Ambassador Summerville turned to me. "May I introduce," he said, "The Honorable Mr. Smith, the representative of the President of the United States. He carries with him a most important message to you from President Porter."

I stood and bowed. "President Ngola," I said most formally. "The message I carry is very sensitive and for your ears alone. May I ask you the privilege of speaking with you, alone."

Following my cue, Summerville and Hardesty stood and walked toward the door. Ngola motioned and the Foreign Minister and Interior Minister stood and likewise exited. I was left in the room with General Ngola and his interpreter.

"Mr. President," I said. "It's preferable that your interpreter also leave. I think we can discuss President Porter's message better if there are just the two of us in the room. When the interpreter finished, Ngola said something in a native dialect and the interpreter also left the room. Ngola and I faced each other across the desk. A smile appeared on his lean face, and I thought it was more of a leer.

"Just what is your message, Mr. Smith, or should I say Mr. Shultz? I know you are the Director of the CIA. You were spotted this morning when you got out of the Air France plane. It's a shame you didn't identify yourself at the airport. I would have arranged for an appropriate reception. You could have inspected my troops."

I realized that in Nogola, I was dealing with an extremely intelligent and competent opponent.

As I thought of what to say, he switched from French into a rather precise English and continued. "What is your President's private message to me? Does he wish to beg my forgiveness for attempting a coup against me? Does he wish to ask me to pardon General Buta? I'm afraid it's a bit too late. I have to tell you that General Buta was arrested and questioned this afternoon. He admitted his involvement in your little scheme and has been executed for treason."

I burst out laughing. "Come now, General," I said. "You must be joking. Do you think I am so stupid as to support a coup against you by Buta? A coup headed by a Christian from an unimportant, minority tribe, who has no access to munitions for his weapons? We knew all about Buta's pathetic little plot and allowed it to proceed to attract your attention. The real plot against you is headed by a Moslem officer from your own tribe and includes officers who have ready access to munitions."

The expression on Ngola's face changed to one of fury. He reached automatically for the revolver holstered on his hip and I thought he might shoot me on the spot.

"'General Ngola," I went on. "There is no message from President Porter. I said there was to be able to speak with you privately. I am here in St. Henri to direct the military coup against you. Unless I order it stopped, by tomorrow you will be dead or hiding in one of the foreign embassies, begging to be allowed to flee the country. Understand General, only I can stop the coup.

Now listen carefully to every word I say!"

"You know that I am the person who put President Porter into the White House. I personally oppose the coup. It is being ordered by President Porter. He and the elites in my country detest the treatment of your political opponents. They claim it is sufficient reason to remove you from power, by force if necessary. You are doubtless aware of the powerful campaign in my country accusing you of all manner of human rights violations. In Washington, the elites think we have the obligation to force every nation in the world to adhere to our views of what is correct."

"What business is it of yours how I govern Bokasa?" Ngola angrily demanded. "Many countries are run the same way. If I am overthrown, do you believe my successor will establish democracy here?"

"Of course not general. But it is easier for my government to seem to do something for democracy in Bokasa than someplace else in the world, where we have more important political or economic interests. A coup here would allow the President to avoid angering more important governments, such as China or Russia by insisting they become democracies."

"Personally," I went on, "I don't give a damn how you treat your opponents. That's your business. But it concerns me when your treatment of them creates so much pressure in Washington that I am forced to organize a coup against you. I don't wish to do so because, frankly, I think it will be easier for me to work with you that with anyone else I might put in power to replace you. But to stop the coup, you must do exactly as I say. I have some power over President Porter, but I cannot stop the coup without your help."

Ngola continued to stare at me. I could see his intelligent eyes, boring into mine. He was carefully considering everything I had told him, but he was not yet decided what do to.

"If you wish to remain alive General, to say nothing of remaining in power, you will immediately do what I tell you. You will summon all foreign journalists and television crews in St. Henri to the Presidential Palace. There you will address them. As befits your new status as a democratic leader, you will be wearing civilian clothes. Pointing to a portrait of George Washington, you will say that Washington, Lincoln and Franklin Roosevelt were your childhood heroes and you have long wanted to establish a democratic government for Bokasa, with a written constitution patterned after that of the United States. You will announce a full amnesty for all political prisoners and the holding of free elections within three months."

Ngola practically laughed in my face. "You are a fool" He said, "And so is your President! Do you really expect me to do all that? My officers would overthrow me if I spoke such nonsense!"

"No, General," I answered. "They will cheer you because you will explain to them first that as a self-proclaimed democracy, Bokasa will be given billions of dollars in aid from the US, the World Bank and other foreign benefactors. A good part of this will end up in their own pockets. You will also receive the latest weapons in military assistance. Think of how pleased they will be to receive modern tanks, jet fighters and other equipment."

"How do I retain power if I give my opponents a chance to throw me out?"

"Very simple," I said. "What you do is not important. What counts is the perception in the US of what you do. For example, take the political amnesty and the release of all political prisoners. How many political prisoners do you actually have in jail, say five thousand?"

He nodded agreement. "Most of them," I explained, "are probably unimportant individuals, constituting no real threat to you. You can always charge the most important opponents with criminal crimes, such as bribery or embezzlement. They naturally would not be political prisoners but criminal prisoners and you could continue to hold them. If any of those you release are considered a threat, you can have your security police carefully monitor their activities. My advice would be to offer good jobs and good salaries to those you release. That way you turn them into supporters. It's expensive, but you will more than make up your costs from the foreign aid you will receive from the US."

"That makes sense," he said. But what about the free elections?"

"That also is easy. As a democrat, you naturally want to allow your people to participate in drawing up the new constitution. There has to be an election for the drafters of the constitution. Permit a free election. It will do you no harm. Most of the people who could vote in Bokasa live in the interior. They will vote as directed by their tribal chiefs. All you have to do is increase the subsidies you already give the tribal chiefs and tell them how you want the voting in their areas to go and whom you want elected."

"When the constitution is finally drafted," I went on, "you will give the voters an opportunity to vote on it. A suitable time has to be given for campaigning. Then once it has been approved, there have to be elections for the new National Assembly. I would suggest you allow free elections in St. Henri. Even if all the deputies elected here oppose you, they will be a small force in the National Assembly dominated by deputies elected by voters obeying their tribal chiefs. In fact, it's helpful to allow some expression of opposition in the National Assembly to act as a safety valve, helping to reduce the likelihood of the opposition taking to the streets."

"Finally," I said, "Have you ever read the American Constitution? It gives the President almost as much power as you have now. The President is Commander-in-Chief and approves the appointment of all the senior military commanders, names the Cabinet, including the Attorney General, and the heads of the intelligence and security services. He doles out money to buy people and votes. If the American President uses his power intelligently, he is virtually unbeatable in any election, no matter how free."

"And if I agree to follow your suggestions, you will stop the coup effort?"

"Of course."

"And you will start the financial and military aid to me?"

"We will start aid quickly," I answered, "But not at once. It takes several months to set up the the required procedures and programs. However, I promise I will do my best to start it sooner rather than later. I may have a limited amount of cash available in the CIA that I can send you until the other government agencies begin their delivery of aid."

"All right," he said. "I accept your deal."

"You have made a wise decision, General," I answered. "I'll write down some notes for you to use in your conference with the foreign diplomats and the media. Since my French is not quite up to it, can you have Colonel Mubaki assist me and translate my notes into French."

"Of course," Ngola answered. He summoned Mubaki into the room and instructed him to work with me on preparing the notes for his presentation. The Colonel's competence and knowledge of English were obvious in the efficiency with which he worked with me. In a few minutes, the task was complete and I showed Ngola the draft.

I held my breath until he finished reading it and signified his approval. As we shook hands prior to my departure, he smiled. "Since I have agreed to everything you suggested, you will have no objection to telling me which of my officers were involved in preparing the coup against me."

Smiling in return, I said, "You have an excellent sense of humor Mr. President. I'm sure that if our positions were reversed, you would not reveal to me who was involved in the plot."

Ngola laughed. "No, Mr. Shultz," he said. "I most certainly would not."

Colonel Mubaki escorted me to the next room, in which Ambassador Summerville and Hardesty were nervously waiting. I flashed them a big smile and a wink, but said nothing. As we said goodbye to Mubaki and entered the limo, I quietly whispered to the Ambassador, "Everything went well." I gestured in the direction of the driver. "It's better that I fill you in when we get back to the embassy."

The return trip to the embassy seemed much shorter than it had when we left it to see Ngola. I felt much more relaxed now that I no longer had to worry about the coup. Of course, I could not relax completely until General Ngola actually announced the moves he had agreed to.

Back at the embassy, we entered the vault, accompanied by Jackson, Barnes and Wilson. I quickly summarized the steps Ngola had agreed to announce. I avoided going into the details of the discussion I had with Ngola about how he could avoid any problems in actaully implementing the measures he was announcing. They all agreed that if he carried out the deal, we had achieved a major triumph, particularly in view of General Bata's arrest and execution.

Our meeting was interrupted by the phone ringing. Wilson picked up, listened for a minute, then smiled. "The Foreign Ministry has just invited Ambassador Summerville to a meeting of the diplomatic corps at the Presidential Palace," he said. "It sounds as though Ngola is carrying out his part of the deal."

Summerville and Wilson left the vault to prepare for the Ambassador's trip to the meeting of the diplomatic corps. I took the opportunity to inform Hardesty, Jackson and Barnes of Ngola's apparent complete knowledge of the coup plot against him. It was probably too late to warn other coup plotters with whom the Station had been in contact, but Hardesty felt obliged to try. I also told him of the ability of Colonel Mubaki and suggested that the Station try its best to recruit him as an agent.

I then left the vault and went to the Ambassador's office. "If you have a minute to spare," I said, "I'll fill you in on went on in my private meeting with General Ngola." After cautioning him that it was all off the record," I gave him a rather full account.

"Is there anything I can tell the State Department officially?" he asked.

"Nothing of what I have just told you," I replied. "But you can inform them that President Ngola revealed he was fully aware of the planned coup against him and of General Buta's leading role in it. He stated that Buta had been arrested and questioned thoroughly, had revealed all of the plot details in his confession and had been executed for treason. Add that Ngola stated he was announcing the adoption of an American-style democracy for Bokasa and a complete amnesty for all political prisoners as proof of his desire to cooperate fully with the US across the full range of political, economic and military affairs. He expects Bokasa to be added to the list of friendly nations receiving appropriate American and international economic assistance. If you feel you can, and here I can't really advise you, you can recommend that Washington provide such aid to insure Bokasa's more rapid progress toward full democracy."

Ambassador Summerville whistled as I told this. "I don't know how far I can go in that recommendation, without permanently finishing off my career in the State Department. Secretary Ashby, to say nothing of the President, will probably be furious. I'll do what I can. In any event, it's been a real privilege to see you in operation, Mr. Shultz. Goodbye and God speed."

When the Ambassador headed off to the meeting of the diplomatic corps, I got hold of Hardesty and told him I would like to leave St. Henri to return to Washington as soon as possible. He spoke to Wilson, and reported there were no flights to Dakar until late the following day. However, he had arranged with Wilson for the Embassy Air Attaché to fly us to Dakar on his plane, so that we could catch an Air France flight to Paris. Jackson, Barnes and I said goodbye to Hardesty and entered the small aircraft.

The trip by to Washington was relatively pleasant. We were all in good spirits as a result of the success of our visit to Bokasa. I found Jackson a fascinating travel companion as he regaled me with anecdotes from his long years as an Agency operative overseas. We arrived in Dakar just in time to catch the Air France flight to Paris. En route to Paris, I enjoyed the especially tasty meal we were served, which combined French and spicy African dishes to perfection.

I had feared a long layover in Paris. However, we were successful in switching our tickets to take a direct flight to Washington, rather than returning by way of New York. The change required us to travel tourist class, which I considered worthwhile as it permitted us to arrive home earlier. Although the discomfort I had felt from the inoculations had disappeared, I was very tired and anxious to get a good night's sleep in my own bed.

Back in Washington, I said goodbye to Jackson and Barnes and we got into separate cabs. They were on his way to their homes in Maryland and I back to my condo in Virginia. I was so tired, I almost fell asleep in the taxi. Arriving at my building, I fumbled trying to get my key into the door lock. I was grateful when the door opened and I found myself looking at Fred's face, which broke into a heartwarming smile.

"Welcome home, Mr. Shultz," she said. "Can I make you something to eat?"

"No thanks," I answered. "I ate on the plane. But can you make me some hot cocoa."

She went into the kitchen to make my cocoa and I carried my suitcase into the bedroom. There I found Pergamon, her back to me, getting dressed. I tiptoed up to her and kissed her gently on the neck.

Surprised, she twisted around. "Oh, it's you, Melvin," she said. "Hurry up and get dressed. We're going to dinner at Senator Watson's. The President and Tammy will be there."

"I'm afraid not," I answered. "I'm exhausted. Why don't you tell them you can't make it and stay home, too? I'd love to curl up in bed with you."

"It's just like you not to go anyplace," she snapped at me. "You go off to Paris and claim you're too tired to go out to Georgetown. Other people go to Paris and relax."

I was about to reply in the same nasty fashion when I caught myself. I had told Pergamon only that I was flying to Paris, omitting any mention of my going on to Bokasa.

"I'm sorry," I said softly. "Something came up while I was in Paris and I had to go to Africa. You go the party and enjoy yourself. I'm really too tired."

Pergamon's critical expression did not change, but at least my answer served to avoid further argument. She dressed, permitted me a brief goodnight kiss on her cheek, and left to go to the party. I gratefully accepted the cup of hot cocoa from Fred, took a hot bath, and got into bed to watch a western movie on TV. The cocoa had relaxed me and the hot bath still more so. I planned to have another cup of cocoa when the movie was over, but instead dozed off.

CHAPTER 9

When I awakened, it was early morning. I found the TV turned off and Pergamon sleeping next to me in bed. I got up quietly so as not to wake her, shaved and dressed, and had my usual light breakfast. As I ate, I realized I had forgotten to make arrangements for the limo to pick me up. Rather than try to do so now, I decided to drive myself in the Buick.

To avoid arguments with Pergamon, I had rented a space for my car in the underground condo garage as far from Pergamon's BMW as possible. I had not driven it for several weeks, and I wondered as I got in whether the battery was still capable of starting the car. To my relief, the engine started at the first try, filling me with a sense of gratitude toward my old Buick. However disreputable it looked, it never let me down.

I drove along the George Washington Parkway on my way to the Agency. The Potomac River, I thought, had never looked lovelier. I found myself singing out loud one of my favorites, the judge's song from Gilbert and Sullivan's "Trial By Jury," something I did only when I was very happy. I turned into the CIA compound and was stopped by the guard. He asked to see my identification badge authorizing me to enter the closed area. This was a unique experience for me. My chauffeur-driven limo had always been waved through by the guards without stopping.

The guard carefully examined my photo on the badge to insure that I was really the individual driving the car. He then scrutinized the Buick before waving me on. He had not recognized me as the Director of the Agency. I wondered what he would have thought if he had realized who it was driving the old, beaten up car.

I didn't think I could park the Buick in the underground garage where the Director's limo was parked. Instead, I drove to the furthest parking area, where the spaces were not reserved, and parked the Buick there. It was still so early that I encountered no one else as I walked to the entrance, showed my pass to the guard, and took the elevator to my floor.

The Director's suite was empty except for the night file clerk, who looked up from her work as I entered the office. I had not met her before and she did not recognize me.

"Could I have the traffic for the Director, please," I asked. "I'm Melvin Shultz." At the same time, I showed her my driver's license as identification.

She jumped up, embarrassed, "I'm sorry, sir." She said. "I didn't recognize you."

"That's quite all right," I answered. "I'm back from my trip. Please tell Mr. Churchill as soon as he arrives."

She handed me a bundle of traffic, as well as my copies of the morning newspapers. I walked into my office and sat down at the desk. It felt good to be back. I was halfway through the pile when there was a knock at my door and Tom Churchill entered a big smile on his face.

"Welcome back!" he said, sounding as though he really meant

it. "I've never been so glad to see anyone in my life!"

"It's good to be back," I answered. "I didn't realize you'd miss me that much."

He looked a bit sheepish. "Of course I'm very glad to have you back," he said, "But what I really was referring to were the calls from the Secretary of State and the White House demanding to know why the start of Project Venus was being delayed. That excuse about waiting for proper weather did not satisfy them for long. I was afraid I would get a direct order from the President to begin the operation, and I was uncertain whether I could deliberately ignore it. Until General Ngola made his announcement, I was dodging calls from everyone outside the Agency, with our office saying I was not there."

"Tell me," he asked, "How did you persuade Ngola to shift his policies so radically."

I gave Churchill a detailed account of my meeting with General Ngola. "Good Lord," he said, "You really took some risk."

"I had to," I answered. "I had no other choice. Fortunately, it all worked out."

Churchill briefed me on the other important matters that had come up during my absence, and how he handled them. I agreed with his decisions, and praised him for the excellent job he had done in my absence. He left my office and I returned to my reading when there was another knock on the door and Ann and Don Collins entered. They both expressed pleasure at my safe return. We had some friendly conversation before they left to get about their work.

I settled into my regular routine as Director, but I felt very uneasy. I heard nothing from the White House or from the Secretary of State about my successful effort to torpedo Project Venus. My call to the White House to set up a meeting with Buck to speak with him about it elicited the response that his calendar was very full and that I could have an appointment only if something truly urgent had come up. The next regularly scheduled Cabinet meeting, after which I hoped to be able to talk to him for a minute or two, was cancelled at the last minute.

The one favorable event during this period was my briefing of the Senate Intelligence Committee. I did not go into detail concerning Bokasa in my meeting with the committee members, but did so in a private conversation with Senator Manley. He expressed great pleasure in the termination of the coup preparations, and was more pleasant to me than in any of our previous meetings.

On the personal side, things at home were going reasonably well. Pergamon remained transfixed by her involvement in Washington social life, particularly her almost daily association with Tammy and the ladies of her court. This was not something I liked. However, it had the advantage of keeping Pergamon occupied. Our relations were only slightly better than they had been in recent years in Watsonville, but at least she was no longer nagging me daily about Lust Cosmetics and its advertising.

The first meeting of the National Security Council after my return from Bokasa was on the subject of the Middle East. I arrived early, hoping for a chance to speak with Buck privately about Project Venus before the meeting. He arrived after the other participants were already there, and so I had no opportunity to raise the subject with him. I did provide an intelligence briefing of the latest events in the Middle East.

I then quickly interjected some comments about Bokasa, noting President Ngola's discovery of a planned military coup against him and his decisive move to transform his nation into a parliamentary democracy. Secretary of State Ashby looked sourly at me, but said nothing. Buck commented that the United States had unfortunately lost an unparalleled opportunity to spread democracy in West Africa and then moved quickly back to the subject of the Middle East.

When the meeting was over, I went up to him and said quietly, "You are aware that Ngola knew all about Project Venus and our involvement in it. He had already arrested General Buta and forced him to divulge all of the details. He had all his forces ready to crush it brutally. If we had gone ahead with it under those circumstances, it would have been a failure worse than the Bay of Pigs.

Buck looked sulkily at me. I did not think I had convinced him. "Tammy thinks we made a serious mistake in not going ahead with it. She is sure we would have prevailed."

"I was on the spot," I said. "Tammy was not. If she had been, she would have agreed with me."

He nodded as though he could appreciate that argument. He then changed the subject to ask me to arrange for a firm owned by one of his old Oklahoma City supporters to receive a contract the Agency was letting for the purchase of some new equipment.

What remained of my complacency was shattered late one afternoon, as I was getting ready to go home. Ann entered my office with a worried look on her face. "Alice Kramer called," she said. "The President wants to see you at 6 p.m."

Alice Kramer was Buck's secretary. A call from her was the equivalent of a direct call from the President. I was puzzled. I knew of nothing that would warrant such a sudden invitation, or rather command to see him.

"Did she say what it was all about?"

"Alice didn't say. When I asked her, she said it was something he wanted to take up with you personally."

I thanked Ann and asked her to arrange for my limo to take me immediately to the White House. After she left, I gathered several documents dealing with matters which might conceivably have sparked Buck's interest. None seemed of sufficient importance to require an immediate meeting, but it was hard to tell with Buck. I opened my personal safe and removed the attaché case I normally used when I was carrying highly classified documents. It was not only secured by a small combination lock, but also had a secret compartment in its base. I had found the compartment extremely useful for concealing documents I considered the most sensitive. I put some material into that compartment and closed the case.

Rather than taking time to read the materials I was taking which might have been the subject of the President's summons, I went straight down to the limo and started off on the trip to the White House. I dislike arriving to any appointment and make it a point to leave early enough to have a substantial margin of time to cover any unexpected delays en route.

Riding along the George Washington Parkway, I chose to enjoy the scenery rather than attempting to read the documents. The Director's limo was equipped with a reading light and portable desk. However, reading in a moving vehicle frequently gives me a headache.

As I expected, when the limo dropped me off at the White House, I reached the President's office early. Alice Kramer, the gatekeeper to the Oval Office, looked up as I approached her desk. She was about thirty-five and reasonably attractive. A native of Oklahoma City, I had added her to Buck's campaign team at Tammy's insistence shortly after the New York primary. Of all of the Oklahomans Tammy had inserted, Alice Kramer had been the most competent. Our relations had always been relatively friendly.

"Good afternoon, Alice," I greeted her. "The President's expecting me."

"Yes, Mr. Shultz," she answered. "Please have a seat and I'll inform him you are here."

I sat down, unlocked my attaché case, and quickly read the documents I had brought with me. I felt confident I could answer any questions Buck might raise. None of the problems described in them seemed to be of a nature to pique Buck's interest. The Middle East was again experiencing a minor crisis, but that was endemic to the area. The possibility that the Russian Premier might be replaced was always with us, but that would make little difference since the Russian President actually held all of the power in that country. I put the documents back in the attaché case and looked at my watch. It was 6:20 p.m.

I was becoming hungry and wondered how long I was going to have to wait. I dislike being kept waiting and on several occasions at a doctor's office have gotten up and left after waiting what I considered to be an excessive length of time. I thought it unlikely that Amy Vanderbilt had ever provided an answer to the question of how long one had to wait before walking out on an appointment with the President of the United States.

To divert myself, I picked up a magazine lying on the coffee table, an old copy of "The National Geographic." One of the articles described a trip to the Inca ruins in Peru. Peru was at the top of the list of vacation spots I was interested in visiting. Pergamon and I had discussed going there a few months before my trip to New Hampshire and my meeting with Buck there. With regret, I had deferred to Pergamon, who wanted to visit Berlin first. I could understand her interest in that city, as she had wanted to personally visit the museum in that city after which she had been named by her antiquities loving father.

As I read about Peru I thought, not for the first time, what a mistake I had made installing Buck in the White House. I had come to enjoy serving as Director of the CIA. In retrospect, however, I realized that I should have walked away from Buck in New Hampshire and never looked back. The country might have suffered from worse Presidents than Buck, but I personally could not imagine how.

By the time I had finished the article on Peru and several others of interest in the magazine, it was almost 7 p.m. I glanced at Alice Kramer, who was busy working on her computer. My patience, never good, was about exhausted. I seriously considered finding out if the sky would fall down on me if I got up and walked out of the meeting with the President.

Fortunately, at 7:13 p.m., two minutes before I planned to carry out my intention to leave, the intercom on Alice Kramer's desk buzzed and she looked up at me.

"The President will see you now," she said. I arose and walked into the Oval Office.

Buck was sitting behind his desk. I had to admit that he looked presidential. He gave me the customary grin and said, "Good evening Melvin. I'm sorry to have kept you waiting."

His use of my first name even more than being kept waiting made me realize that something was amiss. He had never referred to me by anything other than "Mr. Shultz."

I sat down and smiled back. "Good evening Buck," I said."What can I do for you?"

"You've done a marvelous job at CIA. However, I've decided to make a few changes in the administration. I'm going to accept your resignation as Director to permit you to return to running your company. Naturally, I'll make it clear in my letter accepting your resignation how pleased I am with the excellent job you've done."

I stared at him, amazed and furious at the dismissal notice I had just received from someone I regarded as my creature.

"I appreciate your praise and would appreciate such a letter," I said. "However, there's just one minor detail."

"What's that?" he asked, preparing to be gracious.

"You've forgotten. You won't be the one who decides if and when I resign. I will!"

His grin vanished. "You can't speak like that to me! I'm the President of the United States!'

"As far as I'm concerned, Buck," I said, not attempting to conceal my contempt "You're a bankrupt little cab driver who skipped to New Hampshire to escape being forced to confess in court to committing adultery."

Buck stood up and walked toward me. I had heard people who knew him in Oklahoma describe his bad temper, but I had never seen it before, myself. His face was flushed and his eyes blazing. "Get out!" he yelled at me. "I'll have you thrown out!"

"Have you discussed this with Tammy?" I said calmly.

He stopped at the mention of her name and looked at me. "Of course I have. I never do anything important without discussing it with her. She said you have no place in this administration."

I suggest you send for her," I said. "I see no reason for me to waste my time repeating to her what I'm going to tell you now."

I wondered if he would listen to me, and relaxed when he did so. He walked to the door, opened it, and said something to Alice Kramer. He then walked to the window and stood there looking out, apparently trying to regain control of himself.

Tammy entered a moment later. Her quick stride made me think she had been waiting nearby to await the outcome of my meeting with Buck.

"How nice to see you, Tammy," I said sweetly. "Would you please explain to your husband why it's impossible for him to fire me."

"I'm happy to say you're wrong," she replied. "Not only can he you. He has just done so. And it's something he should have done a long time ago."

Her satisfaction convinced me that she had orchestrated the entire affair, instructing Buck to appoint me as CIA Director in order to be able to publicly humiliate me. It certainly would explain Buck's surprise offer of the CIA job.

Tammy's hostile attitude strengthened my determination to keep my post as Agency Director. "I thought I made it clear to you in Oklahoma City," I said, "What I would do if you crossed me."

"You could pull that when Buck was a presidential candidate," she replied smugly. "Now he's President of the United States and you are out on your ear."

"I'm afraid I have to disappoint you," I said, opening up my attaché case and removing from the secret compartment one of the photos I had take from George Terrell's hotel room in Oklahoma City. It was the one showing Buck and Peggy Terrell naked in bed, with her hand on Buck's penis.

I put the photograph on Buck's desk. He started to pick it up, but Tammy grabbed it first. She stared at it, then whirled and struck him on the face. The blow was so hard that despite his size, he reeled back.

"You fool!" she shouted. "You damned fool!"

"If you ever suggest again that I resign," I said, "I'll make sure this photo is spread across the front page of every newspaper in the country and shown on every TV screen. If I have to, I'll pay them to do it, just as I paid them to support your campaign. And I'll do the same thing abroad, in Britain, France, Russia, in any nation you plan to visit."

"It won't work," Tammy said defiantly. "Nobody will believe you over the President of the United States."

Buck stood there impassively, following our conversation as Tammy and I spoke. The imprint of his hand was still visible on his face. It was clear that whatever she decided, he would go along.

"Don't flatter yourself, Tammy," I said. "You can use the facilities of the White House to attack me and the photo, but I have a lot of money and know how to use it. You'll lose. I'll hire people the same way I did to attend Buck's campaign rallies. Only this time they'll be carrying large plastic penises. I'll have them chant slogans like 'See Buck, see Buck's prick, get him out of the White House, quick, quick, quick!' Just how long do you think you'll be able to stay in the White House? Buck will be impeached before you have time to pack."

"Tammy," Buck said. "Maybe we ought to let him stay on." His voice sounded pleading. I had convinced him. His wife, however, was tougher.

"Never!" she declared. "We can win!"

"I'm afraid not," I said. "I forgot to tell you. I have sworn statements from the Terrell's that the photo is genuine."

Tammy glowered at me. I fervently hoped she would not think to check with the Terrell's and learn that only George Terrell had given me a sworn statement.

She still clutched the picture. I realized that I had stupidly never made copies of the three photos. There was nothing to stop her from tearing up the photo she had in her hand. She could order the Secret Service agents outside to search me and seize my attaché case. Without question, they would carry out her orders to destroy the other two incriminating pictures I had of Buck and Peggy Terrell.

To forestall such a move, I decided to risk everything in a bluff. I opened up the secret compartment and removed the second picture, handing it to Tammy.

"This is another good one," I said. "You can add it to your collection. Please keep them. The originals are even better. I took the precaution of leaving copies with various people I trust in places around the country. You had better pray that nothing happens to me. Because if I die or simply disappear, whatever the circumstances, they have orders to carry out my instructions to publicize the photographs and destroy you."

I turned and walked deliberately out of the Oval Office, wondering if I would be stopped by the Secret Service. To my relief, I was allowed to leave unhindered. I took the elevator and walked to where the limo was waiting for me, and told the driver to take me home. In my attaché case was the one remaining incriminating photo I had of Buck and Peggy Terrell. I hoped I would never have to use it.

On the ride home, I felt my stomach tied up in knots and I had a splitting headache. It was the tension of having wrestled in the mud with Buck and Tammy. It's astonishing how strong the prestige is of the President is in your mind that it takes so much will power to actually oppose him, even if the President is a clod like Buck Porter.

Entering my apartment, I was surprised to find Pergamon seated at the dining room table waiting anxiously for me. Her face had a despondent expression. I remembered that it was Fred's day off and Pergamon had volunteered to make dinner. On the table were pork chops cooked the way I liked them, the way Milly had made them for me in Watsonville,

My heart went out to Pergamon. I was touched that despite her dislike of cooking, she had gone to so much effort to surprise me and make me happy.

"Dearest," I said, kissing her. "I'm so grateful to you for going to all this effort. I'm sorry to have come home so late. The White

House called me to go there immediately. I had to go."

"Was I anything important?"

If I had not been so tired, I would not have been so blunt with Pergamon. Before realizing it, I said, "Yes, it was. He fired me."

Pergamon's demeanor changed. "How could you let this happen?" She said, her voice cold and bitter. "You've made a mess out of your life and now you're making a mess out of mine. I told you not to antagonize the President. I told you we ought to go to affairs at the White House. But no, you had to be different. First it was that damned Lust Cosmetics. Now it's this. Well, I don't want to go back to Watsonville! I want to stay here!"

I had never seen Pergamon so angry before. It struck me how similar her words and attitude were to those Tammy had used toward Buck when she saw the photos. However, there was nothing to be gained by answering her in kind.

"Relax, Pergamon," I said. "I think I convinced Buck not to fire me."

"Thank God, I'm glad you apologized to him."

"Pergamon," I said, trying to conceal my annoyance. "I did not apologize. I had nothing to apologize for."

For a moment, I was tempted to tell my wife the tactics I had used with Buck and Tammy. Pergamon was a very intelligent person, and I both enjoyed and benefited from discussing problems with her, when this was possible. However, I concluded this would be foolish in the extreme.

"I think I convinced Buck," I went on, "That if he replaced me as Director, the reforms I have started would be reversed. I explained that he really had no choice but to retain me."

"So you managed to keep the job?"

"I think so," I replied, trying to sound more confident than I felt.

My words calmed her and she looked at me. "You know," she said thoughtfully, "Yesterday Tammy said something strange to me. I thought that she was acting in an unfriendly fashion all day. Then she approached me and said sarcastically, "Tell Melvin I'm glad he enjoyed himself in Bokasa. What was all that about?"

"When I was in Paris, I had to go on to Bokasa. The President, General Ngola, had discovered a military coup against him. He told me to my face that the United States was behind it and threatened all manner of reprisal. I finally was able to convince him we didn't want to overthrow him and that he would do better to announce he would turn Bokasa into a true democracy and cooperate with the US."

"Then why were Buck and Tammy displeased with you? It doesn't seem logical?"

I decided the time was right to tell Pergamon the truth about the reason for my appointment as CIA Director. "Honey," I said, "Pergamon has hated me from the start. She tried to force me out of Buck's campaign. When I blocked that and he was nominated and elected, she persuaded Buck to name me as Director of CIA. She intended to have me publicly humiliated by the Senate's refusal to confirm my nomination. That's why the White House did such a miserable job with the Senate to secure my confirmation. It was all deliberate. Now she thinks that Buck is in a strong enough position politically to force me out."

"My God," she said softly. "I've been such a fool. I thought she really liked me."

Pergamon looked so apologetic I gathered her in my arms and kissed her. She hugged me and kissed me back. It was one of the happiest moments of my life.

The next morning I awakened early and rushed to listen to the radio to see if there was any announcement that I had been fired. That there was none gave me little comfort. My replacement as CIA Director might not be considered important enough to be included among the few snippets of news inserted among the many commercials.

The arrival of the Director's limo to take me to the Agency left me slightly more confident. However, I was apprehensive when the car entered the Agency compound. I half expected the guard to stop us, take my identification pass and bar my admittance. It would not have been beyond Tammy to humiliate me in that fashion. She might very well have made arrangements for the limo to have driven off, leaving me to walk back to the highway and attempt to flag down a taxi to return home.

I felt a similar sensation when I excited my elevator and entered my office. To my relief, everything appeared normal. The file clerk greeted me with her customary "good morning" and handed me the stack of incoming traffic and the morning newspapers. All day long, I waited in vain for the phone call telling me I had been dismissed.

In the evening, as the limo took me back home, I felt somewhat more confident that my bluff had worked with Buck and Tammy. I estimated that the odds of my retaining my post had risen to about two to one, from the even money I would have given at the start of the day.

Pergamon rushed to greet me as soon as I entered the apartment. "How did it go today?" She asked. "I hope you are still the Director."

"I heard nothing," I replied. "In this case, no news is good news."

The week passed with no further word about my status. Early the next week, I called Bob DePorte and arranged to have lunch with him at the National Press Club. I thought that he might have picked up some useful information. Over hamburgers, he fished delicately for information on various foreign affairs matters that had been in the news. Rather than answer him, I switched the subject and told him some juicy pieces of gossip about various Cabinet members that Pergamon had picked up at social gatherings with the other Cabinet wives.

Bob seemed to find this information useful. I was wondering how best to bring up the subject of my status when he raised it himself. "How are things going with you at CIA?" he asked.

"Off the record," I said, "Not well. The President tried to fire me last week. I think I persuaded him to keep me on to avoid scuttling the reforms I have initiated at the Agency, but I'm not sure."

Bob nodded. "That jibes with what I have been told. Off the record, Tammy Porter has been telling people that the President made a big mistake naming you CIA Director and that you were doing a rotten job. If I were you, I'd never turn my back to her."

"Thanks," I said. "I'll try to follow your advice."

CHAPTER 10

The next Cabinet meeting gave me an opportunity to further gauge my position. I arrived to find the other participants seated around the table. Although I had spoken to all of them at one time or another, my reception was as friendly as that of a narcotics agent at a drug traffickers' convention. Buck was in animated conversation with Secretary of State Ashby. He took a look at me, grimaced, and resumed his discussion with Ashby.

Vice President Atwood scowled at me from across the table. Since the inauguration, his attitude toward me had not improved. Apparently, my "persuasion" to drop out of the presidential race and support Buck still rankled him more than any pleasure he garnered from serving as Vice-President.

I sat down in an empty chair next to Harold McAndrews, the Secretary of Commerce. McAndrews had been relatively friendly on the few occasions we had met. I gathered he was quite satisfied with the deal which allowed him to relinquish the Illinois Governorship in exchange for his Cabinet post. He gave me a quick smile, then turned back to his conversation with the

Attorney General.

When Buck finished speaking with Ashby, he tapped the water glass next to him several times to signal that the meeting would begin. He then launched into a long, singularly inappropriate prayer which conveyed the impression that he was on a first name basis with Almighty God. His voice was rich and mellow. I thought he would have made an excellent television revivalist.

The entire exercise struck me a hypocritical, given Buck's questionable morals and ethics. I glanced under lowered eyes at the other people around the table, wondering of any of them found the proceedings as inappropriate as I did. All had suitably pious expressions on their faces, whether from deep conviction or from more practical motives I could only guess.

At length the prayer was over, amid a chorus of sonorous "Amen's." Buck turned to Ashby, stating that the Secretary of State would discuss the first item on the agenda. Ashby launched into a lengthy discussion of the problems afflicting the less developed nations. He graphically described the high infant mortality rates, starvation, and rampant disease. Whenever he paused for breath, Buck would give him a look of encouragement.

Ashby's remarks were long and lachrymose. I wondered where he was headed. When he came to his conclusion, I had to admit that it did in fact warrant the buildup that it received. "What this country is morally required to do," he said, "Is to embark on nothing less than a new Marshall Plan for the benefit of the less developed nations of the World." The total cost to the US taxpayer for the program, he added in an afterthought, would be one percent of total US Gross Domestic Production annually. "Ask not," he declared with a flourish, "What you can do for yourself, but what you can do for the world!"

I wondered if Ashby realized he was paraphrasing President

John Kennedy. There was no doubt in my mind that the Secretary of State was totally sincere in his comments. However, that did not overcome in my mind the complete impracticality of his suggestion. One percent of US gross national product was not a sum so insignificant that it could be added to the other demands on the US budget without serious consideration. I glanced at the others around the table. From their silence, I gathered all were ready to go along with it.

"Good," Buck said. "Then we're agreed."

I knew voicing an objection would be extremely risky for me. Ashby's proposal was not a program that would involve the CIA directly, so that strictly speaking, it was none of my business. Even more important, attacking a policy initiative so dear to Buck's heart would be an invitation for him to fire me. The hold I now had over him was tenuous; it would take little to rouse his anger against me. By temperament, he was prone to act on his emotions, no matter the ramifications.

Still, I felt I had to try. I was the one responsible for putting putting Buck into the Presidency and I was the only one who could stop him. Just as the coup plot to overthrow Ngola risked catastrophic danger to US foreign relations, this ill-thought-out move to spend billions on a new foreign aid program risked grave danger to the US domestic economy.

As I began, my voice seemed to resonate throughout the Cabinet room. "There's no doubt," I said, "That conditions in the less developed nations are truly as horrendous as the Secretary of State describes. However, it would be fiscally unsound for us to embark on such a massive effort without considering how it may impinge on some of the other policy initiatives we are considering."

Buck stared at me, his face crimson, always a sign of his anger. I glanced at the others around the table. They seemed shocked at my audacity. I gathered that at no previous Cabinet session had anyone had the temerity to question one of Buck's proposals.

In order to prevent Buck from cutting me off, I rushed to complete my comments. "The President," I said, "has proposed a large-scale public education program, for which we have to find financing. The budget for the coming year is already in deficit and we are unlikely to show a surplus for at least the next two years. With the deficit we already have, we lack the additional resources necessary to finance the grave problems we face, such as the coming exhaustion of the Social Security trust fund."

I was speaking from the heart and hoped my sincerity would convince some members of the Cabinet to go along with my objection. None appeared ready to do so. I then played my trump card. "The President," I continued, "Campaigned on a platform of abolishing the federal income tax. He has not repudiated that position. I suggest that at a minimum, we defer Secretary Ashby's proposal until the special commission looking into the income tax termination puts out its final report."

The commission I was referring to was one whose establishment I had orchestrated and whose members came from across the political spectrum. I had designed it specifically so that it would find it impossible to produce a report and thus give Buck the fig leaf he needed not to implement his campaign pledge to eliminate the income tax.

Glaring at me, the President turned for support to Treasury Secretary Everett. "Josh," he asked, "Do you have anything to say about how we can best finance Secretary Ashby's program?"

Everyone turned to look at the Treasury Secretary. I knew nothing about Everett other than that he enjoyed a good reputation as a conservative banker before taking the treasury post. If any member of the Cabinet was willing to risk Buck's wrath by supporting my position, I thought Everett would be the most likely.

I was in for a sharp disappointment. Evert paused for a minute before answering, his appearance reminding me of an owl. "There is no doubt," he said, "That the state of the inhabitants in the less developed nations is unsatisfactory and that the US is morally obliged to do something to help them. I will have my Department look into our financial situation and see what might be feasible."

Buck appeared satisfied with Everett's response. He turned to the next item on the agenda. I slumped own in my chair, saying nothing for the remainder of the meeting. I felt as though I had found myself at the Mad Hatter's Tea Party and wished only to be able to return to the world of the sane.

When the meeting was finally over, I stood up and walked out of the room without speaking to anyone. Behind my back I heard fragments of conversation in which my name was mentioned. I walked past the secret service agents standing watch in the corridor to the elevator and stood there waiting for it.

Unexpectedly, someone tapped me on the shoulder. I turned around and found myself facing Joshua Everett.

"Mr. Shultz," he said, "his voice betraying his Massachusetts upbringing, "Would you have a few minutes to spend with me?"

"Certainly," I replied, looking at him expectantly.

To my surprise, he said nothing, but stepped back several paces and stood there silently. Several other members of the Cabinet arrived, waiting for the elevator. The Treasury Secretary turned to them and engaged in friendly chatter, ignoring me.

The elevator arrived and I entered, followed by the others. When the elevator stopped and the door opened, Everett stood back allowing the others to get ahead of us. He then turned to me.

"Shall we have a cup of coffee?" he asked in a low voice.

I nodded in agreement, wondering at his behavior. We excited the White House, went through the gate and turned onto Pennsylvania Avenue.

"There is a lunch place nearby," he said. "Let's go there. It will be more private than my office."

We walked along Pennsylvania Avenue, crossed Fifteenth Street, and Everett led me into a small restaurant. I had walked past it several times before. It was crowded at lunchtime, but was now virtually deserted. We sat down at a table and ordered coffee.

Everett turned to me. "I must apologize for seeming rude back there. I thought it wiser that no one see us talking together."

I nodded slightly, saying nothing.

"You were absolutely correct in your criticism of Ashby's proposal," he went on. I couldn't have agreed with you more. It's financially irresponsible, however well intentioned."

"Frankly," I said, "I was disappointed that you didn't speak out to back me."

"I very much wanted to. But I was afraid the President would have asked me to resign as Treasury Secretary. "

Everett looked carefully around the restaurant to make certain that nobody could overhear us. I wondered if he was paranoid. Satisfied that we could not be overheard, he continued.

"The President intends to privatize the entire Federal Reserve System. It has to be stopped! I desperately need your help!"

"You must be joking," I said. "It's not something Porter would think up by himself. For one thing, he doesn't have the brains."

"The force behind the plan, I am pretty sure, is that of his wife. I gather it was thought up originally by some of her banking friends from Oklahoma City. They are thoroughly corrupt and ready to do it in order to be able to control interest rates and the marketing of federal bonds. They've persuaded many of the large banks to go along with the scheme I know it's hard to believe, but consider the fortunes that will be made by the commercial banks that take over the Fed's responsibilities. "

"I don't like Tammy Porter," I said, "But she's very intelligent. She's smart enough to realize the damage the abolition of the Federal Reserve System would do to the country, even if the President isn't. Just mentioning such an idea would cause the stock market to crash."

"To say nothing of what it would do to interest rates and the value of the dollar," Everett interjected.

"What about Baxter?" I asked. I was referring to the well-respected Chairman of the Federal Reserve.

"Baxter's been bought off. His wife went into a nursing home over a year ago. It's wiped out all his resources. He needs cash to pay for her care. Not only that, Baxter has two teenage daughters he wants to send to college. He's been promised a seven-figure salary at one of the major banks and valuable stock options if he signs off on the plan."

"What does Tammy get out of it?" I asked. "She doesn't strike me as someone who is primarily interested in money."

"She's not," Everett said. "What she wants is a massive increase in government spending for such things as welfare, medical care and education. Under current conditions, Congress would never agree to such increased expenditures because of our already large deficit. Tammy believers, probably correctly, that in the event of a financial collapse, Congress would agree to increase spending for the programs she wants."

I could now understand Everett's urgent approach to me. "If this is true," I said, "I'll do everything I can to help you block the plan."

"Thank God!" Everett said. "Your influence with the President gives us a chance. Do you think you can persuade him to change his mind?"

I shook my head sadly. "I'm afraid I have very little influence over the President any more. He would fire me today if he thought he could get away with it. He might very well do so tomorrow. You saw the way he treated me at the Cabinet meeting. I'll do what I can, but it may not be enough."

"Anything you can do would help," he said. I'm planning to resign from the Cabinet when he announces the plan. I'll describe the disastrous effects it would cause to the country and try to organize opposition to it."

I was impressed by his determination and sincerity. "I'm curious," I said, "How did you get tapped for the Treasury post?"

"Through my wife. Dorothy met Tammy when they were on the same committee of the Radcliff Alumni Association. After Porter won the New Hampshire primary, Dorothy persuaded me to contribute to his campaign. Naturally, neither of us suspected what kind of a president he would turn out to be. I think that Tammy asked the President to name me Treasury Secretary under the impression that she could influence me through my wife.

I laughed and said I was sorry my support for Buck's campaign had not been as limited as his. In that case, I added, I would not have felt so personally responsible for all the damage Buck was likely to inflict on the country. We shook hands, agreeing to keep in close touch, and I walked back to the White House, where my limo was waiting. On the drive back to the Agency, I kept going over in my mind what I could do to block Buck's Federal Reserve plan. For the first time, I was so preoccupied that I paid little attention to the beautiful vistas of the Potomac River.

Back in my office, I opened my attaché case and looked at the one remaining photo of Buck and Peggy Terrell. If used properly, it could certainly embarrass Buck. Unfortunately, there was no great chance that by itself, even with Everett's support, it would be sufficient for me to force Buck to abandon his plan.

I clearly needed some additional leverage to successfully pressure Tammy and Buck. I considered asking Alan Barnes to resume his investigation into their past activities to see if he could obtaining derogatory information. I decided not to do so as it would cause too much of an uproar if it leaked out that the Director of the Agency was investigating the President and the First Lady.

As a substitute, I turned to the large amount of material Alan had previously furnished me about the Porters. Carefully re-reading the files, I found useful tidbits. There were several indications of extramarital affairs by Buck and reports that Tammy might have been associated with a radical student group while in college. Nothing emerged, however, of the magnitude I required.

One afternoon, I returned home early, planning to once again work on the Barnes reports before dinner. I found Permagon in our bedroom crying. Taking her in my arms to comfort her, I asked her the cause of her distress.

"I've never been so humiliated," she said sobbing

I kissed her reassuringly on the forehead. "What happened, Honey?" I asked.

"I was manning a booth at the antique show raising money for the retarded children. Tammy and two of the other Cabinet wives were also there. When we closed the booths at noon, the three of them discussed going out for lunch together. I was standing there with them, but they ignored me as though I wasn't there. Then they said goodbye and simply walked off, leaving me standing there."

I felt a sense of outrage at the shabby way they had treated Pergamon. "I'm so sorry, I said. I haven't seen Tammy since last week. I can't understand why they were so mean to you." I kissed her again and hugged her. That evening, for the first time in several weeks, we made love.

As Pergamon slept peacefully beside me, my mind turned again to the problem of Buck and Tammy. I decided I would have to take the risk of ordering another investigation into Buck and Tammy's background. I would have preferred to use Alan Barnes for the purpose, not only because he was already familiar with the material, but also because of my confidence in him. I discarded the idea, however, believing his scruples would deter him from investigating a sitting President of the United States.

Reluctantly, I turned to Joe Devine. Based on the material he had obtained for me on Atwood, he would not turn up empty handed, even if what he obtained was suspect. My anxiety to block Buck's plans was now so great that I was willing to use any means available.

Devine agree to fly the next day to Oklahoma City to begin his investigation. It was fortunately that I had called him. The day after arriving in Oklahoma City he phoned to report that George and Peggy Terrell had left the jobs I had arranged for them. I was concerned over the collapse of the arrangements I had made for them and even more over the fact that I had not been notified immediately.

Not entirely trusting the accuracy of Devine's report, I had checked it out independently and confirmed the information. Peggy Terrell had given no reason for her resignation. Her husband, however, had boasted that he was getting a better paying job. When I had Devine check further, he reported that Terrell's new employer was a friend of David Ames, the senior partner in Tammy's former law firm. I realized, not for the first time, that in Tammy I was facing a dangerous and very capable opponent.

If Terrell repudiated his sworn statement and he and his wife claimed the photo of Peggy and Buck was faked, there was little chance it would be of much good in pressuring Buck and Tammy. I arranged to meet with Everett in the hope he had been more successful. He told me he had had no luck in his meetings with members of Congress. I didn't have the heart to tell him about how little I could contribute to the effort to block Buck.

Each day at the Agency I feared would be my last, expecting to be informed at any moment that Buck had fired me. It was with great difficulty that I forced myself to go through the piles of documents brought in each day for me to handle.

CHAPTER 11

Late one afternoon, as I was preparing to leave for home, Ann brought in two extremely thick files for me too look at. "It's the Leonov Case," she said, placing them in my in box.

I was familiar with the case. Churchill had briefed me on it when I took over as Director. Since then, the case had continued to grow in importance until it split those elements of the CIA dealing with it into two warring camps.

I opened the first folder and began to read. Yuri Nikolayevich Leonov had been a colonel in the Russian Army Intelligence Service assigned to the embassy in Washington. The colonel had asserted, and this claim had been supported by other reliable intelligence, that he had been in charge of all Russian military intelligence operations in the US at the time of his defection. Unlike most such defections, Leonov's had been widely reported in the American media because of the unusual circumstances surrounding it. He had walked into a Russian Orthodox Church in downtown Washington and asked the Church to arrange a press conference for him. Before assembled reporters and TV camera crews, he declared that his growing appreciation of the benefits of American democracy had motivated him to publicly repudiate Russia authoritarianism and to disclose the multitude of Russian intelligence operations in the United States.

Leonov's comments were widely publicized. Realizing that the defection could not be kept secret, the normal procedure during which the defector's information was collected and evaluated, the administration had trumpeted it as a triumph for American intelligence. This evaluation was widely accepted. Many conservatives had pointed to Leonov's description of on-going Russian intelligence in the US as revealing how little post-Communist Russia had departed from the previous Soviet practice of conducting massive espionage operations in the US.

Because the Russian Operations Unit of the FBI was regarded with disfavor by the previous administration, Leonov was turned over to the CIA for debriefing and handling. At a luxurious estate in the Maryland Eastern Shore turned into a safe house for the purpose, teams of officers from the Agency's Russian Affairs Division questioned Leonov at length concerning his knowledge of Russian intelligence operations in the US.

The extent of the information furnished by Leonov to his debriefers led the Agency's Russian Affairs Division to evaluate him as the most valuable Russian defector ever obtained by CIA. Among the large number of Russian intelligence operations he revealed were several important ones of which the Agency had no previous knowledge.

In accordance with understandings reached with Leonov by his debriefers, the Russian Affairs Division recommended that he be accorded permanent residence in the US, be employed as a consultant by the Agency at a large salary, and be guaranteed a generous benefits package for the rest of his life. In a signal decision, it further recommended that the Colonel be awarded a medal for his exceptional contribution to American security.

The folder I was reading had been prepared by the Russian Affairs Division. It essentially contained documents supporting this evaluation. The top sheet in the folder, opposite Leonov's photo, was a memorandum for my signature approving the Division's recommendations for his future handling. It had already been signed off on by Arch Henley, the Chief of the Russian Affairs Division.

As I read the folder, I had to admit that the supporting material provided a sound argument for approving the recommendations. Unfortunately, its findings differed as day does from night from the recommendations in the second folder concerning Leonov, sent for my approval by the Agency Counter Intelligence Division.

The conclusions in latter folder were that the Colonel was a false defector, ordered by Russian Army Intelligence to appear to defect as part of a Russian deception operation. According to this analysis, the Russian Army Intelligence Service planned by this maneuver to conceal its most valuable operations in the US by diverting US attention to either imagined operations or real ones of limited value that could be dispensed with.

On first reading, I found the Counter Intelligence Division's arguments as persuasive as those of the Russian Affairs Division. I had just finished reading the folder when Ann entered my office.

"The last traffic has been distributed, sir," she said. "Is it all right for me to leave now? It's by son's birthday and I would like to take him out to dinner."

I looked at my watch and realized it was past 6:30 p.m., far later than I usually stayed in my office. "Certainly," I said, "By all means go. I'll take care of locking up the folders myself. And wish your son a happy birthday for me."

Ann said goodnight and left. I telephoned Pergamon and explained I had to work late and not to hold dinner for me. I then began to read the folder again. I was not particularly concerned with whether Leonov was a real defector or the star in a plot to deceive American intelligence. Either way, I thought, I might just have something which might allow me to defeat Buck and Tammy.

By the time I completed by study of the folders, it was close to 9 p.m. I placed them in my personal safe, made certain it was properly locked, and took the elevator down to the garage, where my limo was parked. My regular driver had already gone off duty, but one of the standby night drivers drove me home.

I found Pergamon in bed reading. "You're late," she said, looking up from her book. "Anything important?"

"No," I answered, kissing her on the cheek. I would have liked to have been able to confide in her, as I did regularly during the early days of our marriage. However, what I had in mind was far too sensitive to disclose to a living soul, even my wife.

It was so late, I no longer had any appetite for dinner. I had only a quick beer, then a hot bath, and relaxed in bed next to Pergamon, watching a western on TV. My sleep was fitful. I awakened several times during the night, my brain whirling with thoughts of how I could best utilize the Leonov case.

The next morning, I arose early. Skipping dinner the night before had left me feeling ravenous. A hurried search of the refrigerator disclosed some leftover ham, which I warmed in the microwave and used to make two sandwiches. I ate them with considerable pleasure along with some potato salad I found hiding in a corner of the refrigerator.

My impatience to get to the office made it difficult for me to wait for my limo. I regretted not having arranged to be picked up early this morning. After what seemed like an eternity, the car arrived. As we drove along to Potomac, there was little doubt in my mind that my tenure as CIA Director was almost over.

In my office, I went through the morning stack of traffic, finding it hard to concentrate on what I was reading. Issues that normally would have seemed of monumental importance shrank to insignificance compared to what lay ahead. Several times, I picked up my phone to call Arch Henley. Each time I replaced the phone without calling, forcing myself to wait until Ann arrived. For me to place the call myself, I knew, would seem unusual to Henley and might create suspicion.

As soon as Ann arrived, I asked her to get Henley on the phone. When she reached him, I picked up the phone and said, "Arch, I read that memo you sent me on Colonel Leonov. It was extremely interesting."

"I hope I made clear," he answered, "Just how valuable Leonov's information is and how crazy the Counter Intelligence Division is to claim he is a deliberate Russian plant."

"You make a strong case," I replied. "However, before signing off on your memo, I want to talk to him myself. I'd like you to set up a meeting for me with him this morning at the estate."

"Nothing could make me happier. He's even more impressive in person than our memo makes him out. "I'd be glad to come with you and introduce you."

"That won't be necessary," I said. "Let me know as soon as it's arranged."

Henley called back in a few minutes to inform me he had arranged my meeting with the Colonel for noon. "We've got a super French chef at the estate," he added. "I thought it might be a nice chance for you to enjoy a fine meal as you chat with Leonov over lunch. I've already alerted Cal Foster, who's handholding the Colonel."

When I thanked Henley and hung up, I asked Ann to order the limo ready to take me to the estate. I then went over in my mind who I wanted to take with me. I decided Don Collins was a good choice because of his discretion and his knowledge of the Russian language. I understood the Colonel to speak almost flawless English, but it was possible that a translator might be desirable. My second choice was Chuck Madden, one of the young lawyers assigned by the Agency's General Counsel to provide legal assistance to the Operations Directorate. He had impressed me with his ability. Equally important, he held a very high security clearance, so that I could go into sensitive matters with him if necessary.

I told Tom Churchill to handle the fort while I was gone and went down to the limo, accompanied by Don and Chuck. I did not reveal to them the purpose of my trip until the limo left the Agency compound and we were traveling on the highway that led to Annapolis and the Bay Bridge. It was clear my companions were having a difficult time concealing their curiosity as to the purpose of the trip. Feeling sorry for them, I explained I had arranged to have lunch with Colonel Leonov to get a better idea in my own mind about the case. "Your job," I said, "is to assist me with this and to carry on a conversation with any others who might be present, to permit me a greater opportunity to speak with the Colonel."

Don and Chuck seemed happy about the outing. I took the opportunity to ask Don what he thought about the Leonov case. He responded that he believed the Colonel to be a genuine defector, but admitted that his opinion might have been influenced by the fact that he had served in the Russian Affairs Division.

After crossing over the bridge onto the Eastern Shore, we left the highway and drove along a series of increasingly more rural side roads. I had been informed at the Agency about how magnificent the estate was, but I was nonetheless unprepared for the spender of what I saw.

We drove for perhaps twenty minutes along the front of the property, which was protected by a high, ivy-covered stone wall that looked as though it dated back to colonial times. The car stopped at a large stone gatehouse which guarded the only break in the wall. Two armed guards wearing civilian clothes emerged and approached the limo, their hands resting on their holstered revolvers.

They carefully examined our identification badges, then checked a list of names to make certain that we had been previously cleared to enter the compound. Finding our names on their list did not suffice. One guard retreated inside the gatehouse, where he confirmed our clearance by phone. Satisfied, he unlocked the massive steel gate that guarded the portal and waved the limo through. Turning around, I saw him carefully securing the gate behind us.

The road from the gatehouse to the mansion was almost a mile in length, flanked on either side by a row of century-old trees. We passed a large pond on which geese swam. The road then began a climb to the top of a small hill, on which stood the mansion.

My first glimpse of it made me think that I was back in the English countryside. Although the mansion had been built in the late 1920's by a millionaire industrialist, it more-or-less resembled an eccentrically built nineteenth century manor-house. Its stone walls were covered with ivy. Turrets rose at each corner of the building, looking down on the slate roof. To one side of the mansion were several fenced tennis courts.

The estate had been donated to the government by the industrialist's heirs when the US entered the Second World War.

One of my predecessors as Director had used his influence with the President to have it turned over to the Agency. CIA used it routinely for seminars and weekend conferences by senior Agency officials. Occasionally, it was utilized for debriefing important defectors. The Russian Affairs Division's use of it for Leonov had required the transfer to other sites of several previously scheduled seminars, provoking protests from the head of the Agency's Training Division.

The limo stopped in front of the mansion's entrance. Ed McGuire, manager of the estate, stepped forward to open the door for me. He had been introduced to me at a conference some weeks before, where his presentation had convinced me to overrule suggestions that CIA reduce expenditures by relinquishing the estate for the use of other government agencies.

"Ed," I said, "I'd like to compliment you on the tight security precautions you maintain here. Your guards really are doing an excellent job."

McGuire smiled and thanked me. He then introduced me to a second man who had joined us. "This is Cal Foster," he said. "He's handling Leonov."

Foster shook my hand, then introduced Colonel Leonov to me. I carefully scrutinized the man who had become so important to me. The first thing that struck me was the incongruity of his dress. I had not expected a former Colonel in the Russian Army Intelligence Service to be wearing well-tailored white tennis slacks, an expensive tennis sweater and tennis shoes.

Leonov was slightly under six feet in height, well-built, with blond hair clipped in a crew cut and blue eyes. He looked about five years younger than his age, fifty-four. All together, I thought, he resembled a Madison Avenue version of an American millionaire on his country estate, rather than a Russian defector.

"I'm glad to meet you, Michael Nikolayevich," I said with a smile, addressing him in the Russian fashion. "I appreciate all the assistance you have given the Agency."

Leonov smiled in return, thanking me politely in virtually unaccented English. He did so with such confidence and poise that I thought he was either a consummate actor or a boa fide defector.

After a few minutes of polite conversation, McGuire led us into the interior of the mansion. The rooms were richly decorated, with dark wood paneling on the walls. Thick Oriental carpets covered most of the parquet floors. Nineteenth century oil paintings in gold guilt frames lined the walls. The furnishings, McGuire explained, had been left by the estate's original owner.

I was amused by McGuire's playing the part of a proud host. Several times, he stopped to point out various objects d'art and related interesting anecdotes about them.

We walked through a magnificent living room, featuring a massive stone fireplace, and into a smaller dining room. The dining room table, covered by a fine linen tablecloth, had been set for six persons, although it could have been extended to seat sixteen.

I accepted McGuire's invitation to take the seat of honor, motioning Leonov to sit on my right and Don Collins on my left. I felt guilty about relegating Chuck, Cal Foster and Ed McGuire to the far end of the table. However, I thought this arrangement would provide me with the most convenient arrangement to have a lengthy conversation with the Colonel, without having to take time for polite interaction with the other guests.

The meal we were served would have done credit to a fine French restaurant. An expert, black-jacked waiter served us the courses on gold-rimmed plates. McGuire proudly told us that the estate chef had once headed the staff of a famed New York restaurant. I found the food too rich for dinner, to say nothing of lunch. I contented myself with stirring the food on my plate to give the appearance of eating, while my fellow dinners cleaned their plates.

We were served a white wine with the fish appetizer and a red wine with the meat. I thought of asking for a beer, but desisted to avoid looking gauche.

Throughout the meal, Leonov and I carried on a lively conversation. His dossier had noted that he had specialized in American studies during his university education in Russia. In addition to a grasp of American history and culture which would have done credit to most US college professors in that area, he displayed a broad knowledge of European art, music, history and foreign affairs.

When we finished eating, I waited the minimum interval necessary to appear polite and then invited Leonov to join me in a walk around the estate. I indicated to the others that I wished to have a private conversation with the Colonel. Leonov and I walked out of the mansion and down to the river, which flowed by the estate on the side opposite the gate. I observed that Agency guards discretely patrolled the river bank to insure security from that direction.

As we started our return to the house, I stopped and turned to Leonov.

"Michael Nikolayevich," I said, "I hope you are comfortable here."

He smiled. "Yes," he said. "We don't always eat as well as we did just now, but I can't complain about my treatment. My accommodations are comfortable and the food good. I would not be living as well back in Russia."

"That's good, "I replied. "My people tell me you have been very helpful and we are most grateful."

Leonov smiled again and made a depreciatory gesture.

"As you are aware," I went on, ""I have been sent a recommendation to approve, proposing that you be appointed a special consultant to the Agency on Russian affairs at a suitable salary and that your long-term future be assured. I find such a recommendation reasonable and am ready to give it my final approval."

The Colonel's smile broadened. "You are most generous. Anything I can do to help my new country would be welcome."

I smiled in return. "There is only one minor detail," I said."I'm sure you will be able to quickly clear it up."

Leonov looked at me, the very picture of sincerity. "Of course," he said. "What can I do?"

I dropped my previously friendly manner and said coldly, "My Counter Intelligence people tell me that your defection was ordered by the Russian Army Intelligence Service, that your cooperation is a pretense, and that you have been sent to us in a deception operation to confuse the Agency and conceal your country's most important operations in the US."

The Colonel recoiled as though slapped brutally in the face. "That's a damned lie," he began.

"Calm yourself, Michael Nikolayevich," I interrupted him, reverting to my previous friendly attitude. "Naturally, I do not credit such a view. You know how counter-intelligence people are. They are paid to be suspicious even when no suspicion is warranted."

Leonov relaxed slightly. "What can I do to convince you?" he asked.

"Michael Nikolayevich," I began. "I know you were responsible for overseeing many intelligence operations. It is understandable that a few of them may have slipped your mind."

He stared at me, trying to fathom my meaning.

"It is also possible," I went on, "That your superiors in Moscow may have kept the details of some ultra-secret operations in the US from you. Alternatively, We are both men of the world. There may be some agents whose identities you still wish to protect for reasons of loyalty, gratitude or affection. That, too, is understandable."

I stopped and placed my hand on Leonov's shoulder. Looking him directly in the eyes, I said slowly and deliberately, "There is only one operation I am interested in Michael Nikolayevich. I already know all of the details. You need only to confirm them. Please listen very carefully to me. Your response on this matter, and this matter alone, will determine my attitude toward you."

Leonov listened to me very carefully, his intelligent eyes staring into mine. There was no doubt that I had his utter attention.

"Last year," I began, "A few says before the New Hampshire Republican Primary, you personally recruited President Porter to serve as a Russian agent."

"Leonov looked at me amazed. "That's ridiculous! Whoever told you that made up the story."

"You recruited him," I continued, ignoring his words, "Using a female Russian agent named Tanya, who was employed as a maid in the hotel. She seduced Porter. You then blackmailed him, using pictures you had taken of them in bed, to obtain his cooperation."

Leonov seemed for a moment to fail to understand what I was saying. He obviously groped for the best means of convincing me of the idiocy of what I had just said.

"Mr. Shultz," he said finally, "I have never been to New Hampshire. Beyond that nobody ever expected President Porter to win the New Hampshire primary. We would have had no reason to blackmail him into becoming a Russian agent."

I went on, ignoring his words. "To help cement Porter's cooperation, after you recruited him you put twenty thousand dollars into his account to finance his campaign." This sum represented the payment I had made covertly into Buck's campaign account before Sol Sugarman had established more formal, quasi-legal mechanisms for me to use. Nonetheless the dates jibed with my construction of the Russian recruitment story and my own involvement was sufficiently veiled, I thought, to stand up to the less than thorough scrutiny I expected it would receive.

Leonov shrugged his shoulders in despair. "Is there nothing I can do to convince you that this story is false?"

"Nothing!" I said. "If you refuse to confirm that you recruited Porter, I'll have no choice but to conclude you are a Russian decoy and order your immediate deportation to back to Moscow. You should understand Michael Nikolayevich, that if I do so, I will at the same time arrange for the arrest of several Russian agents whose identity you did not reveal to the Agency. I will make certain that the Russian Intelligence Services believe you cooperated with CIA by revealing the identity of those agents to us. If you are not executed back in Russia as a traitor, you certainly will have no job and no future there."

The Colonel remained silent for a minute, considering his options. I didn't think you did things like that in America," he said finally.

"You know a lot about history," I answered. "You know it is written by the winners and becomes the truth, no matter what the actual facts may have been. One does what one is obliged to do."

"All right," he said at length. "I will confirm your report about Porter."

"I am very glad," I answered. "You will have a long and happy future in the United States. Let's go back to the house. They'll be wondering what's keeping us."

We walked back in silence. Leonov seemed deep in thought, his previous jocularity gone. As we approached the mansion, Foster came out to greet us. "I hope you enjoyed a pleasant walk," he said. It was clear he hoped my impression of the Colonel had been favorable and that I would concur in the Russian Affairs Division's assessment of his bona fides.

"Yes, thanks," I replied. Michael Nikolayevich has been most helpful. I would appreciate it if you could provide us with an office in which he can write down some details about an operation I am interested in."

"Of course, sir."

Foster led us into the mansion to a library off the living room. Handing me a large yellow legal size pad of paper and pointing to a mahogany desk by the window, he said, "I hope this will be satisfactory."

I thanked him, gave the pad to Leonov, and motioned him to sit down. "Please tell Don and Chuck to stick close," I said to Foster. "When we're finished, I'd like them to join me here. You, too.

Foster left and I carefully closed the door behind him, leaving me along with the Colonel.

"Now, Michael Nikolayevich," I said to Leonov, who was seated at the desk with a resigned look on his face, "These are the facts that you recall. Please write them down."

"Do you want me to do it in Russian?"

"No, English would be preferable."

As I dictated, the Colonel wrote down the details of the story I had concocted concerning Buck's recruitment as a Russian agent. It was fortunate, I thought, that Tanya had opportunely turned up in the hotel to be bedded by Buck and that I had made the clandestine payment of twenty thousand dollars into Buck's account shortly thereafter. However, I was under no illusion Leonov's statement would bear up under close scrutiny. It was a chance, but only a chance, and had to be handled deftly. And I had to be lucky.

"There's no doubt about it," I said, when the Colonel handed me the finished statement and I read it. "The counter-intelligence people were completely wrong about you. I Don't know how they could have had such as mistaken impression. You obviously deserve political asylum in the US. I will make certain that you are well-treated."

Leonov smiled wryly. He took out a package of cigarettes and lit one. I was amused to see he was still smoking Russian cigarettes. Although smoking was theoretically prohibited in the mansion, I decided to overlook the fact.

I walked to the door opened it, and asked Chuck, Don and Foster to enter. "Colonel Leonov has been kind enough to collaborate in writing some additional information about an operation. He will now date and sign the statement to certify its authenticity. I would like you to also sign the document as witnesses."

I handed the pad back to Leonov and watched as he dutifully signed and dated the statement. I then handed the pad to the other three, who signed in turn.

"Thanks" I said, indicating I would like them to leave the room again. When they had done so, I ripped the sheet with his statement from the pad and carefully inserted it in the secret compartment of my attaché case. Turning to the Colonel, I continued, "Some day in the future, you may be tempted to repudiate your statement. That would be a most dangerous error for you, Michael Nikolayevich. In addition to being Director of CIA, I am also a very wealthy and powerful industrialist. Many people owe me favors. I can be a ruthless enemy and would take strong measures against you if you cross me. Do you understand?"

Leonov nodded sullenly. "On the other hand," I added, "If you cooperate with me, I will be a most generous and helpful friend. There may be occasions when CIA or the American government is too bound my regulations or to slow to respond in time to meet your needs. I will personally insure that your well-being is guaranteed."

The Colonel looked hard at me. "I understand," he replied. "You may be certain of my continued cooperation."

"Let's go join the others," I said, walking to the door. He followed. In the living room we found Foster, McGuire, Don and Chuck waiting.

"I'm afraid it's time for us to get back to headquarters," I said, looking at my watch. I thanked McGuire for his hospitality, then turned to Foster.

Shaking his hand, I said, "You take good care of the Colonel. He's been most helpful."

Leonov smiled slightly at my effort. I tried once more to leave him in a good mood. "If you have trouble getting those Russian cigarettes, let me know. I'll make certain you are supplied. Or if there's anything else, just get in touch with my secretary, Ann Welch. She'll get the message to me."

My words had the desired effect on the Colonel. He smiled more broadly. As we shook hands, I thought I had been partially successful in finishing up my meeting with him on relatively favorable terms.

We bade goodbye to Foster and McGuire, entered the limo and drove off. I found it hard to avoid thinking of anything but the statement I had hidden in my attaché case. To avoid Chuck or Don realizing the significance of my meeting with Leonov, I began a lengthy discussion of the excellent meal we had been served at the state and the difficulty in obtaining equivalent service at Washington's restaurants.

Fortunately for my nerves, we made good time returning to the Agency. Back in the Director's office, I removed from my attaché case the statement Leonov had written. I knew it might attract unwelcome attention if I made copies of it myself, but I could not take the chance of someone else reading it. Trying to act as though it were a routine matter, I left my office and walked to the file room. I courteously declined the file clerk's offer of assistance and made several copies of the statement. I then returned to my office and placed them back in the hidden compartment of my attaché case, which I carefully locked.

The next few minutes seemed an eternity. I read and signed the documents that had been sent to me for my approval. I repeatedly checked my watch to see if it was time to leave. I stepped into Churchill's office and determined he had nothing urgent for me to look at. Saying goodnight to Ann, I went down to the limo, tightly clutching the attaché case. I relaxed as the driver took me home.

Fred greeted me when I entered the door and told me that Pergamon would not be home for dinner. She inquired what time I would like to eat. Normally, I would have been annoyed at having to have diner by myself. This evening, however, I had so many things on my mind that I felt grateful not having to put on a show of normalcy with Pergamon.

"Just make me a hamburger," I said. "As soon as you can. I'll have that with a beer."

I greatly enjoyed my dinner. I was pleased that I had avoided the rich fair at lunch, in favor of the plain food I was now eating, which was much more to my taste. After a hot both, I made myself a cup of hot cocoa and got into bed to watch a western movie. Although these activities usually were successful in relaxing me, I found it hard not to think about Leonov's statement. I was acutely conscious of the fact that in challenging Buck and Tammy, I was taking a desperate gamble. They had at their command all the power of the federal government. Despite my wealth and influence, I was a puny David, taking on a colossal Goliath.

I got out of bed, retrieved my attaché case, and removed from the secret compartment a copy of the Leonov statement I had made. I folded it, placed it in an envelope, sealed envelope and on it wrote "Most Private, To Be Opened Only By Mr. Sol Sugarman." I then inserted the sealed envelope into a large Manila envelope, on which I wrote Sol's address.

Although it past 9p.m., my phone call found Sol still in his office. I had not spoken to him for several months, so I chatted with him for a bit about his work and family before getting to the object of my call. He listened in silence as I explained I would be mailing him a Manila envelope. I instructed him to keep it unopened in his office safe.

"If I should die for any reason or disappear," I said, please open it and turn over the envelope inside to the editor of the 'Chicago Tribune.' Tell him to open it and make the contents public. Add that I personally vouched for the authenticity of the information."

Sol expressed no curiosity concerning the envelope's contents. He said only, "I trust this will not involve me in anything obviously illegal?"

"Of course not." I reassured him. "If you end up in jail, who would keep me out?"

"Just checking," he replied with a laugh.

When I hung up, I went downstairs and out of the condo to a mail box at the corner of the street. Mailing it, I retraced my steps. I had done all I could that day to protect myself against possible action by Buck and Tammy. Feeling more relaxed, I turned in.

The next day was Friday the thirteenth. I am not superstitious. But as I shaved and dressed, I wondered if the day would prove unlucky for Buck or for me. Please God, not for the country, I prayed.

When I finished my breakfast, I went into the bedroom. Pergamon was still asleep. Trying not to wake her, I put on my suit jacket, took my attaché case from the closet and opened it. I removed a copy of Leonov's statement on Buck and checked carefully to make sure that the original was still there. I removed one of the copies I had made and concealed it inside one of the books in my bookcase. It was not a good hiding place, but would evade detection in any quick search of my apartment.

As I turned around, I was startled to see Pergamon awake, staring at me.

"Good morning, Dear," I said. "I hope you slept well."

I kissed her affectionately on the cheek.

"Fine, Melvin." She answered. "You know, I had the most wonderful dream about you. How would you like to make love?"

My heart sank. There was nothing I wanted so much at that moment as to make love with my wife. I always was eager to do so, but particularly on that morning, because of what I knew would be in store for me. In the early days of our marriage, before going off to deal with a difficult situation, I had often made love with her for luck. I had done so before I went off to conduct the difficult negotiations, which had resulted in my taking ownership of the bankrupt Lust Cosmetics Company.

As much as I wanted to, I knew there was no way I could accept Pergamon's offer. The Agency limo would be at my door in a few minutes and I had far too much to do today to be late.

"Pergamon," I said regretfully, I have to go. I can't tell you how much I'd like to take you up on that offer. How about tonight?"

She nodded in agreement. At that moment, she probably meant it. I sadly realized that when I returned home, there was little chance she would still be in the mood.

I walked to the door, then stopped. I decided I was being a damned fool. Regardless of what happened during the day, my career as CIA Director would be over by midnight. I picked up the phone and called my office. It was too early for any Ann or Don to be in, but I told the night file clerk to inform Ann that I would be coming into the office late this morning and to have her tell Churchill that he would handle the morning senior staff meeting in my place. I then called down to the front desk of my condo.

"This is Mr. Shultz," I said. "Please ask the doorman to tell my limo driver when he arrives that I will be a few minutes late. Have the car wait for me."

As I walked back to the bedroom I quickly and quietly undressed, slipping under the covers naked and embracing Pergamon. I kissed her on her ear and she cooed. "Oh Melvin," she said, "I thought you had to go to the office. This is a wonderful surprise."

"Some things," I replied, kissing her again, "Are far too good to pass up."

CHAPTER 12

As I entered my limo, it occurred to me again that this would be my last day as Director. I felt sentimental for a moment. Then I concentrated on the steps I had to take today.

In my office, I quickly scanned the traffic I had obtained from the night file clerk. I had arrived there early enough to take the morning staff meeting, but decided to let Churchill handle it. I carefully scrutinized the morning papers searching for anything that might suggest a move by Buck against me or to announce his Federal Reserve scheme and was relieved to find nothing. When Ann arrived, I asked her to set up a meeting for me with Vice-President Atwood as early in the day as possible. I also requested her to arrange a meeting for me with the President no earlier than ninety minute after I was to meet with the Vice-President.

It took Ann more than an hour to secure the meeting for me with Atwood. "He'll see you at 5 p.m. in his office at the Old Executive Office Building," she said. "His secretary told me it was the earliest he could do and that it could last for no more than five minutes. I'm sorry. I tried to persuade them to make it earlier. But they wouldn't budge."

"That's fine," Ann, I told her. "I know you did your best. Now please set up a meeting for me with the President for 5:30 p.m. If Atwood is only going to allow me five minutes, I should have no problem getting to the White House by then."

Ann left and I opened my attaché case and took out from the secret compartment the original copy of Leonov's statement, folded it and put it into an envelope. I sealed it and on it I wrote, "Most Secret, For the Vice-President's Eyes Only." Then I carefully put the envelope back into the secret compartment and locked the attaché case.

Ann returned, looking very concerned. "The White House absolutely refuses to schedule an appointment for you to see the President," she said. "Alice Kramer was absolutely rude. She didn't even pretend to provide a polite excuse."

"Don't worry about it," I replied. "I'm not very popular with the White House right now." She looked so sad for my sake that I tried to console her. "I'll handle it. It will cause me no difficulty."

I gave her a reassuring smile, which I did not feel, and she left. Sitting at my desk, I pondered over my next moves. This was no time to despair. I repeated to myself the comforting words I had been told us a young reporter. "God looks after fools, idiots and Mel Shultz."

I looked at my watch. It was getting close to lunchtime. I got up, told Ann I was going to lunch, and took the elevator to the ground floor. I was not hungry and decided to walk outside, along the paved path that surrounded the Agency.

Here and there along the path there were tables which employees could use to eat their lunch outside when the weather was pleasant. During the lunch hour, the path was also used by people walking around the building for exercise. It was still a bit early for lunch, and I found the path deserted.

When I had completed my circuit, I re-entered the building and returned to my office, feeling much more relaxed than when I had left. I tried to read the new traffic in my in box, but my mind wasn't in it. Finally, I got up and went out to Ann's desk.

"Ann." I said. "Please have the limo ready to take me into town. Tell Mr. Churchill that I am leaving for the day. Give him anything in my in box and tell him to handle it."

"What should I say if the White House or the Vice-President calls?"

"Tell the White House that I am gone for the day and you don't know where I am. Tell the Vice President's office that I will be there at 5 p.m. as scheduled."

I said goodbye, took my attaché case, and went down to the garage and got into my limo. The drive into Washington took less time than I expected. As we approached the Old Executive Office Building, I asked the driver to stop and let me out on the corner of Seventeenth Street and Pennsylvania Avenue. I looked at my watch. I had about four hours to kill before my meeting with the Vice President. Just across from the old Executive Building, on the other side of Pennsylvania Avenue, was the Renwick Museum. I decided it would be a comfortable place to wait.

I was a bit afraid that the guard at the entrance would insist on examining my attaché case, but he paid me scant attention as I entered. Ignoring the displays on the first floor, I took the stairs to the second floor. Virtually all of it was devoted to one huge room, decorated with classical paintings. I sat down on a comfortable armchair, enjoying the atmosphere. This spot had always been one of my favorite places in Washington, dating back to my early days in Washington as a reporter. The room was dark, with heavy drapes over the windows, and most restful. I shut my eyes and relaxed.

From time to time I dozed. There were no other visitors. When I got tired of sitting, I would stand and walk around the room, examining the paintings. Finally, my watch told me it was time to go to my appointment with Atwood. I exited the building, crossed Pennsylvania and entered the Old Executive Office Building. After examining my Agency pass, the guard allowed me to proceed. At exactly 5 p.m. I stopped at the desk of the Vice-President's secretary.

"Good afternoon," I said. "I am Melvin Shultz. The Vice-President is expecting me."

She buzzed him, then told me to enter. I found him sitting behind a large desk in a magnificent office, decorated in the style of the Nineteenth Century. I had never been in it before. It was essentially used as a ceremonial office. I had heard rumors that Atwood was using it more than most recent vice-presidents because of his dislike of Buck and the White House staff.

"Good afternoon Mr. Vice-President," I said, addressing him formally.

"What do want?" he asked. There was no cordiality in his voice. We had barely exchanged words since my meeting with him in California, when I had persuaded him to switch his support to Buck in return for the vice-presidency. I gathered his opinion of me was as low as mine was of the President.

"May I ask you a question?" I said. "Have you heard about the President's plan to abolish the Federal Reserve System?"

"I have heard about it. He has not discussed it with me. I realize now I made a colossal blunder when I let you persuade me to accept the vice-presidency. The Federal Reserve plan, as I understand it, is in line with most of his other policies, all equally flawed."

I relaxed. I had been hoping Atwood would say that. "It may

surprise you Mr. Vice-President," I replied, "That I completely agree with you. And if you made a mistake in accepting the vice-presidency under Buck, I made a far graver mistake in putting him into the White House,"

"It's a bit late to realize that now," he said.

"No, it's not. There's a very good chance that before midnight, the President will resign and you will be sworn in to replace him."

"You're crazy," he said. "Porter would never resign. He loves the job. And even if you could convince him, Tammy would never let him do it. She enjoys the power even more than he does."

"Just in case I'm wrong about Porter," I answered, "There's something I want to give you."

I opened my attaché case and from the secret compartment extracted the sealed envelope containing the original statement signed by Leonov. I handed the envelope to Atwood. Please put this in your safe," I said. "I want you to promise to destroy it unopened when you are sworn in as President. If I am wrong about Porter," I continued, "And he announces his Federal Reserve Plan, please open the envelope and use its contents to block him."

"I won't be part of any of your efforts at blackmail, Mr. Shultz," he said, "Even to stop Porter."

"Governor," I answered, reverting to his old title in my anxiety to convince him, "I really do have a conscience, despite what you may think of me. I took an oath to preserve, protect and defend the Constitution of the United States. I take that pledge seriously. Buck Porter has to be forced out of the White House, for the good of the country. I intend to do it. I am the only one who can do it. You have no choice but to do the same."

"Besides," I added, "you will not be blackmailing the President. All you have to do is make the contents public. When you do so, you then can truthfully say that I gave the envelope to you."

"One more thing," I added. "You will be pleased to learn that tonight I am resigning as Director of CIA."

He appeared surprised at the news. "Why?" he said. "I thought that you were planning to stay in that position to block Porter?"

"Mr. Vice-President," I answered, "When I resign, I will give one of two possible reasons. The reason I choose to give will depend on whether or not Buck resigns as President. One more thing," I continued. "When you are President, I want you to nominate Joshua Everett as Vice-President."

"So you can then force me out and have him take over as your puppet."

"Don't be foolish," I said. "I don't get my kicks out of making and breaking presidents of the United States. I don't know anything about Everett other than that he's the one of the few honest and efficient people in the administration besides you. He is ready to resign as Secretary of the Treasury to fight Porter's Federal Reserve scheme. I want him as Vice-President to prevent another oaf like Porter being elected when you leave office."

Atwood was silent for a minute. Then he said slowly, "I don't believe for a minute that Porter will resign. But if he does, I will look into what you said about Everett. If it's true, I will consider your request."

I realized I would get no further with the Vice-President. I was about to extend my hand to him when I realized it would probably be counter-productive. I stood, said goodnight, and walked toward the door. Then a thought struck me and I turned to him.

"It's ironic," I said. "Just think. I spent all that money and effort to have you enter the White House. Still," I mused out loud, "In retrospect, I might have done a lot worse."

I left the Old Executive Office Building and exited onto Pennsylvania Avenue. I was reviewing in my wind the best method of meeting with Puck when I spotted a telephone booth and recalled I had failed to inform Pergamon that I would be arriving home late for dinner. My call was answered by Fred, who told me my wife was out. I asked Fred to pass on my message, hung up and continued on to the White House.

I was worried that Buck or Tammy might have instructed the guards to deny me entry, breathing a sigh of relief as they examined my identification and permitted me to enter. I thought of going directly to Buck's office, but decided against it. In his state of mind, he might well impulsively order the Secret Service guards to throw me out. Tammy hated me as much as he did, but she was far less emotional and much more intelligent than her husband. She would probably decide to see me, both to learn what was on my mind and to gloat. Accordingly I headed to the First lady's office.

Betty Herman, the First Lady's secretary, was seated at her desk outside Tammy's office. I had never spoken with her and thought it unlikely she would recognize me. Approaching her desk, I asked for a sheet of paper and an envelope. She handed them to me with a cursory glance.

On the sheet of paper I wrote, "Tammy, unless you see me for a minute, I will immediately provide the press with evidence resulting in Buck's impeachment, indictment and imprisonment. Melvin Shultz." Folding the paper and inserting it into the envelope, I sealed the envelope and handed it to Herman.

"Please give this to the First lady," I said. "Tell her it's from Melvin Shultz, that it's urgent that she read it immediately and that I am waiting her to see her. Tell her also that that if she doesn't read it immediately, I won't be responsible for the consequences."

The secretary gave me a strange look, rose and went into Tammy's office. I waited for a few anxious moments, wondering what I would do if Tammy refused to see me. If I was forced to give the story of Buck's alleged recruitment by the Russians to the press, I faced a serious risk of ending up in jail. On the other hand, if I failed to do so, there was virtually no chance of blocking Buck's calamitous plan to abolish the Federal Reserve System, to say nothing of whatever other disastrous schemes the two of them could come up with.

It was with considerable relief that I saw Tammy's secretary reappear and beckon me to enter the First lady's office. I entered, shut the door, and smiled at Tammy. She was seated behind an impressive oak desk, which was covered with yellow legal pads. I had to admit she looked far more presidential than Buck ever had.

"How nice of you to see me, Tammy," I said. "It's always a pleasure."

"Don't waste my time!" she snapped.

"I trust you read my note?"

"Yes," she said a nasty sneer on her face. "Why don't you explain it to me?"

Although she had not bothered to ask me to sit down, I sat down unasked in the chair by her desk, ignoring her obvious annoyance.

"It's quite simple," I said. "Either Buck resigns as President before 10 p.m. tonight or I get him impeached."

The sneer on her face turned into a smile. "And just how do you propose to do that?"

"The first thing I'll do," I replied, "Is to make sure those photos I have of Buck naked in bed with Perry Terrell are carried widely in the media."

Tammy looked like the cat that had swallowed the canary.

"I hate to disillusion you," she said, "But the Terrell's will say the pictures are composites put together by you for the purpose of blackmailing the President."

"Oh," I said, "I know that you recruited the Terrell's and that they are now on your pay role. However, I still have their written statements confirming the validity of the photos. I'll make damn certain that the photos and the statements appear on the front page of every newspaper and are featured in the new broadcasts of every TV and radio station In the country. As you know, I have the money and the advertising experience to mount a very effective campaign."

"That isn't enough to get Buck impeached."

"You're right." I said. "If I stopped there, Buck probably would be able to escape impeachment, although it would be close. Of course, many people will believe they are genuine. The rest will half-believe. It will leave Buck a laughing stock. Buck will be a political eunuch and the political power of this administration will be irrevocably destroyed."

I could see my words were having some effect on Tammy, but not enough. She was a hard, determined person. She would fight as ferociously and stubbornly as possible to retain the political power she possessed as long as Buck was President.

"However," I went on, "I must tell you that the photos of Buck are intended to buttress my primary effort. If he does not resign by 10 p.m. tonight, I will call a press conference and announce my resignation as CIA Director."

"And you expect that threat will persuade Buck to resign? You must be joking."

"Not at all. I will state my resignation is due to my discovery that Buck was recruited as an agent by the Russian Army Intelligence Service shortly before the New Hampshire primary."

"I would have thought you could have made up a better story than that," she said sneering.

"Unfortunately for you," I have a written statement giving all the details of the recruitment from Colonel Leonov, who was head of Russian Army Intelligence operations in the US at the time. He has been evaluated by the CIA Russian Affairs Division as the most important Russian defector ever to fall into the Agency's hands. The statement was witnessed by three Agency staffers, all of whom will testify as to its validity."

Removing from my attaché case a copy of Leonov's statement, I handed it to her.

"Read it for yourself," I said. "The original, of course, is in a safe place and will be given to the press."

She read it carefully.

"This is nonsense," she said slowly. "The Russians wouldn't have recruited Buck before the New Hampshire primary. Nobody thought he had any chance of winning it."

I detected note of doubt in her voice. She was beginning to fear it might be true.

"The Russians," I went on, "took measures to insure his winning the primary," I said. "Did you see the part about their putting twenty thousand dollars into his campaign funds? I have confirmed that the clandestine payment was made. Beyond that, I saw Buck in bed with the Russian maid, Tanya, with my own eyes."

"You're bluffing," she said. "It won't fly."

"If you still don't believe me, call him in here and ask him yourself."

I could see from her expression that my challenge had hit home. I knew this was the decisive moment. To convince her, I had to press my advantage for all it was worth.

"Use your brains," I said. "If Buck doesn't resign, by 10 o'clock tonight, I think there's a very good chance the photos, the Leonov statement and my resignation to lead the campaign against him will force him out of office. At a minimum it will oblige him to delegate running the country to the Vice-President while Congress investigates. Even if manages to escape impeachment, he is a spent force as a political figure. Can you imagine him being able to push anything through Congress? And when his term is up, who is going to give you or him a job?"

"Then, there's the other scenario. Buck resigns tonight because of ill health and the two of you fly back to Oklahoma City to permit him to convalesce. I resign quietly an hour later to go back to running my company in Watsonville. I don't think you will have any problem returning to your old law firm. As a former First Lady you will probably be invited to join numerous company boards as a director. So, too, will Buck. If you should have any financial problems, I will assist you generously."

"Moreover," I added, "I give you my word of honor that all copies of those photos will be destroyed as will all copies of the Leonov statement. As far as history is concerned, none of that will have ever existed. Should Buck recover his health and wish to run for office in any future election, I will not become involved in any way. The days of my participation in national politics are over."

"Just think, you are a brilliant and capable woman. If you wished, you could have a promising political future. You could easily be elected in your own right to the US Senate or to be Governor of Oklahoma. As far as I can see, it's a no-brainer."

I stood and walked to the door. Before, leaving I turned to her.

"Just remember," I said deliberately. "My offer expires at 10 p.m."

I excited the White House and walked out past the gate onto Pennsylvania Avenue. Passing a group of obvious out-of-town tourists, I wondered what they would have thought if they had been aware of the high-stakes game I had just played with the First

Lady. Turning the corner onto Seventeenth Street, I hailed a taxi and rode home.

When I entered my apartment, Pergamon rushed to greet me. "Melvin," she said. "Is anything wrong? I had the most awful premonition all day that you were in difficulty. Are you in any trouble? Why are you so late?"

I felt responsible somehow for her distress and took her in my arms. "No, honey," I said kissing her. I am in no trouble. I hugged her and felt her hug me back."

"What kept you?" she asked.

"I had to go to the White House to see Tammy."

"Why" she persisted? "Are you sure there is no problem?"

I thought for a minute about how much I could tell Pergamon without worrying her.

"You know," I explained, "That Buck tried to fire me and I persuaded him to keep me on. Today I went to see Tammy and told her the conditions under which I would agree to give up the post."

"Why did you do that?" Pergamon asked. "I thought you felt you had to keep the CIA job to prevent Buck from doing anything that would be harmful to the country."

"Unfortunately, I have lost any influence I ever had over Buck. In plain fact, he can fire me at any time, with little recourse for me. There is just one thing I can do to block him, and I would hate to have to resort to that. I will know by 10 p.m. today whether or not Tammy accepts my deal, which would permit us to end our relationship on a friendly note. Let's wait until then and I will explain it all to you."

Pergamon stared at me. "All right," she said. "I guess I can wait till then. Would you like to have some dinner?"

"Let's have some fun," I answered. "I'm going to take you out for dinner. Leaving her little opportunity to refuse, I put my arm around her and headed for the door."

"Wait," she said. "What kind of a restaurant are we going to? What shall I wear?"

"It's very informal," I answered."You are dressed just fine."

We stopped at closet for her to get her coat, walked into the corridor and took the elevator to the garage. I would have preferred driving my Buick, but decided to avoid the likelihood this would irritate Pergamon. We climbed into her BMW and I drove out of the garage.

"Let's try Chinese," I said. I had seen a neighborhood Chinese restaurant named the Canton Garden located in a nearby shopping center. It struck me as similar to the neighborhood Chinese restaurant I had taken Pergamon to many times during our early married life in Watsonville, when I could not afford anything more expensive. I loved the place, but my wife had ruined it for me by remarking, albeit truthfully, that the food was not really authentic Chinese.

The interior of the Canton Garden looked very similar to our old standby in Watsonville. When the waiter brought us the menu I had to laugh. It prominently featured the family dinner for two, with one choice from column A and one choice from column B.

"Do you think," Pergaon, I asked in a mock serious tone, "They will throw us out if I ask for two dishes from column B?"

It was something I always asked at Watsonville. Pergamon chuckled.

Melvin," she said, a smile on her face. "Sometimes I think you will never grow up."

"I hope not," I answered. "It's fun being young, as long as I have you here with me."

The food was not inspiring, but I enjoyed the meal much as I did during those nights out with my wife in Watsonville so many years ago. I paid the bill and we got back into the BMW. I thought of going to a movie, but looked at my watch and realized there was not enough time to see more than a few minutes of a film. I wanted to be home by 9:30 p.m. in case Buck made his announcement early.

We drove back to our building, parked the car and took the elevator back up to our apartment. I hung up Pergamon's coat and my own and turned on the TV set. Normally I would have watched a western movie, but I didn't think I would be able to concentrate on one.

"Would you like to play chess?" I asked. Pergamon had been taught to play the game by her father and was a relatively good player. It was something else we had done frequently during our early married years, until it had gradually stopped. I took out the chess set, thinking how glad I was that I had somehow decided to bring it with us from Watsonville. We put the pieces on the board and began a game. It was hard to concentrate, as I kept on looking at the TV, urging it silently to produce the news report I so desperately wanted to hear.

I kept looking at my watch to check the time. Finally, I realized it was well past 10 p.m. It seemed clear that Buck and Tammy had called my bluff. I stood up. I now had to decide whether to carry out my threat to her, with all the personal risk it involved, or to slink out of Washington, a beaten and disgraced man. I shook my head. I simply couldn't choose that path. I had unleashed the Porters on the country. There was no other way to stop them and I had to do it.

"Pergamon," I said, despair obvious in my voice. "I have to make a phone call."

I decided I would first call Bob DePorte and give him the story.

After a few minutes, to give him a slight advantage in filing it, I would then alert the wire services of my resignation, including all the lurid details about the photos and the Leonov statement.

I had started dialing Bob, when the program on the TV was suddenly interrupted. The scene switched to the network news. A breathless announcer stated, "We have a flash announcement from the White House. President Porter has resigned tonight because of ill health. He and the former First Lady are flying at this moment to Oklahoma City for an extended period of convalescence. Vice President Atwood has taken the oath of office and is now President of the United States."

I breathed a sigh of relief. "Thank God!" I said out loud. I experienced a feeling of jubilation quite unlike anything I had ever experienced before.

Petrgamon turned and stared at me. "Did you have anything to do with this?" she asked.

"Yes, probably everything."

"I'll tell you if you really want to know, but I'd prefer not to. I had to say and do some pretty nasty things. He was going to privatize the Federal Reserve System. The consequence would have been catastrophic. It was all my fault that Buck was President and I had to stop him. There was no one else who could it and so I did."

I was surprised to find Pergamon's hand grabbing mine.

"Scoop," she said. "I think I may have misjudged you."

It was the first time in many years that she had called me Scoop. I looked at her. The years seemed to have melted away. She looked like the beautiful young woman I had married in Watsonville so many years ago. I bent down and kissed her tenderly. She returned my kiss.

I turned the TV off. Still holding her hand, we walked together into the bedroom.

"Pergamon," I said. "I love you very much. We're going to have a grand life together. I promise you."

Lust takes the White House

31290095076212 BH

CPSIA information can be obtained at www.ICGtesting.com
Printed in the USA
LVOW131903280313

326545LV00001B/50/P

9 781468 0939